D1090013

NATURAL LAW

A NOVEL

2019

Aug!

To Brandi
Thank you for your
wonderful care
Best Wishes
Wren Richards

NATURAL LAW

A NOVEL

WREN RICHARDS

Copyright © 2018 Wren Richards.

All rights reserved. No part of this book may be used or reproduced by any means, graphic, electronic, or mechanical, including photocopying, recording, taping or by any information storage retrieval system without the written permission of the author except in the case of brief quotations embodied in critical articles and reviews.

This is a work of fiction. All of the characters, names, incidents, organizations, and dialogue in this novel are either the products of the author's imagination or are used fictitiously.

Archway Publishing books may be ordered through booksellers or by contacting:

Archway Publishing
1663 Liberty Drive
Bloomington, IN 47403
www.archwaypublishing.com
1 (888) 242-5904

Because of the dynamic nature of the Internet, any web addresses or links contained in this book may have changed since publication and may no longer be valid. The views expressed in this work are solely those of the author and do not necessarily reflect the views of the publisher, and the publisher hereby disclaims any responsibility for them.

Any people depicted in stock imagery provided by Getty Images are models, and such images are being used for illustrative purposes only. Certain stock imagery © Getty Images.

ISBN: 978-1-4808-6086-5 (sc)
ISBN: 978-1-4808-6084-1 (hc)
ISBN: 978-1-4808-6085-8 (e)

Library of Congress Control Number: 2018904884

Print information available on the last page.

Archway Publishing rev. date: 04/23/2018

CHAPTER 1
ADVENTURE

The track of West Lake High School in Austin, Texas, awaited our Nike-shod feet and many laps of walking as my friend Molly and I prepared for the Team in Training marathon in October. Molly's English accent filled the cool, pleasant twilight air as we completed our training around and around the track. To keep count of our mileage, I tossed a penny into a cup each time we passed the mile marker and made it possible for conversation to flow. Our words wouldn't be interrupted by the mundane training routine. Thirty percent of our attention was given to our workout, but 100 percent of our effort was given to our chats. The report given to our coach was 130 percent total training effort.

My name is Sun Wren Richards, and I was seeking adventure. But little did I know when I started it would escalate into such a frightening ordeal. I am a mother of two grown, independent children with demanding careers and young children of their own, and they didn't need my help. My ex-husband lived in Montana. Although we were still good friends, he didn't need me either. As I walked, I looked to the horizon and pondered my future. I was comfortable and didn't need a job, but my life lacked goals. My restless soul was older than my body and needed to be challenged to realize its potential.

I sighed and stretched my legs on the stadium stairs. I was in good shape for my age, and it would be when Wyoming became overpopulated before I told you *that* number. My legs were made for dancing, my heart was made for loving, and my emerald-green eyes were full of sparkle and life. My five-feet, two-inch body might be petite, but it contained a fire and determination larger than a charging bull. Yes, I needed an adventure. The world was waiting for me, but where to start?

Dr. Seuss provided the answer many years before as I remembered some of the words from *Oh, the Places You'll Go.*

> So be your name Buxbaum or Bixby or Bray or Mordecal Ali Van Allen O'Shea, you're off to great places! Today is your day! Your mountain is waiting. So ... get on your way, and will you succeed? Yes! You will, indeed! (ninety-eight and three-fourth percent guaranteed). Kid (or grandmother) you will move mountains!

"You know, Molly, I have always wanted to go to Costa Rica," I stated as I tied my shoes. "I think I need a relaxing visit to that country to see what it is all about."

Both Molly and I had seen the movie *The Bucket List,* and now it was time to start doing the things I had always wanted to do.

After our successful marathon in October 2008 in Nashville, I announced to Molly that I had arranged to rent a house in Costa Rica from my friend Carol, who owned an animal hospital in Austin and could only travel to Costa Rica on holidays or planned vacations. The remainder of the time, the house was vacant and rentable. Carol had taken an investment class from a University of Texas Continuing Education program, where she learned about investments in Costa Rica. The instructor, Paul Phillips, gave Carol and her class the name of a trusted Costa Rican developer, Pablo Meza. Carol bought the house from Pablo, who served as her property manager while she lived and worked in Austin.

Twenty days passed from the blueness of the Nashville Marathon sky to the torrential rain of steel gray sky scratched by bolts of white lightning that left marks etched into its surface. The kettledrum thunder shook the ground like active volcanoes as my feet learned the feel of new country.

It was a saturating rain in Costa Rica when I arrived at the San Jose airport. Carol's house was located in Heredia, province of Alajuela, near the airport, which to be precise was in the city of Alajuela and not San Jose as a tourist might be inclined to believe. The streets of Alajuela were winding, narrow, and without street signs or addresses. Any tourist, even the most seasoned traveler, would be confused in the maze of houses, markets, and tangled streets lined with pedestrians and street vendors.

Pablo Meza graciously agreed to meet me at the airport to show me the location of Carol's house. All connections were successful. My flight was on schedule, and Pablo Meza waited patiently outside of customs.

The first sight of Pablo Meza gave a lasting impression. The man was elegant even though the day was overcast and drenched in rain. He had the calmness, reverence, and composure of an aristocrat and looked like the epitome of a successful businessman. He exhibited a comfortable, leisurely style, wearing his sand-colored silk suit, a chocolate-brown shirt, and a hand-painted designer tie. I instantly felt at ease as he kissed me on both cheeks in the friendly

Tico tradition. He was a large-boned man in his early fifties with plentiful, well-groomed hair ready for a photo.

As I looked into his black eyes, I knew his extra pounds were caused by medication, diabetes, or possibly both. Experience taught me to recognize the signs of these symptoms. Mr. Meza helped me with my luggage and ushered me toward the exit. He explained it was necessary to introduce me to his daughter Mercedes, who would show me the way to Carol's house because he had unexpected business that demanded his attention. I couldn't believe he could be so calm in his state of urgency. I was impressed he personally took the time to meet me. I commented on this.

He replied, "I told Carol I would meet you, and I wanted to welcome you to our country."

The introduction to his daughter further confirmed his graciousness. Mercedes was as elegant as her father and extremely beautiful. She was in her midtwenties and had medium-brown, thick, naturally curly hair. Her skin was a pleasant almond color, she stood about five feet seven inches tall, and she had a radiant Colgate smile, appropriate for her job as a part-time model. She was not the New York skinny kind of model but the organically healthy type that attractively filled out her beige pants and matching turtleneck sweater. Her mannerisms were demure, humble, and pure. She, like her father, was friendly, warm, eager to be helpful, and attentive.

Mercedes made the car rental process effortless. I followed her dark-blue SUV with a touring company logo on the side— "ALEGRIA," meaning "fun or happiness"—into a covered parking lot and parked behind a large white SUV. The floor had an incline, and as I pulled into the space behind the big white van, my foot slipped from the clutch. The little, red, rented Mazda lurched into the back end of the white van.

Oh, good grief!

I set the parking brake and scrambled out to examine the damage.

The Mazda's right headlight was broken, and the hood and fender were marred with a dent and scratches. I stood there helpless, unable to speak the native Spanish, and I couldn't remember the Budget Rental Car location.

Mercedes saw what had happened, assessed the damage, and shrugged her shoulders. "Tranquella, your rental car is so small that it did no damage to the white van." She looked at the rental car and said, "This is small injury. Not to worry!"

"Shouldn't we report this to the police or to the car rental?" I probed.

"Por qué? It will only take up vacation time. You do it later." She sounded amused.

I planned on being in Costa Rica for six weeks. Would the report take up that much time? She shut the door and linked her arm through mine, and then we veritably skipped through the parking lot and across the street to the grocery store.

"Let's go buy you some groceries you will need to take to Carol's house," Mercedes chirped.

The Auto Mercado was a beautiful grocery store—the equal of Austin's Whole Foods with bins of organic fresh fruit and vegetables with many European products to choose from. The produce section was full of items I had never seen before, much less tasted. Shopping was a great tasting adventure, and one of my favorite newly experienced tastes was *pyejveji*. This was a small, gold-orange, round fruit that tasted more like a vegetable but had a seed at the center of its juiceless flesh that was similar to the texture of a baked potato. The fruit was slow boiled in water for a long time until softened and then served with a dollop of mayonnaise. I thought it was delicious, but I was risk-taking food adventurous. After checking out of the grocery line and loading the bags into the back of Mercedes's SUV, she said, "I would like to show you a typical Tico restaurant you can enjoy. Are you hungry?"

"Yes, after the four-hour flight, two hours in customs, and car rental, I am starving."

Juan's restaurant had a Tico decor, a blend of many primary colors, handmade wooden tables and chairs, and a wait staff well acquainted with Mercedes. The spacious, open-walled seating area accommodated groups or families, but the waiter selected a smaller table for us. It had a great view of the entire valley of Alajuela, San Jose, and Heredia. It was dusk. The setting sun echoed the restaurant's decor and each embellished the other's beauty. I didn't think this was a conscious choice of artistry. Nevertheless, it was complementary for both restaurant and sunset. The cool, refreshing breeze added to the relaxed glow of the fading sun.

Mercedes talked openly about her family, their roots, and her ancestry. She was from pure Spanish bloodlines, and her aging grandfather still lived in Spain. She explained that her goal was to travel to Spain and live with him. Mercedes's father and her mother had been divorced since she was two years old. Pablo remarried a woman named Katerina, who was currently minister of justice for the country of Costa Rica. Pablo financially supported Mercedes's upbringing and college education, but she lived with her biological mother, who remarried early and had two half brothers who were a few years younger. Mercedes graduated with a business degree and married a handsome computer geek, who she loved, named Apollo.

The colorful sunset disappeared into the panoramic view of endless twinkling lights from the three cities below. It was getting late, so I paid the check while many staff and management came to shake hands and give hugs to Mercedes. I continued to follow the Alegria-advertised blue SUV up high hills into an area no longer of tropical forest, but that reminded me of a mountain setting in Encampment Wyoming. The wind whipped through the tall pine trees, and my thin tropical clothing was uncomfortable. Truth being I was freezing!

Mercedes and I hurried quickly inside carrying as much as we could and unloaded in one trip. She was more comfortably dressed in her sweater than I was in my clothes. I dropped bags of groceries, luggage, and purse where ever possible just to get inside to quiet the chatter and clatter of my teeth. Inside was not much warmer. There was electricity but no heaters or furnace; at least I was out of the wind.

The spacious house was designed with a very modern Frank Lloyd Wright look, but no furniture. There were no beds in any of the four bedrooms and no kitchen except for a new stove and refrigerator. The house was in a state of renovation. Mercedes called her dad, who sent over the housekeeper with inflatable air mattresses. There were no curtains, but she brought sheets, towels, and blankets. Carol had only recently bought the house and hadn't owned it long enough to furnish it.

In retrospect this was a humorous situation. Here I was in the middle of Central America, a tropical country, freezing like I was up at tree line in the Wyoming Rockies. This was Heredia, a part of Costa Rica like no other, and I had rented this house for six weeks. Mercedes, the housekeeper, and I hung sheets for curtains and made other makeshift accommodations.

"I will call you tomorrow, Sun," Mercedes said, as we walked to the front door while I remained wrapped in a blanket reminiscent of my heritage. She explained, "Your cell phone will not work in Costa Rica because the government owns all the phone systems, but the house phone works and is included in the price of the rent."

We rushed our good-byes as I thanked her. After the door closed, I made a jet stream dive and landed in the warmth of the bed.

The next morning was as glorious as a crisp mountain-air campout. The smell of the pine trees and hickory smoke emanated from the neighborhood fireplaces and truly gave the ambiance of an October Wyoming hunting camp morning with the makeshift accommodations in Carol's house. The one distinguishing difference was the sight of huge bushes of hydrangeas. They were the most vivid color of blue-violet. Seeing their splendor was worth enduring the frost-like rain and wind of Heredia. I dressed in layers of every available warm piece of clothing I had including mittens and ear-muffs that Carol told me to bring. Woolied up, I jumped into the sun-warmed, wrinkled, red rental and scurried down the pine tree lined roads toward the little town of Heredia.

Not five minutes from the driveway of Carol's house, I was sweat-ing. I removed the mittens and earmuffs first. A few miles more, off came the sweater, and soon I squirmed out of my shoes, socks, and pants. What was I thinking wearing all these winter clothes? Now most inappropriately unclad, I knew I couldn't explore the cozy little town in this state of undress. I did a U-turn and retraced my path back to Carol's house, but as I climbed the higher hills again, I put back on the socks, pants, and shoes. I added the sweater without mittens or earmuffs and upon arrival ran into the house to escape the painfully icy rain and stabbing wind. Once inside, protected from the tortures of weather, I packed a bag of shorts, sleeveless shirt, and sandals. Back down into town I went ready for a day of exploring.

The people of Heredia were happy, friendly, and always ready to be helpful. I was looking for a particular historical sight and needed directions. After asking for directions and following them, I still couldn't find the location, so I asked another person. The second in-quiry sent me back many miles in the same direction I had just come. Again, I couldn't find it. I asked yet another person, and this time a young student told me about a wonderful art gallery I should visit. I found it without any problems. Not the historical landmark but the art gallery! I spent a wonderful day experiencing modern Tico art.

Later that afternoon, when Mercedes called to see how I was doing, I told her about the difficulty with directions. She laughed, "Tico people will never tell you they do not know where something is located because they do not want to disappoint you. Directions are given in a local style using landmarks, 'turn left at the green house, no that's not right because that house is now pink. Turn left at the pink house,'" she explained.

The lesson learned today: maps were useless without addresses, and GPS didn't work in the cities. It was best to wander around without any particular destination in mind and be continuously charmed with the minute-by-minute discoveries of unfurled events.

Mercedes arranged tours all over Costa Rica for me, and I traveled alone sometimes, but more often we traveled together. She and her husband, Apollo, owned the Alegria touring business, but previously she had a high-ranked position with Scotia Bank. Pablo Meza, Mercedes's father, was proud of her when she worked at the bank, but now there was friction. Pablo didn't think Apollo helped Mercedes enough as the breadwinner of the family.

I knew Mercedes tried to earn money, so I did my best to pay her well. We used the red rental car while Apollo drove the Alegre SUV for other tourists. I paid all the food costs, lodging, and gas plus giving her wages of sixty dollars a day. We were great travel companions. She knew the words to American pop music and the Beatles' songs. We sang together, laughed, and enjoyed each other's company. Mercedes knew many lively places, and everywhere we went throughout the country she commanded center stage with her attractiveness and poise. The thing I appreciated most: Mercedes never hurried me along the way other tour guides did, giving ten minutes to do this or that and always pushing the schedule. I hated that about tours.

If I wanted to take a two-hour lunch, fine, we did. Mercedes never said, "Okay, let's go!" She always waited until I indicated I was ready for a change of scenery or location. I observed that Mercedes knew how to read her clients, meaning me. She was an expert at this.

We laughed so much, confided in each other, bonded as friends, and she told me she wanted a baby but Apollo didn't.

"Mercedes," I said, "I feel very close to you. You could be my daughter." She smiled and gave me a hug.

CHAPTER 2
TORTUGUERO

W e traveled together for over three weeks to both coasts of the little country, no bigger than the state of West Virginia, and we continued to use Carol's house as home base. One of the most memorable trips was to Tortuguero in the extreme northeastern shores of the country. From Alajuela, we traveled nine hours until we reached a canal waterway that separated a long strip of land between the inlet and the Caribbean Sea. The resort was casual luxury in a setting of individual cassitas with a central dining area and gift shop. When we arrived, we were introduced to an interesting native named Juan. He accepted the job of tour guide from the Tortuguero Resort to provide the finances for his children's education and simultaneously enabled him to further his interest in saving the endangered leatherback sea turtle.

Our first day, torrents of rain poured upon the Tortuguero Resort and flooded the leatherback nesting beaches. The young hatchlings would be buried under the weight of the saturated sands, unable to dig themselves free and migrate safely to the sea.

At daybreak there sounded a knock on my Tortuguero cassita, and tiny Juan stood there dripping in pools of knee-deep water. Juan's grief-stricken eyes projected his compassion as he pleaded for my help. He explained that out of the thirty tourists, he only found five people willing to help rescue some of the nesting baby sea turtles.

"Of course I will help, and thanks for asking me," I said, energetically.

My knee-high boots were totally of no help or protection from the rushing heights of water. I followed Juan to the beaches with bare feet and learned that my job was to protect the tiny turtles as they made their way to the sea. Juan knew exactly where the nests were; he dug the turtles free from the saturated sand like a gopher and carefully placed them down upon their paths to the sea. He wouldn't allow us to carry them to the water's edge. He explained that each turtle needed to map his mind for the future return as an adult to lay the nesting eggs for offspring. He said it was absolutely necessary they crawl every inch of the way on their own because they were imprinting. The newly hatched turtles obtained endurance for their survival in the sea, and the journey helped them gain the needed strength.

The five of us were like proud parents. We cheered as our guarded baby turtles reached the sea. We worked until we were exhausted. I did a significant task for Mother Nature, and I felt a strong bond with the integrity and kindness of tiny Juan and Mercedes.

As Mercedes and I drove back to Alajuela radiating satisfaction and happiness, my mind probed the experiences and wonders of natural law. The sun comes up in the east and sets in the west. That was natural law. The turtles were hatched and returned to their own nests to lay their eggs, and that too was yet another example of natural law. All creation had at its core an innate creative intelligence. Plants accomplished their photosynthesis, grew, reproduced themselves, and followed the creative intelligence that was locked inside their seeds. Animals hibernated, grew or shed protective insulation, knew directions in unknown areas, and knew their young among thousands of look-a-likes, but what about man? It would be simple for humans to connect to creative intelligence (natural law). This connection automatically produced use of intuition and spontaneous right action. If all individuals governed themselves from the level of natural law, how could there ever be hate, anger, crime, or war? The human brain was capable of such innate skills, but humanity had lost interest in its development. I assumed Mercedes knew about natural law and poetic justice because she grew up in this vibrant environment and understood. I felt kinship with her, and I vowed to myself I would try to discover and operate from the level of natural law. As we drove, my thoughts went around and around thinking of ways to become more in tune with my own creative intelligence and natural law. Being guided by creative intelligence instead of the intellect would produce pure truth. The intellect or mind seemed to be full of its own ego. Decisions made from the egotistical level would only produce selfish, murky, scattered decisions and thoughts. I hoped Costa Rica would become a good school to find more of my creative intelligence, and each trip served as a classroom to experience natural law. In a few days my marathon friend, Molly, would arrive, and the three of us would explore the central area of Costa Rica and provide other opportunities for my development.

The days passed very quickly, and I picked Molly up at the San Jose Airport late in the afternoon. We took a quick trip to the Auto Mercado for groceries. Molly was as fascinated by the array of produce as I had been. We stopped to gaze at the chiote, a vegetable unknown to both of us. We stood there asking each other what it was. I blurted out, "it looked like a squished up butt hole." Our laughter rocked the sedate Tico heads, and all dark eyes were upon us. We couldn't control our laughter, and the other shoppers thought we were drinking the many brands of beer from the aisles we roamed.

We made our purchases and quickly departed for Heredia. I smiled to myself in the dark car as we drove up hills toward Carol's house. I heard Molly's teeth chatter, and I glanced at her groping for her jacket to cover her skinny long arms.

"I'd fancy it a wee bit warmer in Costa Rica," she shivered. "I think I would also do well with a steam 'n' warm shower," she added.

"Yikes," she shouted in her British accent, from the upstairs bathroom, "Sun, how do I turn on the bloom'n' hot water?"

"Sorry, Molly" I shouted back, "the hot water heater hasn't been installed yet." I chuckled at her continued unintelligible mutterings.

In the morning, we got ready to go to the beach of Manuel Antonio. I suggested to Molly: "It gets very hot in that area of Costa Rica."

If you think I would be taking off my down-filled jacket and not wearing my leggings, you have just become a loony bird," she shrieked. "I have never been so cold in all my life. I cannot bear the thought of being ice blue in a bikini."

In the balmy Manuel Antonio beach sunshine, however, she did put on her bikini. We stretched out in the warm Manuel Antonio sunshine where the sound of the howler monkeys was riveting. As we lay on the soft sand soaking up the sunshine, we realized we were between two groups of howler monkeys that seemed to be communicating with each other. One group of monkeys on our right somewhere deep in the rain forest would howl, and another group hidden to our left would answer. These sounds resonated to the depths of my bones in stereo. Their deep baritone voices in unison were spellbinding, and perhaps the conversation between them was more sophisticated then we knew. I wanted to speak better Spanish, but now I wished I could speak "Howler"! This primate choir equaled "EL DIVO"! I loved the sound and listened to it for hours.

The next adventure in the wrinkled red rental took us to Volcano Aranal. Molly, Mercedes, and I were at ease in this brisk clean village enlivened with frivolity like a US college town during spring break. It was named La Fortuna. In the past, the volcano erupted and covered many square miles with hot lava. It destroyed everyone and everything in its path, but not the town of La Fortuna. It was named "the fortunate one." Mercedes knew of a quaint, inexpensive little Tico motel at the base of the volcano available with three separate sleeping quarters. Her reserved smooth business skills kicked into practice, and the motel rooms were ours for two days. It was charming, clean, and quiet. Perfect!

In the evening we trekked to another hotel, located on the west side of Volcano Aranal. This multimillion dollar hotel required special permits to be built high on the side of the volcano. The hotel used the volcanic run off to supply its elegant spa. We took a tour of this gorgeous resort including the posh bedrooms and private suites. The dining room was refined with native wood floorings, royal blue carpet, and gold table place settings. We savored a delicious expensive candle-lit dinner served by expert servers. The view from the all-glass ceiling-to-floor windows showed us the red-hot lava rimmed volcano's cone top. The darkness of forest and sky outlined this beautiful deadly ring of fire.

"Royalty" was my status as I descended the wide curving stairway between my two tall friends Mercedes and Molly onto the paved parking lot with surrounding beautiful sloped landscape. The night was still and soft as the three of us felt suspended in the velvet blackness. We gazed up into the star-sprinkled cavern-dark night sky when the volcano suddenly let out a deafening roar. It shook the ground under our feet like a steroid super-sized vibrator, and I toppled down with the rush of exiting hotel staff running to their parked vehicles. Mercedes was already in the car. Molly shouted for me as she waited for me to get up and then—complete silence. We were the only people left in the parking lot, and the silence was comforting after the commotion of volcano and people. Whatever had happened was over. In my room that night I could see the top of Volcano Aranal. It seemed quiet and contended without the angry red-orange hot ring at its top.

The next morning we three were excited to experience the thrill of the Aranal zip lines, or canopy tours, as they were marketed. When we got to the ticket window, Mercedes reported the cost of the tickets had doubled. I budgeted fifty dollars per ticket, and now the total would be three hundred. I wouldn't pay the price. I explained that I could pay for two tickets but not three. I expected Molly and I to go on the zip lines, since Mercedes was the guide and would wait for us. Mercedes said, "That's fine." She bought two tickets, took Molly's hand and dashed to the wait line.

I stood there alone and surprised about Mercedes's aggressive-ness. Well, now what should I do for three hours? Lucky for me, I had the car keys. I decided to go back to the Volcano Aranal Park Reserve by car and walk the trails around the volcano. At the entrance, I asked a park ranger, "Did you hear the volcano's loud noise last night?"

"Oh yes," he answered." Did you know there were a total of three burps, last night?"

"Good grief! I didn't know. I intended to walk the trails today. Should I do that? Was there any danger it might erupt today?"

"No, today is a very safe day because we like Volcano Aranal to burp and relieve her pressure. She will be contented. Have a good hike," he encouraged.

I started walking the trails around the base of the volcano and heard the volcano's inner workings boiling. All the trails circled around the volcano, gradually taking me higher up its side. The sound of this giant boiling pot grew louder and louder as the trails became steeper. The ground cover changed from the black sand to black lava boulders. While I climbed over these boulders, a lava-colored melancholy mood climbed on me. Perhaps the zip line event was my first clue to Mercedes's monetary aggressiveness. I was very much into my mind instead of my heart when my ego whined for attention and sucked up my energy. While I climbed over large boulders, my ego and intellect yakked away! Why would Mercedes not graciously volunteer to stay behind? Was this a cultural trait common to Ticas? Was I experiencing Mercedes's manipulative business strength? Wasn't she required to plan the trips for me since I was her employer? Yes! It would have been the prudent thing for her to do!

The larger the boulders, the harder the climb and the more my mind grumbled in tune with the boiling sound of the volcano. Good grief! Was I ever in tune with nature. With my head down to navigate the black lava boulders, I suddenly saw a pair of male bare feet. I looked up and saw the most handsome young man standing on a large boulder wearing nothing but white briefs. Oh thank you, Goddess of Attitude! This sight certainly snapped me from my grumbling thoughts. This tanned skin, well-built, dark haired beautiful man had his arms wide open to the sky and his back to the cone of the volcano. He looked like a god in search of his own world. I sat down on the boulder beneath me and stared while I breathed hard, not from passion but from exertion. What I stumbled upon was not a god but a model for Haines underwear. The camera crew moved into place, changed his pose, and continued their photo shoot. Good grief! You poor girls on the zip lines, have I got a story for you.

Completely rejuvenated and lighthearted, I made my way past the model and his camera crew in search of whatever was down the path, but I halted in front a large sign:

DANGER
ALL TRAILS CLOSED AHEAD
DO NOT GO BEYOND THIS POINT DUE
TO VOLCANIC TOXIC GASES.

Oh, sadness. This meant I had to retrace my steps past the model and his camera crew again. My black lava-colored mood and grumbling thoughts disappeared. I was excited to greet my friends from their zip line escapade.

Mercedes and Molly were exuberant with their stories and chatter about their zip line thrills. I had pent-up energy left over from my lava boulder climb and needed to dance like a wild woman. We three made our way to a nightclub that Mercedes knew. She was in search of good music for herself, good food for Molly, and great dancing for me. It turned out to be just like that! We strolled into the Tico restaurant and bar where a man was singing a beautiful ballad. Mercedes turned heads as usual while we paraded through. We found a table and sat down.

The singer was a short, heavy-set, plain-looking man with a voice like Pavarotti. He asked Mercedes her name. She answered, and he began to sing songs to her. It was a great taste of Costa Rica, "after five." The singer asked Mercedes to come on stage to select tickets out of the box for a drawing and join him in singing a song. We three had such a fun evening due to Mercedes's great stage presence and charm. A table of men sent over drinks and compliments. I didn't drink because of diabetes, and Molly only liked wine. Many drinks came to our table, and we gave them away. Our act of generosity made new friends for us. We got back to our hotel late, and the entire volcano was behind cloud cover, disappeared as if it hadn't existed at all.

The next morning, we trekked to the La Fortuna Waterfalls. The falls were tucked away beneath a stairway of one thousand steep steps carved out of the granite mountainside. The hundred-foot falls were viewed only by those who were physically fit or tenacious. Molly's experience as team coach for marathons and her nursing education were lovingly given to appreciative tourists who needed encouragement and a bit of Brit cheerleading. She gave helpful directives to an older Brazilian woman who had trouble breathing. She gave water from her own bottle to a running teenager who became dehydrated. I had long ago named her "Angel" Molly when she became my caregiver during foot surgery. Her concern for humanity was only equaled by her love for animals and the environment. She rescued stray birds, turtles, dogs, cats, and rabbits and took them home. She nursed them to health and released them back to the wild or found them good homes. Molly picked up litter and detoured two blocks out of her way to put it into receptacles.

Once we reached the La Fortuna Waterfalls, it became an inhalational experience. The human breath was replaced by the spray of rain forest emerald green purity and mist. Nature's constant thunderous roar of cascading water reduced the human figure to a diminutive size. I knew my size was either a minus zero or a number large enough to reach infinity or maybe both. The falls and I were linked to the same source.

Mercedes jumped into the ice-cold pool at the base of the waterfall to swim, and I followed. I hadn't felt such ice-cold water since we left Carol's shower in Heredia. We coaxed Molly to join us, but her long skinny body didn't have the insulation necessary for enduring these cold temperatures. I too couldn't enjoy the swim for very long.

On the way back to the motel, Mercedes pulled the car over to the side of the road beside a once elegant vacant hotel.

She whispered, "Benga, benga." We followed her to a place in the wall hidden from public view and climbed over. The property once had beautiful fountains, gardens, and large tiled verandas with many benches and stone sculptures. Mercedes dashed to a natural creek, removed her shoes and clothing and jumped in. She reclined on a comfortable round rock.

"Come on in."

"Mercedes, I haven't gotten warmed up from the waterfalls," I whimpered.

"You will like this," she encouraged.

"You Ticas must be equipped with a special thermostat, and what I fancy is a cup of hot tea," Molly protested.

I looked into Mercedes's pleading face and caved in.

"All right," I removed shoes and clothes and cautiously ventured in. What a surprise. The water was as warm and soft as Cleopatra's milk baths."Good grief, Mercedes. This is great," I yelled.

Molly looked at me and said, "Oh, right, you lot have gone daffy, and I'm not falling for your tomfoolery."

"The water is the volcanic runoff that feeds the creek beds," Mercedes explained.

The three of us enjoyed this unexpected luxury for over an hour.

"I think I haven't enjoyed trespassing so much," Molly announced. "Just think what benefits we get from this mineral water, and we hadn't to pay a hundred-dollar bill for it. Trespassing is quite lucrative."

A harsh Spanish male voice interrupted our private spa reverie.

"It is the security guard," whispered Mercedes. "Come on; we have to get out of here."

We dressed as we ran to the opening where we entered in the wall and slid into the car, laughing loudly after our successful escape.

"*Oh no*, I think I lost my knickers," Molly squealed.

"Mercedes, we are middle-aged women running like juvenile delinquents, and you turned us into American fugitives," I said with a laugh. Our fugitive laughter melted into our regular routines. Molly's return to the San Jose Airport was the end of an extraordinary week of reconnection with my lanky redheaded friend, and it marked the midpoint of my own six-week vacation.

CHAPTER 3
INVESTMENTS

The next two days I spent alone in Carol's cold house and pondered my future. The economy in the USA sagged. I wanted to work as a sculptor but knew art rarely survived in poor economic times. I was an aging woman on my own, and accumulation of wealth was of no interest, but taking care of myself was important. I didn't want to depend on friends, family, state agencies, or government. Happiness outweighed the value of money, and Costa Rica seemed to be where the real treasure of happiness was hidden.

I reached a contented plateau in my life. I achieved my educational goals by earning hours toward my doctorate, raised my children well, resigned from a successful theater career, and traveled to many countries while I remained physically strong and healthy. I possessed contentment with involvement in political positions and contributed to improving my country and community. My social love-life was a void, and all I had to show in that department was a basket full of M&Ms (married men and monks) and a garage full of "G Gs" (gay guys). I guess I should pay more attention to this area. I had no regrets about my spent years, but it was time for self-reinvention.

The phone rang, and Mercedes explained she had time for us to go sightseeing again after we had reorganized ourselves from adventures with Molly.

"Mercedes, I know what I want. I love your country, and as we look at points of interests as tourists, I want to look for property to buy,"

"That is possible. I will look online. Sun, let's continue to scenic spots and simultaneously look for real estate. I will arrange for this soon. Do you want to start this week?"

"Yes, I do. This week would be good. I need to create a future, and being a tourist is fun, but I need to be more productive."

Every day for the next two weeks, Mercedes and I traveled to different locations. We saw property on beaches, in mountains, near rain forests, by lakes, in small villages, and in the largest city of San Jose.

Pablo Meza, Mercedes's father, was a developer and wanted to show me his gated developments in Guanacaste, but I declined. I currently lived in West Lake, a prestigious subdivision of Austin, Texas, and I didn't want to move to another country to choose similar property. I believed buying in a newly developed area was counterproductive to saving the pristine forest when I could buy an existing property without causing further vegetation reduction for Costa Rica.

Pablo phoned me many times during my stay in Heredia to see if I needed anything. He inquired how I got along with his daughter (my guide). The Pablo Meza Developments were of interest to Americans, but I wanted to experience diversity and become acquainted with Ticos. I knew if I looked at his developments and didn't buy it, he may construe this as an insult of his workmanship, design, or demographics. I was already obligated to him for his kindness, and my best option was declining the invitation and avoidance. I remembered an attraction I wanted to see and phoned Mercedes.

"Hi, Mercedes. I called to see if it was possible to visit a sculptor. His name is Tony Lopez, and the location is La Uruka. Can we make an appointment?"

"Sun, this is your lucky day. This is like a stroke of magic. I know this sculptor, and I will find out if he will invite us to his studio," Mercedes said excitedly.

The following day, Mercedes and I were on the ribbon of potholes toward La Uruka to Tony Lopez's house. The area was composed of small homes of the middle-class Tico neighborhoods. There were no zoning regulations in Costa Rica, and that fact produced some very tidy well-kept homes next to ramshackle heaps strewn with litter.

As we approached Tony Lopez's home and studio, the La Uruka area became lush with vegetation, manicured gardens, and many tall trees producing a variety of fruits. In the center of a hector of land (about three-plus acres) set a charming, long, elegant Spanish colonial home. It was whitewashed stucco with a deep burgundy-red roof. The charm of the area was graced by gentle hills and walking paths made from cement stones the same burgundy-red color as the roof. All of this was augmented with other bodegas that matched the house. A thatched-roof tiki hut and a gazebo were completely covered with large burgundy-red passion flowers with black centers that matched the black wrought iron house window coverings. It had a large inviting swimming pool, an outdoor bar and kitchen (rancho), and, of course, his large, seventy-by-thirty-foot open air studio perched on the descending hillside where any artist could enjoy the view of the rain forest and the river.

Our little, red, winkled, rented Mazda was guided down a tarmac driveway by burgundy-red, five-foot-tall thick-leafed plants that matched the entire decor. Our car stopped under the entrance portico in front of three-inch-thick solid mahogany handcrafted doors.

We stepped out of the car and rang the large mission bell hanging in the center arch of the portico. Mercedes and Tony Lopez exchanged the usual kiss on each cheek, and Mercedes introduced me.

"Tony, this is my American friend, Sun Wren Richards." I extended my hand and he shook it.

"Please call me Tony."

I was aware of the soft limp hand that barely touched mine. I grasped his hand a little harder, and he promptly withdrew. Tony was a good-looking Tico, rather gaunt befitting the cliché "tall, dark, and handsome." He was totally uninterested in me as a fellow sculptor or human being. He spoke only to Mercedes and showed her his new art pieces as I tagged along. His sculptures were very reflective of his handshake—limp, pointless, uninteresting, and without a message. I was a "buyer" for his art, but he clearly didn't care. He lacked sales skills and had no business finesse.

He was polite and spoke English. Occasionally there was a Spanish word thrown in that I understood, but he was aware my Spanish was nonexistent. I didn't believe he felt any cultural discomfort nor did I. Tony ushered us into the kitchen where one-half of an uncovered chocolate cake sat on a plate. The house itself had many charming aspects but was in disarray. It held a decided "day after party" atmosphere. Despite the untidiness, the graceful architectural features showed themselves impressively.

The house had eight bedrooms, eight bathrooms, a large living area, dining room, halls, and sitting alcoves. The beams, doors, and trim throughout the house were mahogany. The Spanish colonial style was accentuated by the many arched interior doors. It had two-foot-thick wall construction that made the doors and windows into deep lovely recessions similar to old castles. The reddish-burnt-orange tile floors were of an old world pattern throughout all levels of the house. I knew these floors would polish to a high vibrant shine. The light fixtures were of the same black wrought iron that matched the windows. I liked this house!

Tony escorted us into the office. The phone rang, and he left the room. His absence gave a perfect time to confide in Mercedes.

"Mercedes, I don't like his artwork at all, but I really like this Spanish colonial house. Would he sell it?"

Mercedes rose from her chair beside the computer as Tony came back into the room. She gracefully strolled about the kitchen in a leisurely parade.

"Tony, would you consider selling this place?" Tony looked surprised.

"We would. This is a lucky day for us both." He stood up, walked to the fax machine, and ripped out a sheet of paper.

"Here is the listing. We listed it yesterday."

Mercedes handed me the fax as we picked up our sunglasses and purses that we left in the living room and strode to our car.

"Thank you, Tony," she waved and shouted from the car window. We were both excited and chattered about the possibilities of buying Tony's house.

"Mercedes, if I bought Tony's house, I think you should receive one half of the real estate commission he paid his broker. A part of that commission should belong to you since you are the one that introduced me to the seller. He asked over $520,000, and half of the commission would be a big chunk of change for you. I appoint you as my Realtor."

"I appreciate that very much," she said with a nod and soft smile.

In Costa Rica, anyone can buy and sell real estate. Real estate agencies were a relatively new business system, and it was lawyers who completed the paperwork and registered the sale with the Costa Rica Public Registry.

It was mid-December, and the rest of this month would be a busy family month for both Mercedes and me. Christmas in Costa Rica was celebrated until mid-January for most government agencies and offices. Mercedes would be busy with the high season of her tourism, and I had to get my Austin house ready to sell. I wanted to list my Texas property by January. I was so excited about this new adventure that words couldn't describe my enthusiasm. Of course, negotiations needed to be conducted, but Mercedes and I both had a computer, and we could phone. I really didn't know what price my house in Austin would sell for, but I knew I would never buy the Costa Rican property if I needed to take out a mortgage. I wouldn't risk going into debt just to have an adventure.

Mercedes and I made a schedule for continued communication. Both of us were consumed by the momentum of our future plans. As I locked up Carol's house and loaded the car, I was apprehensive about the rental car return and needed to explain its wrinkled little body with the broken headlight. I hoped my lack of Spanish and the Budget Car Rental associate's limited English would be enough to peacefully resolve the accident.

"*Hola,*" I said and smiled as I handed the associate the keys.

"I have something to show you." The associate followed me to the car.

"Look what I did."

He leaned down and peered at the light and the fender.

"How was your vacation?" he asked.

"It was absolutely wonderful, I love your country, but I am concerned about the cost of damage."

"It is not so bad. How does fifty dollars sound?" he asked. I quickly handed him my credit card before he changed his mind.

The plane trip back to the USA was restful and uneventful. I was glad to see Molly as she picked me up at the airport. After we loaded the bags into her little sports BMW convertible, I gave her a hug. I flailed my arms wildly into the air and shouted, "*I'm moving to Costa Rica!*"

CHAPTER 4
TRUST

The next month was a blur of house painting, cleaning, yard work, and Realtors. Negotiations with Mercedes and the CR sellers continued although we were $20,000 apart. Before I made a binding offer, I had to sell the West Lake property, and to my amazement I had a committed offer in February for more than I anticipated. I narrowed the offered gap between what Tony Lopez asked and my original bid.

It seemed to me during this period of negotiations that Mercedes represented the seller's position rather than mine. "Oh, Sun, why not give him what he wants so we move forward?"

"I met his demand halfway, and he needs to meet my offer in the middle. It is right for us both to compromise if he is interested in selling to me," I firmly stated.

"Okay, okay. I will tell him what you say," Mercedes pouted. After a few days she called back to inform me, "He said he wants you to pay off his mortgage on the house."

"How much is that?" I asked.

"It is $7,000."

"Mercedes, I increased my original bid by $10,000. I certainly *will* *not* pay off his mortgage."

"It's only money," interrupted Mercedes.

"It's easy for you to say when it's my money. I won't continue with these talks. He either accepts, and I come to Costa Rica, or I remain in the States. That's it Mercedes. He needs to relent!" I hung up.

Several days passed, and finally she called.

"Why you had not called me?" she asked in nervous English.

"Because I gave you my final offer, and I waited to hear if he accepted or not," I stated.

"Okay, Tony said for you to send $60,000 into an escrow account, and the balance you should pay two weeks before closing."

"Thank you, Mercedes. I guess we have a deal," I concluded.

"I will email you information for the money to be wire-transferred in about one hour. Ciao." Mercedes hung up.

The email arrived: Send the wire transfer with this information:

> Bank: HSBC Bank USA, NA, New York
> ABA: 823021004
> S.W.I.F.T MAODUS66
> Address: 101 Park Ave, New York City, NY 10178
> Credit Account; HSBC Costa Rica, SA
> Account Number307567445
> S.W.I.F.T. BXBACRSJ
> For further credit to: 605892

I took the email to my bank and made the transfer. Overseas shipping companies were contacted, garage sales were held, and stuff was given to friends. My cars were sold, other assets liquidated, left over things from garage sales were given to Good Will, and I had a light and free "non-attachment" attitude.

Mercedes called to inform me that the wire transfer didn't arrive in Costa Rica. I went back to the bank and found she was correct. Due to some US bank error, the money didn't get transferred. My bank researched and found the $60,000 was still in my account. I wire-transferred it again. Two days passed while I had great fun attending going-away parties hosted by thoughtful friends.

The telephone and computer were operable in the empty house when I received the email from Mercedes explaining she hadn't received the money. I gave her the information from my bank wire transfer confirmation receipt.

"Mercedes, I will check with my bank and ask them to trace it," I promised. On Monday I went back to the bank again and was told the money had been sent, but the receiving bank returned it because there was an error in their escrow account number. I telephoned Mercedes and requested the correct information. We both agreed we tried to have patience with the Costa Rican banking system. Mercedes gave me the account number again, and I returned to my bank for the fourth time with the corrected number. I received another email from Mercedes explaining; the receiving bank's communications for international wire transfer experienced technical problems.

"We have done this so many times, why don't you send the $60,000 to my bank account, and when I receive it, I will hand deliver it to the escrow account personally. This, I think, is best to do," explained Mercedes.

"You might be right, Mercedes. What is your account number?" I reluctantly asked.

Thoughts chased around in my head. No one in their right mind would ever send $60,000 to a person in a foreign country they knew for only six weeks. Could I trust her to deliver the money? What were my options? Why did we have continued banking errors? Were these problems common to a developing country? I needed to relocate.

Should I stay, or should I go? Was natural law testing my belief system and philosophy about unplugging from the status quo of acceptability? Were these negative thoughts binding me to a lower level of collective consciousness? Was my intuition in harmony with the universe?

It became a question of trust as I struggled with my thoughts. Did I trust my own path? Did I trust the common good in human nature? Did I trust there was a reason for going to Costa Rica? Did I trust creative intelligence in humans? This was a $60,000 lesson in life, and I was gambling. If I didn't go, my future would be my past. It was safe in status quo, but what was the shortest path to really learning life's lessons?

Trust, trust, trust. I sent the money directly into Mercedes's bank account. Preparations toward the move continued, and now my phone and computer were boxed and shipped. Communications between Costa Rica and me were relayed through my friend Molly. Days of waiting for the news finally arrived in an email from the bank's escrow account manager. My giant release of breath was heard all over Texas. Mercedes hand-delivered the money and made the deposit into the escrow account. I was a big risk taker and received the support of nature.

Final good-byes were said to family, helpful friends, and neighbors. Arrangements were made with my bank for the last wire transfer to pay off the Costa Rica house in full. I spent my last night with Molly and her husband Jack to facilitate my scheduled departure in the morning. Jack prepared an elegant farewell dinner in my honor, and Molly raised her wine glass and said, "To your success and happiness." Jack raised his glass and toasted, "To your safety and well-being."

CHAPTER 5
TRANSITION

April in Costa Rica, the beginning of the rainy season, was my favorite for experiencing strong bolts of lightning and the crashes of dramatic thunder commanding attention. This year of 2008 the performances of the drenching heavens was calmer, and I missed the anticipated spectacle.

Mercedes picked me up at the San Jose Airport and took me to a hotel on the north side of La Uruka. She arranged to my specifications something clean, inexpensive, and within walking distance to restaurants and the barrio. Mercedes greeted the owners, Mark, a blond American in his early fifties, and his wife, Carmen, an unattractive large Tica, who dressed in sleazy fashion equal to Fredrick's of Hollywood, indicative of the sex-tourism hotel that it was. Mercedes met the hotel owners in the same hurried manner she greeted me at the airport. For some reason, she was smartly dressed in business attire instead of the more casual touring clothing and seemed to be in a frantic rush.

"I would like you to meet my friend Sun Richards from Texas.

We are not acquainted with your hotel, and her stay will be an exper-
iment for my touring company," which meant in unspoken words,
treat her well, or I won't use you again.

Mark and Carmen were both friendly, and a staff person carried
my bags down around the courtyard to a room on the end. Mercedes
received her commission from the owners at the front desk. She told
me the house closing would be delayed for another week, and she
would give me more details later. Mercedes pirouetted in her red flat
dress shoes and dashed to her car before I had the opportunity to pro-
test the delay or to ask questions. She seemed flustered, preoccupied,
and in a business mood during her departure. My intuition stabbed
me and told on Mercedes's self-serving mission.

I could easily entertain myself while I waited for the closing, but
Molly took time off from her work and planned to come help me
move into the house. We looked forward to shopping and decorating
for life in my new country. The delay was a great inconvenience to
us. It meant Molly may not get a chance to see the house because of
her work schedule, and this delay added to my expenses. It entered
my mind that Mark and Carmen's hotel rented with a two-week
minimum and was the reason for the delay. I inquired with the
hotel staff, and they confirmed the policy of a two-week minimum.
Mercedes changed the house closing date to accommodate her hotel
commission, which exposed her business shrewdness, again. I suspected she contrived a much larger prize. She showed no concern
for our circumstances, and I calculated my house closing would
therefore be around April twentieth, and I must wait. I roamed the
streets of La Uruka as I waited for the closing and Molly's arrival.

Arrangements were easily made for Molly's visit with hotel
owners Mark and Carmen. We got Molly settled into our small
two-bedroom quarters, and she cheerfully "made do" with what
was available. That night we left our room opened to the breeze for
fresh air and walked to a restaurant for a seafood dinner and three

desserts each. When we got back to our rooms, we discovered Mark and Carmen's dog entered, climbed upon Molly's bed, and left his deposit.

"Bloody hell," shouted Molly. "This is disgusting."

"Lucky for us, I bought an air mattress from a man who returned to his homeland. The mattress was to be used in my new empty house until I received my shipment of furniture from Costa Rica customs, but it's a good time to use it."

It was too late for us to complain about the state of our room and the intrusion of the dog to the owners that night, but the next morning we showed them the mess, which we hauled out the back door of our rooms. Their response showed no alarm, and they casually sent staff to freshen and replace mattress and bedding. Mercedes arrived midmorning and drove us to the Spanish colonial house for final inspection. In route to the property, Mercedes inquired, "After you buy your new home, would you be interested in hiring someone to help you with the gardens and maintenance?"

"Yes, that would be great. Do you know someone?" I probed.

"Tony has a young man who will be at the property this morning for you to meet. If you like him, you can talk to him about working for you."

Tony met the three of us. I introduced my friend Molly, but Tony's indifference was a replay of our first meeting. Tony introduced us to a shy, mild-mannered, neatly dressed man named Amon, who gave a positive impression. I was eager to see the property and requested Tony lead the way. Tony talked enthusiastically to Mercedes while Molly and I followed his procession, leaving Amon waiting on a bench in the shade. Outside in the gardens beside the art studio piles of discarded art projects, remnants of building materials, debris from car repairs, and garbage from inside the house were obviously abandoned to become a new owner's responsibility. This mess was an embarrassment. I was glad nonjudgmental Molly saw only the beauty of the flowering tropical plants and the curving sloped red painted meandering walkways that led down paths to the bar and lounge area.

Inside the house, an unfinished move-out was in progress. There was clutter everywhere, heaps of clothing thrown into piles in the corner, a single shoe here and there, and trash and dirt concealed the beauty of the floor tiles. Molly strolled through the many arched doorway throughout the house, and I beckoned to Mercedes for words in private.

Tony looked out the window and showed no interest in talking to me directly as I expressed my thoughts to Mercedes.

"This place has to be cleaned up before anyone would buy it. All piles of garbage outside must be removed, and the inside must be prepared for 'move in.' I guess he accepts you, Mercedes, as the spokesperson and doesn't want to talk directly to me. Would you relay my words to him?"

Mercedes nodded. "He is sad about having to move, but I will tell him."

"Maybe he is sad, but that is no excuse to leave this mess for a new buyer to deal with," I said.

Molly and I finished examining the house, and her comments were welcomed.

"You found yourself a rare jewel. I know you will make this place into a breathtaking showplace, but you have your work cut out for yourself, especially if that young man sitting on the bench would rather sit there instead of work."

"Oh, good grief! I forgot about him," I whispered and ran to Mercedes.

"Forgive me for interrupting you and Tony, but will you please come and translate so I can get better acquainted with Amon?"

The translation process was slow, but I liked this polite guy, and I agreed to hire him. I would pay $100 per week, which was more than he expected. He would work from 7:00 a.m. until 4:00 p.m. I would give him breakfast at 10:00 a.m. and lunch at 2:00 p.m. (depending upon the rain). He was appreciative and expressed himself with smiles and a pleasant handshake. He would start work two days after closing. Mercedes would call to let him know when he was to start.

The house closing delay gave Molly and me three extra days to explore the area, and the volcano of Poas was near. Mercedes agreed to be our tour guide and her Alegria blue SUV carted us up the steep, winding hills. The atmosphere was different from the cold blustery elevations of Carol's house in Heredia, less than forty miles away. These mountains were soft green velvet-covered slopes and canyons blanketed with strawberry, orchid, and coffee plantations. The air was misty, wonderfully cool, and made our skin supple under the refreshing breeze, which tasted of mint. The air from the heightened hills gave an unusual effect of blue haze film, like saran wrap, to the spectacular views. This soft translucent coating made everything appear unreal by melting the shape of the cows and houses without defined edges and blurred them together as one giant softness. This was to be my new home, and I loved it.

"Would you two like to stop and visit a coffee plantation?" asked Mercedes as she drove in front of the elegant plantation home. She didn't need our answer and read our eagerness. As we strolled through the rows of thick coffee bushes with their bright red berries and thick green leaves, we saw hundreds of coffee pickers working in rows of coffee where the berries were of a darker color. The workers were men, women, teenagers, and some children, all dressed in colorful work clothes moving quickly up and down the rows of coffee. Some of the workers, mostly from Nicaragua, worked picking the berries so fast that you couldn't see their fingers move, but the baskets of coffee beans grew deep and heavy. It was a competition between the workers to develop their skills and become recognized for speed. A worker who developed a reputation as a skilled coffee bean picker earned a valued status and brought in higher revenues for both coffee pickers and the plantation owner.

We learned coffee grown in the sun produced a different flavor than the coffee grown in the shade. We were ushered into the coffee tasting room of the plantation and served samples of their product. Molly and I weren't coffee drinkers. I wouldn't know a good cup of coffee if I held it in my hand. We were sitting in the spacious lovely room reserved for coffee distributors and world vendors, sipping our coffee when Mercedes exclaimed, "I think these cups are Demitasse Bezique! Molly in her excitement grabbed her cup and turned it over to read the signature on the bottom. The cup was still full of coffee and drenched her white skirt.

"Bloody hell," she whispered. The expression on her face was a lasting memory. Our uncontrollable laughter rang throughout the plantation, and the memory of this sight made us laugh all afternoon.

We three continued our ascent to the highest elevation to reach Volcano Poas. The entire area of this Central Valley Costa Rica was perfect in every way for human comfort. The temperature was always a pleasant range of seventy to eighty, the humidity was moist without making you feel wet, and the breeze was like the soft wind from a Japanese silk fan. For me, the Central Valley area was the most comfortable of all Costa Rica, and soon I would belong as naturally as these tropical trees.

Volcano Poas was different from Volcano Aranal. It was another type of beautiful and reminded me of the geysers of Wyoming where I grew up on the Wind River Indian Reservation. Poas was a volcano where its cone had caved inward and remained a crater full of three hundred feet of rainwater. The water kept the eruptions from spewing fire and lava and sent up fountains of boiling water not unlike those of Old Faithful in Yellowstone National Park. Perhaps these images gave me comfort from my childhood memories and made me feel at home in this area.

We stood on the rocky rim of the volcano and peered into the boiling "mud pot" watching it churn. The smell of sulfur was so strong it made our eyes and nose run, but it didn't detract from the beauty of plants with umbrella-sized leaves that covered our pathway as we walked the volcano's five mile trails.

On our way back down the mountain, we stopped to sample some of the country's best cocoa.

"Hey, Molly, be sure to leave your cup upright until your cocoa is finished," I snickered. She allowed my words to drip onto her skirt like the previous coffee stains. Good-natured Molly took my jabs with humor, and we finished our pleasant evening reminiscing about past marathons.

By ten o'clock the next morning, we had the first phone call from Mercedes, who announced she was coming over to talk. Hmmm, it sounded serious. Mercedes walked into the courtyard of Carmen and Mark's hotel. She didn't ferret them out to exchange the usual stream of Tico pleasantries but moved with purpose directly to the table where we shared breakfast by the pool.

"How was your evening?" she politely asked, masking her intensity.

"Do we really want to talk about our evening when I think you have bigger matters on your mind?" clipped Molly.

"Yes, of course. Sun, I am sorry to tell you the money you sent from the USA was returned because our Costa Rica receiving bank had trouble with the escrow account numbers. We were all set to close on April 22."

"Well, let me call my US bank and ask them to send it again. What are the correct account numbers?" I asked using the hotel phone to make the call.

Mercedes rummaged around in her purse and gave the numbers as I carefully wrote them down. "Good morning, Bank of America. This is Sun Richards. I tried to wire money from my Texas account to an account in Costa Rica. Can you check the records? I sent it April 8, and it was returned … when Mercedes?" I asked, impatiently.

"It was returned April 14," said Mercedes.

"April 14 … could you please check to see if it was returned to my account? It was returned! Would you confirm the account numbers that were used? The numbers are not a match … I have the correct numbers for you to resend … you won't accept any over-the-phone wire transfer from a foreign country? Even if you determined that I was the owner of the account making the request? I am in Costa Rica now and request it be wire transferred … only in person? That means I must return to Texas … Isn't there any other way? I don't understand this … no, I know … it isn't your fault. Okay … thanks." I hung up Mark and Carmen's phone.

"Mercedes … this is crazy. I have to go back to the USA to make the transfer, and I don't think I should bear the expense of travel to compensate for your country's mistake. I have to travel to the United States and return by April 20. I shouldn't pay for this! If you want this sale to take place, your sellers and you have to share my travel expenses."

"No, Sun, I can't pay for this ticket … you must buy your …"

Molly's London accent cut her words into shreds. "Well, for me I return tomorrow anyway, so I can use my own ticket, but you bloody well be for buying Sun's roundtrip ticket, or she can go home with me *and stay*.

"Okay, okay," relented Mercedes, "I go to the airport now and buy the ticket. I call you and let you know the airline schedule. Molly, what flight and time do you leave tomorrow? I try to get Sun on that flight." Mercedes spoke in nervous English, quickly jotted down the information, and left even faster than she arrived.

We waited for Mercedes's call, but we both packed and got ready for tomorrow's flight. Conducting business in Costa Rica was difficult, and dealing with Costa Rica banks was frustrating. Was this the norm or was it only problematic for foreigners? I questioned if this was the unrest of a spoiled American.

The phone rang.

"Hi, Mercedes, were you able to get a ticket on Molly's flight? You should give me the correct wire transfer information now, if closing is next week. It must be correct because we don't have time for more corrections."

"Sun, I think you should send the money to my bank account like you did the down payment. It worked out before, so I will give you my bank account number, and you can write it down."

"Mercedes, this is highly irregular. It is a larger sum of money, and it should go into the escrow account not your personal account. I am uncomfortable with this idea."

"Sun, why don't you trust me? After all, you know the other money was delivered without problems. I don't understand why we shouldn't do what we know will work, especially when we have a deadline. You aren't accustomed to Costa Rican banks, and I am more efficient than they are, don't you agree?"

"Yes, so it seems. Give me your account number, and I will send it to you directly, and you can deliver it before I arrive. What are the numbers? Slowly, please! I will read them back to make sure they are correct. Is my return flight on April 20? That gives me two days in Costa Rica before closing on the twenty-second. Will you explain to the sellers that I was here two weeks before closing, and the delay isn't my fault?"

"Of course. The sellers welcome the extra time to get the house prepared for your move-in. Have a good trip. Ciao," she clicked off.

Molly and I had a good return flight to Austin, Texas, even though I was frustrated about the delays. Molly was a good traveling companion, and we chatted as usual.

The next morning, I experienced the ease of the US banking system, and the wire transfer was made to Mercedes's account. I had renewed appreciation for our country's high standards of efficiency. I completed my business and took the next flight back to Costa Rica. When I arrived at Carmen and Mark's hotel, Mercedes left a message with information and directions about closing for the following day.

CHAPTER 6
COURAGE

Some magical power turned on the illumination of day. The golden-bronze light was spectacular accompanied by a startling symphony of chirping birds. A surge of energy propelled my legs to spring board to the cold tile floor. I stood by the closet and carefully looked at the wardrobe to choose for this celebrant day. I wanted to convey the proper image, as an American in my new country. I didn't want to present the "arrogant American look" or the American slacker image. I chose a simple black and white print wraparound skirt with a white modest blouse, a wide white cinch belt, white shoes, and purse. This attire seemed reasonable for April. One last look in the mirror before I caught a taxi reflected a middle-aged woman aging fairly well who owned a successful investment business, possessed creativity, and had a flare for adventure. Yep, girl, you are ready.

The taxi ride was pleasant, and my first look at San Jose was quite a surprise from the modest, clean but poor neighborhoods surrounding the area of the hotel I occupied for the past weeks. San Jose was modern with tall glassed buildings, tropical landscaping, and wide, clean busy streets. The window fronts of the stores were tastefully decorated to display a modern array of merchandise. The ambiance of San Jose wasn't the staccato pulse of New York or Dallas, but it was more peaceful and relaxed equal to Sacramento, California. San Jose was comfortable, non intimidating, and welcoming.

The driver parked in front of the designated bank building. Mercedes explained she would meet me outside beside the grand fountain at nine o'clock. It was eight forty-five, and I had a few minutes to tour the gardens and building. The bank was like other US banks, with large expansive lobbies, carpet, tellers' cages, officers' desks, and drinking fountains. This was a replica of any bank in any modern worldwide city and was unexpected for an undeveloped third world country such as Costa Rica. I sat down in the lobby with a clear vision of the fountain where Mercedes agreed to meet. It was just now 9:00 a.m., and I was on time. I waited until nine thirty, and still no Mercedes. Did I misunderstand the time? Was this the right place? I had no Costa Rican cell phone. Only Costa Rican citizens had them because of the high demand. She was probably just running late. Why was I feeling ill at ease? Did she take the $520,000 and run?

Ten a.m. and still no Mercedes. What could I do? No choice but to wait! What else could I do? At ten minutes after ten, I saw the dark blue Alegria SUV pull up and park. I leapt to the entrance and out to the fountain.

"Mercedes," I shouted, "I'm over here!"

She barely acknowledged my presence with a brushed-off wave. Her morning must have been a bad one. She rushed into the bank and told me to take a seat while she briskly walked to a teller's line. She caught the eye of Mr. Gonzales in another office, and he motioned her to the front of the line. I had no clue, Mr. Gonzales (the name on his name tag was to be the officiating escrow manager for our transaction). Mr. Gonzales and Mercedes didn't want my money going through the proper bank escrow account, leaving a paper trail for the Costa Rican government's prevention of money laundering. They also avoided paying income tax. It was Mr. Gonzales who prevented the successful transfer of funds between our two banks. He placed the money directly into Mercedes's account from my account and made it appear as a gift.

Mercedes was stunning wearing a pink pinstriped tight business pantsuit. Not only was I ill at ease, but I looked like "the little brown hen." My skirt and blouse blended with the black, gray, and white color scheme of the bank. Good grief! I was environmentally correctly matched. Mercedes rushed to the vacant chair beside me and sank down. "Are you ready to pay the remainder of the balance?"

"Mercedes, what balance are you talking about? I wire-transferred the entire amount. Paid in full!"

"Well ... Well ... do you remember the sellers had a $7,000 mortgage to pay?"

"Yes, and do you remember, when I was in Austin, I told you I wasn't going to pay their mortgage?"

"Well ... they wouldn't pay it."

"Well ... neither will I. I guess we have no sale," I said as I stood up to leave.

Mercedes moved from her chair like a slinking pink panther to the office where she had previously been conversing with Mr. Gonzales. My mind was in a frantic jumble. I sat back down. Mercedes and the bank had my money in her account. How could I retrieve the funds from Mercedes's account? How could I prove the money in her account wasn't hers? I had no home in either Costa Rica or the United States. Where would I go?

"Sun, I talked with the bank manager, and he said everything would be okay. My stepmother did the paperwork for Tony and Rodney, and she offered to do everything in duplicate at no charge to you, or you can choose to hire the man in the office, Mr. Gonzales. He is the bank escrow manager and would represent you for $400."

"Is your stepmother a good lawyer?"

Mercedes made a little smile. "She is the best! She is minister of justice for Costa Rica."

"Good grief, what a choice, the bank manager for four hundred, or the minister of justice for free. I'll take your stepmother." I accepted like a stupid contestant on *Let's Make a Deal*, grasping greedily for the best option.

We climbed the stairs to the conference room where Tony Lopez and Rodney Lewis (sellers), (their Realtor) Ben Kelly, Mr. Gonzales (the bank escrow account manager), Katerina Meza (minister of justice), Mercedes Meza (translator), and I made the seventh person who arrived at the oval table where the room on the fourth floor overlooked the fountain below. Tony and Rodney looked well and lighthearted. I was the only person who had a tangled bag of ropes for a stomach and lungs like two dried-up over-ripened bananas that wouldn't allow air to flow. My heart pounded like a bird's wings flapping against a window pane. I knew something was wrong, but I couldn't discern what it was.

Katerina spoke in Spanish, and Mercedes translated. "She said, first, she had Tony and Rodney sign over the property to you. They would sign, and then she had the escrow manager write out the checks from the escrow account (it was in my account first, and he transferred it to the bank escrow account)," translated Mercedes. She whispered the translation. "Now, Sun, this paper that you need to sign is for the purchase of the corporation. This paper, sign here for the land. This paper, sign it also for the house and buildings. This paper, you sign too for the *plano*."

"What's a plano?" I asked.

"A plano is what you call the survey. This paper, please sign for the city electrical easements. This paper gives the bank permission to release the escrow funds to the sellers. This paper you signed was for prorated taxes, and this paper sign for agreement to pay the closing costs," Mercedes explained.

The papers were whisked in front of me and whisked away after my signature was placed. Later I learned the rapid translation prevented me from reading and realizing all these pages of signatures authorized bank accounts to be opened in four other countries in my name for the intended purpose of future money laundering.

"Mercedes, you went too fast. Let me see the numbers on the closing costs. Is this in colonies or dollars?"

"This is in colonies; you can check on today's exchange rates later and figure it out. We can only use this room for a short time. Look out there ... all those people waited for this room, and Katerina needs to be in court in twenty minutes. She is a busy person. I will explain the closing costs after the meeting," she urged.

"How much are the closing costs? I need clarification now," I demanded.

"Tranquella, Tony and Rodney share them with you. I will explain to you after the meeting. Let's sign these two last papers and meet out in the hall," she said as she put the remaining papers in front of me, while the other six people waited. My intuition attacked my mind, but my intellect was too slow to grasp the pressure that was applied. Why was everything rushed when I was faultless by being on time when no one else was?

"Good. That's good! Finished. Let's go!" Mercedes said.

"Just a minute," I said. "I want some proof I bought a house." They all looked at me, like I was a crazy person. I stared at the escrow manager and demanded a receipt.

"Okay, yes, he will bring a receipt to you."

"In English?" I added. Mercedes asked Mr. Gonzales. He nodded his approval, and Mercedes quickly moved into the hallway.

"I signed at least ten papers," I protested.

"Yes, well ... this is Costa Rica! Later in the week we will meet at Katerina's office, and she will give you your copies of the paperwork. Ciao!" Mercedes disappeared on the run.

Mr. Gonzales, the bank manager, returned with the receipt, and I quickly scanned the numbers. Yes, this was the right amount we agreed upon for the purchase. Now let me look over the closing costs. A charge for the use of the room, a charge for the escrow account, prorated taxes, a charge for the survey. There was a charge for each paper I signed. Total closing costs equaled one half of Tony's mortgage. Humph, so that's how they did it! I was manipulated. I stood alone in the empty hallway when Tony approached with outstretched hands and held the house keys.

"All yours," he said. "Please take good care of it!"

What an unusual remark! Yeah, well, this is Costa Rica!

I overheard Tony say to Rodney, "I bet Mercedes is on her way to lunch at Martineo's." I knew Martineo's was an expensive restaurant, and Casino and I was aware of Mercedes's unfriendly departure. I watched the conference people disperse before I walked down the steps to the grand fountain entryway. I loitered outside of the bank and waved for a taxi to take me back to Mark and Carmen's hotel. In the cab, my thoughts returned to the morning events. I was fortunate Mercedes had integrity to properly deposit the money so the house sale completed. Thank goodness for that. Yet, I felt used by her manipulation with Tony's mortgage payment. I felt alone, lost, and disrespected.

I returned to Carmen and Mark's hotel and packed my two bags and air mattress in fifteen minutes. Carman and Mark gave me a ride to my new home. We traveled the winding streets of the city while Mark gave a commentary and pointed out different locations that might be helpful.

"This area, we pass now, is one of the most crime-riddled areas of Costa Rica. Never drive or walk into this area, day or night! It is called the *Inferno*. The people who live here are violent criminals, and the police won't enter this area. They target foreign people for kidnapping. They take them to ATM machines, force them to remove all their money, and sell them to Colombians for human trafficking or whatever," Mark, explained, as he drove through the green, upper hill side roads of more rural open pasture and farm land to avoid the Inferno. The Inferno warning is good information for me to remember! We drove another two miles, and I gave a jovial shout at the sight of my beautiful, green sprawled lawn and new home.

Mark and Carmen's gray van descended the driveway and dropped down into the bowl of rolling hills to my officially acquired property. I gathered my pile of sparse belongings, shoved them out the car door under the portico onto the tiled walkway, fumbled for the keys in my purse, and waved my thanks.

"We enjoyed you. Call us if you need us," waved Carmen, as they turned around in the driveway, ascended the hill, and were gone.

US Realtors explained to new buyers about "buyer's remorse." I had no regrets about buying this beautiful property, but I experienced loneliness without someone to share it with. I wanted to companionate dreams of its transformation into a beautiful mini-resort and bond with someone in its beauty and peacefulness. It was definitely aloneness not remorse that I experienced. This detachment was "foreign" from prior lonely occurrences. I wouldn't allow my loneliness to consume adventure. This new project gave a chance to exchange loneliness for adventure! I vowed to peel off lonely feelings, like peeling paint from an old Wyoming barn, and set my direction toward my new enterprise.

I hesitated by the door with the keys, two suitcases, two beach towels, and my air mattress. I drew a deep breath. No, I inhaled three deep breaths in anticipation of what I might find inside. I unlocked the thick mahogany, heavy, hand-hewn front door, stepped inside, and jumped straight into the air when the security alarm blared with painful ear-rupturing intensity. After what seemed an eternity, I found the control panel and managed to disarm it. Good grief! That's definitely got to go. Well, I experienced another blessing. The house had been purged of others' belongings and was clean, not shining clean, but passable. I dragged in the suitcases and the air mattress.

Sun Wren Richards, where would you like to sleep tonight? I wandered around the house and selected the best room suited for the air mattress. I followed the hallway down a beautiful set of mahogany steps lined on both sides with ceiling to floor glass windows. The long hall with picture mosque tiles led to three bedrooms with three bathrooms, and each had a patio balcony. This part of the house was at garden level, and the tall windows looked outside to the tropical vegetation as I descended the stairs. This was a perfect place for my sculptures. The sloping level of the hills placed this lower part of the house at ground level. The burnt-orange tile flooring was throughout the house and accented its ambling graciousness. The house was charming! My spirits lifted as I reassessed my purchase, which strongly banished buyer's remorse and loneliness.

The bedroom I chose was a Jack and Jill with spacious closets and built in drawers with closet rods. I could live without furniture for a while because of this practical design. The bathroom was large and had double vanity sinks, toilet, and shower. I would flourish in this house!

Let's see if there was hot water! Yep! Hot water! What more could a girl want? I set up the air mattress beside the electrical outlet for the little electric air pump. Electricity! Yeah! The bed filled to an invited shape. I had no sheets or blankets, but with this pleasant weather I didn't need any. I had two large beach towels, and I used one for a lower sheet and the other for my shower! I unpacked some belongings into the drawers, but I was excited to check out the art studio and gardens. I left the rest of the unpacking until later.

Outside, the gardens were even more beautiful than I remembered.

I loped down to the art studio that was cleared of all previous debris. This studio was my joy and inspiration. I walked the trails, admired the giant nudo-de-india trees that Mercedes taught me to recognize. These trees had massive, slick, graceful trunks, and were named for the color of their trunks, which looked like naked skin, and their shape was curvy like a woman's body. I counted seven of these trees.

The light of day slipped away. The house was settled into the bottom of the bowl made from the surrounding hills. I couldn't see sunset because the house was low behind the hills, which concealed the sun. This was different because now it was dark. There was no twilight. It was like someone switched off the light. I have never experienced living on the equator where the sun turns on at day-break and off for night. I made my way back through the blackness, stumbled over tree roots, and groped the pathway with my hands. I reached the house and flipped the light switch on, but no lights came on. What was wrong? I knew there was electricity. I used the air pump and the blasted burglar alarm went off. I groped my way into the selected bedroom and flipped the switch, but nothing turned on. If the breaker was tripped, at least one light in this house should come on. I didn't even know where to feel for the light switches in each room because of the darkness. I groped my way back down the stairs to the garden-level rooms and felt the walls for the bathroom light. I flipped the light switch. Blackness engulfed the entire interior, and the only light came twinkling from the homes on faraway hills.

I had no choice but to find my bed and lie down. I was peaceful with the blackness full of its wonderful tropical night sounds. This was heavenly! From the breeze-caressed blackness came the most unusual bird sound. Its cry was lonely, begging, mournful, and beautiful. I hadn't heard anything like this sound. It was a sad, haunting cry, a pleading for something, perhaps attention, or love. It was not unlike the cry from a neglected child. This bird made its tearful cry throughout the blackened night and cried me into sleep.

CHAPTER 7
LESSONS

Maybe this morning I would see what the sad bird from last night looked like, but its mournful tune wasn't heard among the loud din of morning birds. There were more birds in these thick tropical forests than were at Mark and Carmen's hotel. What a glorious sound! I couldn't possibly sleep through this little beak chatter. The sun was full bright; the window of my room faced northeast, and by USA time of light was about 10:00 a.m., but guessing by Costa Rican time, I estimated it was 5:00 a.m. I had no way of knowing what time it was because I wore no watch and had no radio, TV, or cell phone. My life now was clearly without technology. It was just nature and me.

Outside in the gardens I was amazed by the wildlife that presented itself for my entertainment. I watched two iguanas on the art studio roof lying there sunning themselves. There were many colorful large and small birds that seemed at home eating the fruits from the many trees. An armadillo churned about in the lower coffee grove, and I spotted a Quetzal a rare bird even for Costa Rica. The

Quetzal was small compared to other tropical birds I watched. The Quetzal was a brilliant lime green color with a cute round face and a three-foot-long plumage of tail. What a beauty he was sitting on the railing of the tiki hut located on the highest point of the property's elevation. I named this property Casa Ave. My Native American culture selected names from nature, and so would I.

I felt unworldly not knowing the species or even the names of all the creatures I saw. I looked forward to learning about their habits and how we would habituate. The animals and birds all rooted, pecked, and foraged for their breakfasts. Good idea! I had a sack of granola bars, but I wanted to retrieve the existing growing stuff.

Mangoes were ripe on four of the mango trees, two lime-bearing trees, cashew fruit with the cashew perched on top of each fruit, which gave the appearance of an aristocratic garden party. I wouldn't have believed the way they naturally grew if I hadn't seen it. No wonder they were so expensive to buy. It took one entire fruit to produce one cashew. The cashew fruit had a strong perfumed aroma that filled the kitchen and dining room when I placed them into a bowl I made from a fallen palm leaf. The fruit wasn't as tasty as its rich aroma. I definitely had food. I wouldn't go hungry, but being diabetic limited my selection. I splurged this morning and ate a banana loaded with carbohydrates. What a rich experience breakfast had been. I already planned my lunch menu. I harvested fully ripened avocados from one of the two trees. I enjoyed playing primitive food gatherer, but it was time to get busy.

I found a wobbly step stool left in the art studio and hauled it into the house to investigate the electrical problem from last night. I sat the stool up in the bathroom and removed the coverings. No bulbs ... well that much was solved. I moved the stool into the main rooms and checked the chandeliers. All wires had been cut. I moved from room to room, and the result was the same. What a mean-spirited thing to have done. Who would do this annoying, deliberate act? Why was it done? This deliberate act was small-minded.

I slipped into a sensible dress and walking shoes and grabbed my Spanish dictionary that Molly had given to me. I walked up the driveway hill to a street where vendors and little grocery shops were tucked. I studied the pronunciation for the words lightbulbs ... "bomba luz." I said it. I entered the first little cubbyhole, designed as a food store, and said my new Spanish words. The shopkeeper understood and replied something really fast in Spanish. I looked perplexed, but she took me by the hand, smiled at me kindly, and pointed to another small shop down the street. I thanked her and strolled off in that direction.

This neighborhood was in a poor area. The residents had made the front part of their homes into some sort of selling space. Some sold baked goods, fruits, school supplies, vegetables, or meat in iced cases, while others were selling shoes, clothing, and pots and pans. One space on the corner sold laundry and cleaning supplies. I tried to remember these tiny spaces and the available items. One man sold barbecue chicken. I would buy some on my way home to eat with the avocados from my property's trees.

I found the "sort of" hardware shop and asked for bomba luz, por favor. He understood! Victory! Triumph! Winner! I took the bag of bulbs and started retracing my way. I bought lettuce, tomatoes, cucumbers, small green onions, and barbecue chicken. I would feast for lunch, and if the refrigerator worked, my comfort level would inch up a little higher. I spotted a telephone booth very near where I bought the lightbulbs. Another day, I would call Mercedes, but right now I could only think about lunch.

Lunch was tasty, and I ate it out in the bar lounge that over-looked the pool. I had enough food to last for several meals, and I could buy supplies by walking to the nearby stores. The refrigerator worked and was reasonably clean. That afternoon I replaced sixteen lightbulbs in the eight bathrooms, and tonight I would have some light available. It should be enough to navigate my way around. I had the luxury of time and intended to use a major part of the day doing a full meditating program. I started with one hour of yoga, one hour of meditation, and one hour for either walking or swimming. I had nothing or no one to interrupt my routine.

Before the sun turned off, I checked to see that all twenty-two doors were closed and locked. Last night it was so dark that I didn't even know where the doors were located, let alone to know if they were locked. I secured fifty-four windows and learned the floor plan of the house and grounds. My comforts and security became more stable while time lapsed.

The house closing took place April 24, 2008. Two weeks passed without communication aids from radio, telephone, television, clocks, stereo, and I had no visitors. I didn't mind the void of such noise products. I became victorious in conquering loneliness, and I noticed remarkable personal changes took place.

I became accurate in determining the time of day based entirely on the sun's position, the color of its light, and the smell of the vegetation. In the morning around sunrise, the smell was a light sweet odor like cotton candy, and as the sun climbed higher into the afternoon hours the plants' fragrance changed and became stronger and pungent like cooked spinach. When the sun moved into the west before dark, the scent was soft and faint again like the early dawn, but with a bitter aroma similar to Burt's hand cream. The nighttime had a different bouquet emanating from the jasmine flowers and night lilies that opened. From midnight to dawn there was a plant called Titan Arum; its color was purple trimmed with green, and it produced a bad rancid smell similar to dirty feet. The natural smells of vegetation were my digital clock.

As a child, I was aware of the smells of the land where I grew up. I knew the smell of draught, the smell of dust, the smell of fields after a hay harvest, the cutting of the sugar beets, the smell when rain was coming, the smell of our tribal Native American sun dances, the smell of a sweaty horse, and the smell of an angry person after drinking too much wine or Vitales hair oil. The Native Americans drank hair oil before civil rights granted them the rights to drink liquor in bars. Being without the technology of time made me realize what an American trait time had played in my life. I got rid of that trait. What difference did knowing the time have upon our personal development, significant knowledge, or spiritual evolution? Not much!

This two-week solitude of Costa Rican life sharpened all five senses and my intuition. I walked up to the phone booth, renamed "my office," many times and attempted to reach Mercedes. The telephone lesson, without knowing what was said in my ear hastened my Spanish education. I remembered one word at a time, looked it up in my dictionary, and tried to understand what the operator told me. Seven trials of "Spanish speaking public phone lessons" eventually produced a positive connection with Mercedes, but she hadn't returned my call even though she was aware of my situation. I felt something wasn't right and had a foreboding feeling. I was ready for Mercedes's explanation.

The new worker, Amon, was to begin work two days after closing. Was he coming? Should I search for a new worker? While I waited, my time was used to study Spanish and to design the house into a hotel and a sustainable food garden. I was ready for Amon's help.

Tony Lopez told me at closing that he would transfer the utilities into my name, but it required both of us appearing together at the separate utilities offices to make the transfer. I learned that all offices were dispersed throughout the barrio. I couldn't transfer these necessities into my name without Tony's signature and his presence. I was ready for Tony Lopez. Where was everyone?

The elements of the universe heard my questions, and by

afternoon a taxi arrived with a letter from Tony Lopez. He summoned me to meet him in two days, on Tuesday at 2:30 p.m. at the city cemetery. I sent back a note of confirmation with the taxi driver. Maybe now I would progress to transform this big house into a hotel for tourists.

With the light from the bathrooms at night, I learned Spanish from children's workbooks used to teach them English. I bought them from the school supply store three blocks from the top of my driveway. These workbooks were helpful, and I wrote out a one-week schedule for Amon when he came. Every night the sound of the sad bird accompanied my Spanish lesson, and tonight after estimating a two-hour study session, I turned off the bathroom light and went to the air mattress. The house was in total darkness, even with the windows and drapes opened; the thick jungle surrounding the house prevented any light from penetrating. Sometimes light came from the moon, but tonight there was no moon, and the thick tall trees prevented a view of the stars. Out of this pure licorice night came a loud crashing sound! The sound jolted me up, and I listened. I couldn't tell where the sound came from, but I thought it was from upstairs, maybe the living room? Had someone broken into the house?

I had no way to call anyone for help. I slid out of bed and walked into the hall without turning on any lights. My nights without lights made my navigation confident. Now I knew the house floor plan, and I could find my way in its blackness. I needed to find out if a drunk driver slammed into the house or if something in the house had malfunctioned. *Crash,* rumble, rumble, rumble, thud. There it was again. I crept up the stairs into the living room. I was careful not to allow my shadow to fall across the open windows and expose my whereabouts to whomever or whatever was out there.

I grabbed the iron poker from the fireplace and slid close to the walls. I looked out without being seen. Everything out in the front driveway was quiet. No car accident and no parked cars. I stood by the window with butterflies in my abdomen. I felt vulnerable. *Breathe deeply, breathe deeply; you are worthless if your fear keeps you from functioning. Stay still and breathe. Breathe deeply, breathe ... breathe ... breathe deeply.* I needed to cross to another window to know what was out there on the other side of the house.

Crash, rumble, rumble, rumble, rumble, thud. Was it only tree debris falling onto the tile roof? I slid close to the walls as I made my way to the east side of the house to look out into the thick tropics. I made my eyes adjust to the exterior darkness and stared into its shadowy depth. I saw something move. I stayed still and waited. I could see the outline of a man wearing dark clothing, stepping forward, and throwing something onto the roof of the house. The hilltop where he stood was nearly level to the roof. *Crash*, rumble, rumble, rumble, thud. I think, he threw boulders onto the roof, which explained the crash and the rumbling sound as the rocks rolled their way down the tiled roof to thud on the ground.

My thoughts chased around in my head as I continued to check the nearby four exterior doors to make sure they remained bolted. Did he wait for me to come out of the house to examine the source of the noise? *Stand still, and see if you could tell who it is.* He was tall and slender. I squinted into the distance. Those identified qualities were only a guess because my night vision wasn't sharp, and my left eye was worthless. *Crash*, rumble, rumble, rumble, thud. I still had two more exterior doors to check. I lay down on my belly and slithered across the floor so I would not be seen. I wore nylon-acetate pajamas, and they easily slid across the slick tile floor where I reached the stairway and hallway. The doors were locked, and all the windows throughout the house had black wrought iron bars to prevent burglaries.

I had mind chatter. He didn't know what part of the house to find me as long as I didn't turn on the light. If I stayed quiet, he might think I wasn't home. Maybe he didn't want me at all but wanted to know if the place was vacant to burglarize. I had nothing for protection if I revealed my whereabouts. My best protection would be to hide and if discovered to run like hell. *Crash*, rumble, rumble, rumble, thud. I knew where I would hide. There was an indentation in the straight walls where the draperies folded and stored while they weren't covering the windows. I would hide there if he was able to enter the house. I knew I would hear him enter, and then I would run. If I ran, where would I go? I would exit the lower exterior door by the pool and run up toward the town. Surely someone would help a screaming woman—or not—in this neighborhood! After checking all the exterior doors, I crawled back upstairs, slithered across the floor, and watched the man. I lay down beside the window and looked for him in the shadows. There he was.

What did he want? Why was he doing this? Maybe this was just a game to scare me—and it worked—but why? If I made no response, maybe he would get bored and go home. *Crash*, rumble, rumble, rumble, rumble, thud. Tomorrow at first light I would find what he threw. I waited for thirty or forty minutes, but there were no more crashing sounds. I carefully looked out and no longer saw him. He was gone. I remained on the floor and slithered back down the stairs in case he had moved into a different position. It was quiet as I slid onto the air mattress.

Listen to that silence! The bird with the sad song no longer sang. *Think! When was the last time I heard him singing tonight?* He sang all through my Spanish lesson until I turned off the bathroom light. That's when the crashing sound began, and the sad song of the bird stopped. Maybe "the man" knew I was downstairs because he saw the light. I would choose a different study place every night from now on, or not study at night at all. The bird started his song again. I had a natural watchdog outside. Little bird, with your sad song, you were my angel bird, and I listened for your song of protection. I fell asleep to his pensive, mournful cry.

The next morning (Tuesday), I went outside to investigate what had been hurled at the rooftop. Five or six lava rocks were strewn about on the grass. I ascended to the area where he stood, and at the base of a large tree was a stash of large rocks that were carried and left in a pile. These lava rocks weren't the same type of rock common to this garden. I picked up arm loads of these rocks, carried them to the base of the garden trees, and arranged them into an artistic border. I went up and down the hill many times and removed his stash. These rocks, even the ones that rolled off the roof, went to good use. They would not be left in position as ready ammunition to be hurled for another night. I sniffed the air. It now smelled a little bit like cooked spinach. I looked at the position of the sun and decided it was time for me to meet Tony at the cemetery as he had requested.

I began my journey to the city center cemetery where we were to meet. I walked four miles before I found a taxi driver who spoke English and could read Tony's note. I peeked at the clock in the taxicab, and it read 1:45 p.m. I had plenty of time to arrive at the cemetery by two thirty. The taxi dropped me at the entrance, and I waited in the shade provided from the entrance's main gate. I waited. I walked four of the seven miles and was careful to watch where the taxi driver drove after he picked me up. I counted on Tony helping me return home since this was a country without addresses. I waited. Two funeral processions arrived and departed. I waited.

"Miss, can you please tell me what time it is?" I asked a young business Tica, sure she would speak English.

"Yes, certainly. It is ten minutes after four," she replied.

"Thank you!"

I was lucky to have worn my old marathon walking shoes because I knew I couldn't give a taxi driver directions to where I lived. I retraced the three miles of my taxi ride plus the four miles I walked to reach the beautiful welcomed sight of my home. I walked a total of eleven miles today to meet Tony, who was a *no-show*. I was tired, disappointed, and angry but glad I reached the comfort of the air mattress.

The following early Wednesday morning, I heard a man's voice yelling, "Señora Sun, Señora Sun." I looked up at the driveway entrance and saw Amon. I ran up the steep driveway and gave him a heartfelt welcome. It must be about 7:00 a.m., which was his agreed starting time. He wore a watch, and I took his arm and looked at the time. I was pleased with both of us—him for being on time and me because I knew it was nearly 7:00 a.m. by the smell of the plants. I indicated for him to wait while I ran back into the house to get my handwritten (in Spanish) work schedule for the week. I handed him the list, and he looked at it for a long time. He glanced at me, smiled, and handed it back. He remained standing, so I handed him the list again. He handed it back again and smiled. Good grief! I don't think he can read.

I took the list and read with the best Spanish pronunciation I could muster. He nodded, and I tried again to give him the written list. He waved it away and tapped his forehead to let me know he had it. I strolled back into the house to begin my morning routine of yoga, meditation, and exercise while he changed his clothes in the gardener's bathroom. I watched him emerge from his lavatory. He wore only a pair of cutoffs, no shoes or shirt, and carried his machete. As the day progressed, I was aware of his whereabouts, and he was everywhere! He was the most efficient worker I had ever observed. He was up in the trees and trimmed out the dead branches, and on the ground cut the grass. He fixed the water well and repaired the leaking roof. I was delighted to turn on all the lights where the wires had previously been cut and now repaired. I was astounded by his work ethic because he completed the week's work in one day. His movements were strong, effective, and efficient.

Amon taught me about the many plants and their medicinal purposes. Some plants were for headaches, for use as shampoos, to make a tea for improving diabetes or flu, and plants the young girls ate after a pleasurable night with a man to prevent pregnancy. Amon told me about a plant that if you stood near it or touched it while breathing or talking, would produce a terrible rash, but if someone held his or her breath, closed the mouth, and touched it, the rash wouldn't appear. I thought this was strictly Nicaraguan superstition, and I reiterated the story to a Costa Rican biologist who confirmed the story as fact and explained that the gasses from the plant affected the respiratory system and indeed produced a nasty rash equal to poison ivy.

I learned about nature and plants from Amon. He was twenty-five years old and had the stature of a pit bulldog. I was five feet two, and he was only a few inches taller than me, reaching a maximum height of five feet four inches. He was a handsome guy with thick black hair and deep black mischievous eyes. He had a great sense of humor and expressed ample nonsexual affection by hooking up our arms, or hand holding as we strolled through the gardens which he was proud to show off.

He had the agility of a monkey and walked up a tree to retrieve any mango or cashew. He was always barefooted despite my warnings about foot injury. Amon told me his nickname among family and friends was Mondo, or monkey. His balance was next to superhuman. He walked a tiny rail not much thicker than a rope and carried two gallons of paint in each hand and one balanced on the top of his head. He loved to have his picture taken, and his pride of his good looks was humorous.

"You look nice today, Amon," I complimented him. He would grin and respond, "Yes, I do, and I am very pretty." I assumed there was no Spanish word for handsome, or he knew my Spanish was lacking and used words I understood.

Amon was an exceptionally hard worker. He loved the gardens and referred to them as "Amon's gardens." When I first arrived in Costa Rica we had no tools. Amon did all of his garden work with a machete. He mowed three acres with this long-bladed knife, and the grass was even and beautiful. He was also very artistic, and he made bold red and white rock designs in various star patterns around all the bases of trees. He painted their trunks white, which matched the designs of the surrounding rocks and discouraged insects. Amon loved flowers, and most every day he made a bouquet for the tourist's rooms and for me. I would come into the hotel lobby to find splendid arrangements a US flower shop couldn't equal.

When we finally bought a lawn mower, Amon was like a child. He wanted to mow all the time! He was the groundskeeper and maintenance man. I hadn't known such a fast and efficient worker. He worked from seven in the morning to four in the afternoon, and we ate together for breakfast and lunch. It usually rained in the afternoons, so I planned lunch at 2:00 p.m. during heavy downpours. If it still rained after lunch, we turned on his old stereo and danced! What fun that was! Good grief, could that kid dance! We were a wild dancing pair.

At the end of the day, he showered in the "gardener's bathroom" and left looking like he was groomed for the screen or stage. His clothes were pressed to perfection, and he took pride to wear the latest fragrance of perfume. He "out aromaed" the flowers in the garden.

Amon was married; no, that's incorrect; he had a woman. Many Costa Ricans never married because they didn't want to promise God to be married "until death do us part." It seemed even well-educated Ticos didn't marry but only stayed together for many years because they were afraid of lying to God about fidelity. Amon later told me that he and his woman, Maria, had tried for a long time to have a baby. It seemed strange to me that it was a greater sin to divorce than to have sex and live as common-law. I questioned which was the greater sin. I guessed the Central American Catholic Church's rules and doctrine accepted love without marriage before it accepted divorce.

By four o'clock, Amon knocked at the hotel door and presented his backpack for inspection. I didn't know why he wanted me to look into his backpack. I made this event into a large theater production. I admired his comb, smelled his perfume, looked at pictures of attractive Maria, and remarked about his leftover lunch. He couldn't understand a word I said, but he knew I didn't understand the reason I looked into his private bag. Amon had a great sense of humor, and he laughed loudly at my theater mime and over exaggerated antics. Later, I learned that presented backpacks or purses for Patron's inspection was normal procedures for Costa Rican workers to prove they hadn't stolen anything during their workday. Amon always gave me a hug and wished me a good night. I tried to thank Amon for his industrious day's work; whether he understood remained questionable.

CHAPTER 8
INDEPENDENCE

My new Spanish colonial house was located in a part of the city that was borderline poverty where few people spoke English or would speak English. Amon and I got along with the help of the Spanish dictionary, mime, theater, and drawings in the dirt. I still had no electronics, and to acquire them would demand knowledge of the Spanish language and travel into the central city many miles by taxi. My concerns now were to establish communications with my family and friends, and transfer the utilities before the supplying companies terminated services for nonpayment.

I gained some sense of independence with the opening of a bank account and post office box, but reliance upon others' kindness and my helplessness was uncomfortable. Growing up in a remote area of Wyoming, I accomplished things alone. My self-image was structured into knowing the strength of my own character, and now I struggled with insecurities. The loss of my language was paramount because expression was the need of my soul. My ignorance concerning policies, governing rules, or acceptable social graces hampered my actions and social liveliness. Being forced by my own insufficiency to rely, trust, and wait for others' help drove me into a negative place. Worst of all, the plummeting of my self-image and self-assurance was a foreign experience.

I was out of sorts waiting for Mercedes all day when she told me she would be here to help transfer the utilities by 10:00 a.m. It was now nearly 4:00 p.m., and Amon would be leaving soon. My dependency upon Mercedes was magnified by the previous event of the eleven-mile walk and a two-hour wait for Tony, who never arrived.

Amon finished his work and was up at the driveway gate when Mercedes's blue Alegria SUV arrived. They talked for a few minutes. Amon went on his way, and Mercedes came down and parked under the portico. I was ready to accomplish our utility transfer task, and I jumped into the car. We drove into the city while Mercedes explained. "I was delayed all day because I interviewed for a job as an events coordinator for one of the computer companies in San Jose," offered Mercedes, without my asking.

I was forced by my dependent position to tolerate Mercedes's lateness because my future depended upon utilities. I was in the receiving position for charity, and to make strong demands was not a wise option.

"That's wonderful, Mercedes. I think you would be great as an events coordinator! Do you think you got the job?"

"I don't know. I interviewed with many department managers. Some were warmer than others. It really doesn't matter to me (she shrugged), because if I don't get the job, I am thinking of moving to Spain to be with my grandfather. Why didn't you meet with Tony? He said you never showed up at the cemetery?"

"Mercedes, what he told you is not true. I walked eleven miles, and I waited for him for over two hours." I quickly changed the subject to avoid an argument. "How can we transfer the utilities without Tony's presence and signature?"

"Tony was angry with you because you didn't meet him, and he refused to come, but he gave me a permission letter with his signature to make the utility transfer. I have a letter of authorization and a notary from Katerina. We can make the transfer," Mercedes said.

"Would it be possible for us to talk to the telephone company today? I really need a telephone."

"People in Costa Rica wait a very long time to get telephones. The wait is sometimes two or three years. You are a foreigner and last on the list." Mercedes added the control for continued dependency, but I didn't take the bait for confrontation.

"Amon asked me to ask you if you wanted to hire a woman to help you with the house cleaning."

"Great! I would like that. Does she speak English?"

"No, not a word, but I will tell him to bring her over to your house. She is Nicaraguan, and most Nica's are hard workers."

We stepped into the ICE (electric company) office. Over one hundred people were ahead of us. There were two hundred chairs in a row, and the procedure was to sit in the empty chair at the back of the waiting group. There were two desks up front, and when the chair at the desk became vacant, the next person from the sitting group moved into the vacated place to receive attention from the person managing the desk. This was a highly inefficient method of customer service.

We took our chairs, moved up the line, and waited our turn.

"How are you liking your new home?" questioned Mercedes, as she looked me directly in the eyes.

"I love it, and I really like Amon. He is a good worker."

"Aren't you afraid to be in that big house all by yourself?"

"No, not at all. I sleep very well, and there is a sad, mournful bird that sings every night. What is the bird?"

"He is called Diablo de Noches, meaning 'devil of the night,'" she explained, as she moved up to the next available chair.

"Why is he named that? His song is sad but beautiful."

"He only comes to harm people. He comes only at night, and you will never see what he looks like. I have never seen him nor has anyone else."

"Mercedes, do you believe that?" I asked, not believing that any educated person of her stature could hold such a superstitious view. She looked ahead with downcast eyes and shrugged her shoulders.

We finally had our turn at the desk, and the electricity got transferred into the corporation name (corporations were required by Costa Rican law for owning investment property), and later I would receive the papers from Katerina.

"You need to come into the office every month to pay your electricity bill," Mercedes advised.

"How will I know when to come and how much to pay?" I wanted to establish correct business practice.

"You know to come every month before the tenth, and they tell you how much to pay. You need to ask your neighbors where to go to pay for your water. You go to another town called Cacow. You need to go with a neighbor, or take a taxi, but it is only every three months, and you have to ask your neighbor when your next payment date is due," Mercedes explained, as we left the electric office.

"Isn't that procedure difficult to keep up with your bills?" I asked, grateful for any information.

"Yes, well—this is Costa Rica. Aren't you afraid at night, by yourself?" She repeated her former question.

"No, I love the house," I said, emphatically.

I suspected Mercedes knew about my nighttime events. I didn't tell her about the five or six times a man came to the house between midnight and sometimes as late as 3:00 a.m. to throw rocks onto the roof. I became reluctant to share information with her. I perceived Mercedes as one of my stage actresses who attempted to play a character's role, but her own attributes bled through, and the audience saw the intended character's nature, but the actress's true self peeked through the thin fabric and made her acting role unconvincing.

"We need to make an appointment to go to Katerina's office to finish the paperwork from the house closing. How would this Thursday be for you?"

"I have no other urgent business. Any day would be good. I also want a will drawn for the property. Can she prepare that for me?"

"You need to pay her." Mercedes stated demandingly.

"Of course, and I will bring the Social Security numbers of my heirs."

"Once you said I was like a daughter to you. Am I an heir?"

I laughed. "You have a quick wit, Mercedes." I joked, thinking she was being lighthearted.

Mercedes didn't laugh but suddenly pulled the car over and parked. She got out of the car and said, "Let's go!" I got out of the car and followed her like a stray puppy.

"Where are we going now, Mercedes?" I asked, completely puzzled. We walked for about a block before she answered.

"We are going to your bank because you need to pay me $150 for today's help with the utilities."

"Mercedes, we made no such agreement. I didn't know this transfer for electricity today was for your hire. I thought you were being kind to help. I don't have $150, and besides, the bank is closed." I looked around and hadn't a clue where I was or how to get back to my house. I didn't even know how to tell a taxi driver where to take me. I would have walked home if I had known the way, which I didn't. I guessed we were still in San Jose. To me this was a kidnapping. I was aware of Mercedes's abilities to smoothly manipulate others to her demands.

"Mercedes, I had fully intended to give you money for gas, as a gift for helping me today because it is the right thing to do, but not because you demand it."

"How much were you going to give me?" she asked, stopping her walk to the closed bank.

"I planned to give you $50 because I know gasoline is expensive, and we needed to travel into San Jose."

"Okay, you can give it to me in the car," she relented.

On the way home, we drove for miles in silence before I asked her, "Are you going to charge me to go to Katerina's office on Thursday?"

"No. I told Katerina I would take you to her office because she asked me to do it as a favor."

"Mercedes, I learned a valuable lesson today. While you drive, I will write down the directions to my house so I can tell a taxi driver, if I need to. What is the name of the area of the house?" She told me, and I wrote it out.

"What is the closest landmark?" I felt childlike learning pertinent information a parent would teach to a child in the event he or she became lost.

It seemed impossible to anyone who had never been to a Costa Rican city to understand my helplessness. Most businesses didn't advertise or have signage on their stores, and the ones that did may not be known to taxi drivers. Being unable to read Spanish augmented my helplessness. If there was a well-known landmark that locals knew, the taxi driver might know the location. There was no zoning in any of the cities, and residences were sprinkled among businesses, which complicated travel. People lived in the area a long time before successful navigation was possible.

If you asked a Tico directions, he wouldn't tell you he didn't know but sent you anywhere just to give you an answer. The customs office was also another problem for me. My shipment of household belongings arrived in Limon or Puntarenas and then traveled to the customs warehouse in Alajuela by truck. Foreigners didn't have telephones, so customs was unable to notify or deliver.

"When should my shipment of furniture arrive from customs?" I asked.

"I will give you the name and telephone number of customs, and he will tell you how to pay. The phone number is 2284-2283, and his name is Rogelio Ortiz. He will tell you when your customs delivery arrives." Mercedes answered far too compliantly. Intuition poked me again. How was it that Mercedes had this information so readily available? Was this another of her self-promoting plans?

It was difficult for me to understand Mercedes's moments of unkindness. She didn't express gratitude for the employment or Realtor position bestowed upon her. I wished she wanted to be helpful out of kindness instead of monetary expectations, but now I understood how someone took advantage of others who need help. Helping someone came with the expectation of reward. I became cognizant that Mercedes realized she overplayed her business aggression, and she fell back into her demure refined tourist guide role. She sang her favorite Spanish songs and told me a story about another tourist she took on a boat ride at Playa Manuel Antonio.

The story began as Mercedes and the tourist stood on the deck of a boat. A bird flew overhead and pooped onto the tourist's sunglasses. The tourist, in horror, removed the glasses and put them to his lips to blow breath onto them to clean them, as Americans did. The tourist accidentally got the bird poop on his tongue. He stood there with his tongue hanging out. Mercedes's infectious laugher was strong, and it was impossible not to enjoy the slapstick humor of her story. It provoked peals of laughter from us both and served as her method to erase the tension between us. It was at this juncture of time I realized I hadn't spoken English with anyone in over a month and how I missed it. I knew I needed to eat a plateful of humble pie until my dealings with Mercedes ended, and I was independent. When we arrived home, it was already dark, and I paid her $50 for the gas.

"Thank you, Mercedes, for helping me today." I was relieved to have secured utilities. "What time will you pick me up on Thursday to go to your stepmother's office?"

"I will be here between 9:00 a.m. and noon, depending upon the schedule of Apollo (her husband) with his tourists. I will see you Thursday. Ciao!"

I entered the dark house, turned on the lights, and made sure all doors were securely bolted from the inside. Diablo de Noches bird sang his forlorn melody as I prepared for bed. I had a warm sense of well-being, believing my standard of living had improved. I drifted to sleep listening to Diablo's doleful solo.

Bang, bang, bang. Someone had pounded on the main entrance door. I bolted upright, startled, and as rigid as a freeze-dried shirt on a Wyoming clothesline. I remained in bed, aware that Diablo's song was gone. The knock at the door was repeated louder and in more rapid succession. My thoughts came like swift, uncomfortable strobe lights bringing pain to my eyes and lungs.

Costa Rica had an epidemic of burglaries where the thief knocked at the door, and when the homeowner responded, the thief either shot or robbed him at gunpoint. *Are those knocks from the man who threw the rocks? Are his actions becoming more aggressive and closer to his target? Was I the target?* My thoughts screamed in my mind.

Breathe, breathe, deep breath. Why did I always forget to breathe? *Be calm and listen.* I didn't hear any more knocking at the front entrance, quiet … listen … listen … I heard the rattling sound of the metal entrance doorknob. He had become aggressive enough to enter. I knew the doors were all bolted with deadlocks from the inside as well as key locked from the outside. Could he possibly have keys? Tomorrow I would have Amon call a locksmith and change the outside locks. The rattling knobs revealed that the intruder examined all exterior doors and windows. He looked for entrance and continued to knock on each exterior door. I was damned well certain I wasn't going to answer the door! My thin short nightgown was saturated with perspiration, and my entire body behaved badly. My heart raced, and my skin dripped wet. My breath was held, and I needed air. Breathe. Breathe. Breathe, deep breath, deep, deep breath. *Sun, stop this fear now!* Something needed to be done to take care of this nighttime saga!

1. Change all the locks. 2. Double check the bolts on the windows. 3. Build a security fence with iron safety gates to keep intruders at a distance. 4. Get acquainted with neighbors. This was a good list, and it redirected my mind away from the dark fear tunnel I had fallen into.

The intruder had one more door to check, and he would have been all the way around the house. He had attempted entry on all twenty-two exterior doors. It was odd; he hadn't shouted or approached stealthily and noiselessly as a burglar might be inclined to do. *Listen. Listen.* More silence. *Just relax.. Wait. Relax. Breath. Silence. Silence. Silence was good. Silence was good. Try to meditate. Relax and meditate.* After meditating for about twenty minutes, I was aware of Diablo's song. *Relax. Diablo's song indicates he has gone.* I sank down into the air mattress and was comforted by Diablo's continued song.

CHAPTER 9
CASA AVE

The next morning, at seven o'clock, Amon brought the new woman who wanted to work as a maid and cook. I couldn't share any of the nighttime events with them because I couldn't speak enough of their Spanish language, and I knew Amon was superstitious and might be afraid to come to work. Amon left the new woman positioned in the kitchen as he marched to the gardener's room to change for the day's work.

"Como se llama?" (What is your name?)

"Wyoming," she said.

"Yes, I am from Wyoming. Como se llama?"

"Wyoming," she repeated.

This went on for several more times, and then I enacted: "Yes, yes, I am from Wyoming. What is your name?" I said as I pointed to her. She stood still and looked at me wide-eyed.

I pointed to myself and said, "Sun."

She then pointed to herself and said, "Wyoming."

This was so silly, and I laughed out loud, pointed to myself and said, "Me Tarzan. You Jane." She got my joke; evidently she watched those old movies too, and our introduction ended in mutual laughter.

Wyoming was a short, portly woman in her fifties with graying black hair and dark brown eyes. She maintained a guarded warmth about her demeanor and looked at me with suspicion, willing to be of service but not willing to trust. I felt she was trustworthy, but I needed to earn her confidence. Amon and she had known each other for many years while working in the coffee plantations. Wyoming, like Amon, was from Nicaragua, where she worked cooking in a restaurant until the Sandinista government violently closed the restaurant, killing her father and two older brothers. She fled to Costa Rica and married a Tico who left her to raise four children by herself. Her oldest daughter was married and lived in Nicaragua. The two boys learned abusiveness toward women from their father. They made financial demands upon Wyoming and often beat her. Her one joy was the youngest daughter, fourteen-year-old Tania. When I looked into Wyoming's cocker spaniel eyes, I knew she needed someone to love her.

I hired her. I asked her to begin the workday at 10:00 a.m. and finish by 4:00 p.m. so she could walk home with Amon. They needed to walk through a rough neighborhood to the bus stop. The bus took forty minutes to reach their homes, where they were neighbors.

Amon and I established his self-directed work routine by the time Wyoming was hired. He knew what needed to be done and took the initiative to work independently, continuously improving the property. He worked without needing "the directive list" from me. If I requested something to be done, he completed that task first in the day. Wyoming, being older and having worked under strict plantation owners longer than Amon's young years, was lost without direction. She expressed frustration without knowing what she should do when she finished her list, and I wasn't home to provide more directives. The first days of her employment she was insecure, but I knew she talked to Amon. The following days proved Wyoming was an efficient, hardworking, knowledgeable woman, who possessed the gift of service. She became a self-directed dynamo like Amon. The beautiful artistically designed floors shone to a reflective brilliance. Her speed and concern for her work brought great benefits for both Amon and me. She cooked our breakfast, lunch, and prepared my dinner before she left at four. She did laundry, ironed my clothes and table napkins, polished my shoes and handbags, cleaned and organized the kitchen to suit her meal preparation, and did the dishes by hand to save electricity. Our dishes were pewter and hand-washing achieved the same brilliance as the floors.

When she completed her tasks, she worked outside in the gardens. Wyoming planted beautiful flowers she and Amon collected from their mountain homes to make new flower gardens for our prospective hotel. She harvested plants from our gardens to make special noni tea, beneficial to lower blood sugar for me. She picked fresh fruit each morning for our breakfast.

Wyoming, Amon, and I pleasantly adjusted into a productive work routine. I stayed busy and studied the administrative order and what was necessary for the legal requirements of Costa Rica. I had one more legal matter to attend to, and that was receiving papers from the lawyer, Katerina Meza, later this week.

Thursday at ten thirty, Mercedes arrived, and we drove into the city, where Pablo Meza and his ex-wife Katerina Meza had their offices together in a beautiful two-story brick building with terraced gardens and a reception room, including coffee and comfortable chairs. We waited for thirty minutes before we were ushered into Katerina's office. Katerina was the coldest woman I had ever met. Besides being short and stout, with short graying hair and very unattractive facial features, her attire was drab and unfashionable, which was unimportant to one's character, but in her case magnified cruelty. She refused to look in my direction and avoided eye contact even though we had met at property closing. Mercedes translated as I signed three more papers. Mercedes explained these papers were for registering the property into the National Registry and for filing my will designating my two children as heirs. I was told these papers required much of the attorney's time, and the bill was more than I was originally quoted. Katerina scowled as she pushed the bill across her desk in my direction.

"Mercedes, were you the victim of the 'ugly stepmother syndrome'?"

Mercedes raised her head in surprise and without answering looked me directly in the eyes, as if to say, "How did you know?"

Katerina emanated revengeful hatefulness in her every move and facial expression. I couldn't remember ever feeling so uncomfortable in someone's presence. I abruptly stood, walked to the receptionist, and paid the required fee. I was finished here and was glad Mercedes suggested a shopping spree at Tips, a Tico store equal to the US Crate and Barrel, for the many household items I needed.

I found contentment buying a radio, clocks, sheets, towels, and many items that provided comfort for the property. Everywhere we went, Mercedes received a commission from the store managers for bringing them a valued customer. I didn't resent her for using entrepreneurial skills to raise both of our living standards. It was a joy to soften my living environment with the new store-bought items.

Later in the week, the delivery truck from Tips arrived with the house and garden supplies. Amon and Wyoming squealed in delight like children waving Fourth of July sparklers at a parade. Wyoming used the new cooking utensils to prepare delicious gourmet meals of ceviche and cordon bleu, and Amon mowed everything in sight with the new lawn mower, which was much faster than his long-bladed machete.

One morning Amon came and stood by my side, took my hand, and walked up the driveway toward the markets, dragging me along.

I had no idea what was happening as I listened to his rattle of Spanish as we walked to the telephone booth. He made a phone call, jabbered, and handed the phone to me. To my surprise it was Mercedes.

"Sun, why are you not having Wyoming come to work earlier than ten each morning? I think she should come earlier to do more of a day's work."

"Mercedes, thank you for your interest, but what happens between me and my employees is my business. Just so you know, I meditate until 10:00 a.m., and I don't want the noise of a maid disrupting my practice. Amon works outside, so his work doesn't bother, but I don't speak enough Spanish to explain to Wyoming the type of required silence. Mercedes, why did Amon call you? Does he understand I am his employer and not you? I really don't think you should be the authoritative figure my employees seek to solve their problems. It is difficult enough to be without language, but I must bond and develop a strong employer relationship to earn their respect. Did you give Amon your number and tell him to call you if he had problems?"

"Sun, I only tried to help by translating."

"I appreciate your help, but we must muddle through the best we can—alone. I need to speak better Spanish, but we have to do this the best way we can without your help. I am giving the phone back to Amon, and you should translate my displeasure."

When Amon replaced the phone into the booth, I mimed and used a gruff voice tone that he was not to call Mercedes anymore. He got it! I also explained I was his boss, and he understood.

It was clear that Wyoming arrived at ten to facilitate meditation. As the days passed, Amon became curious about meditating, and I knew he stood outside my window and watched me. I ignored this intrusion because I wanted him to know I wasn't hiding something. Meditating wasn't something secretive. He may have thought I was in prayer. Sometimes during his meal hour, I observed him sitting in the gardens imitating my sitting position with closed eyes. This imitated gesture made me smile. Wyoming too began to imitate me in other ways. She changed her hair color to match mine, and Amon pointed out she wore makeup. We both told her how beautiful she was.

When I hired them, they ate their meals separately from me. I thought this was a silly routine, and it definitely made more work for Wyoming fixing separate meals and preparing two settings. One day before mealtime I sat the table for three. Wyoming's eyes were wide with amazement. I went to the gardens, took Amon by the hand, brought him to wash in the maid's bathroom, and sat him down at the table. I then pulled the chair out and held it for Wyoming. She sat down with great hesitation. Amon smiled and sat as proud as a blue ribbon winner at the State Fair. Wyoming let out a gusty belly laugh neither Amon nor I had ever heard before. This became our regular mealtime procedure and a great benefit toward my Spanish lessons. They both talked freely, and I asked questions that needed explanation. My vocabulary grew each meal.

I ignored their table manners, and in time they both began to imitate a more refined style of eating. Wyoming and Amon told me stories about how past employers fed them outside sparingly with the dogs. I told them the employer was very stupid because hungry, wimpy workers couldn't make a beautiful home and garden. I wanted to feed them well so they would work hard, and I got my money's worth. They understood my humor. I paid both of them on Saturdays at noon and gave them a half day off as well as Sunday. Each Saturday we had a payday tradition where I served them a special payday treat as they signed a receipt showing proof they had received their week's pay.

I understood why Wyoming didn't trust me. She experienced employers who conveniently forgot to pay her or refused to pay after she gave her diligent labor. She explained how employers demanded jobs to be completed instantly. They gave new directions for new tasks, leaving the first job unfinished, and punished her for uncompleted work. Amon told stories about the brutality he suffered working on the banana plantations. His stories rivaled the southern black slave days that occurred in my homeland hundreds of years ago. It was hard to grasp that labor brutality still continued today. Amon, since his first day of employment, gave me a hug and a good-bye each day, and today Wyoming gave me a Saturday hug. I always thanked them both for their good week of work and told them I appreciated their help.

The three of us became a strong working team, and I decided to start the renovations for our hotel. We redesigned the Spanish colonial house by changing bedrooms to be more accessible with outside entrances. We removed walls, enlarging the living room into a lobby. We made new arched doors leading into a new office area and transformed the dining room into a separate formal area. We plastered walls and ceilings and created a laundry space appropriate for a hotel. We painted roofs of the art studio, lounge, outdoor kitchen, laundry house, toolroom, and sentry a dark burgundy red. We finished by painting the walkways to match our burgundy red, white, and black color scheme. The house quickly transformed into the showplace I envisioned, creating a beautiful mini-resort. Wyoming assisted the renovations with Amon and me. She did 90 percent of the interior painting and completed her regular housecleaning and cooking. She proved to be a superior house painter. Next Saturday I gave her a raise equal to Amon's weekly salary.

CHAPTER 10
NEIGHBORHOOD

I became acquainted with my neighbors and inquired about the nighttime intruder. Monica and Dave were a handsome Canadian couple, raising two children, who lived at the top of the hill.

"Is this nightly intrusion some type of cultural ritual I need to learn about?"

"We have random burglary, but the type of repeated nightly visits you described is something we have not experienced," Monica replied.

"Should I contact the police?"

Dave scoffed. "That would be a total waste of your time and money. We caught a burglar and held him while we called the police. They arrived and told us they needed thirty dollars for gas money they spent to answer our call. It seems they have new beautiful patrol cars, but they don't have enough budget for gas to use them. We gave them the gas money, and they took the burglar off in the car, but when I went to the market, I saw the same man we caught burglarizing our house thirty minutes earlier at the store. The police let him go, and I was out thirty bucks."

"The parents of our children's classmates told us the cops are as corrupt as the burglars and want to see the inside of our house so they can take things later for themselves, or hire the burglars to take things for them," Monica lamented, as she continued combing her daughter's long blonde hair.

"I don't have a phone or means of communicating and no way to call the police even if I needed to call them."

"You need to take Wyoming to the ICE office with you, and she can get a phone for herself. Ask her to give it to you, and you pay all the phone bills. I bet she would help you. That's how we have a phone. Our maid, Yolanda, gave us her phone," Dave advised.

"That's a great idea. I will ask Wyoming. I think I understand most of the billing process, but how do I pay the water bill, and when do I pay it?"

They both laughed in unison as they related being foreigners also. "Isn't that the most backward process ever experienced? You can go with me when the bill is due," Monica invited.

"Anytime you have questions, I will be glad to help. We have lived here eight years, and we only understand just enough to get by. Living in Costa Rica is not for the faint of heart," Dave sympathetically consoled.

"You are my closest English-speaking neighbor, and I know I will have a ton of questions. Thanks for your help." I walked back home just as Wyoming and Amon were leaving for the day. I asked Wyoming if she could get me a phone. This question took several tries combining mime, imitating a phone conversation that equaled an equity theater production, and Amon's help to make her understand what I wanted. She agreed to help. Thank goodness Amon understood my Spanish better than she did. Maybe he understood better because he had been with me longer or because he was younger and very bright.

That night my Spanish study was interrupted at 9:00 p.m. by gunshots. Someone was shooting at the house. I knew a little about guns, and these shots were fired from a pistol. I knew from growing up in Wyoming these were not sounds from a little BB gun, .22 rifle, or a .30-06 rifle. These were clearly high-pitched pistol shots. I recognized the sound to be from a .26 Magnum Glock. I believed the "man in the shadows" changed his ammunition from rocks to bullets. He knew when I was alone, and these happenings always occurred at night. I experienced my body mixing adrenalin and sweat so often that this anxious state became the norm. The prior door knocking and rattling knobs had happened three more times, but now the man seemed to be farther away, (which I preferred), but the pistol shots created imminently greater danger than before. Good grief. I wanted this harassment to stop.

I raced throughout the house, closed curtains, turned off lights, and dead-bolted the doors as well as key locked the exterior. I was glad we rekeyed the locks, and I had the only set. The bullets pinged against the cement exterior, but bullet penetration was unlikely since all exterior walls were two feet thick, but the windows would be vulnerable, and bullets could easily strike flesh.

Stay away from the windows. Yes, yes! Sun stay away from the windows! The rock throwing came from the front of the house, but the bullets came from the back. Maybe the man was down by the river hidden in the tropical jungle and shot toward the house. He shot two or three times in a row and then waited before he shot again. I remained crouched in the maid's bathroom, the farthest room from the river that had no exterior windows.

Oh, how I resented this situation! The shooter continued for two hours, with the bullets pinging against the back of the house. He must be down by the river! I was pinned down in the bathroom, too afraid to move and without a phone to call for help. As I sat there without my Spanish lesson workbook, I tried to find a more comfortable position so I could meditate while I endured this vicious act.

Forty years of scientific research had proven Transcendental Meditation significantly lowered the resting heart rate of people who practice the technique. Heart rate reduction lowers the chemical in the brain that produces fear. I used this technique many times since I arrived in Costa Rica to control and erase my fear.

Meditation not only helped to pass the time in a positive way, but scientific evidence proved meditation changed the "energy field" surrounding the meditator. I experienced fear, but I needed to experience peace. If a meditator transcended, it was scientifically recorded that meditation influenced other people within the "energy field." I understood about affecting the "field," but I needed to affect the "jungle" where he was hidden. If this intruder felt peace and happiness of his own, then maybe he would be less inclined to create unkindness.

After an hour of meditation, I stretched out on the cold hard floor and relaxed into a deep rest. I hadn't heard any more shots, so maybe I could go to bed. I crawled to my room, undressed, and slipped into my new Tips bedsheets without Diablo de Noches's song. My thoughts shifted toward a vow of continued regular meditation and better security. A gated entrance would be the next step, I promised as I fell asleep.

The property had an eight-foot fence around the hector boundary line, but the entrance had swinging chain-link fence gates, secured only with a chained padlock. A skinny bandit could squeeze between the two gates by extending the chain and entering the property. It was my assumption the intruder who knocked on the door and rattled the door knobs at night entered by forcing the gates apart and squeezing through the opening. Gate security was a high priority on my to-do list.

Our next project was to build an attractive entrance with a roof for guests to stand under out of the rain while they communicated through the intercom announcing their intentions. The gates would be operated by remote control boxes that only Wyoming, Amon, and I had. The gates would be fifteen feet high and constructed from wrought iron to match the security bars on the windows of the house. This new design provided more security. Day or night, Casa Ave residents and workers stood at the gate and opened the padlock with a key, which made everyone vulnerable for attack. The new gates offered more protection. I drew up the plans, and we started construction.

The construction project was to be completed in three or four days, but the property remained wide open facing Juan and Isabella's home at the top of the driveway. Today, I trudged up the driveway to visit them about the gunshots from the river. They were polite in our introductions and invited me into their courtyard but didn't extend a warm greeting. Both Juan and Isabella showed the same hesitation of friendship Wyoming had shown to me months ago, and I understood their distrust. I was a foreigner, and my Spanish-speaking skills were limited. I was aware of their reluctance for an open friendship, but I was tenacious about receiving answers concerning last night's bullet rampage.

Isabella, a beautiful teenager, held a young baby and spoke good English, while her husband, Juan, in his late sixties, held cruel anger and darkness.

"I came to ask if you heard the shooting last night?"

"We certainly heard it," replied Juan.

"Why was the shooting happening?"

"Señora, this is a hungry country, and many people hunt down by the river for food to eat," shrugged Juan, as he attempted to withdraw into his house.

"Please call me Sun," I quickly interjected to thwart his retreat. "What would they be hunting?"

"Nicos eat anything that moves: iguana, soopotti, birds, skunks, anything. You have a couple of Nicos working for you, don't you? Maybe they are hunting," snapped Juan.

I ignored the racial dig and continued my line of questioning. "I only heard one type of gun. Do you know about guns? Do you know what kind of gun it was?"

"Señora, it was a pistol," Juan said, disgustedly.

"I counted 115 shots. Someone must be very hungry or be a very bad hunter," added Isabella with a sly smile. I laughed at her good sense of humor, but her husband was annoyed with her joining the conversation.

"Should I have called the police?" I asked.

"It probably is a policeman high on drugs, out of his mind with his department-issued new pistole. The best thing to do with a thief was what we did, right, Isabella?"

"What did you do?" I asked with curiosity.

"Señora, we cut off two of his fingers, put him in the back of the old truck, and dumped him out at the emergency hospital. We haven't seen him around here again, right, Isabella?" Isabella nodded.

Isabella might become a friend, but it had to happen when Juan was at work or gone. I sensed she was married out of necessity and probably needed a friend.

"You have a beautiful baby, and if you need for me to babysit anytime, just ask. I enjoyed meeting you as neighbors, and if I can be of help to you in return, please let me know."

"We don't ask anyone for favors. We take care of our own." Juan ended the visit by going back into his house. I turned to leave as Isabella placed the baby on a blanket in the grass. She looked up at me and smiled. "I am glad we are neighbors."

"Thank you, Isabella, I am glad too."

I returned home to progress my business plans.

Last week, Wyoming and I managed to visit the ICE telephone

office, and I bought the phone in her name and cedula (Costa Rican citizenship) number.

"I don't need a phone because all four of my kids have phones, and if I need a phone, I can use our new phone when I come to work."

"Oh, thank you! Thank you, Wyoming! Now we can be a business and at least call for help in an emergency."

I spent the remainder of the day watching the construction progress and wrote an ad in the newspaper to find a renter for the newly remodeled suite. It read: La Uruka area: Looking for a special person with a high level of consciousness, loved nature and Costa Rica to rent a small 2BD, 1BA. Beautiful gardens, gated, pool, bar, and rancho. Environmentally pure. No smoking, No loud drinking or music. No pets. 1 BLK to bus. $600 per month. Call 2288-9593 (the number of our soon to be installed home phone).

Today the ICE truck arrived and parked in the driveway and waited for me to return from the market. When I saw him, I lunged down the driveway in a wild welcome and thanked him with gusto for the phone.

He was angry and shouted, "You will not receive a phone until you return the transformer you have stolen!"

"Sir, forgive me, but I don't know what you are talking about."

"The *transformer, the transformer,* the one on that pole," he shouted angrily, waving his arms, and pointed to a telephone pole thirty feet high.

"I can't possibly have climbed that pole," I tried to reason with him. "I don't know what a transformer looks like, and why would I steal it if I need it to make the phone work? I require a phone!" I attempted to communicate in my best Spanish.

"I will have you arrested! That transformer is worth $400, and I cannot install any phone without the transformer. You have stolen ICE property!" he challenged.

Be calm; do not absorb this man's angry energy. If both of us share negativity, then nothing will progress toward receiving phone service. I hailed Amon to talk to the ICE man in Spanish and tell him that I didn't steal the transformer.

"Amon, please tell him that the former owner cut all the wires to the house lights, and maybe he also removed the transformer." Amon and he talked in Spanish for forty-five minutes. Amon explained that he knew Tony removed the transformer and took it to his own house for quicker phone installation. Amon gave directions to Tony's house. I was surprised and impressed Amon knew Tony's location. Amon showed the ICE man throughout the house to prove we didn't have any phones and convinced him the former owner, Tony, Antonio Lopez, removed the phones and the wiring.

It was another week before the ICE truck returned to install the phones. We three danced wildly, celebrating our giant step into the world of technology. The phone enabled tourist business for the hotel, eased worried minds of family and friends, and established communication for the newspaper ad, customs, and security. The phone was our new family member, named Precious, and it only took six long months compared to the two to three years other foreigners waited. I progressed.

I called the phone number Mercedes gave and spoke to Rogelio Ortiz at Customs and inquired about the delivery of my cargo from Texas. Yes, he said, it was there, and I could go directly to Bank of Costa Rica and deposit the $6,000 I owed. They would deliver it to my house and unpack it for me. I went to the bank, made the deposit, and the bank teller curiously remarked: "Do you know this account number is in Spain?" she asked. I knew Costa Rica and Spain had special connections, and I assumed Costa Rica outsourced its customs service like its toll roads.

"Thank you for telling me this information," I replied. I called the customs representative Mercedes had given, told him the deposit was made, and I was ready for delivery. He promptly delivered my long-awaited belongings. This was an exciting time because the hotel and gardens were completed. The sculptures I previously created and bronzed were placed into our beautiful gardens while tables and beds completed the hotel's readiness.

I decided to administer special marketing. I visited nearby hotels, introduced myself, and invited the owners to a dinner party at our new hotel. I wanted the other hotel owners to become familiar with Casa Ave, and give recommendations to their guests in the event they had no vacancy. Wyoming, Amon, and I made lavish plans for the upcoming celebration. I sent out invitations to people who helped me relocate to Costa Rica. We planned for a grand opening for Casa Ave.

It was Friday night, and Wyoming left for the bus, but Amon wanted to stay to finish a roofing project. It was beginning to get dark, and he was at the door to say his good-bye when we looked up to see a well-dressed man coming toward our house through the unfinished open entrance. The man was about five feet eight inches, thirty-five to forty years of age, short legged, rather plump, wore dress pants, a pink short-sleeved shirt, and carried a folder. He was a light complexioned Tico with dark blond curly hair and brown eyes. He introduced himself as Jorge Vargas, employed with the San Jose municipality. He began speaking in Spanish and asked if I was the owner of the house. I responded, "Yes," and he spoke rapid Spanish that was not understood. Amon helped me understand that he asked to see a permit for the gate construction.

He and Amon got into an argument and talked a blazing blur. I understood only about three in ten words. Their argument lasted for twenty minutes, when I suggested he speak English.

"If you do not show me your permit or pay the required fee, there will be a wrecking crew to come Monday morning and demolish your new construction. You pay the fee now, and I will file your permit to stop the demolition."

"How much are the fees, and where is the permit?" I challenged.

"The fees are seventy-five dollars, and I have a permit in my folder," he retorted. I got my purse, and sat it on the table inside the door where we stood. I asked him to show proper ID. He handed Amon his card, and I suggested we call his office to check his authority. Amon dashed through the lobby into my office, where "Precious" phone was located.

"There might not be anyone at the office this time of evening. They may have closed," Jorge Vargas shouted to Amon.

"Why are you here late on a Friday night?" I questioned while I stood at the hotel entrance as night began to turn on.

"Because this is my job to check permits. There is much new construction going on in the area, and I have to meet with people when they are home from their work," he professionally responded.

I knew Amon's reading skills were nonexistent, and he had trouble reading the man's cedular and locating the phone number to his office.

"What is your office phone number? Write it down here, please, so Amon can call," I instructed.

"I can't find the phone number!" Amon shouted from my office.

"I have the phone number here," I answered as I rushed back to the office and gave him the written number. We called the number, but there was no answer. I came back into the lobby, and Jorge Vargas was positioned in the center of the lobby with his hands behind his back.

"What are you doing in my house?" I shouted! "You were *not* given permission to enter." He backed out of the door and fled up the driveway. He was gone, and so was my purse.

I darted back into my office, where Amon still tried to reach the phone number given for Jorge Vargas's office.

"Call the police, Amon! He stole my purse!" Amon called the police and gave details of Jorge Vargas—his description and his cedular number from the card he still held in his hand. While we waited for the police, Amon searched the garden area to make sure he wasn't hidden somewhere on the property. Amon was gallant and sped to the bodega and armed himself with his machete. He locked all the doors, closed the curtains, and told me to wait for the police.

"I want to leave this machete for you by the door. Be careful because it is very sharp. I am going home to tell Maria I will stay here at Casa Ave because you should not be alone tonight. I will be back in one hour and a half," he explained as he dashed to catch the bus.

While I waited for Amon and the police, I canceled my credit cards and applied for a new one that took two months to arrive in Costa Rica. I had the week's salaries for staff in my purse and money to pay the month's bills. This was the beginning of the month, and the cash in the purse totaled $700. The worst thing of all—my passport and ID were inside. Tomorrow was Saturday, and I wasn't able to pay the staff. How would they survive without their pay? This would be a terrible setback in gaining Wyoming's trust.

The way my banking system worked here in Costa Rica was that I used a Visa card at the ATM to get cash each week to pay the salaries, and once a month I extracted enough cash to pay the utilities. The utilities companies accepted only cash payment, and Wyoming and Amon used only cash for all their needs. I paid utilities in colonies, and Amon and Wyoming wanted to be paid in dollars because they benefited extra money with the rate exchange. Tomorrow I would beg the bank to allow business to continue.

I begged and pleaded with the bank officials, and their answer was a mandatory: "Wait for proper ID or passport."

I had a checkbook I could write a check on the American bank and then deposit it into the Costa Rican bank, but the bank wouldn't process any transactions without a bank card with the account number and passport. I couldn't write Amon or Wyoming a check because it was on a US bank, and it took over fifteen days for the check to clear, and they didn't have bank accounts. The Costa Rican bank didn't set up a checking account until an account holder had lived in their country for four months. I had money in the Costa Rica Scotia Bank but no way to get it out without proper ID.

After a disappointing bank meeting, I walked up the hill to Monica and Dave's house and explained the financial situation to them, and they graciously exchanged a thousand dollars in cash for my thousand-dollar check on the American bank. I was grateful they were willing to help. This would pay the utilities for a month and get me through this pay period until I could get a new passport. It would be troublesome to keep cash at home, but I had no other choice. I was relieved I wouldn't need to postpone payment to Amon or Wyoming. I also experienced and confirmed Dave and Monica's story about the police. Last night the police arrived after one and a half hours. Two very polite young officers arrived and took a "leisurely home tour" and admired the latest remodeled home improvements. I thanked them for coming, but they decided searching the grounds would produce no thief.

I called my two sisters and told them about the complicated money situation. They cleverly devised a way to send me cash. They sent thick greeting cards with hundred-dollar bills tucked inside. My next hurdle was to replace the stolen passport, and that task required a trip to the American Embassy in San Jose.

I challenged my skills to understand the bus systems to reach the American Embassy. That process required walking three or four blocks in between bus stops. These few blocks were in the heart of San Jose's pedestrian-crowded section near the main bus terminal. The Pavas bus stops were known for petty crimes.

This morning was a clear beautiful day. I wore practical walking shoes, slacks, and a loose-fitting blouse with a necklace of sentimental value given to me by Clair, a dear employer who was a good friend. We both had worked at Zachary Scott Theatre in Austin,

Texas. Working together in the arts formed a close emotional bond. She gave the necklace as a going-away present when I left for Costa Rica.

"The jewel of the necklace is not an emerald, but it is emerald colored and matched your eyes." I held the warmth of her friendship whenever I wore the necklace, which was most every day.

I walked quickly with purpose through the throng of people to reach the Pavas bus stop and kept a tight grip on my shoulder purse looped across my body. With no warning, I felt a hand grip my throat. I screamed, and a woman walking in front of me turned and saw a man rip the necklace from my neck, breaking its gold chain, and run off into the crowd. She said he was so fast she didn't even get a good look at his face. I didn't see him at all but only felt his hand on my throat.

I had been on a mission that morning to recover from the passport crime. Now I was victimized by another. My neck had been cut and bled from the jerked necklace chain, but I was wounded even more by a deep gash of sadness concerned with the integrity of our human race. The necklace meant something dear to me. How could one human cause such injustice to another? Why did our culture perpetuate and stimulate such low consciousness? What caused this low level of consciousness to slap me twice? What was the lesson I was to learn?

The paperwork to replace the passport took the entire day at the embassy, and I was told to return in three weeks to receive the new one in person. I retraced my bus route and walked through the same crowded streets to return home just a bit before dark.

I arrived home and found the staff had already gone for the day but thoughtfully closed the house in protective ways. The curtains were drawn, and all exterior doors were dead bolted and key locked. Only one door remained unbolted but locked for me to open with my key. One lobby light was turned on in case I arrived home after dark.

This thoughtful house closing made it difficult for any intruders to know if I was home or if the house was vacant. I was refreshed to know my staff cared about security after my awful unnerving day.

I went to my room to change clothes. My room was now located on the main floor off the lobby near the hotel office with a comfortable bed while the air mattress resided in a closet to be used for overflow guests. I undressed, and my mind jumped into reassessment of the proverbial battle between good and evil. Today I plunged into the energy of a low-consciousness vibration that sucked my spirits to the same level. I was a confirmed believer of natural law that created a higher state of consciousness and corrected out-of-balance activity in our world. I removed my bra, and there lodged in "natural cleavage" was the emerald portion of the snatched necklace with part of the broken chain. The thief got nothing! I couldn't help but smile to myself about this humorous definition of natural law. This was a perfect example of poetic justice and natural law.

Today in the midst of regular routine, Precious rang!

"Good morning, Casa Ave. How may I help you?" I answered.

"Good morning. This is Tony. How are you enjoying your new house?"

"Oh, hi, Tony! I love it! Thank you for asking. Are you moved into your new location?"

"I called to tell you that you bought a service contract for the security system, and the monthly payment is due," Tony explained.

"Are you talking about the annoying alarm system that went off all the time?"

"When you bought the house, the security contract was for three years. The No Thief Alarm Company wants its payment."

"Tony, I disconnected the alarm the first day I bought the house. I don't like alarms, and I don't want it."

"I signed a monthly contract for three years with the alarm

company, and they will force me to pay the entire amount now if the monthly payments are not up-to-date."

"I am sorry for your troubles Tony, but this is not my responsibility or concern."

"The house is in your possession, and so is the alarm," he said as his tone intensified.

"*Oh*, well that's an easy fix. Just call them, and have them come remove it. I don't want it. I am sure they will understand when you tell them you sold the house."

"I have to pay off the full three-year contract," he insisted.

"Tony, I don't want the alarm system."

"You must buy the alarm system contract. Do you hear me?" he yelled.

"Just because I bought your house doesn't give you the right to tell me what to put into it. I won't have an alarm."

"You must do as I say, or I will really hurt you," he screamed.

"Just how will you do that? Tony, I am not afraid of you. Pay for your own alarm system; I don't want it. Good-bye.

I hung up the phone while he talked. I had difficulty understanding Tico logic or reasoning. I had a good conversation about Tico logic with a delightful taxi driver, who said there was no logic available to a Tico. He told me their drive to acquire money was stronger than their logic. Perhaps this was true in Tony's case.

CHAPTER 11
BUSINESS

The taxi driver and his wife befriended me. He had proven to be a reliable taxi service even though he spoke no English. His wife spoke fluent English and became my Spanish teacher. They were in their early thirties with an adorable five-year-old boy who gave me hugs. I soaked up the affection like a dry sponge left in a dusty Wyoming barn. I missed my own grandchildren, and this child's sweetness was welcomed.

This couple took me to many clothing and appliance markets, and to car dealers. After many car shopping visits, he introduced me to a man who wanted to sell his car. His wife translated for me during the bargaining process and requested the car be sold with new tires. I bought a 2000 white four-door Suzuki with new tires, and now I experienced some real freedom. I picked up tourists at the airport, drove to supermarkets at night, went sightseeing, and took up to four passengers on outings. Life in Costa Rica was good, and happiness abounded.

Friday night was one of the most pleasant Costa Rican experiences.

Amon and I, and occasionally Wyoming, went to the farmers market to buy our weekly supply of fresh fruit, vegetables, fish, chicken, and bread. The atmosphere was festive with the wonderful rows of vendor stalls lined up under an open-air roof the size of a football field. Everyone was jovial, pleasant, and encouraged shoppers to sample their goods. There were so many kinds of fruits and vegetables that I had never seen or tasted before.

The first time I went to the market, I heard Native American music played by people who wore Native American dress. These singers made me homesick and reminded me of my childhood growing up on the Wind River Indian Reservation of Wyoming. I was disturbed by the sights and sounds from my life. Why were they imitating Western, Native American culture at a farmers market in Costa Rica? I found this seeming imitation offensive to my heritage. Upon closer examination, the beadwork on their leather clothing was different from mine, and the music was of a slightly different rhythm, but the similarities were curious. I learned these entertainers were from the Malekus indigenous tribe of Costa Rica. I had forgotten my middle school and high school history lesson of Central America conquest. I stood with people who had the same blood linage. I read about a scientific study conducted on Costa Rican Clovis children, and it was determined their DNA showed common ancestry with most contemporary Native Americans.

I wished for more knowledge about our Pre-Colombian ancestry. I had mistakenly thought of myself as the foreigner in Costa Rica. As a child, my unique heritage in my own country made me different from my friends. The realization that all Indian tribes were linked at our roots startled me. I thought that, coming from such a remote area of the world like Wyoming, my heritage was unique only to me. I stood at the farmers market of foreign Costa Rica and listened to music I knew well. I danced the dance from my childhood while Amon watched in fascinated stares. I danced with confidence and sheer delight. He had no idea about my youth or why I was enamored with this occasion. He didn't understand why I couldn't leave this music to continue our shopping. I danced in rapture for two hours, and he stayed with me. The idea that all people of the world were related smacked me hard. I knew I wasn't a foreigner in a foreign land, but I was at home in my soul. All people on this earth came from the same source, and I was living proof.

Amon loved to go shopping with me on Friday nights, and I enjoyed his company. There was a large dance hall on the grounds of the farmers market, and after our shopping bags were placed into the car, Amon and I went dancing. The music was Latin American, and I learned to dance Nica and Tica. He was a wonderful dancer with the Latin moves, and we danced until we dripped wet with tropical equator perspiration. Our dance was "pure dancing," as art, style, and skill without the usual purpose of sexuality.

Amon and I were well suited by any standard of ballroom dancing judges. We were visually well matched in height, weight, and agility. He was strong and muscular while I was well proportioned with long slim legs. I had no exposure to Costa Rican or Nicaraguan dance, but I could follow any male lead. I danced in small town community dance events since I was four, and by age eight I watched and danced powwows. I didn't have a singing voice for auditioning for abundant musicals during my theater career, but I relied upon my skills for the musical dance chorus line or other dance groups. I learned the steps like my next meal depended upon it, which it did. This dance background provided lifetime movement happiness that I enjoyed sharing with Amon.

I was told by an English-speaking Nica at the dance hall that white women (meaning me) weren't to dance with Nicaraguans like Amon. The Tico men resented our dancing together. I was aware Amon pranced like a pinto pony on a lead line when we shopped while he pushed the grocery cart and hauled the bags. I was amused because I saw him as a young man who experienced pride for his job and himself. He showed bravado for me as my protector. All of this was good for his self-image, and I had no idea of the underlying racial structure or cultural norms we broke.

We continued our Friday night dancing at the farmers market many times until one night while in the dance hall Amon told me to run to the car. He said, "Go now!" I left at record speed and reached the car. I saw Amon escape from three Ticos who had given him a beating. He received bruises but pushed away from his threatening crowd and ran safely to the car. This was the year 2009, and it was hard for me to believe racial injustice still continued. During the sixties, before civil rights and racial equality emerged, our Indian tribes had endured the same kind of racial prejudices as the blacks. I was exposed again to the socially imposed disparity between races. I understood why, when Amon and I went to restaurants, the parking attendants let the air out of my tires.

"Why would they do that?"

"Este mi! Este mi culpa!"

"Amon, what do you mean, it is you; it is your fault?" Our language skills between Amon and I were limited, and I never understood the racial disparity between the two countries of Nicaragua and Costa Rica. Now I got it!

We never went to the farmers market or the dance hall again, but in the rainy season we three, Amon, Wyoming, and I, turned on an old stereo and danced until the sun shined. Wyoming laughed so hard that tears ran down her cheeks, and Amon's passion for dancing changed into a fascination for the car.

Every Saturday he washed, polished, and hand-brushed every crumb from the interior (because we had no vacuum). He sprinkled drops of his perfume in it like a priest flicked holy water.

"Doña Sun, will you please teach me to drive? I will have my lessons on my time-off days, after pay time on Saturdays or Sundays?

We can do the lessons from your house? Would this be possible?" he begged.

My Saturdays and Sundays were quite empty except for Sunday Mass. Saturday afternoon included swimming or driving to a golf course where I walked five miles.

"Okay, Amon, we can do that." Wyoming piped up that she wanted to learn too.

"Okay, but only one of you at a time. Amon will be first, and after he learns, then it will be your turn, Wyoming."

Wyoming came with us on our first few lessons, but she was too nervous and afraid of the car crashing. She jumped and squealed at every wrong clutch lurch or brake jolt, and it made us all a nervous wreck. I decided Wyoming learned nothing from her fearful experience and shouldn't attend Amon's lessons.

Over the months, Amon became a driver, but I wouldn't allow him to use the car alone. I got him a driver's manual that included a copy of the driver's test and told him he must study and couldn't drive until he had his driver's license. He carried the book with him everywhere, and his wife, Maria, helped him with reading skills. Amon's fascination was the car, but my interest was promoting business for the hotel.

Precious (the phone) in conjunction with a beautiful website (constructed by professional web masters and gracious US friends) brought us tourists from all over the world. The ad in the newspaper advertised our suite as an apartment and resulted in guests who rented for three to five months. We entertained guests from Canada, Brazil, Germany, Poland, and the USA. We designed tours for our area and took guests to canopy tours, national parks, plantations, herb farms, waterfalls, farmers markets, nearby villages, and three of our nearest volcanoes. Our nearby zoo, botanical gardens, and orchid parks were also popular. We were doing fine and had great fun. Our house had transformed into a beautiful mini-resort as the website portrayed. I felt accomplished and counted on the success of our future open house. I invited nearby hotel owners to promote Casa Ave. I intended to feature our beautiful hotel and procure their referrals if they had overflow reservations. The dinner was part of the promotion campaign.

Our Casa Ave open house and dinner had been planned for weeks, and we were ready to entertain some Costa Rican businesspeople. I found beautiful handmade Costa Rican colored vests and shirts with black background fabric for the three of us, and we wore them with attractive-fitting black slacks. We all looked great. Wyoming and Amon learned to make margaritas in salt-rimmed margarita glasses, which were served to the guests as they entered the hotel. Amon managed the large pewter trays balancing the drinks like he balanced paint cans. I greeted the guests and ushered them to our outdoor mahogany bar and lounge where they were served a delicious crab- and lobster-filled pastry. The stained glass lanterns in the bar looked atmospherically romantic, and the guests got acquainted with each other. Everyone seemed to be relaxed and enjoyed themselves.

The dinner was served in our formal dining room with swinging mahogany doors leading into the kitchen where Wyoming prepared the plates, and Amon learned the proper methods of serving. I sat at the table with the invited guests but looked into the kitchen where Wyoming and Amon saw me giving them cues for clearing the used dishes or serving the next course. When Amon served, I only unobtrusively reminded him to serve the food from the left side of the guests and remove the dishes from their right.

Wyoming's cooking was superb. The dinner began with ceviche as the appetizer. I never had ceviche anywhere in the world as good as Wyoming's. Amon served a garden salad with our signature house dressing of roasted sesame oil, apple cider vinegar, parsley, and a dash of cream mixed with brown sugarcane. He served white wine to complement the main course of cordon bleu. The sides were *pique-guio* (a Nico speciality of tiny cut green beans with red peppers and seasonings known only to Wyoming). The cordon bleu was served over long-grained rice with a white sauce that was to die for. For dessert we had Costa Rican tres leche cake. The meal was prepared beautifully by Wyoming and served elegantly by Amon.

The owners from the other hotels totaled six couples and included Mark and Carmen, who housed me while I waited for the house closing. Pablo Meza and his new girlfriend were in attendance, but Mercedes and her husband, Apollo, had moved to Spain to be with her grandfather. Katerina Meza could not come. Everyone seemed to be at ease, and the dinner conversation was robust and friendly.

Throughout the evening, I observed Pablo Meza's discomfort from symptoms of diabetes. When I first met him at the airport many months ago, I suspected his condition when I looked into his eyes, and now his symptomatic behavior confirmed my diagnosis. Pablo Meza didn't select his eating and drinking choices to minimize his symptoms of the disease. He needed an injection of insulin three times during the evening to control his heat flashes, perspiration, and equilibrium. He had my silent sympathy.

It was especially surprising that our usually shy and humble (around strangers) Amon was uncharacteristically jovial, witty, and familiar with Pablo Meza. Amon blossomed into a self-confident, charming young man, but of all the dinner guests, I wondered why Pablo Meza and Amon had closeness. The evening ended, and hopefully the hotel owners would remember to send their overflow business to Casa Ave. Pablo Meza, a Tico, was the last to leave, and he and Amon, a Nico, shook hands like familiar business partners before they departed.

CHAPTER 12
ATTRACTION

The morning turned on with virescent-tinted splendor, and I viewed the array of greenness like standing in the middle of a giant kaleidoscope of geometric-shaped glittering shards of green. Sage green fused with bronze green contrasted with the bright emerald, aquamarine, kelley, and lime greens to outline the shadows of pea-green, sea-green, moss, and pine green. The morning breeze moved the apple green into new designs as the kaleidoscope changed its shapes to olive green and grass green, and accented the chartreuse with bottle green. It was definitely a chlorophyll morning, and I knew it would be a special virility day.

During the sea-foam greenness of morning before noon, Precious phone rang.

"Casa Ave. Good morning. May I help you?" I lilted into the phone.

"Yes," responded a beautiful baritone male voice, "I am calling about the apartment for rent. Is it still available?"

"Yes, it is, and I would love to tell you about it," I responded with excitement at finding a prospective renter.

"To save us both time, may I come to see it? I am in your area, and if it is convenient for you, I could be there in less than thirty minutes."

"Great! Come on over. I am eager to have it rented. Do you need additional directions? It is in a rather obscure location."

"No, the classified ad is clear, and if I need extra directions, I will call you. I look forward to meeting you. I hope you enjoy this beautiful day. See you soon."

As I hung up the phone, I had an unexplainable electrical surge enter the core of my body. I had rented the apartment on three previous occasions and reasoned it wasn't excitement due to the possibility of monetary gain for the hotel. It was caused by the sound of that man's voice. The apartment, the hotel, and I were all in "ready to show" appearance, and that was what I felt—the excitement of "opening night" at one of my theater productions. I was amazed at this energy ignited by the vibrations of a beautiful male baritone voice. *Sun, get a grip. You have been alone in the jungle way too long!*

In response to the apartment ad, a well-kept 2008 slate blue Honda pulled up to the new electric gate and stopped. A well-dressed, dark-haired man got out and pressed the intercom speaker button.

"Hi, I called about the apartment, con permissio."

"Mucho gusto," I replied as I pressed the control button, and the gates eased open. The Honda descended our sloping driveway. From the polite response, I knew he was a Tico, Latin American, or a well-traveled European. I met him at the entrance of our hotel lobby and extended my hand in greeting:

"Hi, I'm Sun Richards, and I'm glad you are interested in the apartment." He extended his hand and clasped mine in both of his as he looked directly at my eyes.

"I am Angelo Orlando Andres Lopez." His grip told me volumes.

He was a person with authority, intelligence, compassion, and strength of character who demanded respect (almost military-like). I felt his commanding magnitude. His appearance was handsome and pleasing, but his energy field was about strength, mystery, and kindness coated in steel intensity.

"Please come in. I will get the keys for the apartment." I returned to the lobby where he stood.

"Would you like to look around the gardens and pool area first, or would you like to see the apartment?"

"I would like to see the apartment first," he said.

Oh, good grief! I thought the pool, lounge, bar, and gardens were more impressive than the small apartment. I sensed this man's elegance and believed he might not be impressed with the apartment, but if he could see our peaceful grounds first, it might make a better presentation.

"The apartment is small but clean," I said. *Why am I already apologizing?* I walked under the portico to the apartment entrance. He followed, and I could feel his warmth. We entered through the thick mahogany doorway, and the apartment floor tile matched the shine of our brilliant lobby. *Thank you, Wyoming.*

"This is charming and so very clean. I will take it," he announced. His decision happened so suddenly. I was prepared to elaborate on the apartment's attributes, and his words left me suspended in midair.

"Okay, would you like a cup of coffee so we can get better acquainted?"

"Coffee would be most welcomed; I have been running from apartment to apartment for a long time today. Your apartment has the seal of approval from *Better Homes and Gardens*, compared to what I have seen today," he explained.

We returned to the house and entered the kitchen, where he took a seat at the kitchen table. *Coffee. Coffee. Of all the days for Wyoming to be sick, this day is not the one.* Lucky for me, Amon had made the coffee for the ten o'clock breakfast break, and there was at least two cups left. I poured coffee into a mug, inquired about cream or sugar, and he shook his head no.

"Just black," he said.

I thought, *Just black; that's quite like an American response. He traveled and knew Americans.* I sat opposite him without coffee and grabbed a glass of water to drink with him to save the remaining coffee in case he wanted a second cup.

"We have a maid, who will do your laundry, cook, or clean. She is sick today, but when she returns to work, you can talk to her if you need any of her services. Most property owners asked additional rent for these services, but I want Wyoming to work directly with the renters so she knows that I don't make a profit from her extra efforts. You and she can talk about the arrangements you require."

"That is a good idea. She will also be directly responsible."

"You'll find her to be very trustworthy. She has been with me for several months now and works exceptionally hard to please. How long do you want to rent the apartment?"

"It is difficult to know for sure but at least a year. It could be longer depending on the success of our project. My company is building the new highway, Autopista Del Sol, you surely noticed. We have a contract with the Costa Rican government, and it is expected to take at least one year to complete. Your property is only five minutes from the job site and will be very convenient for me. I have been staying at the work site with the men, who work on rotating job shifts, and I am not sleeping. They are noisy, and there are many to feed at odd hours. There is always someone asking me questions about his job or about the road. They always tell about problems they run into, and I need some time alone so I could try to sleep," he expounded as he drank his coffee from our pewter mugs.

"Your job sounds stressful, but I think you will find your peace here. The pool, lounge, bar, and outdoor kitchen are available for your use and for your invited guests." I filled his empty cup with the remaining coffee, and I felt his chocolate eyes following my moves as I moved around the kitchen. "This is the perfect place and convenient to have it completely furnished. Is it always this quiet?"

"Yes, always except on some special occasions when the family at the top of the hill has a celebration, and then we hear their music, but usually it is good music."

He asked about me, and why I came to Costa Rica alone. I told him my entire career story and noticed Amon peeking into the open doorway, patting his stomach like a hungry child. I realized my new renter and I had talked for over an hour, and Amon's dinner hour was passing. This man was in no hurry to leave. I tried to conclude our conversation by standing up.

"The classified ad said the rent is $600. Will you take $500?" he asked.

"No, but I would take $550." He gave a faint little smile like he enjoyed the business banter, reached into his pocket and handed me the cash.

"May I have the keys?" he asked.

I kept waiting for him to leave so I could make Amon's lunch.

"When would you like to move in?" I saw Amon pacing outside the kitchen door, and I quickly handed Angelo, the new renter, the keys.

"Right now. I am not leaving!"

"You don't need to move in any clothes, boxes, or stuff?" I asked in wide-eyed surprise.

"Nope; a driver will deal with all of that."

"I'm late in preparing Amon's lunch. Would you like to meet him and join us?" I sort of reluctantly invited.

"Very much, I am starving!" he said. Amon came into the kitchen and both men introduced themselves and began speaking very rapid Spanish. I turned toward the kitchen sink window and looked outside. I saw the most beautiful bird. Please, God, if it is your will let this man be in my life.

The new renter came by my side and looked out the window to see what I saw.

"That bird is a Quetzal, a rare sight even in Costa Rica." As Angelo stood near, I could feel he held an enormous sadness—a sadness for the things he was required to do for innocent people, for victims he knew he couldn't help, and a sadness for the world's wrongs.

I looked up into his eyes and said, "It is high time you know; I am the world's worst cook, and I must now be in charge of two men's hungry bellies."

He laughed and returned to the kitchen chair. I had to make something fast before Amon ate his shoes. Tuna melt sandwiches! That's what I could make. I tried to hurry. I grabbed the silverware, tossed it on the table, and set their hot tunas in front of them.

The new renter, Angelo, took a bite, and with his mouth full, said, "This is the best tuna melt sandwich I have ever had!" He knew my inferiority complex about cooking, and he knew what to say to win my heart. "Can I have another one?"

There was something about Angelo that drew my curiosity to the point of fascination. It wasn't his good looks; I had known many good-looking men. It was his magnetism. In theater, an actor was trained to possess stage presence. The audience wasn't aware that an actor commanded his audience to look only at him. This new renter sitting in our kitchen had great stage presence without a stage. I had never known someone to draw this kind of attention without moving or speaking. He was the king of stage presence, and he was comfortable basking in the limelight.

Amon told him he didn't like my cooking, and he should wait to taste Wyoming's cooking if he wanted to have good food! I pretended not to understand. The two of them jabbered Spanish so fast I couldn't understand much more. They joked, laughed, and were very animated in their voices and bodies. I continued to observe our new renter and hoped he would become a friend.

Our new lunch guest, Angelo, was six feet tall, dark, military short hair, round features with dark chocolate brown eyes, an attractive soft small nose, and the most beautiful heart-shaped full (kissable) lips. His bone structure was not the angular strong bones I was usually attracted to but was medium size and rounded. Maybe the roundness came with the extra fifteen pounds he carried in his midsection. Amon left after Angelo, and he finished lunch to continue his garden work, and the new renter and I talked sitting at the table for a couple more hours.

"I am going to go now to enjoy my new home. Thank you for the delicious lunch." He took my hand and looked directly into my eyes and said, "You have the most beautiful green eyes I have ever seen. I am going to like living here."

The following day was a glorious mint-green Saturday, and Amon and Wyoming only worked half a day. Amon had washed and waxed the car and finished manicuring the gardens while Wyoming completed her ironing and planted the remainder of the mountain plants they brought from their homes. The sun was in midday position, and the smell of the tropical plants was in highest state of pungency when the two devoted staff members came to the house for their weekly pay and treats.

"I'm amazed at the number of birds and butterflies our property seems to be attracting. Look at that one," I said as I pointed to a large blue-bodied bird with a yellow belly. "He is magnificent! Amon, what are you putting onto the garden that all of these new birds like?" I questioned, interested to learn about the country's environment.

"Nothing, Doña Sun. The birds are many because you do not shoot them!"

"What? Of course I would never shoot them! Why would you even think such a thought?" I was flabbergasted.

"Before you came, we never had many birds. Tony shot and used them for target practice."

"What a terrible thing to do! We will have no more killing of anything on this property! What kind of gun did Tony use when he killed the birds?"

"He used a German .26 magnum Glock pistole. He carried it in his boot top and killed many iguanas, soopotie, and snakes." My mind lost a measure of thought. I was no longer focused on conversation with Amon and drifted back to the many horrible nights of shootings. I suspected the shots from the river hitting the house were from a pistol, .26 magnum Glock. *Don't make hasty assumptions.*

"Amon and Wyoming, have a great weekend!" They both gave me a hug and walked to the top of the driveway where Wyoming unexpectedly turned and blew me a kiss. Her small innocent gesture blew great significance into my heart. I had won her over! The new renter, Angelo, watched the staff exodus as I closed the main entrance door.

"Doña Sun," he hailed. I heard his call and reopened the door.

"Hi, Angelo, how is everything going for you?" I asked sticking my head out the door and saw him as he stood in his suite doorway past the portico. He bounded to the hotel entrance.

"It was the most peaceful night I had in a long time. I want to ask you something. My partner and I have an abundance of engineering and communications equipment in the apartment. I wondered what your thoughts might be to electrify your fence?" he asked.

I gasped as my eyes sprang wide, and I replied, "I don't think I can possibly afford to do something like that since this property is a hector in area."

"Would you give me permission to do it, if I paid for it? I will pay for all the labor and materials, and after I move out it would remain for you as my gift."

"What a wonderful gift that would be. Our security would be maximized." I sighed.

"An electric fence would help safeguard our expensive equipment we use, and I would be saddened to lose it to bandits," he said softly.

"You have more than my permission. You have my thanks!"

"The two-bedroom suite is a perfect size for my partner and me to work from home. I will go to the job site to pick him up, and we will return on Sunday. Manuel looks forward to meeting you. I know I will love it here." I watched Angelo walk back to his apartment. He changed his clothes, got his car keys, closed the windows, locked the apartment door, and waved good-bye as he drove out.

Angelo had a very distinctive walk. It was a bold, heavy but smooth gliding movement with his toes aligned outward with each step and was unusually graceful for a man of his six feet, 180 pounds.

He said, "partner." In my theater culture, "partner" meant a same-sex relationship. Oh, good grief, wouldn't you just know it would be my luck! On the other hand, in Costa Rica, it might mean a business colleague. Everyone was gone, and I had the day for my own.

CHAPTER 13
SENSATIONAL

I possessed some satisfaction with the status of our newly transformed hotel, gardens, and administrative organization. I decided to stroll the gardens and walkway down to the neglected art studio. I felt inspired to begin a new sculpture in the relaxing open-air-roof covered work space. The descending burgundy-red-colored terra-cotta pathway leading to the art studio passed Wyoming's eight-foot circular flower gardens of red geraniums with many other dark green plants that provided a border. On the left, the property had a hundred-year-old rare (protected by the government) cork tree. The walk to the art studio was lush, fresh, and peaceful with a cool breeze washing my face.

I entered the studio, took a long grimacing survey, and in my wake of emotional disgust, concluded that every power tool I owned was gone. My small sculpting tools remained, but all large tools used for construction were missing. In anger I searched cupboards, closets, storage rooms, and anywhere Amon or Wyoming might have moved them. The tools were not in the studio. The tools had been stolen. The only reason the small sculpture tools were left was because the thief didn't know what they were. I sat down on the cool studio steps with a hollowness in the pit of my stomach. My creative urge vanished, replaced by feelings of violation and resentment. The only way I had to replace those tools was to return to the States to buy new ones.

I drove to the country club, where it was safe to walk. I needed to void this gripping negative resentment. The country club was thirteen miles away and empty of people except a few from the nearby hotels. My walk was lonely, self-nurtured, and self-comforted. I examined the depth of my inner strength. Some psychologists might call this walk "feeling sorry for yourself," but I knew it was "inner diggings to persevere." I felt better after a five-mile walk and was ready to return home.

I made the right-hand turn down my little lane and saw billowing gray smoke coming from the direction of my hotel. I hurriedly opened the gates, pulled the car to a stop, jumped out, and ran to the art studio. I saw fifteen-foot-high flames engulf the hillside across the narrow river. I raced back up the driveway to Juan and Isabella's house, which was my closest neighbor. Isabella spoke English.

"Please call the fire department," I shouted.

"The fire will not jump a river," she yelled back.

Living in Wyoming most of my life, I had seen fires of this nature consume fields and homes in minutes, and jump large wide rivers.

"Please call the fire department," I pleaded.

Isabella called her younger brother from the back bedroom. She spoke to him in Spanish. He ran outside barefooted, saw the billowing flames, and told her to call the fire department. He ran to my property and scaled our eight-foot-high chain-link fence with his bare feet as easily as a graceful gazelle. He scaled two more fences before reaching the studio. From the studio, we watched the flames reach thirty-foot heights, and we listened to the snap and crackle of the dried underbrush and dead trees. The sound of the fire was so loud it was difficult to understand conversation and remained a frightening roar. We felt the intense heat from the flames bring discomfort to our uncovered faces and hands. I ran back to open the gates in readiness for the fire trucks while Isabella's brother stayed to watch the fire. Isabella and her baby joined us while we waited for the fire trucks to arrive, but she retreated to the house because the heat was too intense for the baby. I was relieved and gratified to know the fire department was reliable. They arrived in record time, entered, assessed the situation, and sprayed down the roof and tree-tops surrounding the property in protective measure.

One firefighter attempted to speak English and assured me the tile roofs protected the wooden structures beneath. He explained that the outer shell of the house was stucco and was fire resistant. The fire billowed snow-like ashes and soot. We covered our faces with wet paper towels I dispensed from our kitchen supply to mini-mize the burning eyes, running noses, and congestion we suffered.

Finally I thought about all the soot and ash being dumped every-where and dashed to close the windows and doors to the hotel, but I was too late. The outside walkways and bar floor were covered with three inches of soot and ash. Inside the house, the eight bedrooms were coated with gray ash on bed duvets, linens, towels, blankets, and curtains. All interior floors had a one-inch slick gray powder covering. Wyoming's hard-earned glossy-polished surface looked similar to dance halls that sprinkled dance dust to make dancing easier. Luckily, the apartment had been closed, but what a mess we had in the rest of the house! The flames retreated as the fire began to burn itself out, and all that remained was floating snow-like ash that continued to be dispensed on everything. The fire brigade stayed and watched the fire while I gave them lemonade and cookies as my humble thanks for their efforts. The firefighters gathered up their equipment and walked to the top of the driveway while I followed them. I shook their hands and expounded my thanks.

I walked Isabella and her brother back to their home and thanked Isabella with a hug for helping me today. The discovery of the stolen tools seemed distant and small in comparison to the day's later events. I looked inside the entrance door at this complete fire filth and knew I must take action against the "open burn" that caused destruction to the surrounding beautiful tropical vegetation. The fire deposited soot to many properties and caused extra expense to owners for cleanup.

I worked on cleanup until dark and made a pathway through the lobby to my bedroom. I replaced the bed linen, towels, and blankets for a soot-free sleep. The beautiful song of Diablo de Noches filled the night air as I carefully locked up for the night and wrote a neighborhood petition against "open burn." The fire was deliberately set to expedite the clearing of sugarcane crops. It seemed unbelievable any country as beautiful as this one cared so little for the vegetation and health of its people. Breathing the contaminants caused congestion and other respiratory problems. The lack of concern for the tropical plants and jungle animals was unacceptable. Most important was the threat to human life and property. Tomorrow I would walk the neighborhood to gather supporting signatures for the "no open burn law."

A soft-lighted Sunday morning gave the day a hushed quietness without the birds singing their usual symphony and everyone at the hotel gone. Perhaps the open burn disrupted the natural order of tropical life. I walked the neighborhoods with my petition and found joy meeting many new people. I saw the result of fallout ash throughout the walked blocks. Many people were eager to show me the condition of their property after the burn and rapidly signed the presented document.

Our property was the most affected, being located at the bottom of the rolling hills, which formed a bowl. I gathered fifty-two signatures by the time I reached Monica and Dave's house. To my surprise, they refused to sign. They explained their fear of repercussions from the owners of the land who lived across the street and who were rightfully responsible for the open burn. I wasn't disappointed with their refusal because I was pleased with the number of signatures gathered in such a short time.

I returned to the hotel and resumed the filthy job of soot cleanup. I swept ash in the front lobby beside windows that viewed the south gardens and was stunned when I recognized the short-legged man who pretended to be from the municipality—the very one who stole my purse and passport. He now struggled to hoist himself over the east side of the chain-link fence. I ran, threw open the entrance door, and used my director's voice to scream his name, which I luckily remembered. *Jorge Vargas, uste alto!* (Jorge Vargas, you stop!) He landed hard on the inside of the fence, picked himself up, and ran as fast as he could across the yard. He looked like a fat, short-legged, windup toy. He scrambled over the fence on the south side of the property and disappeared into the thicket. I made sure all the doors were locked even though it was only midday. I dashed into my office where we kept his identity card and confirmed his name was indeed Jorge Vargas. I didn't want to go outside with him out there. I swept soot into high mounds throughout the hotel and wanted to take them to the compost pile to make rich fertilizer, but fear compelled me to be housebound.

The new renters returned to their apartment late afternoon, knocked on my door, and made introductions.

"Hi, Sun. I hope we are not bothering you, but I want you to meet my partner, Manuel."

"Please come in and sit down. Can I get you something to drink? Angelo, would you like some tea or coke? Manuel?"

"Coke, please," Manuel answered.

"Make that two," echoed Angelo.

"I'm happy to have you both staying at the hotel," I projected from the kitchen. "You're both welcome to make this your home. I want you to be comfortable," I said as I carried the Cokes into the salon. "Will there be anything you need in your apartment?"

"No, we have everything, and if we need something, we can take care of it. Just so you know, our job makes us keep very unpredictable hours and schedules. Some weeks we will be here most of the time and other times we are gone for days and sometimes weeks, but this will be our base, and we will be punctual with our rent money," Angelo assured.

"This is your home, and you are free to come and go as you please without explanation. Manuel, are you Tico too?"

"Yes, Señora."

"Please, both of you call me Sun."

"Manuel is shy about his English, but he knows quite a bit and it will be good for him to speak it."

Manuel lowered his eyes and said, "I will make great effort."

I saw in the intense depth of Manuel's brown Tico eyes a look of friendship. His eyes reflected and radiated pools of experiences not openly shared.

"Thank you both for that! I want to speak Spanish, but your English is better than my Spanish, and if we are to get acquainted and understand each other, we had best speak English."

"What happened here? I told Manuel how clean you kept the place."

"I had quite the adventure while you were gone. There was a terrifying fire, which covered everything in ash. I wanted to clean things up for you, but I didn't want to enter your apartment without your permission. Can you get by until tomorrow when Wyoming comes?"

"Sure. We can shake the bedding outside, and we will be fine," Angelo assured.

"I can give you clean linen for tonight. I have been busy collecting signatures. Please enjoy your Coke," I said, as I ran to get the papers I had worked on.

I came back into the room and presented the petition to Angelo. He took it from my hands and read it carefully.

"This is good. I have to go to the courthouse tomorrow for a meeting about our highway permits. Would you like me to take this and have it filed? Can we both sign it?" he asked.

"Of course! I had no idea what to do with it after I collected the signatures. I hope this won't be an imposition for you." Angelo took out his pen, signed his name, and passed the petition to Manuel, who also signed it.

"Not at all. Sun, I don't want you to be disappointed, but I must tell you, I don't believe any action will be taken because the burned land belongs to a member of the legislature who successfully has a two-year moratorium placed on the 'No Open Burn Law,' which rendered the law useless for two more years. The action by the legislator is rather self-serving! Would you agree?" he asked.

"Is this typical for politicians?"

"You need to live in this country for a few years, and then you can answer your own questions about that," he stated.

"Yesterday and today, there were two occasions when the fence was scaled. A young boy skillfully hurdled it when we were concerned about the fire and called the firefighters, and today another man I recognized as the thief of my passport trespassed into our gardens, saw me, and went over it again on the other side."

"I spoke to Manuel about electrifying the perimeter," Angelo said.

"With your permission, I can start tomorrow. It sounds like we need to make this happen quickly," offered Manuel.

"This is needed protection against thieves, but isn't there a law preventing us from doing it? What if we hurt someone? Wouldn't I be held responsible?" I asked.

"There is a law restricting the amount of voltage that can be used. The power can only give third-degree burns but won't be enough voltage to cause death. The fence must have visible warning signs with the voltage posted. If thieves get burned, it is of their choosing, and we won't be held responsible. The electrical power is strong enough to knock down a large-sized person," Angelo explained.

"After the power is placed on the fence, we won't be bothered by thieves," said Manuel.

"Sun, you are a very brave woman to have faced much adversity today. It is a pleasure to know someone with your strength. Not many women have that courage," Angelo complimented.

I didn't tell Angelo and Manuel about the stolen power tools from the art studio for fear they might worry about their equipment in the apartment, and when the fence was electrified, their possessions would be safely guarded.

"Please excuse our rushed departure, and thank you for the Coke. Enjoy the rest of your evening. We have many hours of work to complete from our computers. We have overdue reports to deliver, and we want to go to evening Mass," Angelo said.

"When you leave for Mass, I will place the clean linen and towels inside your apartment door so you have them when you return."

"Thank you for your thoughtfulness. Good night," Angelo said.

Manuel was opposite Angelo in his physical appearance. He was younger than Angelo's forty-six years. He was in his twenties and built similar to Amon but not as good-looking. Manuel had a rugged exterior like a blue-collar worker rather than the refined, intellectual style of Angelo. His complexion was Tico weathered, and his hands, compared to Angelo's professionally manicured hands, were square, hard, and used for labor like mechanics, or electrical or construction workers. He had no vanity for his looks and was born to be of service to whomever needed his help. When he smiled, his bulb nose crinkled up and revealed his good nature. Manuel had none of Angelo's elegance and upbringing but was streetwise, cautious, and practical. The energy that emanated from him spoke about loyalty, strength, honesty, protection, and trust. I knew I could use his helpfulness in years to come.

The following week, I asked Manuel if he would like Amon to help with the electric fence. He was very appreciative and told me the project could be completed in record time with both of them working toward its completion.

"Angelo has asked me to give you a message. After Wednesday, when the fence is completed, we both will be gone for two weeks. Angelo has a road job that needs some supervision in El Salvador," Manuel explained.

The fence electrification was completed on Wednesday, and I admitted that I had enjoyed the comfort of their presence at the hotel and would miss them, but other unfinished projects needed my attention. Amon, Wyoming, and I had one final project to complete. We needed to paint the hotel's main roof the same burgundy red as the rest of the property's color scheme. The three of us began this undertaking. We sweated, painted, and laughed, with me being the brunt end of Amon's many jokes. I was a slow painter and was positioned on the very top ridge of the roof while Wyoming and Amon painted the rest. I only managed to paint the ridge crown.

Amon sang a song his former banana plantation supervisor sang to make the workers move faster. The gist of the song was that the faster they worked, the faster the work would be completed, and the faster they could get to their wives or girlfriends to have sex. Amon teased me unmercifully about working so slowly I would never earn any sex time. I could tell Wyoming was uncomfortable with Amon's taunting me and feared repercussions, but after I begged him to teach me this Spanish song, she relaxed and knew I absorbed this in good humor and not disrespect.

Wyoming and I had our own "inside" humor about men. One evening on our way to the farmers market, a flock of ugly buzzards (*soapyloaties*) were on the road eating garbage. She commented how ugly these soapyloaties were. I agreed and explained that these birds were as ugly as some of the American men I had dated. She laughed until she had tears and was delighted with our joke. I asked her about the neighbors' gardener that continued to ogle and flirt with her. Her response was that he was a married man, and that made him an old soapyloaty.

Up on the rooftop, she told me I had better look again in Angelo's direction because he was not a soapyloaty. I laughed and agreed. I heard the phone ring. I scrambled down to answer when Amon yelled a warning that I would be deducted pay for every minute I wasn't painting. They drowned out the sound of Precious with their laughter. I hung up the phone to return to the rooftop when it hit!

A 6.7 earthquake less than fifteen miles from its epicenter shook Costa Rica. The hotel shook violently, and its floors moved like ocean waves. The chandeliers swung hard and hit the beamed mahogany ceilings. I stood in "theater freeze frame" in the middle of the lobby transfixed by this astonishing surge of natural power. This was *sensational*. All of my five senses were on red alert, but my electrical nervous system was affected like a depleted cell phone connected to a charger. I was charged to my maximum! How powerful this energy was! I was stunned. The quake released its grip on me, and I recovered. I bolted outside and yelled, "Is everyone all right?" No response. My heart jumped into my throat, and I tried to yell again. "Are you all right?" Silence. Then I realized that I spoke English.

Wyoming was near the bottom of the ladder on her way down from the roof to get more paint when the earthquake hit, but Amon was still up on the crest of the roof. I looked up to see his face the

same color as the ashes we cleaned weeks ago. He gripped the edge
of the roof as I asked if he was okay. He hastened down the ladder,
and the three of us sank to the grass. We sat there for a few minutes,
and then I asked. "Do you need to go home to check on your families?" We discussed the possibilities of bus travel for them both as
we listened to the screech of sirens, medical vehicles, and fire trucks.
Wyoming thought it best for her to remain at the hotel. Her family
was dispersed at various jobs throughout the city, and she would
most likely find an empty house if she returned home. She was concerned for her perched house on a hillside that could have easily slid
down and been demolished. Her house would be a dangerous place
to be, especially if the area experienced echo tremors. She was more
concerned for the safety of her family and wanted to be here in case
they called. She thought her family was safer because they were not
at home. She decided it would be difficult to reach her house with
the emergency vehicles jamming the narrow roads.

Amon, on the other hand, was frantic to reach his home. His
late-term pregnant wife, Maria, was out on those shaking slopes on
a plantation picking coffee. He wanted to find her. He left to try his
luck at catching a bus. It hadn't been fifteen minutes since the earthquake had occurred, and already my concerned son from the USA
established contact with me.

"Son, thank you for checking on me," I gratefully responded.
"We are safe, but we haven't evaluated the property for damage,
which is least important until we find out if everyone's family members are safe. I think we shouldn't tie up the phones, so other expats
can get through to their families. Please call your sister and my
sisters to tell them I am safe. I love you, and thank you for checking
on me."

Wyoming and I walked the pathways and looked for subsid-
ing. Our sloping hills supported our buildings, and we found only
minor cracks in the cement walkways. She and I entered the hotel

and picked up a few broken plates and glasses that were jostled to the floor, but again the damage was minimal. Near Wyoming and Amon's homes, an entire city had been buried by a landslide. A favorite place to take our tourists had a waterfall garden with seven beautiful waterfalls that disappeared. The water was rerouted to other rivers by the quake. Hotels, bridges, roads, and botanical and ecological resorts had vanished. Many people were never found, and the government gave a memorial on the landslide that buried a city of humans.

In the late afternoon after Wyoming left for her home, Angelo called from El Salvador.

"Sun, thank goodness you answered, and I know you are safe. Please tell me what is your property's condition and are Wyoming and Amon able to reach family members in the epicenter area? Is everyone else safe?" he asked.

"I don't know how their homes or family members are. I won't know until tomorrow when they return to work, or even if they can return. The roads are blocked with landslides, and other routes haven't been established."

"The government asked for the use of our road equipment to help with the landslides that blocked roads, bridges, and stranded people who have been cut off from access to water and food supplies. Our Costa Rican highway projects will be greatly delayed while we help clear up this disaster. I am so glad to hear your sweet voice and know you are safe. I will try to call you whenever I can. Ciao."

I was happy I heard from Angelo and was warmed by his thoughtfulness.

The morning brought two faithful employees who were three hours late because of the jammed roads. They gave full accounts of their safe family members. They told about their missing friends and neighbors. A child and mother who sold tortillas were buried alive with the baskets still on their heads. Costa Rica had 365 earthquakes per year. Most of the daily quakes cannot be felt, but they still occurred.

We gave our extra bananas and fruit to the relief fund for the disaster victims. This earthquake happened the first part of January 2009, and for many months following, people remained missing. Angelo's company lost a large road grader and an employee. They were removing dirt when the hillside gave way and pushed the driver and equipment over a canyon wall. President Oscar Aries placed a travel moratorium upon entire areas and dynamited existing roads to keep people from reentering areas that were unstable. I was fond of the beautiful waterfalls we experienced and used for sightseeing, but all seven of them vanished. Hummingbird, butterfly, rare bird, and animal sanctuaries were destroyed along with orchid, coffee, pineapple, and banana plantations. For the future success of the hotel, I needed to be creative and resourceful to find new venues for tourism.

CHAPTER 14
THIEF

Costa Rica had beautiful undiscovered places of beauty, and I managed to find new tourist attractions in spite of the great loss due to the earthquake. Our hotel, Casa Ave, had an interesting American couple that made a reservation to spend their fiftieth wedding anniversary with us over Valentine's Day. This event was good for us to recover from the earthquake's devastation.

Valentine's Day was my most despised day of the year because I never had anyone as my valentine. I decided we would really make their wedding anniversary special. I would hire a band to play for a poolside dance and buffet. I enjoyed visiting different clubs at night, sometimes in the company of Amon and sometimes alone. I found a talented, classy Latin American, romantic salsa band and hired them. The only problem was they couldn't come on Saturday, February 14, but signed a contract for Friday, February 13. This design by nature amused me to the utmost. Friday the thirteenth, a popular day for negativity and bad luck, was perfect for me in my valentine-less situation! I could celebrate Friday the thirteenth as Valentine's Day without any hesitation!

Amon and Wyoming were delighted to help host this grand event due to unfold in less than two weeks. In the meantime, I arranged to return to the USA to comply with the ninety-day Costa Rican visa law for foreigners. This requirement gave me the opportunity to replace the stolen sculpture power tools. If I bought them in the States the replacement cost would be one-third less than buying them in Costa Rica with import taxes. The stolen tools and the ninety-day immigration law caused me great inconvenience, but there was nothing to do except comply. I arranged to travel and placed a "No Vacancy," tag on the website. Amon and Wyoming weren't capable to manage the hotel alone and spoke no English.

"Amon, excuse me, can you come and talk to me for a few minutes?" I asked, as he climbed down from the mango tree where he was cutting the ripe fruit.

"Si, Señorita!" He was down from the tree before he had finished his phrase.

"Amon, I need to be gone for a week, and I wondered if you and Maria would like to stay at the hotel in the maid's quarters until I return. I know Maria is near her due date for the baby's delivery, and staying at the hotel will be much safer for her than to be up in the mountains an hour and forty minutes away from the hospital. You also would be here to make sure there are no burglars at night, and you won't need to pay bus fare to and from your house each day to come to work."

"I am glad to do this. Can we use the pool? Can we cook meat in the outdoor kitchen?"

"Yes, of course you may, and I would like it if Maria would help Wyoming or you with the hotel work while I'm away. Amon, there is one more thing! You are *not* permitted to drive the car except if Maria goes into labor! I left the keys in my office, but you are to drive only if the baby comes. You don't have your license. Do you understand?"

"Yes, I understand, and I am trustworthy!" promised Amon.

"I left a list of jobs for you and Wyoming to do while I am away. Wyoming is in charge of the inside of the house, and you are in charge of the outside. If Wyoming asks you or Maria to do or not do something inside the house, you must listen to what she asks of you. You and Maria must obey her. Do you understand?"

"I have great respect for you as an honest and fair-minded employer, and I want to please you," Amon assured.

"Okay, do we have an agreement then?" I asked. He nodded his head, and we shook hands. Casa Ave staff finished their day's work and returned to their homes.

When darkness dropped into the center of our green, lush, bowl of gardens I heard the sound of a carpenter's hammer. The geography of our bowl made it difficult to tell where the sound came from because the hills caused an echoing effect. The hammering continued until two o'clock in the morning. Other nights during the week the construction sounds began around two in the morning and continued until dawn. I heard the construction sounds at night until the day I left for the States.

My weeklong trip to the United States was productive, but I was eager to return to Casa Ave to prepare for the tourists' arrival. The anniversary couple would be visiting in less than one week. When I arrived at the hotel, Amon had hung crucifixes in every window.

"I am glad to go to my own house. This place has bad demons, who banged, and I am sure they mean to kill me with a hammer."

"Amon, I heard the hammering sounds too, but I think the noise is made by good spirits. There is no need for you to be afraid. It is an echo coming from someone's new project."

Uneducated Nicaraguans were superstitious and believed in all types of voodoo. It was a waste of effort to talk him out of his cultural beliefs. I removed the crucifixes and returned them to Amon. I changed the subject and asked him to help me carry in the new supply of power tools I bought in the USA. We hid them in their unopened boxes in a place thieves would not know about. Only Amon and I knew where they were hidden.

Maria still hadn't gone into labor, and she and Amon wanted to leave for their own home after being gone for seven days. It was four o'clock, the usual end of the workday. They gathered up their belongings in less than five minutes and walked to the bus stop. Something was different. Wyoming waited until they left before she gave me a proper greeting.

"I am so glad you are back," she said, keeping her eyes downcast.

"Me too, Wyoming. We have many things to do before our tourists come. Did everything go all right for you?" I asked as I plopped down on the kitchen chair.

"No!" she said.

"What is wrong?" I asked. She remained silent. "Wyoming, you need to tell me your thoughts," I urged. Silence. I knew Amon and Wyoming were childlike at times, and I tried to dig deep to find my patience. I just sat in the kitchen chair and waited in silence.

"Are you mad at Amon?"

"Yes!" she said.

"Are you mad at Maria?"

"No!"

"Why are you mad at Amon?" More silence."Did he do something wrong?"

"Yes!"

"Are you mad at me?" I asked as I walked over to her. Surprisingly, she threw her arms around me and began to cry.

"Wyoming, do you want to tell me what is wrong? Please tell me."

She took me by the hand and led me in the kitchen to where we keep the liquor we use for the guests' margaritas. She just stood there and said nothing. At first, I didn't notice anything, but then I saw that the liquor looked pale. I understood what she showed me.

"Have these bottles been filled with water?"

"Yes!" she said, relieved that I understood.

"Amon drank the liquor and refilled them with water?" That was the oldest teenage trick in the world, and I got it. "Is that what happened?"

"Yes!" She was reluctant to tattle on Amon and wanted me to see it for myself.

"Wyoming, thank you for letting me know! It took courage to tell me. Did Amon get drunk?"

"*Yes!*"

She took me by the hand again and led me outside to where the car was parked and showed me the passenger's side. The front fender had been smashed, badly repaired, and repainted. I was heartsick. I felt victimized again! I trusted Amon to look after my belongings. I gifted him with driving lessons and enabled him to damage the car that was vital to our business, which produced the income for his salary. The salary I paid was more than the salary Costa Rican gardeners earned. It was my turn to lead Wyoming back into the house and give her the present I bought for her in the USA. I kissed her on both cheeks Tico style and soothed.

"Wyoming, you did the right thing to tell me. Amon won't get away with this, but he won't know you helped me to see the damage. Thank you."

The demons with the hammer he thought meant to kill him were nothing but his own guilty conscious. He needed more than crucifixes to keep safe from my wrath! Admittedly as darkness came so did the hammering, and I understood how he believed demons were after him. The hammering lasted most of the night. The hammering on metal sound was joined with the squeal of an electric drill and indicated two workers. Before I left for the States, I walked the perimeter of the property, looked for new construction, and found nothing. I also walked the neighborhood in search of construction.

I asked neighbors if they heard someone building something during the night hours. No one heard anything except for Amon and me.

At lunch the next day when the three of us were at the table, I said, "It has been a while since you have had any driving lessons, Amon. I think on Saturday you should learn how to parallel park. Would you like that?"

"I would like to learn, but I think Maria wants me to do something that day."

"Whatever it is that she wants must wait because your lessons are important to finish. I insist on this. I demand it!" I was forceful, and Wyoming saw that I had a plan.

"Okay, I will stay on Saturday," he agreed.

"I have more news for us. Angelo called this morning and told me he would be home soon.

"When will Manuel and Angelo come back home?" inquired Amon.

"I don't know; he didn't say." Amon finished his lunch and returned to his garden work, and I noticed he had a new cell phone and made a couple of calls. Wyoming and I cleared up lunch dishes, but she asked no questions regarding Amon.

That night during my Spanish study, I noticed there was no construction noise, and Diablo De Noches was loudly singing. I fell asleep peacefully and woke to a beautiful day. I saw that Angelo and Manuel had silently arrived in the night and were cleaning the pool together. When I opened my bedroom patio doors, Angelo saw me, hurried up the hill, and gave me the special Tico greeting.

"Hola, Sun. I am pleased to see you again," he said softly.

"And—I'm glad you've returned!"

"Will you have time to have lunch with me today?" he invited.

"Yes, I would love to, but today is Saturday. I have to pay the help and give a short driving lesson to Amon. What time are you thinking about going?"

"I too have things to do. I need to drive Manuel to a job. Would you be able to go with me if it were a late lunch, about one thirty?" he asked.

"It is all the better for me. I'm eager to talk with you."

"Oh, me too! We need to get better acquainted!" he said, as he sprinted down the hill to the pool.

I couldn't help glancing in Angelo and Manuel's direction as I did my office work. Manuel remained beside Angelo as they worked on their computers together. They strolled the fence line, checked the electric fence, stopped and examined the grass, and made cell phone calls. Everywhere Angelo went, Manuel remained close. They drove out in one car and returned to their apartment with new items for their kitchen. Wyoming saw new placemats with matching dishes and napkins. What rough and tumble engineers would buy these things? Yep, I think they might be gay!

I thought about lunch (my favorite word) and decided to give the driving lesson early. I paid Wyoming so she could leave on time while Amon and I began the lesson. We drove out to our regular gravel road where most of our lessons had taken place.

"Why is the radio set to the Spanish-speaking station rather than the regular one that I listen to? Have you been driving the car?" I barked.

"Oh no, Sun. I changed the station when I washed the car," he nervously answered. I drove to a rural area and pulled over near a deserted shack. I stopped, pulled out a piece of paper with some numbers on it from the glove box, and handed it to Amon.

"Amon, please read those numbers for me." He read them.

"Now Amon, read and write down these numbers," as I pointed to the odometer on the car. He did as I asked but didn't understand the purpose.

"Amon, do you understand what an odometer is for?"

"No. Does it help with parallel parking?"

"It has nothing to do with parking, but it has everything to do with showing the number of miles the car has been driven. Look at the first numbers that were written in my handwriting and read the date." He followed my instruction.

"The date is the day I left for Texas. Those numbers are the total miles the car had traveled before I left. Now look at the numbers that you just wrote down. They are a 140 miles more. Today we drove twenty miles, so subtract twenty miles, and what is the final number? Amon, answer me, please," I demanded.

"The car traveled 120 miles," he said.

"Amon, how can that happen when you didn't have permission to use the car except for Maria, who obviously didn't need it yet?" Amon looked so scared he was sweating.

"Tell me, did you give the car to someone?" He didn't answer. "Because if you did, that would be car theft. Did you take the car without permission?" He hung his head and didn't answer. "Because if you did, that too would be car theft."

Amon cried like a small child! I was startled by this reaction of a grown twenty-five-year-old man who bawled like a baby. Another of my "American concepts" was awakened.

"Amon, do you have something to tell me?" I asked as he buried his face in his hands.

Through his tears and his sobbing, shaking body, he said, "Sun, I did wrong. I am sorry!"

"Is there anything else you should tell me?" I asked. He sobbed and shook his head no. "Are you sure there is nothing else?" I prodded. Again, he shook his head no. "Well ... I guess we can sit here for a very long time until you remember to tell me everything." I settled more comfortably into the seat and unobtrusively looked at the clock. I would rather be back home getting myself decorated for lunch. We were parked in an ugly part of the city that threatened our safety and that was cluttered with rubbish, which added to the discomfort of both of us. I sat in silence and listened as Amon cried. It was hard for me not to show compassion for him, but I remained stern.

"Amon, when I got home from the USA, I went into the kitchen and saw the liquor bottles were out of order, and the color wasn't the rich quality I bought. Are you sure there is nothing more you want to tell me?"

"I drank it! Maria told me not to, but I drank it," he mumbled.

"Why did Maria need to tell you not to drink it? Don't you know right from wrong by yourself?" I snapped.

"Maria is a good person," he said.

"Maybe she is, but she doesn't work for me. You *do*. Get out of the car," I said in Mafia style. He looked panicked as I quickly jerked open my door and walked to the passenger's side and jerked open his car door. He got out, and I walked to the front fender on the passenger side of the car and pointed to the damaged area. "Do you want to tell me about that?" I demanded.

"Maria and I had a fight because I drank and got mad at her. I drove off in the car. I was drunk and sideswiped a taxi." Amon's words tumbled out of his mouth like foam from a frog-eating dog.

"You have driven the car more than once to have racked up 120 miles," I exploded.

"Yes, I did. Are you going to fire me?" he whimpered.

"Yes, but I'll take my time in deciding what is the right thing to do with you," I said, as I briskly walked around the car and started up the motor. Amon got back into the passenger seat, and I drove him to the bus stop in complete silence.

"I'm never going to help you learn to drive or get your driver's license!" I shouted as he strutted off like a proud Wyoming prairie chicken without guilt or remorse. He believed the matter was closed. I was able to relax and think about a workable financially acceptable termination plan on the drive back to the hotel.

CHAPTER 15
FIRST DATE

I took extra care to get ready for lunch because my social life was a rare occasion. I dressed in a white skirt and blouse, used makeup, and slipped on cute heeled sandals. (Ticos had an attraction for Ticas in high heels.) I even smelled good with a new perfume I saved for a special occasion. I guess this was as special as it got! I took one final glance in the mirror and thought this 110-pound, five foot two older lady didn't look too bad for just dealing with a troublesome employee.

I met Angelo at the front door, and we drove in his car (a different one from his 2008 slate blue Honda he drove the first time he came to our hotel) to The Contessa, a classic Spanish manor resort hotel with fine dining, casino, and golf course. He was elegantly casual dressed, in beautiful silk and linen blend dark gray slacks, Italian charcoal loafers, a soft light gray short-sleeved shirt, and smelled of expensive cologne. His demeanor was relaxed—his conversation was spontaneously free-flowing, which put me into a natural comfort zone without the false push to be engaging. Angelo used his deportment in an effortless gentlemanly way without superficial pretense. His manners seemed to be innate from a long linage of tradition. Our conversation was lively driving to the restaurant through the warm green tropical foliage gracing the roadways.

"Sun, I find you to be a very attractive and interesting woman. You have thought-provoking sculptures that I want to know about. What were your thoughts when you created the winged sprite that sits in the stairwell to the garden level rooms of the hotel?" he inquired as he cautiously careened the curving roads.

"Thank you, Angelo, for the compliment. Most people never consider the artist as they view artwork. You heard the old adage that 'art is in the eyes of the beholder.' Angelo, what do you see when you look at her?"

"Being a male, I first noticed she was beautiful and nude."

I laughed. "Beyond that?"

"There is a precise strength about her even though she is delicate in her features. I think she is you."

"It's impossible for artists not to reveal themselves in their work. Sometimes they embarrass themselves when they exhibit their inner self."

"Are you embarrassed about the message she exudes?" he asked.

"No. For me she doesn't exude sexuality. Does she exude sexuality for you?"

"No, Sun, she does not! She radiates exceptional happiness. There is a story in her creation, and that is what I want you to tell me."

"As an older woman, she reached many of her goals. The flower she holds represents her goals in life. It took her a lifetime to find that one rare flower, and when she found it, she reached contentment, bliss, and happiness. Even though her wings are tattered and torn, her beauty faded, she doesn't care because she possesses inner happiness and is gratified."

"I have always been attracted to older women because they

experienced life. I lose patience with women who are in the thirties age range who seem to be completely self-centered and aggressive," he said as he parked the car in the restaurant parking lot. He walked around the vehicle to open my door and offered his hand to help me out of the car. He was surprised when I took his hand going up the steps to the restaurant's main entrance. The dining room was a sea of creamy white-and-gold-colored table coverings with crystal glasses and chandeliers. The interior furniture was thick heavy Spanish colonial with cream brocaded chairs, one of which he held for me as I slid into place. He walked to the other side of our small table for two. The restaurant was unusually sparsely populated even though the time was still considered to be the lunch hour.

"Would you care for some wine?"

"No, thank you, but I would love a glass of Perrier. Please have wine if you wish," I encouraged.

"No, I prefer Coke. I don't drink anymore. I once had a drinking problem," he said shyly. The black tie waiter brought us menus, and I fumbled for my reading glasses. The waiter gave Angelo a greeting of special recognition as if he was a regular guest.

"Would you mind if I borrowed your reading glasses when you finish with them? I wear contacts for driving, but I can't see to read."

"That's precisely my problem. These little pink glasses will go nicely with your gray shirt!" I teased as he smiled.

"What looks good to you?"

"I think I want the almond roasted duck," I answered.

The waiter arrived, and Angelo assertively announced; "My beautiful friend will have the roast duck and I the filet mignon."

It was rare to find a man who used old-world etiquette. It was considered rude and forward for a lady to speak to a male waiter. He knew social graces, and I respected his refinement and his upbringing.

"Angelo, I want to know more about your Costa Rican contract if you will share it."

"Eureka, there isn't much to tell. The first thing, it is going very badly."

"I'm sorry for that, Angelo."

"The Autopista Del Sol was started thirty-eight years ago, and Costa Rica didn't have the funds to complete the project. Our corporation should never have accepted the contract, but we did, and we are stuck with it. The government insists on using thirty-eight-year-old plans even when the engineered design is outdated. Roads have greatly improved with better and safer methods. The government believes it saves money by using the old blueprints, so they won't need to pay for new designing costs. The problem is that the cuts we make into the hillsides are much too steep for the heavy Costa Rican rains and assuredly will produce landslides."

"Why won't they listen to reason?"

"To make the highway safer requires the government to expropriate much more land to reduce the steepness. This is an election year, and incumbents don't want to anger any landowners. The cost of the road project will quadruple if they use our designs, and the president's financial budget is already in the red. Our corporation will be blamed for everything that goes wrong."

"Angelo, I'm sorry for your stress. You must be under tremendous pressure doing something you know is unsafe and harmful."

"That is why I have such peace and comfort being at your place. I sequester myself away from all the ringing phones, except for one that I must ask you about. President Oscar Arias wants us to have a land line. Would you object if we put a telephone into our apartment? We need special internet lines too, and we will pay for everything."

"I would be honored to help. Getting any kind of technical service for the hotel requires an act of Congress! I guess you have the VIP stamp from Congress." I laughed.

"I guess I do," he said dubiously. "There is something about you that gives me peace. What is it? I find you to be a very calming person to be with."

"Oh, good grief! I am just a little wonder!" I joked. "Tell me about Manuel."

"He has been employed with us for seven years even though he is very young. He is an electrical engineer and our best security person, as you observed by the great job he did with your new electrified fence. He can do anything with electricity. He also loves dogs, and he trains them to be guard dogs even though they aren't bred for guarding. He has packs of dogs that follow him around like the Pied Piper. I remember your ad read: 'No Pets.' Do you really mean that?"

"Why do you ask?"

"Manuel loves his dogs and will feel great comfort if he can bring two of his favorites to your place. When we aren't there, the dogs would be a good source of protection for you. They are well behaved outside dogs and would learn to love you. Manuel trained Rex, a golden retriever, to walk the perimeter of our camp site guarding the heavy road equipment. Rex trained Tico, a black lab to be a guard dog too. I have never known one animal to teach another, but that is what happened. You can meet the dogs before you invite them to stay, and if you don't want them, Manuel will understand. I know it would make him happy. Do I have your permission to bring the dogs?"

"It is only that I am protective of our gardens that I said no pets. I know labs love to dig. Do Rex and Tico dig holes?"

"I haven't seen them digging, and if they did, Manuel could teach them not to, or we can take them back to the job site. I hope you will learn to love them too."

"Okay, you bribed me with this delicious duck dinner and beautiful resort. You have permission to bring your dogs for an introduction meeting."

"Sun, I brought you here only because I wanted the pleasure of your company."

"I only came because I wanted the pleasure of yours."

Angelo flashed me a beautiful shy smile as he ordered the special chocolate fudge pie for dessert. My heart had little butterfly wings of excitement.

"My extra pounds are from the many mountains of chocolate desserts I have consumed. I don't feel a meal is complete without dessert."

We walked back to the car, and he held my hand.

"I have a gift for you from El Salvador." He reached into the backseat on the floor and handed me a large, flat, orange handblown glass bowl.

"Angelo, this is beautiful! It's the same burnt orange color as our floors, and the shape is graceful like a fallen palm leaf. I love it! You have the eye of an artist. Thank you! "I gave him a hug.

"You are very welcome. You are a rare person who deserves quality presents. I want you to know my schedule. Manuel and I will be gone for the next several days, but after that I have a two-week vacation, and I am going to enjoy your peaceful home."

"We're planning a big anniversary party for tourists during the days you will be gone. I look forward to entertaining an American couple from Pennsylvania. That's what I'll be doing in your absence. I have a big to-do list. One of the first things on my list is to become Tica. I need to begin working on my citizenship."

"I have a background in Costa Rican law, and when I return during my vacation I will help you with it if you permit me. I don't believe we have spent almost three hours having lunch!" he said as he glanced at his watch.

"Yeah, I am an exceptionally slow eater," I confessed.

"I don't know when I was so relaxed." Would you enjoy going with Manuel and me to the six o'clock Saturday Mass tonight?

"What an exceptional invitation. Yes, I would love to! Thank you!"

"I will take you home and go get Manuel and the dogs so you can spend Sunday getting acquainted with them, and if you don't want them, we will take them back before we leave."

"Angelo, thank you for the delicious elegant lunch and for my beautiful El Salvadorian bowl."

"You are welcome, and thank you for your wonderful company. See you at 5:45 p.m."

The evening Mass was always beautiful with the soft glow of the lights and reverent people. Our visits to Mass became a regular tradition when Angelo and Manuel were home on Thursday, Saturday, or Sunday evenings, and I began to feel a special closeness. Angelo took me through Lopez providence, named after his mother's family, and to their family church. I learned about the prestige and power their Lopez family held not only in the Catholic Church but throughout this part of Costa Rica.

On Sunday, after Mass, I was introduced to their two dogs Rex and Tico. Rex was an older, kind, gentle, reddish-gold retriever while Tico was puppy-like in his exuberance for fun. Tico was a black lab foundling, the runt of the litter found abandoned with his siblings in a culvert beneath a driveway. Manuel found homes for all the puppies except for Tico, who grew up at the camp job site to be trained as a guard dog.

I watched Rex conduct his patrol of the property once every hour. It was quite extraordinary to see him perform his duties without anyone giving him commands. Manuel told me when he put a collar onto Rex, it was his signal to be on duty, and he patrolled regularly. Tico followed Rex and learned how to patrol. Manuel showed me how Rex upon command stocked and pinned his prey into a corner and held him. Rex knew another command, which meant attack. Manuel told me Rex wouldn't bark at intruders but bared his teeth and growled. Tico barked if there was trouble. Angelo removed the collar when there wasn't any danger and allowed Rex to be off duty, to rest, eat, drink, or play with Tico. He showed me that Rex wouldn't eat as long as he wore his collar. I respected Rex's integrity, and I guessed Angelo was right when he said I would learn to love the dogs.

Angelo and Manuel flew to Honduras for their road construction projects after dog introductions were completed. At night, I placed the collar on Rex and removed it during the day. I knew I was watched by someone because the nights the men were home there was no hammering or other construction sounds. Tonight after they left, the construction sounds began, again. It was a comfort that I had the help of Rex and Tico. I went into the house, locked doors, pulled curtains, and began to study from the Spanish workbooks Molly, my Austin friend, gave me. The hammering and construction sounds continued. I looked outside and saw Tico and Rex in the illumination from Manuel's newly installed security lights executing their patrol.

At two thirty in the morning, I heard an electrical snapping and popping. I peered out, scanned the fence line, and saw Rex crouched nearby with Tico barking loudly. I saw something quickly burn and realized I had witnessed the sizzling of human flesh. The small glow of flames on the outside of the fence was now gone. The dark spot on the ground was dragged off by two running figures. Tico quieted, and Rex stood up and continued his patrol. The sight of someone incurring such injuries was disturbing and made me depressed. The hammering discontinued, but I felt wretched for the violence, pain, and suffering I caused to another. It was my protective fence, the separating factor between the desperate people of poverty trying to gain materialism from those they perceived to have abundance. I caused pain because I was protecting my stuff, or was I protecting myself? Either way, it didn't leave me with good feelings. I couldn't sleep, and at first light before Amon and Wyoming arrived, I rushed outside.

I removed Rex's collar and rewarded him and Tico for last night's work. I scurried to the area where Rex had crouched by the fence. En route, I saw the place Manuel and Angelo examined yesterday. On the ground outside the fence was a scorched place in the grass. A perfect imprint of a human figure. So that's what Angelo and Manuel saw. I hastened on and found the fresh imprint from last night. The scorched grass was the perfect shape of a man's body, his head, neck, shoulders and wide back, hips and thighs, but there was no imprint from the knees down. The electrical shock bolted the body backward on the outside of the fence onto the ground, but the lower legs and feet were not burned. Last night if the intruder hadn't been dragged off by friends, he might have been able to walk on his own to get medical treatment.

I retraced my steps and examined the older imprint. It was exactly the same. The body suffered burns down to the knees, but didn't fry the calves or the feet. If a thief was alone, it was possible he could walk out for help by himself. The impact of last night's violence was subdued with the new thought that survival was possible. I also had a brighter opinion about the protective electric fence. It could lower the recidivism rate for crime. I believed these two thieves wouldn't return and perhaps other thieves who saw their wounds would be detoured. I guessed this method was preferred over the method used by my neighbors who cut off their fingers. I finished inspecting the fried residue just as Wyoming and Amon crested the hill to begin the day's work.

Amon's attitude was bright, and he continued to be an efficient and energetic worker as if his committed infraction didn't exist. It seemed he didn't suffer from remorse or guilt. This was the same attitude Mercedes exemplified during her wrongdoing. Was this a Tico cultural trait? Was my Wyoming upbringing saturated with self-punishment unfounded in other cultures? Was there no right or wrong behavior for Costa Rica? Maybe Amon believed I had forgotten the entire incident, and for the present that's what I did in preparation for fulfilling the reservation with our guests. The house and gardens looked great, and I found ample new interesting tourist places since the earthquake wiped out the others.

The guests, Joe and Wanda, arrived. They were a cute older couple in their seventies. They were supremely complimentary toward accommodations and Wyoming's superb meals. These visitors were content to stay in the hotel and use our pool while they relaxed. I introduced them to the wonderful new archaeology tourism of the Palmar Sur in the Osa Canton near the South Pacific Coast. The United Nations considered this an artifact of world heritage as it was the home of the stone spheres that scientifically had unknown origins. Many theories suggested beings from other planets, but the Costa Rican Native Indigenous Tribes believed they were from their heritage. The round stone spheres, some weighing as much as fifteen tons, were sitting on a complete city yet to be excavated. When I touched the spheres, they felt good, sensual, cool, and peaceful, but I received no jolt of inspiration. This was my first time to this area, and I enjoyed it more than the tourists did.

Wyoming and Amon had everything ready when we arrived back at Casa Ave. The valentine anniversary party was a great surprise for Joe and Wanda. The party took place beside the pool, decorated with white floating candles. The pool deck was naturally colorful with the tropical flowers rooted into permanent landscape. The band was flashy! They were a handsome group of Latino musicians dressed in light blue satin jackets trimmed with silver and dark navy blue tight-fitting pants, and they played upon dark midnight blue metallic musical instruments. Our forty guests danced and met our guests of honor. People represented three generations and five countries. They danced, visited, laughed, drank, and ate together.

I rented a giant carnival-style popcorn machine, which added to the festivity and to the olfactory of Wyoming's tapas. For our buffet, she made her famous ceviche in small cups, tea sandwiches,

Tico cheeses, sausage wrapped in pastries, many tortillas, and dips. Monica and Dave, the neighbors who helped me when my passport was stolen, brought over a heart-shaped red velvet cake.

Amon and I danced until we could dance no more. Wanda admired our dancing and asked me if Amon would dance with her. Of course he would. He was flattered and sashayed over to her like a Wyoming show pony. Amon wore his baby pink new shirt in celebration of his fatherhood and passed out cigars to the men (who mostly didn't smoke), but he enjoyed the attention his new baby girl had created for him. He kept busy serving as the bartender and waiter. Wyoming had her daughter and daughter-in-law help with food preparation. The band left at midnight, and by one thirty everyone had gone. Amon and Wyoming had everything cleaned up and back in pristine condition. The hour was past their bus run time, so I hired a taxi to take them all home.

The next morning after breakfast, I took the weekly garden tour with Amon to check his yard work. We strolled past the hiding place where we stashed the many boxes of new sculpture tools. I gasped at the empty cavity. The tools were gone! I was devastated! I returned from the USA to replace the first batch of stolen tools only to be the target of theft again. I was prepared to go back to work sculpting, but again I had no tools. It was Amon that had stolen them. I sank down and cried! My tears erupted when my trust for him vanished, and his tarnished effervescence eroded into the rust of my great disappointment. Amon was shocked by my outburst of tears.

"It's no big loss; you can just go buy more," he apathetically explained as he shrugged off any guilt from my devastation. I couldn't respond. I was so upset that I sprang to my feet and checked the rancho where we held the anniversary party and found the rented carnival popcorn wagon was also stolen.

CHAPTER 16
EMBOLDEN

"Sun, either he goes or I do!" Angelo threatened as I retold Amon's theft stories. I agree Amon's insubordination with my car, drinking, and theft had reached my threshold of tolerance, and now that the tourists were gone, it was time I exerted authority.

"Amon's last day is Saturday, and this is my plan for termination. I won't fire him. I know the Costa Rican law shelters the employee even in the case of neglect or theft, but I'm not paying a thief severance pay or finding him new employment as required by law. Saturday I will give him his week of paternity leave followed by his week of vacation time. When he comes back, I will offer him a new contract for two days a week at minimal pay for gardeners, and he will refuse. I didn't fire him by law, and it is his right to refuse the contract."

"You have a good plan, Sun, and this afternoon I want to take you to a pawnshop so you can see his signature on the receipts, and maybe we can find some of your sculpture tools."

"Thanks, Angelo. Did you find the popcorn wagon?"

"No; I don't think he pawned it but probably sold it to someone."

Angelo suspected Amon of wrongful acts before I did. When the first power tool theft occurred, Angelo used his corporation personnel to research the pawnshops and discovered Amon's frequent pawning routine. Amon was the only person who knew where the new power tools were stashed, and when they vanished I knew it could be no other thief than Amon. When Amon used the car without permission to take his joyride which resulted in the accident with the red taxi, I knew his employment with me would soon be terminated, but I needed to proceed patiently and cautiously.

"Saturday is his final workday, and you thought being on vacation was going to be peaceful?" I joked.

"This is just entertainment! I am glad to be back from Honduras. Our job went much faster than we thought, and we returned this morning, but I suspect we will return later to give back what we picked up," Angelo explained as he sipped his coffee.

"We are all glad you are back; even the dogs welcomed you."

"Sun, what are the construction noises I heard this morning? Are you building something in the art studio?"

"No. I haven't found the source for the noises that have been going on for a month now." Both of our faces reflected puzzlement, and we remained silent.

"Let's talk about your citizenship requirements for immigration. You have a large investment in this property and getting an investment citizenship is easier and faster. I need to see your corporation books. Can I look at them now?" he asked as he sat his coffee cup on the stone bench under the mango tree.

"Angelo, what books?"

"When you bought the property, the lawyer gave you six books that prove you are the investor."

"Angelo, the lawyer didn't give me any books. What do they look like?"

"They are eight by eleven inches, rather thin, and usually green or blue. Sun, it is against the law for your lawyer not to have given you these books! What is the lawyer's name?"

"Her name is Katerina Meza. I will call her and ask her for them," I said, as I started toward my office phone.

"No, let's not. We need to get them now. We can get them after we go to the pawnshop. Can you find her office?"

"I think I can. I remember her office was near the Costa Rican president's home, but I don't know how to find that area."

"We will find it. I know where the president's house is located. I just left there a few hours ago. Can you recognize the way from there?"

"Yes, I can."

"Good. Let's go!" he said, as he rushed to his apartment for the car keys.

I was aware of Angelo's sense of urgency. Was he connecting Amon to my property purchase? We stopped at the pawnshop where Angelo found Amon had pawned many of the power tools. The pawnbroker was very sympathetic and showed me the receipts for the pawned items.

"Do you have any of these items here, so I can buy them back?" I hopefully asked.

"No, Señora. I am sorry, but these power tools are rapid sellers."

"If you have more items pawned from this man, would you please call me?"

"No, Señora. We make our living from repeat customers."

"Yes, I understand. Thank you," I said, halfheartedly.

Angelo and I left the pawnbroker and continued to Katerina's office. He knew the area, and I remembered the location. Angelo was assertive and spoke into the security box outside the building.

"We wish to see Katerina Meza, please. We don't have an appointment, but we want to talk to her about legal matters. My name is Angelo Lopez. Con permissio." We were granted entrance, and Angelo stepped back and allowed me to make the inquiries while he looked around. Marianela was surprised to see me.

"Hi, Marianela, It is good to see you again! I didn't know you were expecting. When is your baby due?" Marianela was one of the most beautiful Jamaican women I had ever seen. Her skin was as black and shiny as a polished baby grand piano, and her hair was a mass of waist-long ringlets. She was thin and shapely even pregnant and carried her five feet nine inch self gracefully. She was gentle, soft-spoken, and refined.

"In less than two months. We are very happy for this child," she gushed.

"Your pregnancy makes you even more beautiful," I complimented.

"Thank you, Sun. Are you here to see Katerina Meza or Pablo Meza?"

"Katerina," I answered.

"She is not here. Pablo told me, months ago, what a fabulous time he had at your dinner party and how beautiful you made your hotel. He was glad you had invited him, and I was sorry I couldn't attend, but that was the first months of my morning sickness, and I wasn't feeling well," she apologized.

"Marianela, when you are pregnant, there are no explanations necessary. Even though Katerina isn't here, I think you can help me. I want to pick up the corporation books for Llaves de Negocious. Do you have them?" I asked.

"Sun, I am sure Katerina packed them up with her office things because she has relocated her office," she explained.

"Where is her new office? Can you give me directions? Does she have a new phone number?"

"I will have her call you," she said.

"I want to get the books because I am seeking investment

citizenship, and we cannot continue without them. Please forgive my rudeness, this is my friend Angelo Lopez, and he is helping me with my immigration papers," I explained.

"It is kind of you to help Sun. I am sure Katerina wants to talk to you. What is your phone number, and she will call you when she has the books ready?" she asked.

"My phone number is 2254-8230," answered Angelo.

"Sun, what is your number?" Marianela asked.

"It's 2288-9593," I answered. "May I have Katerina's number too please?" Marianela wrote the number on a piece of paper and handed it to me.

"I have business in this area in three days. Sun and I will be back on Wednesday to pick up the books," Angelo, assertively stated.

"Marianela, have you heard anything from Mercedes? Does she like Spain?" I inquired.

"She finds it difficult because the economy is bad in Spain right now. She said the stores don't have enough food to keep stocked. The good news from her is that she and Apollo are going to have a baby too," she revealed.

"I am happy for her; she wanted that to happen for a long time. Please tell her congratulations from me. See you on Wednesday," I said as we left Katerina's office.

On the way to lunch, I told Angelo about my friendship with Mercedes and asked him if Costa Rica outsourced the customs services to Spain. He looked bewildered.

"No. Why do you ask that, Sun?"

"Mercedes gave me the phone number of the customs office. I made the call, and a man there told me I was to place the $6,000 custom fee in the Bank of Costa Rica, and when I did, the teller at the bank told me the account number was in Spain."

"Do you have your customs numbers of your shipment?"

"Yes, I have all of it. I still have the man's name I talked with. Do I need it? I have it right here in my 'Saprissa Sports' notebook."

Angelo pulled the car over, stopped, and looked through the notebook I carried with me.

"This is good, Sun. I think we need to visit customs because Cost Rica doesn't outsource to Spain. You have paid money directly into someone's account. Do you also have the BCR account number where you deposited?" Angelo asked.

I looked over Angelo's shoulder and said, "Yes, there it is. Do you wish to write it down?"

"No. I have it. Thanks." We drove to the customs office, and Angelo asked the receptionist for Rogelio Ortiz.

"We don't have anyone by that name who works here. Could you have the wrong name?" she asked hoping to be helpful. I turned my back, fumbled in my notebook, and rechecked the name. Angelo gave the correct name. He glanced in my direction and gave me a little wink and a smile, as if he already knew the outcome.

The receptionist called to her supervisor, and a man who looked similar to Grumpy of the seven dwarfs came forward.

"Can I be of help to you? Oh, hello, Angelo, how have you been? It is good to see you again!"

"Do you mind if we speak English so my friend Sun understands?" he requested

"Yes, my English is broken, but we can get by. Do you have the account number of your shipment?" Grumpy asked. I turned to my notebook again, but Angelo had spoken.

"It is 778B490AUS2000K7846."

I was astounded that he had remembered. I checked the numbers he said so fast, and I think he was correct. Grumpy asked for them again, and Angelo repeated them more slowly. Grumpy wrote them down and walked to his desk, shuffled papers, came back, and said, "The numbers do not match any of our records."

"May I see your paper?"

"This number should be a U and this number should be four nine zero. Try that please!" requested Angelo.

"Yes, now I found it!" he shouted from his desk. It is an order for a Señora Sun Richards. Is that correct?"

"Yes! When was it delivered?" I asked.

"June 8, 2008," Grumpy replied.

"I didn't receive the shipment until mid-July. Were you paid the customs fees?" I asked.

"Yes, we were paid before the delivery trucks left the area," Grumpy said.

"How much were the customs fees?"

Grumpy shuffled through his papers and said, "There were no fees due. Everything had been prepaid from the United States."

"What was the name of the delivery truck that picked up the order?" Angelo asked.

"Unfortunately, I do not have that information. When a prepaid order goes out, the delivery driver only gives the name on the shipment and passport number. We have many people who pick up their own orders or hire their own delivery trucks, and theft of customs shipments is a common problem. Sometimes trucks come at night and steal shipments. We have no idea they are stolen until months later when the owners have not received their shipments. Look out there. Do you see all of those cargo boxes piled along the dock? We try to warehouse everything inside, but much of the time we have such overflow that we stack them outside, and even though we have security, many orders are stolen," Grumpy explained.

"I have one more question to ask you. What is the number of the passport that was given for my order?"

Grumpy shuffled papers again and said, "The passport number given is 884256617. Was that your number?" I looked over at Angelo, and he seemed to be computing everything like a machine.

"That was my original passport number," I explained.

Angelo and Grumpy exchanged pleasantries in Spanish. I thanked him, and we walked to the car, where Angelo opened the car door for me.

"I am starved! Would you consider having lunch with me?" Angelo asked.

"I am a captive lunch guest and hungry too."

We drove to a shaded, intimate, quiet restaurant with few customers. We agreed to share chicken fajitas because Angelo said they were too big for one person to eat.

"Angelo, it feels really good to have a friend helping me. Thank you."

"It is just a game for me, and besides it gives me an excuse to be with you. I saw the account number in your notebook for the customs deposit to the BCR and texted it to some of my guys. They already researched to see who the bank account belongs to. We should know who received your $6,000 before dessert comes."

"Angelo, are you teasing me?"

"Not at all. When my employees aren't scraping the roads, they loved to play on the computers. I just gave them their game for today."

"I want to tell you something about the hammering and construction noises I hear at night. They usually don't happen when you and Manuel are home. I think my hotel is being watched."

"Yes, I think so too! I know Amon reported what went on at your hotel to someone. He had a sophisticated telephone that wasn't a Costa Rican ICE phone."

"I am disappointed in him. How was I so wrong about his integrity?"

"You aren't wrong. You only see the good in people, and you see people as God intended them to be. In Central America, people are directed by money and how they can profit themselves. You paid him a good salary, but someone else paid him more or promised him more."

"Do you have this trouble with your employees?"

"Always. It is a constant vigil!" Angelo explained as our lunch arrived. "Sun, tell me more about your meditating practice. You are a Catholic, so why Transcendental Meditation?"

"Meditating has nothing to do with religion. If anything, meditating makes it possible to be more worshipful. Meditating is a practice no different from brushing your teeth. You brush your teeth to keep your teeth and your body healthy. This is the same reason for meditating. It reduces the stress of the mind and prevents mind chatter or mind clutter so your decisions and thoughts are strong and accurate with correct right action. It helps the meditator to be in tune with natural law."

"What is natural law? What do you mean?" Angelo questioned

"Natural law is Mother Nature, Universal Energy, God, Mother Devine; all of those words equaled God. Meditating helps to use and develop your full potential or your unique personal gifts and talents. I see your gift as your astounding strong computer-like mind."

"If my mind is remarkable, why should I meditate?" asked Angelo as he shared our luscious fajitas onto two plates.

"Because your mind is where the ego lives, and meditating allows you to separate the intellect from the transcendent. Transcendence is the true conduit to receive natural law. Meditating helps you make fewer mistakes, gives you creative intelligence, and balances the naturally made chemicals in your body. Scientific research shows that during transcendence the mind produces the chemical serotonin, which produces happiness."

"I don't understand the difference between the mind, the intellect, and the ego!" he said as he used his napkin to dab his beautiful mouth.

"Angelo, that is a great question, and it is hard to explain. I'm not sure I intellectually understand it either, but I feel the difference. I experience it. Meditating and transcendence must be experienced before it is understood. How would you describe sleep to an alien if he never experienced it? He must experience it to understand. A seed of a plant has no mind, no ego, but it grows into a plant and into a flower depending upon the design of its natural law. The sap carries its creative intelligence (telling it how to grow)and becomes what is designed in the DNA. Humans are the same," I continued to explain as the flavor of the fajitas bolstered my words.

"The blood contains the DNA similar to our parents. We, too, have creative intelligence; it isn't the mind, it isn't the intellect, and it definitely isn't the ego. It is natural law, but ego gets in the way of our creative intelligence. Ego becomes an obstacle and meditating helps develop creative intelligence, which reduces ego. Angelo, you have a physical brain that I call the mind. Your mind is what some scientists called a photographic mind. You see something, and it imprints on your mind. What a gift that must be! Creative intelligence, on the other hand, develops your connection to the source of energy. I know that your church and your worship are part of that connection. Developing creative intelligence will strengthen the 'sap' to know everything about 'God,' and evolve your consciousness level to the highest level of all possibilities. Transcendence through meditating must be experienced not intellectualized! TM is a meditating practice that has years of scientific research to document the results of lowered blood pressure, reduced heart rate, improved immune system, increased learning skills, and creativity. Meditation produces hormones in the brain that empty into the bloodstream and produce happiness."

"I feel very calm in your company. I experience calmness and don't intellectualize," Angelo said.

I smiled at his words. "I want you to find relaxation, calmness, and happiness of your own."

"I find that with you," Angelo flattered.

"Now, you definitely fed my ego, and it grew to proportions that I need to meditate forever to reduce it."

"Would you like to spend the afternoon doing a bit of sightseeing?"

"I am a wild mustang, raring to go."

Angelo laughed and said, "Well, I guess I better hold your reins a little tighter, so you won't run away."

"Oh, no worry for that! I follow my master that feeds me. Thank you for the great lunch."

Angelo's cell phone rang; he waggled two fingers at me and said, "This is the call we have been waiting for ... yep, please just text the name. Thanks. There it is. Do you know that name?" He held the phone up so I could read the screen: Mercedes Meza Hernandez.

CHAPTER 17
MERCEDES

My heart skipped a beat as my suspicions were confirmed. Mercedes got me for another $6,000 for customs and $7,000 for closing costs, which was the seller's mortgage. I think Mercedes must be very glad she met me. "Yes, how uncomfortable it feels to know that I was so stupid."

"If you don't make mistakes, you aren't learning!" Angelo said, as he took my hand.

"My dad said those very same words to me."

Angelo always exemplified the best of manners, and I felt wonderful that he displayed them to me in an attentive way. He made me feel valued even when I felt unworthy. We were in San Jose, and he showed me the embassies of China, France, Japan, and the United States. He related fascinating history about many beautiful buildings, where ambassadors and diplomats lived, and personal stories that were only known to insiders. He was an encyclopedia of world history that I had never heard, and when we arrived in front of the

American Embassy, he pulled the car over and stopped. "What do you notice about this street?" he asked.

"It looks very wide like an American highway. It doesn't look like the small little streets in San Jose in front of the other embassies."

"Sun, you are very right. The American Embassy's street can be used as an airport runway for quick evacuation. You see that fence over there around the building grounds? It is on hydraulics and drops down to be used for runway lights. The basement of the embassy can be transformed into a special communications center for world communications in minutes."

"Angelo, how do you know all of this? Are you FBI? Are you CIA?"

"No, not FBI or CIA, something else," he said.

I knew not to ask any more questions by the way his body stiffened, and he seemed closed up.

Angelo, are you an engineer working on the Autopista Del Sol?" I asked.

"Yes, of course I am, and I wish I wasn't because it is going badly."

"Do you have a construction company?"

"Yes, I do. I have always told you the truth. My construction company is a front for gathering data for the American government. We implant different chips into the asphalt to learn about transportation and illegal commodities trafficking, and we track people movements."

"Do you work for the United States or Costa Rica?"

"Both."

I didn't want to talk anymore. I was shocked and needed to absorb what I learned. His life was astoundingly different from mine. The gracious gift of the electric fence was, as he said, for the protection of his equipment, and his eagerness to be rid of Amon had also been clarified. Sharing this information with me was his masculine attempt at intimacy. I thought through his relationship with Manuel.

He wasn't gay, and Manuel stuck close to him as his bodyguard. Now his mysteries were beginning to be understood.

"Sun, have you noticed the different vehicles I drive?" he asked.

"Yes, I thought they were your construction company vehicles that belonged to your corporation."

"They are, but look at the license plates. Every one begins with a nine. Not many people know all vehicles that start with a nine are government."

"Angelo, why are you telling me all of this?" I asked as we began the drive back to Casa Ave.

"For some reason I feel close to you, and because of my job, I have never been able to have a lasting relationship. I want you to know my truth."

"Angelo, this responsibility of knowing your truth scares me. What if I mess up? My life has always been transparent, and I don't know how to keep secrets. Expression is the need of my soul. That is why I am an actress, teacher, director, and artist," I admitted.

"You will find a way to share my truth only with me. You are the most thoughtful and courageous woman I know, and I don't think you capable of intentionally hurting someone."

"It is my prayer that I don't ever cause hurt to others."

We arrived home, and he opened my door and gave me a warm hug. My senses were on overload, and my returned hug was genuine. My compassion was for his lifestyle. The reason I felt his sadness when we first met was now understood. The gift of his great mind made him into a machine where he had no life of his own and was only in service for others. My compassion for him overwhelmed me, and I knew it was my desire to help him find peace and happiness.

"Thank you for helping me today, Angelo. I always enjoy our time together."

"Me too. Listen, do you hear those construction sounds?"

"Yes, and you and Manuel are home! Something changed. Good night, Angelo."

"Good night my beautiful woman." He blew me a kiss as he walked to his apartment.

I slept peacefully until 2:14 a.m. when I awakened to Manuel calling Tico in an urgent voice; doors slammed, the outside water ran, and Angelo started his car. I grabbed a robe and ran outside. I saw Manuel carrying Rex, wrapped in a blanket, to the backseat of Angelo's car. He got in and held Rex.

"What's wrong, Angelo?" I shouted.

"Rex has been poisoned, and we are on our way to the veterinarian. Sun, go inside; keep all the doors and windows locked, and don't go near the doors even if someone knocks. I will call you to let you know when we are back. Keep watch out the windows, and if you see people get hit with electricity, call the police. We will be back. Please stay safe." I followed Angelo's instructions, and two hours later, Angelo called.

"Good morning, Sun. We are back, and Rex will live, but we don't know if there is brain damage. It was poison given to him on meat found between his teeth. He was given the meat before Manuel put the collar on him. We guessed it was close to 9:00 p.m. when Manuel wanted Rex to be on duty. Rex came back to the house and wanted water. Manuel noticed he had foam around his mouth and thought Rex had eaten a frog. Manuel cleaned his mouth and gave him two full bowls of water, which he drank and began gasping for air. Manuel knew it was not a frog and called a veterinarian. The veterinarian gave Rex a shot, and he recovered, but someone must be with Rex to monitor his breathing and give him a pill every half hour. We didn't get much sleep," Angelo explained.

"Please allow me to stay with Rex while you both sleep. I want to help."

"Sun, you are kind, and we appreciate your offer, but Manuel won't let anyone stay with Rex. He wants to do it. He won't even let me take a turn, and he told me to go away and go to bed, which is what I think I will do."

"I understand the maternal instinct to be with your sick child, and that's what Manuel is doing,"

"That's it! Good night again." He hung up, and I went back to sleep.

I slept until 10:00 a.m., when the intense light from the open patio warmed my feet. I looked out and saw Manuel sitting beside Rex in the shade of the mango tree. I dressed for the beautiful day and went out to check on Rex. I sat down on the other side of him.

"How's he doing? Is it okay if I pet him?" I asked.

"I think he is better, and he enjoys being comforted. Yes, please pet him," he said.

"Manuel, if you want to sleep, I will take over giving the pills and stay with him."

"No thanks, Sun. This is my job."

"Yes, it is. Manuel, how is it possible for this to happen to Rex? I know you check the fence often."

"I thought about this too. There are no openings in the fence. I wondered if someone cut up small pieces and poked them through the links of the fence. The veterinarian didn't think it was the case. He thought Rex got the poison in one fatal dose. The only other way would be if someone threw the meat over the top of the fence," he explained. Manuel fell silent, and I continued to pet Rex.

"Now that Amon refused his offered contract, and he is gone, you need help with the gardens and pool. Would you consider me for that job?" he asked.

"What a wonderful offer, but how can you help me and do your own job?"

"I live at your beautiful place, and it will be recreation and a workout at the same time. I need to stay in shape, and pushing the lawn mower around here would be a great workout. I find it restful to work with plants and help with the pool."

"What would you charge me, Manuel?" I asked.

"Sun, it would add to my peace of mind and receive therapy at the same time. What will you charge me to have that?" he smiled.

"You are a delightfully crazy man, Manuel! Tell you what, whenever you and Angelo are here, you both may have your meals with us. Wyoming can also cook for you when you want to eat your own menu. What do you really like?"

"I love the American banana split," he said.

"I can do that! Starting tonight, you will have my special, rich, Richards banana split. Nope, I changed my mind. You will get the Sun Sundae Special. Do you want it for dessert, or should I deliver it later in the evening?"

"I work late. Only Angelo is on vacation. I am not, and I would like it around seven or eight so it would power me through the rest of the night."

"What kind of ice cream do you like?"

"I liked it all. You just make it, and I will eat it."

"How is everything this morning?" Angelo asked, as he poked his head from the apartment door. At the sound of Angelo's voice, Rex got up and started to move around.

"Look at that!" Manuel cheered. "I think he will be fine, and I got a new job working for banana splits."

"If you get paid in banana splits, do I get one too?" Angelo asked.

"As long as mine is the biggest," humored Manuel.

"Sun, would this be a good time for us to look over your paperwork you received at your closing?" Angelo asked.

"Oh, yes, I am ready to straighten that out. Do you want to do it right now? Do you guys need some breakfast or something?" I asked.

"No thanks; we ate and had coffee. Can we use your dining table?"

"Sure. Let's go inside and get started. I brought out the file of papers given to me at Katerina's office, and Angelo spread them out on the table. He looked through them and announced, "I think we have enough information. We can start to research your property while we wait for the books. Do you have time to go with me into the city today?"

"Of course. I think this project is a priority."

"Be sure to bring your passport. Let's just bring this entire file in case we need it."

I changed my shoes, grabbed my passport, sunglasses, and two bottles of water, and walked to the car, where Angelo held the car door. I glanced and noticed that his and Manuel's car license both began with a nine.

"Let's begin our day by swinging past Katerina Meza's office and asking for the books. Little surprises are good for people," Angelo said with a sly smile.

We parked in front of her office. He spoke into the security speaker and waited for Marianela to buzz us in. A few minutes passed, and we entered the building, climbed the small flight of stairs, and Angelo approached the receptionist's desk.

"Good morning, Marianela. We were in your area and thought we would check to see if you might have found Sun Richards's books. We haven't received any calls from Katerina, and we hoped you found them," Angelo cheerily said.

"I will make sure Katerina gets your message to call you, and I looked everywhere but cannot find the books," Marianela, said sadly.

"We will wait until Wednesday as you suggested, and maybe Katerina will find them. We have an appointment with immigration and need the books. If we don't receive them by then we will begin to file for lost books with the court. See you Wednesday." Angelo walked away with authority.

As Angelo opened the car door and I slid in, he said, "We will have the books Wednesday. Katerina doesn't want us to file for lost books because it would bring an investigation of her records."

We remained in the car parked outside Katerina's office. He said into his cell phone, "I want a wire tap placed on Katerina Meza's law office phone line and total infiltration of her electronics, please, starting today. Thank you. Sun, look at the corporation ownership papers you bought from Pablo Meza. Do you see these names on the document as members of your board of directors? Do you know any of these people?"

President … Valerina Pachona Uribe

Vice Pres … Leonardo Garzon Serpa

Treasurer … Jorge Manuel Vargas

Secretary … Marianela Barahoama Gonzales

Member at large … Mauricio Machado Santos

I looked at the document Angelo presented."Yes, I recognize two names. Is this Marianela Barahoma Gonzales the same Marianela I know inside this office?"

"The very same one! When we were here a few days ago, I had a file research done on her. Sun, she sits on twenty-two property boards, and yours is just one of those," he informed me.

"This other name, Jorge Manuel Vargas, is the same man who posed as an official from the municipality and wanted payment for the gate construction. We still have his cedular (photo ID) in my office. Jorge grabbed my purse with the passport and ran off, forgetting his ID," I related.

"That is the biggest mistake of his life. You told me about the man running across your yard the day you cleaned up the soot, and you thought he was the same man you recognized from the gate event. I ran a check on him too, and it turned out he is Katerina Meza's brother. Do you know any of the other names on your board list?" Angelo asked.

"No, that's all."

"The others are all Colombians. Do you know what that may mean?" Angelo probed.

I shook my head and looked vacant from all the new information that washed over me.

"Colombia is the world's largest drug traffic, racketeer, prostitution, and human traffic offender. Your property seems to be in the mix of a Colombian operation. If you feel some fear, I want you to 'experience' a little bit of what your intellect tells you," he said teasingly. (He referred the lengthy explanation I gave yesterday concerning Transcendental Meditation needing to be experienced rather than intellectualized to gain understanding.) He cleverly reversed my explanation of intellect versus experience. We both enjoyed our laughter like a musical duet. What fun espionage could be! I found this man to be delightful.

"How about some quick lunch? What do you feel like today?" he asked.

"You know San Jose and the wonderful food places. Feed me, and I will follow you anywhere just like a greyhound. How about someplace that has vegetables or a salad?" I suggested.

"Have you noticed Costa Rica is a country with the longest growing season for fruits and vegetables, and the food establishments served mostly meat? I find that odd. I guess most people live or work with agriculture, and when they came into the city they expect a meat cuisine."

"When I first started working with Amon and Wyoming, they never served or ate salad. Raw vegetables were a new introduction into their lives. Angelo, if you can't think of a salad place, please don't go out of our way. I will eat donkey."

The restaurant Angelo chose was a little mom-and-pop outdoor place that served great leafy green salads with a tasty fish dish. The ice tea was made fresh from rose petals, and we each had two glasses as we talked. The lunch was healthy and reflected the tone of our conversation.

"In today's news, I read where President Oscar Aries commemorated the new hospital. The hospital is a good direction for this country," I commented.

"Sun, the hospital is my oldest brother's project, and he told me the president is being a glory hog because the hospital is nowhere near completion. He wants to commemorate it now for his political campaign. His strategy is to impress the public with a list of his accomplishments, and Costa Ricans think social improvement projects indicate an excellent president."

"If the hospital isn't ready, won't that cause problems?"

"Oscar Aries doesn't care what problems or hardships he creates for others."

"Angelo, is your brother the senior doctor, or is he an administrator of the hospital?"

"Your question strikes directly in the heart of our family. My brother, Horacio, argued with my father throughout his medical education because he wanted to become a doctor. My father wanted his eldest son to be in line to take over our family business and wanted his education to be in business administration. Now he is an MD with nine children of his own, an administrator of three hospitals, and doesn't practice as a doctor. I think, in my brother's case, my father understood his son's abilities."

"Do your siblings have your mind capabilities?"

"All of us have done well scholastically, but I don't know if their minds are like mine. I wasn't with my family during my late teen and young adult years, and as adults we never talk about who is smartest, and all will answer, 'It is decidedly not me,'" he laughed.

"You have an interesting, rich heritage."

"As do you, little Miss Indian America. Are you ready to go to one more office before we head back home?"

"What office?"

"I am going to introduce you to two lawyers that share the same office who will help us get your papers properly filed after we get your books."

We drove for about twenty minutes, and Angelo pulled up to a modest yellow building that had a small room with two desks. Angelo introduced me to an older man who spoke no English but managed to understand a little. His name was Roberto Galverez, and his partner was Luis Marcoto, a municipal court judge. Our meeting was short with the sole purpose of introductions.

On our way back to Casa Ave, Angelo asked, "Was it in your English newspapers today about a rash of kidnappings going on in the cities that took place at the ATM machines?"

"No. I haven't heard about it. Tell me," I said.

"There isn't really much to tell other than to caution you to bank inside and not use the ATM. There have been thirty-six foreigners and one well-known wealthy Tico who were the targeted victims. People were held at gunpoint by local thieves, forced to withdraw their money until the account was empty, and then the victims were sold to the Colombians. I am curious about the Colombians who are your board members for your corporation." We parked Angelo's car under the portico entrance, where Manuel, along with Rex and Tico with wagging tails, greeted us.

"Where's your wagging tail, Manuel? Everyone else shows their greeting. How about you?"

"I will wag my tail when I get the banana split," Manuel said.

"Coming right up, sir," I said as I jumped out of the car. I looked around the newly mowed edged gardens and the sparkling clean pool.

"It is well deserved. The place looks wonderful, Manuel. Thank you."

I made super-sized, artistic, delicious-looking banana splits in the shiny pewter dessert boats Wyoming had polished. I placed the dishes into the freezer so they would be extra cold and delivered them with flare and style. Both men stood up as I entered.

"*Eureka*, look at those!" Angelo said admiringly.

"These are fifteen-dollar banana splits! Which one is the biggest?" asked Manuel.

"You have to decide and make your choice first, Manuel," I encouraged.

"Please join us, Sun," Angelo said as he offered me a comfortable chair matching the settee.

"Where is yours?" Manuel asked.

"My reward is to see you both enjoy them. Please begin," I invited.

"I think Rex has recovered. He followed me around all day. I kept a close eye on both of the dogs. I heard the construction sounds nightly, and today I searched everywhere for new buildings. I walked a mile in both directions down by the river, and I saw or heard nothing. I took Rex and Tico out of the property boundaries and walked the neighborhood, and still we found nothing. I couldn't get a fix on the direction when I heard them at night. The other night I got up and followed the sound, but the hills made an echo, and I couldn't tell the direction," Manuel said.

"Thank you for validating my conclusions, Manuel. I found the same thing!"

"This is such a pleasant, satisfying, and delicious dessert. Thank you, Sun," Angelo complimented.

Our evening and relaxed conversation was shattered by the sound of gunshots from the river.

"I am sure those are the same sounds from the .26 Magnum Glock I have heard in previous months," I assured as the two men looked at me in surprise.

The men made eye contact with each other; Manuel set his

empty dish on the floor, went into his bedroom, and pulled out a machine gun from under his bed. I was unnerved at the sight of a machine gun. I had never seen one up close, and I can't describe the ugliness, harshness, and irreverence for life that the image of this weapon displayed. I thought a machine gun to be in the hands of gangsters from the Mafia, terrorists, or soldiers at war, but not in my own home while having dessert.

Manuel held the machine gun straight in line with his body pointed down at the floor, and it was as long and thick as his thigh. He calmly walked outside and called the dogs. I sat riveted in the cream-colored brocade wicker settee. The disparity of the gentle man who sat, ate, and enjoyed his dessert, the same man who joked about transcendence at lunch, and now in the peace of this lush ambiance was totally undisturbed by the sight of such violent artillery. I suddenly realized I hadn't taken a breath in a long time and gasped for a gulp of air.

"It's okay," said Angelo as he looked up at me. "Sometimes it is necessary to show who has the bigger gun. This will quiet the river pistol," he assured.

A loud and thunderous round from Manuel's gun shook the night air like the 2009 earthquake shook the floors. All sounds from animal and birds, from man and God, were turned into an obtrusive void of sound.

"Your wonderful gift of banana splits is greatly enjoyed. Thank you, Sun," Angelo said.

I picked up the empty dishes and quietly walked to my own front door. The sound of pistol shots, construction sounds, Tico barking, and the sizzling of the electric fence were all regular nightly sounds that silenced the song of Diablo de Noches. Tonight after the rumble of the machine gun, the night sounds were the echo of silence.

I went to the computer for escapism, and my interest was attracted to an article in the morning Costa Rican newspapers explaining that physiologists were concerned for the mental health of Costa Rican children who were encouraged by their parents to be trained in firearms. I felt such an emptiness. Whatever happened to the days of playing Annie, Annie over, or hopscotch with the family? I checked the hotel internet website before bed and saw where an interesting couple in television production from Austin, Texas, had made reservations for next week. That should be fun. I replied a confirmation and thought about their vacation at our hotel.

CHAPTER 18
KATERINA

This morning, I walked to the nearest markets to replenish our common food stock. On the way, I stopped to chat with Isabella and inquired about her happiness and the baby's health. Both topics were reported in a positive response.

"Is there anything you need from the market? I will be glad to pick them up if you do."

"No, thanks, Sun. We have all our needs. See you later."

I walked on, did my shopping quickly, and on the return in front of Isabella's house a man on a motorbike wearing sunglasses and helmet pulled directly in front of my path, pinning me between the high cement wall and a deep ditch. I couldn't go forward because he was menacingly blocking my forward advancement, and I couldn't back up and go around because of the deep ditch. He mumbled something inaudible. I just looked at him and remained silent. My mind thought about the caution Angelo gave about the kidnappings. I was laden with groceries, and I didn't understand how he could attempt a kidnapping with a motorbike. At that moment, Isabella with her two large Dobermans came up the road in the opposite direction and yelled to the rider.

"Let her pass, or I will have my dogs attack." The rider opened the throttle and sped down the road.

"Oh, thank you, Isabella! What would he have done if you hadn't come along?" I asked.

"He would have taken your purse. You should not walk anywhere alone day or night. If you are alone, you need to take dogs with you. Aggressive men usually won't bother you if you have your dogs," she said.

"You came to my rescue twice now! You are a good neighbor, Isabella! Thanks. See you later."

I reached home safely with the groceries, and Angelo met me at the door to help carry in the sacks.

"What was all that about with your neighbor?" he asked.

"I was blocked by a rude man on a motorbike," I said. "Have you heard from Katerina about the books?"

"No. Let's go visit Marianela at Katerina's office. Can you go now?" he asked.

"Yes. I will adjust my schedule to yours to get those books in our possession." I put the sacks down, and we left immediately for the twenty-minute drive into the city. We pushed the intercom button, and Marianela buzzed us up.

She was very friendly and energetic and said, "I have good news for you, Sun. I found your books in a special office drawer marked 'for delivery,' and now you are here and saved me time."

Marianela handed the books to me. Angelo and I shook her hand in thanks and left her office. Angelo walked briskly to my side of the car and opened my door. I slid in, and he nearly galloped around the different car Manuel delivered. It was a silver-colored SUV with a license plate beginning with a nine, and I assumed we were on official government business.

"Katrina moved like I expected she would. We will drop these books off at Roberto Galverez and Luis Marcoto's office. They need all the time possible to get their work done for us."

Before we reached Galverez and Marcoto's law office, Angelo's cell phone rang. He looked at the caller ID, gave a wink and sly smile to me, and said, "It is Katerina." He put the conversation on speaker phone. "What a timely call, Katerina; we just picked up Sun's books from your office. Marianela was very helpful. Thanks. Now we can work on Sun's citizenship."

"Mr. Lopez, I called to advise you to consider moving from Sun's hotel. The reason we withheld her books was because we waited to hear from Costa Rica's Judicial Investigating Organization (JIO) telling us what to do," she said.

"Eureka! What would the JIO care about Sun Richards's corporation books?" he asked.

"Sun Richards is not the lady you thought her to be! She is wanted in the USA for many crimes of fraud, illegal gambling, money laundering, forgery, and parole violation. I think you are a kindhearted Tico to help her, and I want you to know who you are dealing with. If you wish to change apartments, I know a great place and will be glad to make arrangement for you to move," she said.

"I will think about the things you told me, but I really like where I live," Angelo said, as he made direct eye contact with me and touched my hand.

"Call me if you change your mind about a new apartment," she said, as they both hung up.

The things she said about me hurt my feelings. How could I redeem myself in Angelo's eyes?

"Angelo, the things Katerina said about me aren't true," I said almost inaudibly.

"Sun, you are a wacky woman! Of course I know they aren't true! I ran a check on you months ago before I came and saw the apartment for the first time. You don't even have a parking ticket violation. You are one of the rarest people I ever checked and are squeaky clean," he laughed.

"I am glad you believe in me."

"Come on. Let's get these books to Galverez and Marcoto," he said.

We left the books with Galverez and Marcoto, and on the way home, I told Angelo about the new tourists that would be coming in a couple of days.

"Sun, they sound like a fun couple, and I am still on vacation. Will you permit me to be the driver and tour guide for San Jose?"

"Oh, Angelo, would you? We could have such fun, and you know so many interesting things about the city!"

"Let's plan on it. We can go—" His sentence was interrupted by his cell phone again. He put two fingers in front of his lips in a shushing gesture.

"Good afternoon, sir. I hope you are well and happy. May I be of some service today?"

Pause.

"I would love to help out in any way I could, but the road is no-where near completion."

Pause.

"Which bridge are you wanting?"

Pause.

"Neither bridge is ready for opening."

Pause.

"We would have to have our cranes hold up both ends of the bridge, and your safety will be a great responsibility and concern."

Pause.

"Oh, it would not be you in the cars?"

Pause.

"Only staged for a photo shoot, huh?"

Pause.

"A car caravan of nine would be out of the question. Two cranes could not hold the bridge and nine cars!"

Pause.

"I would be nervous with three cars, but I think we can do it. When are you wanting this to happen?"

Pause.

"It is now almost 1:00 p.m., and I agree sunset would be beautiful as a background for the silhouette of the bridge, but I am on vacation, and I need to move all the crews around and relocate them."

Pause.

"I will try to have it all arranged by 5:00 p.m. I will do my best to help you, sir. Good day to you."

Angelo hung up.

"Can you believe that? That was our inconsiderate president of Costa Rica, who wanted to stage a phony commemoration of our highway when we are months away from a final product. Sorry, Sun, but I have to rush you home and leave to go do this! What a ridiculous waste of our time and money. I had a very short vacation, but I am glad to have had it with you. It will probably be early morning before I return to sleep. I need to pick up Manuel, but the dogs will keep you safe. See you in the morning," Angelo said as he ran to his suite and called to Manuel.

—

CHAPTER 19
ALONE

There were no more gunshots down by the river, but when Angelo and Manuel drove out of the driveway in their separate cars, the construction sounds began. I fed both of the dogs and put Rex's collar on when he had finished his food, and the dogs left for their patrol. I had office work, and having the afternoon to myself gave me a chance to catch up. Later I looked forward to going for a swim. Wyoming and I worked on the menu and plans for our Austin, Texas, tourists until nearly 4:00 p.m., when we heard Tico barking and yelping. We saw Rex run to the hotel and then dash away. He ran to the hotel and ran toward the art studio. Tico's barking had changed to muffled whimpering.

"Wyoming, I know it is time for you to go, but will you go with me to see what's wrong with the dogs?" Wyoming was already out the back door and headed down to the art studio. We followed Tico's strange sounds. He wasn't barking anymore, but Rex ran in frantic circles and dashed back and forth, back and forth in front of us, and nearly knocked Wyoming down.

"These dogs are crazy," Wyoming said, as she continued to the studio.

"They really act strange!"

Wyoming reached the studio and let out a scream. I ran the rest of the way to see Tico lying on the floor of the art studio drenched in blood. There was blood on the steps and a pool of blood beneath him. There was blood everywhere. I gingerly approached Tico and saw someone's savage act of torture. I was sickened by the wretched scene displayed before me. My stomach heaved, but I knew I needed to act fast.

"Wyoming, run to the bodega and get the wire cutters." She understood my Spanish and ran. Someone had tied Tico up with barbed wire. They tied his mouth closed to stop his barking, but he tried to bark in spite of his wounds, and the barbs had sunk deep into his under chin and across his nose. All four of his feet were tied together, preventing him from standing. His struggling caused the tendons of his legs to be badly pierced.

I knelt down beside Tico and took the wire cutters from Wyoming. "Sssshhhh, ssssshhhh," I tried to calm Tico so his struggling would stop. I whispered to him. "Easy, boy. Easy, boy. Ssssshhhh, ssssh-hhh." Tico looked at me with his appreciative pleading eyes. I clipped the wire from his nose and mouth first, and I knew it was hurting him. Rex went into his crouched for pinning pose beside Tico. Tears flooded my eyes, making it hard for me to see. The barbs from the wire around his nose and mouth had to be pulled away with my fingertips after the wire was cut. The saturated blood from his fur made it difficult to grip the blood-smeared wire cutters as they slipped in my hand.

"Wyoming, please run to my bathroom and bring the big green bottle of Listerine and a pan of water for Tico and Rex to drink." She knew we used Listerine as an antiseptic. Bless her heart, Wyoming also returned with a box of Q-tips.

Tico's mouth was nearly free as the last few barbs were loosened. He began to whimper, and so did Rex. I glanced over to see if Rex had been injured, but he only whimpered out of sympathy. Wyoming began to put Listerine on the puncture wounds that were freed from the barbed wire. Someone tried to tie his head between his four legs, but Tico managed to get his head free. The struggling gashed his throat and ears, though. I clipped and gingerly removed the wire around Tico's neck and ears while Wyoming applied the antiseptic. I began to free Tico's four legs while Wyoming offered Tico water, but he didn't take any.

"Wyoming, see if Rex will drink first, and then maybe Tico would take some too," I said as I continued to pull the wire from his legs. When I had loosened the last wire and Wyoming had finished with the antiseptic, I was aware the construction noise had stopped.

"Wyoming, we have been so busy with Tico, did you notice when the construction noises stopped?" I asked.

"No. I hear nothing now," she said.

"Me neither, but when did they stop?" She shook her head and shrugged. Tico lay still, and I wondered if the barbed wire had damaged the veins in his neck. The studio appeared as if he had lost quantities of blood, but I didn't see where he was cut to make such a mess. I didn't see any blood flowing from his body. I continued to comfort him by talking to him. The cruelty of this act was unfathomable to me. Who would do such a cruel thing? As I sat on the floor beside Tico, I scanned the fence line to see how someone could enter. Everything was secured, but someone had to have come into the art studio to do this. But how? The electricity on the fence was still active, and nothing had shorted out.

"Wyoming, I think I need to take Tico to the veterinarian. We can carry him on a tarp, but he is such a big dog, I can't carry him by myself. Can you stay and help me put him into the car? I will be back and pay a taxi to take you home. Right now before I leave, we need to make sure no one has entered the hotel while we worked on Tico. Will you call the police? Tell them what happened and have them search the hotel because someone might have gained access. I don't want you to be here alone without knowing the hotel is safe. I know my Spanish is bad, and the police may not understand. Ask them to search and wait with you until I return."

Wyoming and I held the corners of the tarp and lifted together as we loaded Tico into the car. Wyoming called the police. They arrived in less than ten minutes, and I navigated my way to the veterinary hospital.

The veterinarian's assistant helped me unload Tico when I arrived. They began preparing him for Doctor Rivera's examination. I tried to speak my best Spanish, but the veterinarian said, "Hi. I am Doctor Rivera. You may speak English if you like." Doctor Rivera was a fit, slender man who didn't appear to be over the age of twelve and conformed to the Tico national pattern of dark and handsome but not tall.

"You said the dog was tied up with barbed wire, right?" he asked.

"Yes, he has multiple puncture wounds, but I don't see any major cuts that would cause such blood loss, and he doesn't seem to have any flowing blood wounds."

"You did a good job of removing the wire and cleaning the punctures," he complimented.

"Thanks, but why isn't he more active now that the wire is removed?"

"His body physically seems to be okay, but he may be in shock. It may take a few hours for his recovery, but he is not weak from loss of blood. Why do you think he had blood loss?" Doctor Rivera puzzled.

"The floor was covered in blood, and he was lying in a blood pool when we found him. The other side of his body was wet with blood."

Doctor Rivera turned Tico over, shaved some blood-saturated

hair, and took it to the lab next door for analysis as Tico whined from being moved.

"The lab is very fast, and we will have the results of the dried blood in five minutes. Did you give Tico any water or anything to eat?" asked Doctor Rivera.

"We offered it, but he didn't take any," I answered.

Doctor Rivera removed a dog dish from his cupboard, filled it with water, and gave it to Tico. Tico drank.

"I think he will be fine. He should recover from possible dehydration and exhaustion from struggling. He is standing now and already started to recover," the doctor assured.

The laboratory buzzed. Doctor Rivera walked next door and returned with the results.

"It is good news for Tico. Your dog is not suffering from blood loss. It had been confirmed the dried blood sample is not his. This blood is human blood, type O positive to be exact. Don't try to pet him for a few days. He is tender from the punctures that are all over his body. Give him the antibiotic for three days just to make sure there is no infection," Doctor Rivera cautioned.

Tico crept stiff and sore out of the hospital but relieved someone had cared for him. He slowly moved to the car on his own and licked my knees to show his appreciation. I spread out the tarp in the backseat, and he slowly pulled himself up as I boosted him in. He gave a loud whimper but settled down. On the way home, I drove carefully, protecting my passenger from jerks and jolts. I was careful to drive the speed limit, but my mind was uncontrollable and sped forward not obeying its limits!

Who and how did someone leave so much blood on the art studio floor? Why were they in the art studio, and how did they get in there without being seen? There was no entry into the property! All the gates were locked, and an eight-foot-high fence with another two feet higher electric wire was active. I had the only keys, and they had been in my possession. No one had entry except with gate controls. Amon returned his before he was fired, and Wyoming left hers with me when she left for the bus. This was frustrating and impossible for me to reason. I began to have the same superstitious thoughts Amon and Wyoming shared about ghosts and demons. *Sun, stop this useless mind chatter!* I pulled up into the driveway portico and was relieved to see the police were still with Wyoming.

Wyoming and the police were sitting comfortably at the kitchen table, where she had served lemonade like a gracious hostess she had learned to become.

"I am glad you stayed with Wyoming! Did you find any indication someone had been inside?" I asked.

"No. Wyoming knew all the possible hiding places, and we searched the garden as well," the English-speaking police officer answered.

"Wyoming, you have put in a long day today. Please call the taxi, and I will pay for your taxi fare home. Did the police look at the art studio?" I asked.

"*No!*" Wyoming answered with alarm. "We looked in all the other buildings and the hotel." Wyoming didn't want the police to see the blood-drenched studio for fear of implication because she had no trust of men in uniforms.

"Wyoming, I will walk the police to the art studio. Call me when your taxi arrives." We walked down to the art studio, and when we were out of Wyoming's hearing range, I told them the blood in the art studio was not dog blood, but human O positive. They talked in Spanish and deliberated.

"We will take a sample of blood with us. We are local police, but Investigating Organization should be contacted," he said.

I heard Wyoming calling. "Excuse me; I need to pay the taxi," I said as I ran up the hill.

"Wyoming, you don't need to come early tomorrow because

you were here three hours extra today. Angelo and Manuel will be working all night and need to sleep tomorrow anyway." Wyoming looked haggard and nodded. She deserved some time off.

"Thank you for helping me with Tico today." I gave her a hug and waved to her as the taxi drove out of the driveway.

The police officers trudged up to their car. I gave them forty dollars for helping and they were appreciative.

"Please don't clean up or move anything from the art studio until JIO come," the officer, cautioned.

"When will that be?"

"We don't know, but we will call you," he answered.

"I have hotel guests coming in a few days, and I don't think all that blood will be good for Costa Rican tourism."

"We will tell them the situation, and they will come soon," he answered. I walked them out and thanked them again.

Everyone was gone, and I was surrounded by silence. Our green, leafy salad bowl was void of construction sounds and gunshots. I locked hotel doors and checked the fence electricity. Everything was secured. I watched Rex on his patrol, and Tico painfully followed. I closed the heavy metal gates blocking the entrance to the art studio, returned to my office, wrote a note to Angelo and Manuel explaining Tico's condition, and requested restricted passage into the blood-splattered space. I knew Angelo would be alarmed and would want to examine the space himself in the daylight before the investigators arrived. I was exhausted by the anxiety to stay safe. I filled with fear. Someone entered and spilled type 0 positive blood everywhere, and the person could enter again. I was alone, and fear dropped over me like a heavy suffocating steel cage that prevented light or ventilation from reaching my lungs. There was no room to move, and the fear cage pressed on all points of my body. The images of stagnated pools of blood on the floors of the sacred space that inspired my creativity shot riveting bullets of terror into my skin as Manuel's machine gun had shot bullets into the night air. My heart pounded; I gasped for air, and my hair was saturated with sweat like Tico's fur was saturated with blood. Fear was a loathsome unwanted creature. I closed all the drapes and began my Transcendental Meditation program.

When I finished meditating, it was dark outside, and I needed to check on Rex and Tico. I scanned the fence from my bedroom windows with my poor night vision, and it took some time before my eyes adjusted, but I saw the dogs tenaciously patrolling the south fence boundary. Rex looked strong again after his poisoning, but Tico moved stiffly, carefully, and painfully. I was struck with admiration for their work ethics and self-sacrifice. My intention would be that all humans used these dog-like loyal qualities. It was curious what internal chemical gave these dogs desirable qualities. Would it be possible to extract the dog creative intelligence and inject it into humans? The United States did genetically modified foods by taking a gene from fish, resistance to cold, and placing that gene into tomatoes, giving them strength to resist low temperatures. Why couldn't we invent a similar procedure to make better quality humans? I knew humans had their own creative intelligence but chose not to listen to its directives when it spoke about the spilling of human blood in pools upon art studio floors. This was not part of the human creative intelligence or our natural law. So what was it that made humans imitate the raw, animalistic instincts of animals but not the admirable qualities?

While I watched the dogs on the south fence boundary, a flash of firelight ignited on the north fence boundary, and I turned to see an enflamed silhouette of a human plummet to the ground as the flames extinguished. I carefully noted the location and called the police. I watched the motionless figure on the ground. My emotions flashed like the light that ignited the human and roared between compassion, sympathy, and the surreal awareness this had happened.

Was this ignited human my nemesis? In my world, I knew about artistic creativeness, laughter, fun, and peace. I knew nothing about this savage lifestyle.

Twenty minutes passed before car lights arrived at the security gates announcing someone's presence.

"Did you call for police?" a male voice asked into the intercom.

"Yes. I will be right up," I answered from the hotel box. I didn't approach the gate until I knew for sure who was up there, and in this case it was the police. I traipsed up the driveway into the blinding bright headlights of the parked police vehicle and became aware that my own innate trusting nature transformed into guarded caution. There was no reason for the police to come down the driveway into the hotel, since the burned figure was near the wrought iron security gates.

"Someone just got burned on the electric fence and fell to the ground right over there." I pointed in the north direction. The two police officers with their searchlights and I moved to the location where flames engulfed the figure, but the person was now gone. The police ran their hands over the scorched imprint of the human figure. Was this the imprint of my assassin? My fear-drenched spirit further wilted.

"He couldn't have gotten very far since this area still feels warm, and the burned brown grass is still visible. We will search the area and contact the hospitals looking for a patient with third-degree burns on his hands and body," they said. I was relieved the police officers were different from the ones I paid to stay with Wyoming just a few hours ago. I was embarrassed but simultaneously grateful for the number of police frequencies.

"May I give you something for your efforts?" I asked.

"Yes, Señora, we would appreciate that!"

"What would you like?"

"Do you have any beer?"

"I sure do! I'll be right back." I ran to the pantry where we kept the beer for Manuel and our hotel guests and quickly returned with a six pack of Bud Light (Manuel's favorite), which was sought after by the Tico population. The gift of beer was certainly cheaper than the forty dollars given this afternoon.

"Eureka" they sounded the Tico cry of pleasure. "Bud Light is our favorite. Thank you, and please call us anytime you need us. Have a pleasant night," the police said.

My fear persisted, and I slept restlessly until the morning light emerged through the balcony doors.

CHAPTER 20
ANALYSIS

Angelo and Manuel arrived early in the morning to their apartment and slept until noon. I reexamined the scorched imprint from last night's fallen aggressor before I weeded the entrance flower garden. I looked up and saw Angelo bounding toward me. He looked tired, but his khaki pants and butter-cream-yellow shirt were in their usual pristine crispness with brown tasseled loafers. He was newly showered, and I smelled my favorite Armadas after-shave lotion.

"Sun, please excuse my intrusion, but would you come with me into the city? I will explain on the way while we drive."

"Angelo, I will change my clothes and be ready in five minutes."

"Thank you, Sun. I received another call from Katerina this morning, and we must hurry."

"Just watch this greyhound run," I said, as the front door slammed after my heels.

Angelo started his conversation as the engine of the ugly lime green sports car, license beginning with nine, left Casa Ave driveway.

"Thanks for telling me about the art studio, and I received both police reports this morning. It seems the violence and the criminal activities have intensified. Katerina called and said she has an ocean-view condo apartment gifted into my name for the remainder of the month, but I must accept by tomorrow. Now that she knows we have the books, she will move quickly to have the documents transferred into her name or some other name than yours. We are going into the National Building for Lawyer Records. I have a law background, but I'm not a practicing lawyer and cannot legally enter the building; I have privileged clearance and a 'tip' for the security clerk of Records. He will locate Katerina's record books by the time we arrive, and you must look at them to see if she forged your name or if you signed the papers."

"I'm betting it's my signature. At closing, Mercedes translated and explained the purpose of each document. I signed many documents seemingly for trivial matters," I remembered.

"We will be searched upon entrance to the building, and we must leave our cellular phones in the car because they don't want pictures taken of the documents. We have a short clearance period of less than fifteen minutes to do this. Today is a holiday, and Katerina cannot get into the building, so we will be one day ahead of her. I am glad I ran with a greyhound because we have a pack of mean terriers on our heels."

"I don't understand why Katerina wants you in another apartment."

"I don't know why she wants me out of your place, but I know she doesn't want me helping you."

"The many burglaries of my power tools, the lawn furniture, the violence to the dogs, and the three sizzled, charred people thrown from the fence—is that the work of random petty thieves or Katerina?"

"I don't know, Sun. We have *five* fried people off your fence. It could be just random bandits, but I think we will have answers when we see her lawyer's books. She doesn't want an investigation of her books if we applied for 'lost books,' and that is the reason she gave them to us. What does she have in her record books that she doesn't want the officials to know about? We will have a peek at those law records and find out," Angelo said.

We drove the car to the back of a tall beige building and parked the lime green sports car out of sight from the main street. Angelo walked around the car to open my door, and we hastened to the main glass doors in front of the building, where a beige uniformed security guard waved us into the building as he held open the doors. The guard scanned our bodies with a wand and ushered us into the lobby. The building wasn't open for official use; the lights were all turned off, the blinds were closed, and the marble floors echoed our footsteps. The guard directed us to a table with a single dim lamp, and we sat down while he went behind the counter to get the tall stack of record books in purple binders.

"Sun, forgive me for my rudeness, but please don't talk to me while I look at the books. I have much to look over in just a few minutes, and I don't want this clerk of Records to hear your American voice. He might become suspicious and question our activity." I nodded my agreement.

The clerk placed the stack of books on the table in front of Angelo.

"What month was your house closing?" he whispered while the clerk made coffee at the loud machine.

"April 24, 2008," I whispered.

He dove into the stack of books like a Wyoming prairie dog in pursuit of a mate. He shuffled, restacked, and disregarded some of the books until he found one of interest. Angelo leafed through the book and quickly ran his hand down the pages. His eyes and fingertips touched the page edges faster than a computer scanner. He'd read five pages when he let out a long exhale of sound like a whispered whistle. He read and turned pages and asked me in a whisper, "Is this your signature?"

"Yes," I answered.

"Neither the sale of your property nor your will was filed. You paid her, but she didn't do the proper filing." Angelo read until the guard walked toward our table. He closed the book, reached into his pocket, removed some money, and put it into the palm of the security clerk of Records.

"Thanks for your help," Angelo said.

Angelo took my hand and whispered, "Let's get out of here." We almost ran to the car and didn't speak until we were inside with the engine started.

"Sun, this is no longer about helping you with your immigration. This has turned into one of the biggest cases I have ever had. Katerina Meza not only is a dishonest lawyer, but she has scammed 210 foreigners just like you. You are only one victim of a large property scam operation that encompasses all of Costa Rica. I need to get to a computer fast so I can get this information to my headquarters and start researching the other names in the books. We will drive to Galverez and Marcoto's law office and give them the information to begin correcting your property problem. I will use their computer to forward these 210 names to my office and Interpol."

Angelo and I power-walked into the law office, and he explained only the business pertaining to my property to Galverez, who went directly to his desk computer and began working. Angelo asked Galverez, "Would it be possible to use your computer for about an hour?"

"We are not that busy. Please be my guest!"

I was fascinated with Angelo's ability to manifest into the computer what his eyes had seen and what his mind remembered about the information he gleaned from Katerina's books. While he continued to work, I feigned calmness and leisurely conversed with lawyer

Luis Marcoto about theater and about the experiences during my years as a theater director. I served as a front for Angelo's espionage.

Luis Marcoto was younger, smaller, and cuter than his law partner, Galverez. He was humorous, charming, and entertained me with his flirtations. It wasn't enough to keep my mind from probing yesterday's events of guard dog Tico in the blood on the floor of the art studio and the hideous sound of frying skin on the electric fence. Sitting here while I waited for Angelo, in Galverez and Marcoto's law office, opened the foggy path to clearly understanding the fake kindness of the Meza family. Mercedes and her father, Pablo, wrapped me in warm fuzzy friendship to use my trust to feather their own nests for profits. Were they helping Katerina, or was Katerina helping them, or were they all equally participating?

It became clear as the dawn rising in the east why Pablo Meza, eating dinner at my Casa Ave open house dinner party, was familiar and friendly with Amon. Pablo Meza, an affluent Tico, and Amon, a Nico peasant, clearly pointed to what now seemed so blatantly obvious. They were working together on a business project, and the project was me. Amon's careless attitude for me as his employer coupled with the racial animosity between Nico and Tico cultures was now apparent. The friendship between the two of them was a business deal. Angelo discovered Amon's advanced cell phone was registered and given to him by Pablo Meza.

Amon was the best gardener I had known, but honesty and loyalty were more important. Amon's resignation was final, and it brought sadness for the lost goals that could have been reached for both of us. I offered to send him to a renowned, well-established botanical gardeners school for environmentally protecting Costa Rica's beautiful vegetation. His education would give him knowledge to multiply our food sources and to enrich the food quality and health benefits for staff and guests. His education would have helped our gardens to become a beautiful tourist attraction. In the event something happened to me, or to his employment with me, Amon could have used his school credentials to work for the many hotels that continued to spring up. He could have received a much better salary than formerly working in the coffee plantations. My offer was rejected with his reply, "I would rather you buy me a microwave." Amon was sure Pablo Meza was a better bet for future employment than working for a woman. This example represented the Costa Rican view toward women and particularly foreign businesswomen.

Mercedes and Apollo's Alegria touring business and my hotel, Casa Ave, could have produced reciprocally natural benefits for us both, as she and I had discussed. When Mercedes received a request for a tour, she could have supplied me with overnight guests, and if our hotel had guests who looked for events, I would set up tours with Mercedes. Our trip to Aranal zip lines when she forced me to pay for her ticket, the deceptive maneuver of adding the seller's mortgage to closing costs, and being an orchestrator of customs theft were self-serving manipulations. She used friendship as her disguise. She rejected honest business opportunity to grasp for larger profits for herself. The disappointment I felt for the lost friendship with Mercedes left a gap in my soul.

CHAPTER 21
SEDUCED

The beautiful, soft, dark night dropped its warm jasmine blanket around us as Angelo and I drove away from San Jose in silence. Rumi once said, "Silence is the language of God, all else is poor translation." If companions are comfortable in silence, this could be the sign of a strong friendship. My voice quietly lifted the corners of night's fleece cloak when I spoke. "Wyoming left fried chicken, mashed potatoes, and a corn casserole for us tonight. You and Manuel deserve your banana splits. Does that sound good to you?" I asked as we drove from Galverez and Marcoto's office, leaving the city to twinkle in its own lights.

"Oh, yeah. I think we should start with the banana split. I am so hungry." Angelo words spewed from under night's darkness like released captive pigeons.

"My office, JIO (Judicial Investigating Organization), Fuerza Publica, and Interpol all have invested interests in your case. Nearly all the names from Katerina's list are foreigners who bought property in Costa Rica and are unaware they have a property problem.

In some cases they may not even own their property. Many different countries are involved in this case. Katerina's clients are from Canada, Russia, Spain, France, Poland, United States, England, Brazil, and Colombia. The assortment of clients from so many countries indicates she has other people who help her. Two people we know are Pablo Meza and Mercedes Meza, but how do they make their contacts? Sun, how do you know them?" Angelo asked.

"A friend of mine in Texas took a continuing education class at the University of Texas from an instructor named Paul Phillips. During his class he recommended Pablo Meza, a property developer, as a trustworthy person who helps investors. My friend Carol came to Costa Rica and bought a house from Pablo Meza. I rented her house, and she asked Mr. Meza to meet me at the airport. Pablo Meza introduced me to his daughter, Mercedes. Mercedes asked Katerina to be the lawyer for my house closing, and Marianela is Katerina's secretary. Now we have the full circle," I explained.

"We have a circle of Ticos, but 210 property scams indicate a larger circle, or your friends the Mezas are really busy. I checked out the art studio, and whoever was there got wounded. He walked away injured with possible dog bite wounds. Fuerza Publica ran a hospital check for patients who had large open wounds. It is mysterious how an injured person can get in and out of your secured property," Angelo pondered as we drove.

My cell phone rang en route home, and it was JIO telling me they would be coming early tomorrow morning to look at the art studio.

"I don't believe they can tell us anything we don't already know. Do you?" I asked Angelo after ending the JIO call. Angelo nodded in agreement as we parked under the portico. Angelo, always the gentleman, opened my car door, vanished into his apartment to work on the computer, and I disappeared into the hotel kitchen to serve the dinner Wyoming had prepared for us. I placed the mountain of banana splits into the freezer. I gathered up our food-heaped plates for delivery to the apartment when Manuel bounded into the kitchen.

"Come quick; Angelo has a phone call he wants you to hear."

"Manuel, please grab those plates and help me deliver," I said.

We quickly transported the dinner to the apartment, and Angelo signaled for us to be quiet while he switched on the speaker phone. He was in mid-conversation with Katerina.

"Is that why you called this evening, to talk about the highway project, Katerina?"

"No, I called to ask you about your decision to accept the fabulous apartment we found for you," she said in persuasive tone.

"Thank you, Katerina, but I don't understand why I should move when I am comfortable right here."

"I want you to know something," she said and then paused. "We are foreclosing on Sun Richards's house next Wednesday. You won't have anywhere to go, and you seem to be a good Tico who helps out of kindness. We want to help fellow Ticos with your qualities," she construed.

"That's very interesting, Katerina. Why would you foreclose on Ms. Richards?"

"She is a fraudulent person like I've told you before and doesn't have the money to pay for the house she bought from Tony Lopez and Rodney Lewis."

"I heard you say the foreclosure is happening Wednesday, but who is the officiating court judge?"

"It is Armando Morra, one of the best judges in San Jose," she boasted.

"This news gives me concerns about my living accommodations, and with my busy work schedule, I really don't want to be homeless. Let me think about this some more. Thanks for the call, and we will talk again soon." Angelo hung up, quickly looked up a number in his cell phone, and made another call.

"Good evening, Judge Morra. This is Angelo Lopez calling."

Pause.

"Just fine, sir. It has been a long time!"

Pause.

"My parents are happy and well, thank you for asking, and how is Margarita?"

Pause.

"Perfect! I wonder if you have a pending foreclosure next Wednesday on a Ms. Sun Richards by a lawyer named Katerina Meza?"

Pause.

"Please take your time, I will wait. Thank you for checking. Señor Morra, I need to ask you for an extension. Would that be possible? Whatever time you could grant would be appreciated."

Pause.

"Yes, one week will be helpful. Thank you. Please give my regards to your family. Thank you again and have a pleasant evening."

Angelo ended his call.

My stomach was a rope of tangled knots, and my thoughts were pulled in the direction of gratitude and enthrallment toward Angelo's ability to problem solve. I was pulled toward optimism with his possession of power, and I felt proud I knew him. I was infatuated with his abilities to right the wrongs that plagued my life. The tug-of-war pulled me between brightness and darkness. The abrasive rope jerked me into the darkness of panic and fear about the reality of my situation and scratched open raw wounds that allowed black insecurity to seep into my being, which caused me tenseness, suffering, and worry. This tug-of-war going on inside pulled me into disquiet and anxiety. I could be left homeless in a foreign country where I barely communicated. My plans and dreams could disintegrate into ashes, leaving me without security and projecting a dismal future. This tug-of-war had my mind and emotions tied in knots. Hope unraveled the knots inside of me, and gratitude toward Angelo eased anxiety. Angelo looked into my eyes as if he read my mind.

"Please quiet your fears; everything will be all right, but we have much work to do next week to stay ahead of Katerina's foreclosure. Sun, please allow me to help you, and don't worry. It will all work out," Angelo soothed.

"Angelo and Manuel, I am glad for both of your help, and thank you for your efforts. I looked forward to the Texas tourists next week, but now I wish they weren't coming until we get past Katerina's threat of foreclosure," I exhaled.

"We will manage everything," Angelo promised.

"He is a man who can pull out many rabbits from his hat," Manuel supported in his accented English. I picked up the dishes and returned to my hotel office. I opened up the computer and read the emails. "Hoooooobaby!" I jumped up from the computer, dashed back to Angelo's apartment, barely knocked on the door, bolted in, and announced, "The tourist have postponed!"

"You made a believer out of me! Didn't you just wish for a postponement? I accept your weird philosophy and ideals." Angelo gave me a high five. "Nature supports your wishes. Tomorrow after the JIO inspects the art studio, do you want to run in the dog races, my beautiful greyhound?"

"We need to be the first hounds out of the starting gate, that's for sure," I cautioned.

I returned to the hotel office and quickly acknowledged the Texas tourists' postponement. I confirmed their new reservations. I wonder if Angelo and Manuel listen to the sounds of the construction noise that I hear throughout the night.

Morning brightness brought a lightened mood and the police.

"Buenos Dias, I am Chief Inspector Mario de Luisa, with the JIO, con permiso," he said in Spanish into the intercom at the gate.

"Mucho gusto," I replied as I pressed the button, which slowly and gracefully opened the big wrought iron gates. Inspector de Luisa strode down the hill of the driveway carrying a suitcase, as I sprinted to Angelo's door, knocked, and announced the inspector's arrival. Manuel, Angelo, Inspector de Luisa, and I paraded the pathway to the art studio.

En route, I noticed Manuel surveying his garden workmanship. He removed the small encroaching weeds as we passed down the sloping green, lush, grassy hills. The sunlight reflected off something shinny lying under the bougainvillea, and he stooped to pick it up, thinking it was a silver foil candy wrapper from Wyoming's morning snack. Manuel pushed back the plant and saw that the reflection was from a large expensive machete, stained with dried blood.

"Is that one of yours?" the inspector asked.

"No, not one of ours. Is it yours, Manuel?" I asked.

"No, Sun, I only use the weed eater not a machete," he said disgustedly.

"Do you have a plastic bag?" asked the inspector.

"Yes," answered Manuel, as he ran back to the apartment. "I will be right back!"

The inspector took a variety of testing kits from his suitcase and collected several specimens from the art studio. He carefully put on surgical gloves and put them into his case. De Luisa removed the machete from the bougainvillea and put it into the plastic bag that Manual delivered.

"I think I have enough. You can clean the art studio, if you would like," Chief Inspector Mario de Luisa permitted.

"Thank you for helping. Will you give me information about the blood tests when you know something?" I requested.

"It might be possible for my organization to do so," he responded evasively.

Manuel helped the inspector gather his stuff and escorted him up the driveway to his parked car while Angelo and I darted to the house to prepare for travel into the city.

"I will bring the house closing file and my passport. Is there anything else I need?" I asked.

"Make sure you have your passport and a good book to read because the wait at these Costa Rican government offices takes a long time," Angelo instructed.

"Race you to the car!" I said, as I granted myself a sizable head start. I bolted toward the house in my fastest run. I looked over my shoulder and saw Angelo fast on my heels.

"Last one in the car is a decrepit old soapyloaty (Costa Rican for buzzard)," I yelled. We were on the road in record time, in a black Lincoln continental with a license plate beginning with the number nine.

"We need to hurry as fast as we can. Katerina never filed your ownership papers, as we saw in her law records. Now that we have your books, she will file using the former board members, and they can vote to take possession of your property or whatever they want. The first thing we need today is to stop by Galverez and Marcoto's office and pick up a legal document that names you as president. You need to choose your board of directors." Angelo continued talking as we sped toward San Jose.

"You need three others beside yourself. I recommend you choose family members or trusted friends. Each person must sign stating he or she agrees to be your corporation's board member. After that, we will take the document to the Republica De Costa Rica Registro Nacional and get your Certification Literal. If we can get that much done today we'll be able to slow Katerina's efforts. She will be crazy with anger if we are able to get that paperwork completed. To save time, I called Galverez. He is expecting us, and after you give him the names and Social Security numbers for your new board members, in a couple of days, we can move on to the Registro Nacional."

"Days ago, I realized the necessity to obtain my own board members, and I emailed family members and Molly. I received their faxed acceptance letters. I have them with me today," I reported.

"Eureka, Sun Richards! Smart woman! You have saved us at least four days. We can file all of this at the same time! We have a chance to win this dog race! You are a greyhound after all." He laughed.

We wasted no time in reaching Galverez and Marcoto's office. Galverez greeted me with a kiss on each side of my face and directed me to a single straight chair beside his desk. Angelo explained to him in Spanish that I had the information for my new board members. I removed the papers from my file; he accepted them and nodded with approval. Galverez's English was difficult for him. I understood a little of his Spanish, and he understood some of my English, but both of us appreciated Angelo, who remained standing and translated for faster communication. Galverez and Marcoto's office was so small that there was only enough space for their two desks and the one chair that Angelo gave to me. The office door remained opened onto the sidewalk, and Angelo spent his time on his cell phone outside on the street while I waited for Galverez to prepare the needed documents. Galverez explained that he had to be very careful preparing the documents because the clerks at the Republica de Costa Rica National would refuse them if they weren't perfect. He excused himself for being focused on his work instead of involved in conversation with me.

"I am glad for your attention to detail. Please, Mr. Galverez, take the required time."

When Angelo wasn't on his cell phone, I stepped outside onto the sidewalk and asked, "Angelo, how much is Señor Galverez charging me for this paperwork?"

"Nothing, Sun; he is on a retainer for our construction company, and we pay him a salary whether he has legal work or if he sits there and reads the newspaper. You gave him a reason to be a lawyer at this moment. My corporation doesn't need him, but his idleness is about to change. My road project is in serious trouble.

"Angelo, I'm sorry. What's wrong?"

"Do you remember when I was required to hold up a bridge with a crane and open the entire new highway for a commemoration for the presidential photo shoot when the highway was still unfinished?" Angelo asked.

"*Yes*, of course, I remember."

"The unfinished prematurely opened road caused nine deaths and eleven other serious injuries. The roads have no markings and no reflection lights or signs of any kind. The road has no warning signs cautioning of curves to drivers, and I am required through political maneuvering to accept the responsibility. The roads have landslides, with the increasing rains, because the cuts in the hills are too steep, as I explained to the Road and Highway Authority, which is determined to save money by using the thirty-six-year-old, outdated design. More deaths are foreseen because the Road Authority is unreasonable. Our construction company must defend itself against the fatalities and injuries."

I wanted to give Angelo a hug and say something that assured him. I believed in his efforts toward rightfulness, but his body language and demeanor signaled me to keep my distance and not give him the sympathy I carried. He was closed up, unapproachable, and stressed. I couldn't express what my heart wanted to say. He helped me with many things, and I wished there was some way I could bring him the calmness he deserved. I imagined the remorse he endured every time he heard the news of another highway fatality due to faulty road construction. How could he withstand the agony of involvement with such careless disregard for human life? I stepped

back into the law office and watched Señor Galverez apply paste to
the official stamps. He placed them on the documents authenticating
his official license to manifest the completed papers. He looked up,
handed me the papers, and encouraged me as he spoke in his struggling English. "Go with great speed," he said.

"Thank you for your help, Señor Galverez." I hastened to the car
where Angelo waited holding the opened car door and jumped in. We
drove quickly through traffic to reach a very beautiful, tall, modern,
dark blue glassed building, off the main city square. Angelo found
parking in the indoor parking lot, and we entered the gray granite
highly polished tile floors and walls with many offices. Angelo knew
exactly where to go and wasted no time searching for the correct
office location. He opened the double glass doors to the Republica de
Costa Rica Registro National office, and we waited in a short line in
front of a clerk behind a counter, not unlike the cage of an American
bank teller. Angelo looked at me with his humble shy smile.

"You look very elegant today, but you always look elegant because you are an elegant lady."

"Thank you, Angelo; it is an honor for me to stand next to such
a creditable illustrious man, who helps me." I tried to erase the un-
worthiness he experienced from his highway problems.

"I think you stand beside a slow-running old soapyloaty."

"Not a chance," I laughed.

It was our turn at the counter, and an attractive young woman
with beautiful hair asked in Spanish, "How may I help you today?"

"We need the Certification Literal for Llaves de Negocios #3–
101–453024, por favor."

"I have it already from the vault! I spent one and a half hours
looking for this corporation. A woman left here, not ten minutes ago,
by the name of … (she looked at a business card) Marianela Gonzales.
She didn't have the correct completed documentation. She said she

would get them with the correct stamps and be right b —— " Angelo interrupted her.

"Yes, we know. She called us on her cell and told us what was needed. I hope we have the correct documents now." The clerk took the papers, looked them over, and requested, "I need to see a cedula from Sun Richards." I presented my passport; the clerk looked intently at me and matched the name with my documents and said, "Please wait for your Certification Literal; it will take a few minutes." She left her counter cage, and my wide alarmed eyes met Angelo's, but no communication was needed as we moved away from the counter.

"Angelo, that was very quick thinking to tell her that little white lie about Marianela telephoning us to bring the correct documents. That was genius!" I hoped Angelo recovered his sense of value from his disabling troubles with his road construction.

The clerk returned with the Certification Literal, and I looked it over. I was greatly relieved to see my name as president and the names of family and Molly that supported my position as president. I looked up at the attractive clerk with the beautiful hair and said, "Thank you so much for your efficiency, and, by the way, you have beautiful hair." She gave me an appreciative smile. She would remember me when Marianela returned.

I felt twenty pounds lighter, and my breathing was noticeably more regular. I wasn't even aware how much tension I had accumulated until now, when it was gone. I took Angelo's hand as we left the counter and strode down the granite floor while I listened to the beautiful sound of our footsteps. I knew Angelo was aware of the warmth from my gratitude and friendship.

"Angelo, thank you a million times over for helping me. You are Angelo, 'My Angel Man,' and I want to treat you to a lunch of your choice. You deserve a banquet befitting an angel. Where should we go?"

"Let's go to an elegant place befitting our celebration."

"Do we have time for that?" I asked.

"We most certainly do. You provided board documents that afforded us the time."

"Excuse me for a moment." Angelo called someone on the cell phone and talked in very rapid Spanish. He ended the conversation, and we walked to his black Lincoln Continental, where we had parked in the inside parking lot at the Registro Nacional. He opened my car door, and I slid into place. He drove to a home outside of the city, in mountains similar to the area I rented from Carol when I first came to Costa Rica. The vegetation was no longer tropical but more like a Colorado forest. We traveled up the winding, narrow, gravel roads, which presented a panoramic view of San Jose and Cartago.

"When we were teenagers, this was the place we called 'Lovers Lane.' Kids came to this road to test their driving skills and to make out," Angelo reminisced.

We came to a very sharp curve in the road. On the driver's side was a steep, solid granite, sheared-off mountain that made a wall in front of us, and Angelo became sullen and tense. I sensed a change in the level of his energy and his mood. Angelo slowed the car and said softly, "This is the place where my older brother, Cristian, died instantly when he crashed my Mercedes, given to me by my father for my seventeenth birthday present," Angelo memorialized.

"It must be difficult to return to this place and have a birthday reminiscent of such an emotional tragedy," I comforted.

"I brought you up here to replace a bad memory and make a pleasant new one with you. It's time for me to let go of the past," he said as he gingerly drove the car around the twisting curves.

"Today is a glorious day for celebration. I am astounded by your abilities and accomplishments to make my life better. Thank you, Angelo, for being there for me."

"It's you who deserves my thanks. Your friendship changed me to become a different person."

"*Oh, no!* Angelo, there is nothing wrong with the Angelo I know."

"You know an Angelo that doesn't exist! Everyone in the office tells me I am a different person. My secretary said I was much calmer and not grumpy or snappy anymore. I know it is because of you that I am more relaxed. Other people are more relaxed around me because I am calmer."

"I don't believe people change unless they change themselves, and their old habits no longer serve them. You changed yourself. I also think you are getting more sleep, and deep rest erases stress and heightens personal good qualities. You remain the same Angelo, but you learned to like the new and improved you. I know; I like you!" Angelo patted my hand in response.

We arrived at the very highest mountaintop to find a Spanish hacienda with a gorgeous view for hundreds of miles. Angelo leaned across me and pointed out cities from all over the center of Costa Rica. "Look there; that's Puntarenas, Jaco, and over there is Alajuela, Grecia, San Amon, Esparza, Zarcero, Sarchi, and in that direction is Cartago.

"This is absolutely magnificent," I said breathlessly.

"This restaurant is known for all its specialities from Costa Rica. They have wonderful crab dishes, or any seafood, and a good variety of vegetables and salads. Let's go. I'm hungry."

"Señor Angelo, I'm glad to see you again. Your table is ready," invited the waiter.

He directed us to a table with a full view of the green lush valley below. This open-to-nature restaurant was elegant with a natural feel that erased the "pinched" feeling some stylish restaurants emit. The decor was a gradation of blue and white table coverings with dark blue and white napkins. The tables and chairs were natural Costa Rican mahogany and rosewood beautifully hand-crafted hardwoods.

"I love this place, Angelo. What a good place to celebrate the good fortune we had today."

The waiter delivered two glasses of sparkling water. We placed our order of shelled crab in drawn butter with vegetable medley and sweet potatoes.

Angelo raised his glass and said, "To your wonderful company."

"What a pleasant thing to say! To your happiness," I replied.

"Sun, I said it with the most sincerity. I have enjoyed spending my leisure time with you. My job is full-time, spring-loaded bullets ready to be discharged every minute, day and night. I'm never alone. I'm on vacation now, and things are a little less tense than my regular workdays."

"Angelo, we have been alone all day."

"Sun, I'm never alone. It appears we are alone, but we are not. Since I am on vacation, I have fewer people around than I normally do. I have a team of bodyguards night and day. The people that protect me (us) blend into the surroundings. Do you see the two businessmen having lunch at the table in the corner? They are not businessmen, but they are my guys."

"Why can't you have alone time, and why are bodyguards needed?"

"My area of responsibility is the total of Central Wyoming, and I have many projects and teams of people that work simultaneously. Each project and team has a new code for obtaining instructions and information each day. It is necessary for me to know these codes to give orders, answer questions, and dispense current vital information pertaining to each project for each team. If the code is incorrect, entire areas are without knowledge and instructions. I'm the lock for the security system. If something happened to me, the system would be broken until my replacement could be installed. Each code is different for each team each day, and this information must be remembered exactly."

I remembered months ago, Angelo told me his construction company was a front. I was beginning to fit this puzzle together.

"Angelo, how do your protectors keep track of you? I have been with you many times, and I haven't noticed any bodyguards."

He gave a little smile and said, "Good, they know how to do their job. All day today we were followed. If we are in the car, we are followed by car and sometimes by helicopter. If you noticed people following us, they aren't doing their job. Today while we drove, a car followed us for only a few blocks, and then another car would follow us, and then another took over so no car was behind us for very long attracting our attention. They usually change at intersections, at stoplights, or when I change lanes. Sometimes, I play games with them, and it drives them crazy." He chuckled.

"If you can be very discrete and not obvious, look for my security. Why don't you take a trip to the ladies' room and see if you can count how many people work for me in this restaurant," Angelo playfully directed the rules of his game.

"Will you please excuse me for a few minutes," I said as I stood. He stood up in courtesy and held my chair. I walked to the restroom and cast my eyes over the other diners. The restaurant wasn't a busy place, so I thought my task would be easy. I made use of the bathroom while I had the chance, and coming out, I noticed two men by the entrance outside smoking. Okay, plus the two businessmen Angelo told me about made four. I walked back to the table; Angelo stood and pulled out my chair.

"I've got it! There are four people here that are your people. The two businesspeople you told me about and the two men, in tropical print shirts outside the entrance smoking, make a total of four."

He laughed. "You are rather good, Sun, but you missed some. There are six. The two tourists smoking outside are not mine. The two businessmen I told you about, the waiter who showed us to the table, the romantic couple at the south windows holding hands, and the woman in the blue dress who followed you into the ladies' room."

"This is incredible. Are you teasing me, Angelo?"

"Not at all! If we are going places together, it is important you know that we are never alone, and your conduct is always on display. Now you know why I am glad you are an elegant woman," he confided.

"It must be very hard to always be on display."

"I am not always on display, and that is what I love about your peaceful home. The security fence, the electric gates, the security lighting, the guard dogs, and Manuel allow me to relax without the security team. It gives them extra time off as well."

All the added security for my property, at his expense, isn't just for my security and his equipment. Who is this man? What is his position and with whom?

"You are the most interesting man I have ever met, and even if all this is untrue, and you are playing games with me, you remain the most entertaining man," I said.

"Sun, I am not playing games with you! I want you to know my life and the job I am married to."

Our food arrived with a different waiter, who I assumed was the real one. The lunch was as wonderfully delicious as the ambiance was beautiful.

"Thank you for bringing me here to see this wonderful place, Angelo."

"It is selfishness on my part, Sun, because I enjoy being with you."

"When you leave Casa Ave and go to work every day, sometimes in different countries, isn't it difficult for the security to follow you everywhere?" I asked.

"Yes, it is, and that's why our top-ranking agents have tiny electronic tracking devices surgically implanted into their scrotums. Sometimes those devices cause impotence and sometimes not, depending on the mood of your surgeon. It is a good idea to stay on the good side of your surgeon," he said, blushed, and laughed.

I had a thousand more questions to ask about the scrotum implants but forced my "elegant lady-like behavior" to restrain my scrotum questions.

"When you travel to other countries, isn't it expensive for your security to go along unnoticed?"

"We have many different security teams, and they work harmoniously together like a tag relay. Each team has its own area and boundaries. For example, when I travel to Nicaragua, the Costa Rica team (we have three CR teams) will hand off to the Nicaragua team, or El Salvador, or Panama, and so on. It is a very orderly system. Sun, it is important for me that you know I am truthful with you. I want to tell you how my team works today, so you can determine the truth for yourself. The two businessmen will leave first. When we get ready to leave, the man who ushered us to our table (the waiter) pretends his work shift has ended, removes his apron, folds it neatly, gives it to the other waiter, says something about "coming to work another day" and leaves the restaurant ahead of us. The romantic couple holding hands will leave right behind us, and the single woman will probably return to the ladies' room and wait for our car to leave the parking lot. Later she will take an alternate road and join the car-following exchange. Can you observe this without being obvious?" he asked.

"I won't waste my acting career unwittingly, and this seems the perfect time for you to witness my performance." I said, as Angelo flashed a big smile and showed his beautiful teeth.

"Sun, I know you invited me to lunch as a way to show your thanks for the help I gave, but I can't allow my team to see you pay the bill. They will tease me and say I am a 'kept' man. I want my team to know you to be as refined, poised, and beautiful as I know you. When we get home you can show your appreciation with banana splits or taking care of the dogs. It is also a cultural Tico tradition for the man's status to remain in place. In our country the man takes care of his woman, and my pride will be damaged if you don't allow me to assume this role of responsibility."

"I'm not competitive in this field. Angelo, I love to be pampered, and I soak up attention like a dry sponge."

"This topic is the reason I have always been attracted to older women. I cannot tolerate the arrogance and flip attitude of women under fifty. Especially American women; they are the worst."

"Angelo, you are an attractive man with position and style. You can have any woman in the world you want." As I said this, he looked down at his shoes. I believed there was an interesting story hidden in his past.

"Want to share a dessert?" he asked.

"OOOOYeah, but you choose, and I will only have your last couple of bites because my will power for sugar and dessert is non-existent. If I get started on a dessert, there won't be anything left to share because I will eat it all!"

"Why not share with me equally? You are not fat. You do yoga every day, and you have a good figure."

"Thank you, Angelo, but I am a sugar addict and diabetic. I will enjoy that dessert vicariously through your enjoyment, if you promise to really savor the flavor, smack your lips, and make sounds like, mmmm oooooh, and aaaaw."

He laughed and ordered the Chocolate Mint Mountain. It was a big piece of chocolate cake topped with two inches of handmade chocolate fudge, pecans, and a drizzle of cream de mint liquor. Oh, good grief, was it ever good!

The same waiter who ushered us to our table brought the check and presented it to Angelo. While Angelo paid the bill with his credit card signature, the pretend waiter strolled to the receiving podium, removed his apron, folded it up, and handed it to the other waiter.

He simply said "Hasta luego" and sauntered to his car parked in the parking lot. The romantic couple left their table and edged in front of us to their car. The single woman in the blue dress stood by the window admiring the view. I was so enamored with the chocolate cake that I forgot to observe the two businessmen's exit.

Angelo and I walked to our car, and I quickly noticed all but one vehicle in the parking lot had a license beginning with a nine. I assumed Angelo paid the bill for everyone's lunch today, and I knew if the large bill was presented to me, I would have upchucked my crab lunch on the restaurant tile ever so unladylike.

We drove down the twisting, winding roads, and I couldn't observe the car exchange that followed us because I was too small to see out the rearview mirrors without stretching up to peer. My movements would have telegraphed my awareness and certainly been obvious if I had turned around and looked out the back window.

"Sun, you have been my muse today; let's continue to one more office to gather the Plano Catastrado (survey) documents we need. This office stop will be lengthy because they prepare papers for us as we wait. If you want to bring your book and read, I won't be offended."

"I enjoy our conversation, which remains more exciting and interesting than my book, but if you have other work, I understand."

"Not at all, I am on vacation, and it would be easy to get sucked up by the system, if I allowed."

We traveled back into the city, and our conversation reverted to his job.

"Do you enjoy your job?" I asked.

"Sun, I have told you before, I am an engineer, which is the truth, but my real job is crime. I once loved my job. I have been an agent for thirty years, and I am tired of it. This job is the only thing I know. When I first began, I knew clearly what was right, and what was morally and ethically wrong. Nowadays, the problems and solutions are complicated, making right and wrong boundaries blurred, and I'm not sure if what I do is helpful or causes more harm and confusion. A United Nations affiliated organization reported Costa Rica as having the highest rate of robberies in the Western Hemisphere in 2010. There were 43,000 robberies. How can we control crime with statistics like those?" he rhetorically asked.

"One of my first missions was under my current mentor, JoSam. We were on a job, transporting criminals (cargo) to their trials by air. JoSam solved crimes involving these criminals on previous occasions and knew much of our work was like a fishing expedition of catch and release, catch and release repetitively, making our job meaningless when we tried to make the world less corrupt. We had in our possession pre-signed papers stating that the cargo had been delivered. JoSam opened the cargo bay of the airplane and pushed the screaming criminals out. He closed the hatch, and we never said a word about that event. Ever. I knew it was wrong, and I mentally suffered from the cruel shock of my mentor's actions. When I was young, I thought if we cleaned up a hornet's nest of criminals I would feel the sunshine of a brighter place, but my job of solving and cleaning up a crime became a revolving door. I cleaned up one mess, and then I was caught in an avalanche of more that took their place."

"I feel no satisfaction and only see more violent crimes. After working thirty years in this business, I know the futility of my job and understand the actions of JoSam's disposal of cargo. I asked myself: Is it right, or is it wrong? I don't know anymore where right and wrong begin or end. In this job, I know the US diplomatic and political pressures add to the murky boundaries of right and wrong. I know JoSam better than I know anyone, and he is my mentor, but he is too old to still be in this job. He is in his mid-eighties and still in the top command position of our secret government agency, which is privately funded and invisible from any authority, and he has dementia. We had a very sensitive project in the Middle East he needed to monitor every second. He forgot about them, with tragic results. Instead he watched a football game on television. One of our female ambassadors who traveled by motorcade was ambushed and assassinated by sprayed bullets from machine guns at the hands of our own American men. It was nothing but a preventable mistake that left her infant riding in the car an orphan."

"Everything I experienced, every fearful horrifying violent crime I witnessed, can't measure up to the fear I have of JoSam. He is the epitome of cruelty, and there is no predicting what wrath he brings to his victims. If he is angered, he becomes insane, and it doesn't matter if it is one of his ranking officers or a hardened convicted killer. He can't discern between who is honorable and who isn't, and his punishment remains the same for both. He holds total power and is not accountable to anyone. Only a few of us under his command know of his atrocities. His anger controls his actions. I saw him assassinate his own agent. I fear this man. At meetings in Washington, I sit beside JoSam at the conference table, help answer questions for him, and keep him awake. I don't know how long this can continue. I help prop him up in the eyes of the board. He has no life other than his job. He was married eight times. All the women left him, and each took a helping of his fortune. He has children, two daughters, he doesn't even know by his first wife. I know I don't want to imitate his life, but I think I am."

"JoSam knows his position is at risk, and he doesn't know how to live in this world without it. He asked me the other day, when he is certain he is going to be released from his job, if I will help him commit suicide. What a thing to ask. Huh? From the time I was seventeen years old, JoSam looked after me. If love exists in me, I know I feel obligated to help him not commit suicide but to live at least one day in happiness."

We drove the black Lincoln Continental into an available parking space in front of the government office building, Tierras y

Agrimensura Land and Agriculture in San Jose. We climbed the stairs to the second floor, which was a large open space with many desks and scattered comfortable overstuffed leather chairs for visitors. Angelo ushered me to a small coffee table with two chairs. He walked to an open desk and talked to an older official customer service clerk. The man behind the desk looked distinguished in his mid-sixties and appeared amiable. I realized I held the file and walked to the desk and offered it to Angelo.

"Thanks, Sun. I gave him the needed information."

"You both can wait over there, and I will bring the Plano Catastrado to you when it is finished," the clerk replied.

"Thanks," we both replied in unison and walked back to our chairs. Angelo moved his chair closer to mine around the table as we waited. After we settled into our chairs, I rekindled our former conversation.

"I know this isn't the place to talk about our private topics, but I want you to know I understand your difficult position, and I see parallels between your work and my efforts. We both are warriors of two different kinds. You are a government agent warrior; I am a peaceful warrior, and we both try to accomplish the same goals. We want to rid the low consciousness plaguing our countries and to free it from crime, fear, and all the human negativity bottled up in our societies. If our efforts are accomplished, we won't have the repetition of continuing crime. We approach the solution of this topic in different ways. I sit for four hours a day effortlessly, with my eyes closed, while transcendence emanates through my body and calms the stressful energies in our countries. This practice manifests peacefulness that brings personal comforts and harmony to me and others." Angelo listened to my words.

"You use guns, handcuffs, great personal effort, and self-endangerment to reach your goals. You face great frustration and discouragement with the recidivism rate of crime while I face frustration and discouragement because humans are slow to embrace meditation.

"I question if Costa Rica or the United States will ever understand my efforts. Your penal code of crime and punishment is necessary because our world isn't refined enough to understand and accept meditating alone. Someday soon we will use meditating without the needed force of punishment to gain a higher level of societal consciousness. Others would never call me a warrior, but I believe I am. I devote much of my time to this cause, and I am a crusader for individual inner peace. I think we both are crime fighters of a different kind."

"Sun, I know your strength, and I have witnessed your dedication to the practice every day for these past twelve months. I want to ask you about a portion of your Transcendental Meditation program that seems untrue to me. I went online and read about it, and they gave a snippet of information about yogic flying. Is that for real?" he asked.

"Oh, yes! It is true and scientifically explained. Using the yogic flying technique is where the power of societal consciousness reform takes place. Quantum physics explains the mathematical equation; if one percent of a country's population uses the yogic flying technique the entire population receives benefits. One of the most important benefits is the reduction in crime. Using this technique is part of my four-hour-a-day routine, two hours in the morning and two hours in the evening, to help our countries.

"Do you fly around your house and gardens like a witch without a broom?" he asked with wide eyes.

"Oh, good grief, no, I don't," I said, and I laughed. "Angelo, I know yogic flying seems as strange to you as placing a tracking device in the scrotum of your agents seems to me. This topic is a very humorous collision between your world and mine. During the practice of the yogic flying technique, brainwave synchrony is maximized as the body spontaneously springs forward in short hops. Internally, the experience is accompanied by exhilaration, expanded awareness, bliss, and happiness. If criminals learned to meditate and did this technique, they would find happiness. They would no longer find the thrill of crime so alluring."

Angelo sat there for a few beats and just shook his head in disbelief. "I know you to be a very calm person, I have known you for months now, yet this yogic flying business seems very strange to me," he confessed.

"Yes, and you seem to be a regular guy, but you store masses of information in your brain without taking notes, which seems very strange to me." We both laughed, and he reached over and hugged me.

"Angelo," I exclaimed in surprise, "have you forgotten that your staff is watching us?"

"You know what? I have. I was so interested in our conversation that I forgot about them."

"There are different people working for you than the ones we had at the restaurant. There are five of them," I said, without looking around the waiting room. "The man with the unusual haircut that looks like an American who is reading the *Tico Times*, the college kid who got a drink at the water cooler, the woman who is eating a Snickers candy bar, the older gentleman with Italian shoes, and the very young skinny girl with the long dyed red hair are all your team," I smirked.

"You are getting very good at this. There are only four. The very young, skinny girl with the red hair is not ours. Do you want to know how these people will leave?" he asked.

"Yes, this is fun. How?"

"The American, Tom, who reads the *Tico Times*, and Linda, with the candy bar, will go to the checkout desk and exit first, before us, and Lindell, the older man, will leave with the college kid, and they will be behind us," he explained.

"You think this is a more normal life than yogic flying?"

Angelo's laughter was interrupted by the ring of his cell phone. He excused himself and moved to the distant side of the room. My curiosity was aroused by the movements of his staff. Each moved to another location of the room. I feigned reading my book. I thought his staff repositioned themselves in front of him to block a possible gunshot that could come from a doorway or from a window. I don't know. I give up! This is all too complicated to figure. I really did read my book.

Angelo remained on the phone for an hour as I read three chapters. His staff looked like real waiting people when the Plano Catastrado clerk walked over to me. He told me the certificate was finished and could be picked up at the checkout counter. I asked how much it would cost, and he replied it was about four dollars. I thanked him and moved to the checkout desk. I paid for the document and was amused to see that the older bodyguard, Tom straightened his standing position against the window, and Linda stood up but didn't move to the checkout. They both waited, and I returned to my chair to wait for Angelo. I read my book. Another fifteen minutes passed before Angelo walked over to me.

"Did you get the Plano?"

"Yes, I have it in the folder."

"Good! Let's go home and take a swim; I need one," he invited.

Tom and Linda moved to the checkout counter, said something to the clerk, and exited before us. I dropped the file to the title floor on purpose, turned to pick it up, and saw the older man with the college kid behind us. Angelo told me true. There was no skinny, young, red-haired girl in the mix. Angelo tapped me on the shoulder and said, "I'll get it," as he stooped to pick up the mess of papers.

On the way home, Angelo was quiet and seemed deep in thought. I was contented and allowed him some thinking time as I gazed out the window of the elegant black Lincoln Continental with the license plate that began with a nine. I watched the buildings of the inner city move past and was glad my property had its own park-like atmosphere. The city was far calmer than a Wyoming city but still a city, exuding its emissions, auditory vibrations, and restless din.

"Sun, do you like this car?"

"Angelo, I just had the thought that this was an elegant car. I am amazed at the synchrony of our thoughts."

"This Lincoln Continental is JoSam's car. It is the car he drives when he is in Costa Rica. He always drives a new black Lincoln Continentals wherever he is."

"The car has an affluent look and style to it, and I understand his attraction."

"I was on the phone for a long time today, talking to the comptroller of our construction company. All the highway mortalities and personal injury responsibilities are unjustly placed on our company by the press and public opinion. The comptroller said the total cost is now nearly seventy-five million and might be more after we finish the road. The construction crews—all of them—work around the clock to close dangerous exits, place warning signs, and reroute traffic to other, safer, finished roads. We face bankruptcy. The Costa Rican government won't allow the contract to be dropped, and neither will JoSam. They both have vested interests and personal agendas to fulfill. Our company is left holding the bag."

"I am sorry, Angelo, for your troubles. I wish I knew how to solve them as you know how to solve mine. I really want good things to be in your life and not this mountain of anxiety. All that I have in my arsenal of defense is the desire and intention for eradication of obstacles placed in your path. I will send to you all the energy I can muster and hope you will be clear-minded and triumphant."

"Sun, no one has given me more. Thank you for caring." Angelo remained quiet the rest of the trip home.

CHAPTER 22
VIOLENCE

It was late afternoon when we pulled up to the house, and I knew Angelo was distraught about his roads. "Do you prefer to go for a swim alone?" I asked.

"Not at all! You give me calmness. See you poolside at seventeen hundred hours." I had to count on my fingers how military time converts. That was in fifteen minutes! I dashed into the kitchen to see what Wyoming had prepared for dinner. I thanked her for the chicken cordon bleu for Angelo and me, and for Manuel, who didn't like chicken, she made his beloved rice and beans. I walked Wyoming to the gate, and she blew me a kiss. I went to my room, put on my one-piece black bathing suit, and walked out to the pool where Angelo was already sitting on the edge dangling his feet into the water. I eased down on the edge beside him, and he looked up at me. "You are attractive. You managed to keep your figure."

Angelo wore a baggy, blue, knee-length boxer type swimsuit, but he had good, masculine, strong legs, arms, and chest. His midsection could use a few yoga classes, but I found his looks appealing. I heard

Manuel's car drive in abruptly. He ran down the hill toward the pool, like a wild bird flapping his wings and shouting!

"Stop! Stop! Don't get into the pool." It took me a minute to translate what he yelled.

"Don't get in the pool. Take your feet out now," Manuel urged.

"Manuel, whatever is the matter? We are just relaxing—"

"Angelo, did you get into the pool?" Manuel asked.

"No, but we—"

"It's full of *arsenic* and *strychnine!* Manuel gasped, out of breath.

Angelo and I simultaneous pulled our feet from the water.

"I check the pH of the pool every day, add the correct droplets, and make the water good. Today I checked, and it was all wrong, so I added more drops, and still the water was not correct, so I took a sample to our lab, where Jerry tested it, and it contains lethal-strength arsenic and strychnine. Someone has been here and put these chemicals into the pool. Jerry told me that swimming in this could be fatal, and if it didn't kill us, it would make us very sick because this type of strychnine can be absorbed through the pores of skin. I must completely drain the pool and wash down the inside," Manuel explained.

Angelo and Manuel left the pool area, deep in discussion, and walked toward their apartment. I grabbed up my unused towel and walked to the patio from the pool leading into my bedroom. I sagged on the edge of the bed feeling like a deflated balloon. My thoughts went wild. What if I were alone here, like I had been in the beginning? I went swimming in the pool at 4:00 p.m. every day after the staff went home. Someone knew my routine. I would have been alone not knowing arsenic was in the pool. What if I had tourists who died from swimming?

Wyoming was the only person here today, besides Manuel who was at his work most of the day. Could Wyoming be capable of doing things like this? *No.* She wouldn't know about arsenic or strychnine, and she was with me when Tico was wrapped in barbed wire. Would

Angelo and Manuel move to another, safer, place? I lay on the bed trying to calm my thoughts. *How? How? How* could someone get into this property? How? Manuel's job was to protect Angelo; he had done that today. It doesn't make any sense to think it was him or Wyoming. My heart pounded, my skin was clammy, and I forgot to breath. *Sh, sh, sh, sh, just breathe, lay here, rest, and breathe deeply.* I lay there on the bed and gained control, got up, and walked to Angelo's apartment. As I approached, I heard they were in a deep discussion inside the apartment and speaking very rapid Spanish. I knocked on the door. Angelo answered, "Come in, Sun."

I realized I still wore my swimsuit. "No, thanks, Angelo, I came to tell you and Manuel that Wyoming left a beautiful dinner, and when you get ready, you can come over anytime you want. You can eat in the dining room or take your dinner to your apartment. I'm going to be in my room. I'm not hungry now, but I thought you guys might be."

"Sun, are you all right?" Angelo asked.

"Yes, I'm fine." I turned to walk back to my room.

"Manuel, are you hungry now? Sun, wait. We aren't hungry now either. We will wait for you, so when you are ready, come back, and we three will have dinner together in your dining room. We want to talk to you," Angelo said.

"Are you going to tell me you are moving to another apartment?"

"Not at all." Angelo looked surprised at my question.

"I'm glad for that. I don't want to be here alone," I said, as I walked back across the red pavers, under the portico, through the thick mahogany doors, and into my bedroom.

I finished meditating and felt better. No matter what boulders were to be hurled in my direction, I would endure. I turned on the warmer to warm Wyoming's prepared dinner and walked next door to Angelo and Manuel's apartment and lightly knocked on the door. Angelo answered on my first rap.

"Hi, Sun, are you feeling better?"

"Much better, thanks. Are you guys getting hungry now?"

"We are ready for dinner."

"Come over whenever you like"

I walked back to the dining room, sat a colorful table, lit a few candles, softened the lights, and made a calmer atmosphere. I was mentally drained and couldn't even think about why they wanted to talk to me. I was strong enough to hear anything as long as I knew they would stay.

Angelo gave the informal, Tico call of "whoopee, whoopee" at the lobby door.

I responded, "Mucho gusto." I heard the lobby door open, and Manuel and Angelo removed their shoes out of respect for Wyoming's frequent labor on the polished floors.

"I'm in the dining room."

"This dinner looks inviting, Sun. Thanks."

I sat between the two men with Angelo on my right and Manuel at the end of the table on my left.

"Today, Angelo, I never voiced my appreciation for our celebration lunch and for your help."

"There is no need to always thank me, Sun. You are always welcome."

I was at ease with the lingering silence as we ate. I found comfort in this silence. It was a good sign of compatibility and companionship. I continued to be patient and waited for one of them to begin the conversation. Angelo was about to break the silence when his cell phone rang. He looked at the caller ID and held up his fingers to his lips in a sh, sh, sh, sh.

"It is Katerina." He switched his phone to speaker.

"Hi, Ms. Meza."

"Señor Lopez," she said, "I am going to get right to the point. We hold your expensive condo luxury apartment for you, and we expect you to move in two days. Do you want a moving crew to help you with this?" she asked.

"Ms. Meza, I find your actions aggressive to relocate me. I am not ready to move. Maybe in a few months, but right now I am on vacation, and I don't wish to be interrupted by a move."

"Señor, you have no place to go after Wednesday," she said.

"Are you sure about that, Katerina? What are you going to do if I choose not to move?"

"We will kill you both," she said determinedly.

Manuel jumped up from the table, grabbed a piece of paper, and wrote something down.

"Katerina, this conversation has been recorded, and you may be in trouble yourself." Katerina abruptly ended the phone call, and all I heard was the beep, beep, beep, beep. Angelo switched off the speaker phone.

"I have never, in my life, heard anyone make such strong threats as this. Is this a normal way Ticos get what they want?" I asked.

"No, usually when someone makes a threat, he or she intends to carry it out. Manuel, sorry to interrupt your dinner, but will you get this to headquarters ASAP?" Angelo opened the back of his cell phone, removed a tiny chip, and handed it to Manual.

"I'll be back before my dinner gets cold," he said. He took the chip and the paper he wrote on and disappeared into their apartment.

I felt stunned. It was like I had been hit by the biggest of boulders. It was as if my entire nervous system had slammed shut, and I was mentally transported into displaced suspension. I remembered Tony told me that he would really hurt me if I didn't pay for his alarm system. Perhaps Ticos gave no empty threats.

"Sun, are you okay?"

"Yes; I'm feeling overwhelmed at the moment. I have never known someone who earnestly wanted to kill me or wanted me dead. Thanks."

Angelo smiled. "Sun, even when you are upset, you are still polite," he said with a chuckle.

"Angelo, I feel no humor right now. I'm sorry."

"Sun, I am used to threats. In my job they happen all the time. Can we continue to talk about this?"

"Yes." I sounded vague.

"This is part of what we wanted to tell you. I know you don't drink, but I want you to take a couple sips of Manuel's beer. The sugar might jolt you back, because it is important you hear the things I am going to tell you."

"Katerina's threat escalated your case to a much higher level of danger. JIO has done its follow-up with the hospitals. They looked for the intruders who were fried on your fence, and they have three Colombian men in custody. They were hired assassins, paid a hundred dollars to take you out."Angelo held up his fingers as he listed the questions they were asked:

"'How did you get the burns?'

'Why were you attempting to trespass?'

'How much were you paid?'

'What was proof of Sun Richards's death?'

'Who are you working for?'

"The JIO report included their answers," Angelo enumerated, as if he read from a paper.

"They answered:

'From an electric fence.'

'We were to shoot Sun W. Richards.'

'We would be paid a hundred dollars after we showed proof of her death.'

'Proof of her death was to be one green eye.'

'We don't know who we work for. We received the work order over the phone, and we received travel expenses mailed to our home address in Colombia. We were to be called on our cell phones to meet for the exchange.'

"Those were their answers, concluding the interrogation report.

"The JIO can't hold them for much longer because they didn't trespass, break and enter, or commit any crime. They are immigrants who have legal passports and visas. If they are released, will they try to contact their employer? It is JIO's hope they would. Will they attempt assassination again or would they go home? Their guess that is they will try again. Sun, do you remember the day we went to the National Records of Lawyers?"

"Yes, Angelo, of course, I do."

"Three of the names from that list are murdered, and three are missing. A father and son were found dead in their own swimming pool. That was a JIO case, and we don't know if there was an investigation that included a water test. Manuel is very poised to react and has been sensitive to abnormalities after the experiences with the dogs." Angelo began again after he sipped his Coke.

"Since the Colombians were apprehended, this became our case because our jurisdiction is all Central America, and JIO is restricted to Costa Rica. We continue to work together, but now our department will take a much more active role. Are you sure you want to hear this?"

"Angelo, please, I am just fine. I prefer to know exactly what is happening."

"That's good, because I want you to be clear-minded for the next thing we will talk about." Manuel returned and took his place at the dining room table.

"Manuel, I can reheat your food if you would like. How about you, Angelo, do you want me to reheat yours?" I asked, as I returned to my role of innkeeper.

"I told you, Sun, I would return before my dinner got cold, and

I have." Manuel gave me a wink and a smile with his wrinkled bulbous nose.

"Mine's fine too, Sun," Angelo said as he tolerated the interruption. "We want you to know you need protection, like I have. You will also be 'case bait.' Our department needs proof Katrina's group is linked to the many foreigners who were murdered or missing. You have a choice; you can return to the United States until this thing is over, or you stay and wait until Katrina and her group make their move … on you, or until we can gather enough evidence to stop her," Angelo continued to explain.

"You know she is still minister of justice for Costa Rica. She is able to pull many strings and has high-powered people to help her. It is our bet she is the one that hired the Colombians, and it is our job to know why. Do you remember your former corporate board had three Colombians and only two Ticos? One is her brother, and the other her Jamaican secretary, who sits on twenty-two boards and is Tica because she married a Tico. Sun, this is not just Katerina, but she has some kind of organization behind her or in front of her. She may not be the leader. She may be just a little cog in the wheel. Our strategy is to find enough irregularities to get her out of office to reduce her power. The question you must answer now, Sun, is what do you want to do?"

"Angelo, this is my home! It isn't right someone else has the responsibility to defend it without my help. It sounds like this case will move much faster if I stay. Is that correct?"

"We think it will end faster if they thought you didn't know anything about what is going on and went about your daily routine as always. Will you feel comfortable, and trust us to keep you safe?" he asked.

"I realize there is a danger, but I will act my part to help other Americans and foreigners never to be faced with this problem," I assured.

"Sun, remember what we talked about at lunch? Crime goes on and on, and you will receive no satisfaction from your efforts. Another thing to be considered is: even if we clean up this case, it will only stay clean for a matter of months, and at most maybe three years before underlings replace the crime bosses, and it all repeats itself."

"If I feel things are unsafe, I will leave for the States," I said.

"You are a very brave woman, Sun. Thank you for the dinner; I should go check on the dogs. Con permiso," Manuel said, as he left the table and returned to their apartment.

"I will help you pick up the kitchen so you see how I can be an 'American man,'" teased Angelo.

"Thank you, Angelo, for talking with me openly. I am a person who prefers to know the truth straight up rather than be treated like one of your father's plantation mushrooms."

"Plantation mushrooms, what do you mean?" Angelo asked.

"Fed shit and kept in the dark."

Angelo laughed and blushed.

"Sun, there is another thing I need to tell you about. JIO found that the machete Manuel discovered thrown into the bushes was made by a well-known Colombian metal artisan, and Amon, who no longer works for you, is in the hospital with a stomach wound where he was nearly cut in half. The blood in the art studio matches the blood from Amon. The question is how did he get into the art studio? The doctors said he will recover, and JIO said he will be interrogated."

"I feel better knowing the situation even though the danger level is higher. I know Amon is a skilled tree climber, and maybe he climbed overhanging branches. He could lower himself to the roof of the art studio, avoid the electric fence, and enter. It still doesn't explain the Colombian machete or why Amon could be wounded so severely," I conjectured. "I know his pain, even though he has done many wrongful things. I am sorry for him. I grieve for the wounding of his individual potential. I see clearly what he could have been, but I understand he makes his own choices. I think I will sleep tonight because our talk relieves my mind and gives me clear direction, but this new information reopens so many questions, doesn't it?"

"Yes, Sun, it does, and it makes no sense to get into the 'mangled mind mess'; it is best to wait for the evidence to answer questions. Sun, most people would have bought their airline ticket and headed for their own country, but I am glad you will stay. I have highway concerns to attend to," he sighed. "I will say good night to you." He folded the dish towel.

"Angelo, I have another thought. Maybe this new direction is the reason I am meant to be in Costa Rica. Maybe I am destined to help you with this case. I will send you as much energy as I can for your highway problems. Good night!"

Lying in bed, I had thoughts for Amon's recovery, for Angelo's highway, and for the quieting of Central America's high crime. Before drifting to sleep to the tune of my night bird, Diablo de Noches, my last thought was that for the last three nights, there had been no construction noises.

CHAPTER 23
INTERROGATION

I was rejuvenated by morning with the day's beautiful sunshine flooding my bedroom like amber-lensed Fresnel theater lights. I looked out my bedroom windows and saw the humorous sight of Manuel chasing both dogs around the outside of our property fence. He ran in pursuit to catch the wet, soggy dogs. I smiled at the sight. I had barely finished dressing when I heard knocking on the interior door of my bedroom. "Hello," I said as I opened my bedroom door. "Manuel! What a surprise! Good morning to you! Good grief. Where are your soggy doggies?" I joked.

"Did you see them?"

I laughed and said, "I saw you chasing your wet dogs outside the fence."

"Sun, can you come with me right now? There is something you must see!"

"Sure," I said, as I put on my sandals.

"Sun, I did not want to wake Angelo because he worked very late, or I should say, very early this morning on his road project. A little while ago, I looked out to see our very wet dogs on the outside of the fence. I drained the pool because of the arsenic and strychnine, and it is without water. The dogs never get into the pool, but they were dripping wet," Manuel described.

I continued to follow Manuel in the direction of the art studio as he talked.

"The only other water source is from the river," I reminded him.

"Yes, Sun, the dogs were in the river. Our ten-foot-high fence surrounds the property and is between us and the river. How did they get to the river?"

"They dug under the fence?"

"Sun, my job is security, and every day I check the fence boundary line. The dogs do not dig, and I know they would never dig under the fence. This is what I want to show you. The dogs showed me!" Manuel said assertively.

He knelt down near the foundation wall of the art studio and pushed aside the thick-growing coffee plants. He grabbed a flashlight he had placed on the studio steps and shined it into a beautifully constructed tunnel leading from the art studio under the electric fence and out to vacant property on the other side.

"Manuel, *good grief*! I can't believe this! This tunnel must be sixty feet long, and a six-foot man can walk upright inside. I can't tell from here how wide it is. How wide is it?"

"It is four feet wide and over six feet underground, not counting the height of a standing man, and it is fifty feet long. Come on, I will help you enter," Manuel said.

I remained in place and only peered inside. "It looks like it is a permanent structure, reinforced with side pylons and supporting structure beams."

"It is also nicely finished off so whoever used it would not get dirty. Come on, I'll show you," Manuel coaxed.

"Have you already been completely through it?"

"Yes, it is quite good work. I will go first with the light, if you wish," he encouraged.

I sat down on the steps. "Manuel, there is something I must tell you. You are about to learn of my personal weakness, and I am embarrassed about it, but I have claustrophobia. I will freak out before I reach the end of the tunnel."

"*Oh!* Sun, it is okay. You at least saw the tunnel. Now we know what the construction noise was and why we couldn't tell what direction the sound came from." Manuel sympathized with my affliction and sat down on the steps beside me.

"This is how Amon entered. The tunnel answers many questions about how the dogs were injured and why they were abused. It is a wonder they didn't kill them and dispose their bodies into the river," I said.

"Maybe someone was a dog lover and had compassion for them," he reasoned.

"I hope the compassionate person was Amon, and he received his life-threatening wounds by trying to protect the dogs."

"You always see the best in people, Sun. Maybe he tortured the dogs, and his wife followed him from the outside of the tunnel because he cheated on her, and she decided to whack him in half," Manuel said.

I laughed. "Yep, that is also possible."

"I need to call the JIO, so they can see this, but I want Angelo to see it first, and this tunnel isn't going to disappear before he wakes up. He can sleep a little longer."

"Manuel, have you had any breakfast?" I asked.

"*No*, have you?"

"No, but I think Wyoming has coffee ready for you, and I am low blood sugar and need to eat something. Manuel, you made a good discovery today. How can we block this off so the dogs won't enter?"

"I can move one of the boulders in the coffee grove to block the entrance. You can go back up to the house while I do it if you want," he said.

"I need to talk about this!" I remained setting on the steps. "All these nights we heard construction sounds for over a month have now been answered. This construction reveals just how determined these criminals are to plan for our demise. This tunnel is how the burglaries took place, and it provided the passage for the lawn furniture, the popcorn wagon, and both sets of power tools. They were removed without being seen or fried on the electric fence. The tunnel gave access for someone to contaminate the pool with strychnine, and now with its completion, their next move is to remove one or all of us! I can guess who is to be their victim! Kidnapping has been a priority for whoever is behind all of this. We all, tourists included, are more valuable alive then dead.

"You are right Sun!" Manuel agreed.

"I feel better now I know. It is the unknown that makes me jittery," I said, as I stood up from the steps and called to the dogs, who lay in the sun to dry from their river swim.

"I share your views about the unknown," Manuel said, as he struggled with the boulder.

The dogs and I returned to the house, and as I crested the grassy knoll behind Angelo's apartment, I saw his balcony door fly open, and he popped out.

"Oh, there you are, beautiful woman! I looked for you—where have you been?"

"Good morning to you, Angelo. Were you able to get some sleep?"

"I think it is enough. What did you do to me last night about ten thirty? I had the most unusual surge of energy while I worked on my highway problems that lasted for hours until I discovered a possible solution. I can't tell you about it yet until I talk to the accountant, but I am thinking everything can be resolved," Angelo beamed.

"Angelo, that is wonderful! I am happy for you. Manuel is down by the art studio and wants to show you something."

"What is it?" he asked.

Manuel appeared at the crest of the knoll and called, "Have you told him yet?"

"No, Manuel, I have not. The honor belongs to you, and it is your gift to give," I answered.

"Thank you, Sun; you are thoughtful. Come with me, please, Angelo. I want to show you something." The two men loped down the declining hill with the dogs playfully bounding along.

Last night, I cast my desires and intentions to the universe, and two of them manifested. Angelo reached a possible solution for his corporate problem, and Manuel's discovery this morning reduced crime. Only Amon's recovery had yet to be answered. I strolled into the kitchen and saw Wyoming.

"I have been so busy this morning I didn't even say good morning to you, Wyoming."

"You said it now." She laughed and gave me a hug.

"Wyoming, none of us had breakfast, and I think the guys will be hungry. You should make extra coffee because the JIO and the Fuerza Publica will be here this morning." Wyoming stopped her bread making and looked up at me with fear in her eyes.

"It is good things—Wyoming, do you have time for a cup of coffee? I want to talk to you about Amon."

Wyoming sat down at the table, and I told her what I knew about Amon. She and Amon were friends for many years, and she deserved to know. I watched her response, and saw genuine sadness as she finished her coffee and went back to her bread making.

I met Angelo and Manuel at the door. "You both are invited for breakfast in a little while. Angelo, if you wish to use the dining room table to meet with Inspector Mario de Luisa and the Fuerza Publica, you are most welcome. I have asked Wyoming to make extra coffee for their visit."

"Sun, you read my mind, and I was about to ask you for that. You saw the tunnel?"

"Only a little bit inside the entrance. Did you go in?" I asked.

"Yes. It is designed by engineers. We are not dealing with common thugs or burglars. This tunnel is made for permanence."

"Did you happen to find the popcorn wagon or any of the new power tools stashed inside?"

"No, we did not. Sorry, Sun."

"Angelo and I discussed what should be done. The tunnel is your property, and the decision is yours," Manuel quickly inserted.

"I think it should be removed immediately after Fuerza Publica and JIO see it. We don't know how many people know about it. Anyone has access to the property and makes us all very vulnerable," Angelo assertively expressed.

"It is another entrance that needs security," Manuel added.

"It would be a cool idea to have a secret passageway!" They looked helplessly at one another. I quickly added, "Just joking. I agree with you both; we need to destroy it."

"I am glad we all agree," Angelo said.

"I am amused you Ticos use a democratic system of decision-making and include a woman," I said. They understood my male/female equal rights point of view, but they saw no humor.

"I will give the JIO dynamite from our road construction, and for a few hours we can provide our dynamite experts, who can safely take care of the tunnel for us in a hurry. This needs to be done today. I explained to JIO and the Fuerza that as we now sit, we are very vulnerable," Angelo restated his position.

Wyoming called us for breakfast, and both the JIO and Fuerza arrived as we finished. I helped Wyoming clear the dining room table while Angelo and Manuel greeted the officials at the driveway and escorted them down the pathway to the tunnel.

I needed to work from my office doing hotel business and prepare for the postponed Texas Television tourists from Austin. Disgruntled but with purpose, I refrained from being abrasive to the Latin American culture by intruding into the "men's domain." I swallowed my Wyoming pride and avoided joining the men's parade to the tunnel.

This is the hardest culture adjustment that I must overcome. I resent this Costa Rican custom of segregation between men's business and women's duties. I find it impossible to lose my American traits of women's equality. This country is fifty years behind the world curve, and it stepped all over my Wyoming upbringing as an independent woman. Wyoming was the first state of the United States allowing women to vote. I was raised under the historical tutelage of women's suffrage leader Easter Hobart Morris, who was responsible for women's rights to vote, and Nellie Taylor Ross, who became Wyoming's first woman governor, and now I live in a machismo culture. I can continue to be upset or learn to find some contented balance. I shook off personal injury and dived into my office work.

I checked out the *A.M. Costa Rica* English newspaper online. I looked for current social events where I could entertain my future guests. Instead, I saw a news item that caught my attention. The article described the death of a woman, Valerina Pachona Uribe, a Colombian who was beaten to death with a blunt instrument outside of her apartment in San Jose last night. Her body was found by a deliveryman at 12:40 a.m., and the estimated time of death was between 8:45 and 10:45 p.m. I continued my search for social events, and I scrolled down the screen to find several art galleries that presented professional Costa Rican artists. This would be good! The arriving tourist, Linda, was an art teacher and would love this. My mind tugged back to the crime article, and I rechecked the beaten woman's name, Valerina Pachona Uribe—Valerina Pachona Uribe. Why did I know that name? My heart did the fast heart rate dance as I jumped from my chair and grabbed the file I carried yesterday. I found the paper that listed my former board members, purchased from Pablo Meza, with Katerina Meza as the legal representative. Valerina Pachona Uribe was former president of the board for my corporation!

My mind jumped and thundered without any sense of concentration. I closed my bedroom door. I didn't want anyone to see my display of jangled nerves. My breakfast churned in my stomach, and I felt my blood boil. The raised heat made my face and hands hot, and I sweat. My mind would not calm. I plunked down on the edge of the bed, closed my eyes, and tried to reach the source of my calm. Breathe, breathe, please breathe deeply and find your center for calmness. Experience the calmness, feel the sweet wonderful feelings of peace.

My mind settled down, and I started to reason. Chief Inspector Mario de Luisa was at my house now and inspected the tunnel. Should I tell him Valerina Uribe was on my corporation board, or should I wait until he makes the discovery himself? What if he thought I murdered her and listed myself as president? Would I be suspected? Was I a suspect? These were all scary unknowns. I know the adage "When in doubt, don't. I certainly was in doubt, and maybe waiting was the best thing.

I believe in spontaneous right action, and it is my wish to use it now. Okay, I recovered. I want to emanate love from within, and it was time for me to be a gracious host. I opened my bedroom door, walked through the lobby into the kitchen, and asked, "Wyoming, do we have enough coffee made for everyone?"

"Yes, Doña Sun, and I have fresh bread with mango jelly."

"That sounds so good; thank you." I looked out the kitchen window and saw the "male parade" coming up the hill.

"They are on their way now, Wyoming." I went into the lobby and greeted them at the door.

"Señors Mario de Lisa and Roberto Zamora, 'mucho gusto.' Would you all care for some coffee?"

"That would be wonderful, Doña Sun. Thank you," Angelo said.

"Please sit anywhere you like in the dining room." I ushered.

"Sun, please join us," Angelo invited.

I sat in the middle beside Angelo, who held my chair, and when I was seated, the four men took their seats as Wyoming came with a tray of coffee cups, plates, coffee, and a big graceful bread basket laden with buttered bread and jam.

"Thank you, Wyoming. This looks delicious," I said.

Everyone poured their own coffee and helped themselves to the bread. They were relaxed and so was I—almost.

"Angelo told me about the very efficient and thorough investigation results you found from the blood samples and your findings at the hospital, Señor Zamora. Do you have a health report on Amon?" I asked this question so Wyoming heard his answer.

"Yes; he is a strong man, and we questioned him about his presence in the art studio. He was hired to help build the tunnel with several Colombians, and it seems he requested payment but was refused and, instead, they slashed him with a machete. He managed to reach the emergency room before he bled to death. Amon only knew their first names, and it will take time for us to know who they are. Amon, when fully recovered, will be deported. He has no proper immigration papers, and the prosecuting attorney has charges of burglary, car theft, and trespassing against him."

"Thank you both for doing your job," I said.

"Sun, Señor Zamora, with Fuerza Publica, would like to destroy the tunnel this afternoon. Have you any objections?" Angelo asked.

"Certainly not. It seems a shame to crush such good workmanship, but it has to be done. When will you do that?"

"We will have the dynamite within the hour. Manuel will deliver it, and he and Señor Zamora will supervise the detonation at about one o'clock this afternoon," Angelo said, as he drank another cup of coffee.

"Señora Richards, do you know a woman by the name of Valerina Pachona Uribe?" Mario de Luisa asked.

"*No*, I have never met her. Her name is familiar to me because she was president of the board for the former corporation I bought from Pablo Meza," I calmly explained.

"When did you buy your corporation?" he asked.

"April 24, 2008."

"How was it paid for?" Mario de Luisa asked.

"I paid cash for the property, and the Meza corporation was included."

"Did you receive your books at closing?" he asked.

"No, I didn't know about 'books' until Angelo told me and helped me retrieve them."

"Were you in San Jose yesterday?" he asked.

"Yes, I went with Angelo to the Registro National for a Certification Literal, and we spent most of the day there until about four o'clock, when we came home and went for a swim. Manuel, did you tell Señor De Luisa about the pool?" I wanted to escape from center stage and the limelight. I hoped Manuel would help me out.

"No, Doña Sun, we were busy talking about the tunnel; I forgot." He sounded surprised to be in the position of adding to our case. Whew, this gave me a minute to regroup.

"I will see if Wyoming needs help in the kitchen; please excuse me." I prepared to leave the table, and all four men pushed back their chairs and stood until I left.

"Manuel, what was that about the pool?" Inspector Mario de Luisa asked.

When I returned to the table, Manuel had finished his report about the pool, and again all four men stood until I was seated. I inwardly smiled at the humorous control the role of femininity gave to me. How many times could I do this before they refused to stand? I sat down a fresh pot of coffee and another basket of bread, and I worried about what would come next.

Nothing came next! They ate the bread and drank the coffee, and I talked about the tango version of the *South Pacific* musical; Angelo and I attended in the historic San Jose Square Theatre a week ago. I talked at great length about the creativity of the director and choreographer. I explained that I was a theater director for many years, and I related how tango embellished the emotionalism of the old musical and made it relevant for modern audiences. I stole a quick glance at Angelo, who seemed contended.

I walked the guests to the door when they finished their coffee and said, "Thank you for helping us with our troubles. Will we see you again soon, Inspector De Luisa?"

"I hope to see you at an upcoming theater production," he responded.

"Officer Zamora, will I see you at one o'clock for the detonation?"

"Yes, I will be back soon. Manuel and I will go together to pick up the dynamite and return. Thank you for the coffee," he said.

Our guests drove out the driveway, as Angelo took me by the shoulders. "Sun, I am sorry you were not prepared for the interrogation, but I knew nothing about the death of the Colombian woman until he told me about it in the tunnel. You did very well. You will make a great witness for our case now that you have had this practice." He chuckled.

"Angelo, am I a suspect?"

"Yes, you were, but you are not anymore. What made you talk about the tango version of *South Pacific*? he asked.

"Nervous to talk about anything but Valerina Pachona Uribe's death," I assured.

"Your support of nature struck again. The JIO subpoenaed your phone records and found phone calls made from your phone to Pablo Meza the same night and time as the tango production. The phone records made them suspicious that you and Pablo Meza were a team, but you gave such details about the show that they eased off. They will check on the purchase of your show ticket with the theater box office, and they will dismiss you as a suspect," Angelo expounded with frivolity.

"It means someone came through the tunnel, entered the house, and made the calls," I conjectured.

"You are partly right, but I don't think they entered the house. They used a sophisticated phone tapping device to operate your phone system. I believe they operated your phones from the connection pole outside. Anyway, you are no longer a suspect, and you managed to clear yourself. I need to finish some work on the highway claim, and I want to watch the detonation. Do you want to see it?" he asked.

"Yes, but what about Katerina's threat of foreclosure? Our extension ends tomorrow."

"We will hear nothing more about foreclosure! She must cancel the court date because all of our papers are legal *and* recorded. This place is yours! We celebrated at the restaurant, don't you remember?" he asked.

"Of course I remember, but I thought we would need to go to court," I said in amazement.

"Nope, we are finished, and now we need to solve this case and catch the real criminals, a.k.a. Katerina and Group. See you at one, my lovely lady." Angelo bounded out the door in high spirits.

I requested three intentions from the universe, and they had been answered: First, Amon had recovered. Second, the terrifying experience of being suspected of murder was resolved, and the related interrogation had taught me yet another valuable lesson concerning the power of offered intentions to the universe. I learned I could trust my instincts for spontaneous right action. Third, in today's newspaper, *A.M. COSTA RICA*, I learned about Angelo's resolution to save his highway construction company. The news article read:

> Autopista del Sol, the concessionaire of the San Jose Caldera Highway had filed a ninety- million dollar lawsuit against the Cost Rica Government. Attorneys for the concessionaire had a two hundred and fifty-million dollar investment in the project and claimed the road works were more than what was stated in the government's original proposal. The claim included nonpayment for use of the company's time, labor and equipment to clear landslides from the Carpio and Poas earthquakes and transport heavy equipment to Haiti during their natural disaster as a gift from Costa Rica. The concessionaire further cited Ministry of Public Works (MOPT) and the Highway Authority responsible for fatalities and injuries caused from opening the highway prematurely.

Maybe I helped Angelo in a subtle way.

CHAPTER 24
ESPIONAGE

The following days were a flurry of changes in our security system. Manuel reprogrammed the code for our individual controls enabling the automatic gates, in case Amon sold or gave code information to the Colombians who hired him to help work on the tunnel. Whenever I left the boundaries of the property to run errands, keep appointments, or socialize with women's clubs, I had my own squad of bodyguard protection equal to Angelo's. Manuel placed a tracking chip into my 2000 Suzuki that sounded an alarm to the tracking squad and signaled that I was on the move. I thought that approach was more humanitarian than to place a chip into testicles I was born without.

I assumed all of this was implemented because of the death threat Katerina made into the phone recording, and maybe it was standard procedure for safeguarding the life of an important agent. Anyway, I was grateful to be included with special coverage.

A group of Angelo's men built a camouflaged camp on the outer perimeter of the property facing the river. Our property fence was constructed ten feet from the riverbank and allowed enough space to position two tents, side by side parallel to the river. Any intruder needed to ford the river before reaching the tents, and the electric fence was positioned at the camping men's backs. If an intruder was wet from the river crossing, the wet clothing could cause his demise on the electric fence. This camp prevented any rear accessibility to the property. Across the river was dense tropical jungle, and anyone camped there would be completely hidden. It was possible other camps of Angelo's men had positioned themselves there, but I couldn't see them.

The front of the property was protected by the electric fence and automatic gates, and Angelo's department rented a house across the street from our main entrance for six men from the Arms Squad. They were proficient marksmen with high-powered rifles and scopes. They were on duty in rotated shifts.

All this security was completely hidden and undetectable to anyone who didn't know. Anyone except for Wyoming, who pleaded with me to take a walk down by the river.

"Please, Doña Sun, there are tents down by the river! You must call the Ministry of Housing because homeless people live on your property. Homeless people live in tents. Come with me now to see," she pleaded.

"Wyoming, yes I know about them. I gave them permission to camp there. It is okay. They are fishing tourists, and they camp out! It is an American sport to camp out in the jungle. American men love that sport. They are roughing it. It is a man's thing!" I explained.

I didn't want to lie to Wyoming, but telling her the truth wasn't possible. My level of Spanish proficiency wasn't enough to explain this complicated case, and she was a fearful person. Placing her into fear would be worse than my white lie. If she had known the property was surrounded by agents, her nature was to tell about the activities to friends and neighbors, and it was too risky for our safety.

Wyoming and I laughed about the strange species of American males. She shrugged her shoulders and waved her hands indicating she bought my story. Wyoming was also given protection to and from her bus each day without her knowledge.

Casa Ave Hotel (home for the bird) was now referred to as "The Compound." When Angelo or Manuel left the compound for their road jobs or traveled to other countries for their projects, Angelo enlisted the Fuerza Publica to check on us every half hour at regular intervals. Fuerza Publica reported directly to Angelo that they had personally spoken with me. He called and related what the police had said, to decrease my fear level, assuring me of our protection. Angelo called me from El Salvador and explained, "I will be home tomorrow and wondered if I was the designated tour guide for your tourists."

"I would love that!" I screamed into the static, breaking up conversation. He called from an airplane using the government field phones. "Yes! Yes!" I hoped he heard me. The broken conversations, static, and dropped calls were a regular occurrence between us.

I grew into a deep comfort zone when Angelo and Manuel were home, and I missed them when they were gone. The nights were so beautiful and quiet without the pistol shots down by the river or the disturbance of construction sounds. The demolition of the tunnel brought back silence and the song of Diablo de Noches (Devil of the Night) bird, which I loved. I was wrapped in protection, and I no longer had pangs of anxiety or thunderous fear, even though the danger level was higher.

Sometime during the dark perfection of the night's silence, Angelo and Manuel arrived home. A clean, polished, gold-colored SUV, license plates beginning with nine, and a small gray jeep were parked in their spaces beside the apartment when I awoke the next morning.

The morning was filled with enthusiastic energy as Wyoming arrived at seven o'clock and prepared for our Texas tourists. The hotel was gleaming, shining clean, and we spent the morning going over the food and drink information forms the tourists gave at my request. They didn't eat meat, but fish and chicken were agreeable with plenty of fresh fruits and vegetables.

We decorated our most desirable three-room suite with my mother's oil paintings, which pleased any artistic palate. I sculpted the towels into swans and boats for their bed, wrote a personal note of welcome, and placed it beside the bird creations. We arranged fresh flowers into mint green vases, the same color scheme of the drapes, bed duvet, and rugs. My spirits dropped and sagged with the thoughts about Amon because flower arrangements were his forte. I thought a quick blessing for him when I heard Angelo's beautiful baritone voice give the Tico cry of "whooppee, whooppee." I ran up the stairs to greet him at the lobby entrance and gave him a hug as he held something hidden behind his back. It was a beautifully wrapped box of gold and silver with a big silver bow perched on top.

"I got this for you. It is from Colombia," he said.

"I should give you gifts for coming home because you were greatly missed!" I said, as I opened a beautiful handcrafted pottery vase and placed it on the dining table. "Angelo, thank you for your thoughtfulness, but your safe return is more priceless than this beautiful vase." I gave him another warm heartfelt hug, and he seemed surprised but pleased.

"What time do we pick up the tourists today?"

"In less than two hours. Do you want to play tour guide?"

"I thought of nothing else! I want to show you this vehicle we can use for their tour. It is very roomy, and we will be more comfortable because it gives more leg room." Our eyes met, and I knew there was more information to be told.

"It's a beautiful van, Angelo, but you don't need so many extra things for me and now also for my guests," I humbly uttered.

"Sun, I need to plan for these touring occasions." He looked

directly into my eyes again. "Do you understand what I am telling you?"

"Yes, I know. All our safety is an issue for your department. I am
an expensive witness."

"You understand! Come let me show you. This van looks like any
other touring van on the highway, but it is not. It is fully armored
with bulletproof exterior and glass. It is deceptive in its appearance
because it looks elegant and innocent. It is similar to an army tank
in its all-terrain power and protective capabilities. Look at this, Sun."
Angelo opened the driver's side of the car and pressed a button that
automatically slid out a long drawer that held many high-powered
rifles with scopes from under the front seat. He closed the largest,
longest drawer and opened a few short little drawers that held a variety of pistols and boxes of ammunition.

"This is to be used if we are caught by the assassins. It is important we go about our daily routines without fear, but we need
to take precautions. We also have the tracking team with us, but
never acknowledge them. If you make eye contact with them, they
are trained to immediately disappear. This makes extra work for all
concerned. You are the topic of many of our meetings because your
peculiar friendliness is not a common international personality trait
the trackers understand. In the beginning, they were sure you knew
who they were because of your direct eye contact and friendly smile
and your quick readiness to strike up conversation, which are all
against tracking regulations. It drove them crazy! They continuously
changed teams only to be changed repeatedly. They soon learned
you talked to the street parking men, clerks in stores, postmen, de-
liverymen, pedestrians both men and women, sometimes children,
and your people awareness was large in scope. It was concluded
you didn't know they were trackers, and they didn't need to change
teams. At the meetings they imitated you and enacted situations
where you talked to two or three strangers around you all at the

same time. I laughed out loud. I found their entire enactment to be humorous because their antics were true to your nature," he said with a chuckle.

"Oh, good grief, Angelo, I am troublesome! This trait is blamed on my Wyoming heritage. Growing up in rural areas there are few people. I learned to acknowledge everyone and guess I still do a verbal embrace. I need to train myself to become like a horse wearing blinders." He laughed until his earlobes shook.

"You need to stay your unique, lovable self. Let's just enjoy ourselves. Come knock on my door when you are ready to go to the airport," he said.

I finished up a few hotel details, showered, and dressed for Costa Rican warm humid weather. Together, we made our way to the San Jose Airport riding in the deceptive armored gold van. I spotted our guests waiting outside the airport and gave them a welcoming hug.

"Welcome to Costa Rica! I hope you will be overwhelmed with the country's beauty," I said to the Austin tourists. Linda and Steve were a strikingly handsome couple. Both were exceptionally tall, blond, middle aged, and the epitome of fitness and health.

"Linda and Steve, I want you to meet my friend Angelo, who agreed to be our tour guide for your visit. He is a native Tico and knows the best places to tour, best restaurants, and the most interesting facts about San Jose."

The arriving couple came to Costa Rica to take photos of my property for marketing onto a crafted website to advertise my hotel as a mini-resort. They wanted to create a televised travel show about Costa Rica. At this point, Angelo transformed into a Wyoming cowboy. He picked up Linda's bags, threw them over his shoulders like a pro, and opened her car door as well as mine. It was interesting to observe others' reactions to the sights of Costa Rica. They were surprised by the lack of order with the streets wandering around without street signs or addresses.

"How do you know where you are or where you are going?" Linda asked.

I laughed, knowing exactly her thoughts, and remembered how helpless I was when I first arrived.

"It takes a long time to learn the trails, and if someone paints their house a different color, I am totally lost," I humored.

"The United States gave the city of San Jose $9 million to install street signs," Angelo said with a laugh. "Ticos don't know how to use them, but Americans can find McDonald's much faster. It is a mystery why the American government gave such a gift unless it is their way of protecting American investments." Angelo talked nonstop all the way to our gate.

When we neared the Hotel Casa Ave, Linda gasped! "This is so beautiful." Her response was what I worked toward for the past year realizing again that artists work for praise instead of money. Linda's words just made payment.

"It is our wish that you have the best vacation possible," I welcomed.

The afternoon gave the guests time to settle into the hotel with the help of Wyoming's famous lemonade and tres leche cake. They made use of the art studio, pool, and gardens. I relaxed into my own life with the arrival of the tourists, comfortable with the absence from fear that permeated my system for the past months.

Angelo needed to return to work in Colombia until the day of our San Jose tour. I was alone with Steve and Linda and enjoyed their company. We became acquainted, and I gave them my complete attention.

The second day of their vacation was a beautiful day. I took Linda and Steve on a short scenic drive to a private location that tourists hadn't yet discovered. The property Los Chorros was family owned, and I was fortunate to find it after the earthquake demolished the waterfall garden that I formerly loved to tour with tourists. Linda and Steve were strong, vivacious, and environmentally aware, and I loved to hike with people who enjoyed the outdoors. I drove my little white Suzuki down the curving dirt road that cut deep into the jungle. The vegetation was so tall and dense that it completely hid the sky. All that remained visible was the one lane car path wrapped in greenness. It was like driving in the middle of a large spinach salad. I was rewarded by the awed response from my two travel companions. We continued down the dirt car trail until the vegetation reduced to a walking path. We left the car parked and continued on foot over the small path with gentle hills that paralleled a volcanic-rock-lined clear cold estuary. As we hiked deeper into the jungle, the tamed rivulet widened and transformed into a rapid raging river rushing over volcanic boulders and powered its way beside rare, six feet in diameter, one-hundred-year-old hardwood trees that hid the shy sloths in their upper branches. We heard the faint sound of distant waterfalls.

My tourist friends walked in reverent silence, and I knew they felt the strength of forceful natural law. We were alone, absorbed with the earth's life-healing energies that we put into our lungs, minds, and hearts. Linda turned, looked at me, and put her hands into prayer position and whispered, "Thank you."

Our path crossed a ravine over the pounding savage river by means of a swinging rope footbridge. Now was the true test of their courage. I smiled at the thought. Would they trust enough to go across? Steve hesitated, took Linda's hand, and unsteadily swayed in perpetual motion toward the bridge's opposite end. After crossing the bridge, we were deafened by the roar of a gigantic waterfall to our right, and on our left the path narrowed beside a mountain that leaked a one-hundred-yard horizontal line of water from its middle. The pure water was suitable for drinking and washing your hands or face.

We removed our shoes and left them like we left the car. The shoes were no longer useful. We walked into the water beside the weeping mountain and made our way around the side of the watery hill until the stream we waded in opened to another cascading, thunderous waterfall sending a mist of spray that made a rainbow in the sunshine. Opposite the waterfall was a partly hidden grotto, perfect for swimming or getting completely dampened by mist from the falls. All of this splendor was framed by the vivid variegated shades of tropical lush greens. *Costa Rica, oh, Costa Rica, how could you be so beautiful and yet be so violent?*

These delightful tourists were full of joy, and they plunged into the grotto, raised their arms toward the heavens, and shouted, "I love you" to each another.

I continued to be filled with the same joy each time I came to this magical place. I returned many times, and on each occasion it was different with the changed amounts of rain and light, and with the seasons. I was rewarded when other people loved this place as much as I did.

I perched on a granite ledge that jutted out from the side of the mountain for a perfect full view of both the grotto and the thundering cascading waterfall. Linda and Steve approached me from both sides and gave me a hug, and Linda kissed my face. The roar of the falls was too loud to hear their unnecessary words, and they both scampered away like two mountain goats. They attempted to climb the rocky, craggy side of the grotto. I remained seated on my granite shelf basking in the rainbow from the falls and the warm sunshine. We stayed beside the plunging waters for hours until the pangs of hunger urged us back to metropolitan amenities. We found a typical Tico open-air restaurant and ate ourselves into delirium.

Linda and Steve wanted to spend the rest of the daylight hours preparing for tomorrow's photo shoot of Casa Ave mini-resort. They began at daylight to capture the best light and explored the most scenic places that featured the trees, gardens, and interior of the hotel.

They even photographed Wyoming's meal presentations. They shot their cameras most of the day, and at twilight they photographed the night lights.

"Tomorrow, are you ready to explore the modern-day tourist attractions?" I ask.

"We are, but nothing compares to the experience of your waterfalls," Steve replied.

Precious, our phone, rang after the guests had gone to their room.

"Hi, Sun. This is Angelo, static—crackle—I hope you can hear me—crackle—crackle. I am flying home now—click—in the cargo plane—static—I will be home—backpackers—static—guys—click—workout—today—backpackers—static—helicopters—hard to keep up with you—hello—hello."

"Yes, Angelo, I am here. We will tour San Jose tomorrow with you. Do you need to sleep late tomorrow morning?—static—Angelo—pop—can you hear me?——I heard—static—click—sometime—static—tomorrow. A big kiss—for—static—beep, beep, beep—tomorrow—static—hummmmmmmm."

Wyoming arrived at 7:00 a.m. and prepared a natural breakfast from the fresh fruit harvested from our gardens. I didn't hear Angelo and Manuel arrive in the night, but the big gold van and Manuel's gray jeep were parked in the proper places. By 9:00 a.m., Angelo knocked softly on our lobby door.

"Angelo!"

I gave him a hug.

"Wyoming has fixed a beautiful breakfast for you and Manuel. Would you like to join us? The guests will be ready in a few minutes. Do you want coffee?" I invited.

"Oh, yes! Coffee would be great! Manuel is still sleeping and won't go with us today. It will be you and me and your guests. How are they?"

"They are wonderful people and very appreciative of everything we do. Have you had any sleep?"

"Enough, I think. Would you like to leave about ten o'clock this morning?" Angelo asked.

The guests looked well-rested and bright as they walked up the steps into the lobby.

"Good morning to you, Linda and Steve. Angelo wondered if you would be ready about ten, after we had breakfast?" I inquired.

"Sounds good. Good to see you again, Angelo. Sun gave us a very adventurous day in your beautiful Costa Rica yesterday. We could barely keep up with her!" Linda laughed.

"Yes, I know that is true! She is hard to follow; you might need a helicopter."

Angelo spoke his truth. Both men continued to joke, and the four of us were a good blend of energy. We toured the city with its historical buildings and many embassies. The tourists were fascinated by Angelo's stories about the ambassadors and their unusual personalities and interests. Steve became Angelo's fan.

"How can you remember all the historic dates and their sequence?" Steve asked

"This is my country—my home—and I grew up knowing these things," Angelo replied.

We had lunch and toured the art section of the city in the afternoon, visiting many of the art galleries. Linda and I were in our element. One of the small crowded galleries with dark, poorly lighted rooms was owned by the artist himself. I fell in love with his painting of a Quetzal. Angelo and I admired his painting for over half an hour. Angelo wanted to buy it, but it was a large painting, and Casa Ave didn't have a wall large enough to accommodate its size. The painting was exquisite, and later I regretted my decision not to buy it.

Late in the afternoon, I lived with another regret I wished I had changed. We four toured other streets with government buildings, and we pulled to the curb. Angelo grabbed my hand and pulled me toward the driver's side of the car, opened his door, and said, "Linda and Steve, would you please excuse Sun and me for a few minutes? I want to show her something." We hurriedly made our way across the street and ran up the steps to a beige government building with granite floors and walls. We stepped into the lobby, and a security guard stopped us.

"Sorry, folks, but this building is closed to the public today!"

"Yes, I know," responded Angelo. Sun look up at the names on the walls. "We will only remain in this lobby for a minute, so she can see," Angelo said to the guard as he pulled out his wallet and showed his ID.

The guard looked at the presented credentials and said, "Certainly. Yes, you may, sir."

The building, I vaguely recalled was the Public Building of Justice. It was dark inside and took a few minutes for my eyes to adjust. I saw four hallways leading in different directions, and each passageway had a name in gold metal letters two feet high over the hallway entrance. Angelo Lopez's name was the first name of the four on the left hallway passage transom. I didn't recognize any of the other three names.

"You saw?" Angelo asked.

"Yes. What does that mean?" I questioned.

"We will talk later," he said.

He grabbed my hand, ran out the door, and shouted, "Thanks," over his shoulder to the security guard. We ran across the street and jumped into the waiting car with Linda and Steve.

"Were those names of honored lawyers?" I asked.

"Yes, exactly," he replied and closed the conversation, letting me know not to ask any more questions or to talk about what I had seen. Years later, I learned that the name on the wall, Angelo's name, was really the name of a beloved judge from the 1800s. I was led to assume his name had significance and paid him great honor.

"Would you like to tour some of San Jose's wild side and see some casinos?" Angelo asked.

"I would like that very much!" I loudly said and surprised everyone. I grew up on the Wind River Indian Reservation, and casinos were a way of life. Linda and Steve, would you go with us?" I asked.

"Sure!" they replied.

It was interesting for me to compare the casinos I frequented as a girl and the Costa Rican casinos we toured. The Wyoming smoke-hazed reservation casino's carpets and human clothing reeked of stale smoke, and they were filled with clanging, ringing, bonging, lights flashing, sirens blaring, and frantic and desperate people spending their Social Security or per-capita checks. These Costa Rican casinos were refined and more imitative of the casinos seen in James Bond movies. The floors were polished tile, the walls and ceilings were constructed from natural wood and decorative plaster, and there was no stale smoke odor. The ambience was peaceful, elegant, and much quieter without the din from slot machines. The majority of Costa Rican clubs had only gaming tables that attracted professional gamblers, who used skilled techniques unlike the reservation players, who depended on luck as their weapon.

"Sun, are you ready to become my muse? Shall we try our luck?" Angelo invited.

"Do you want to play, Angelo? I am an unlucky lady when it comes to my own gambling. I will watch you, and you can be my teacher," I encouraged.

"Oh, no, you must play too. I want to stake you with a hundred dollars worth of chips and see what happens. If your tourists don't want to play, they can wander off somewhere or watch the music performance on stage. What do you want to play first?" Angelo asked.

"Let's try roulette."

"Okay. You are lucky because this casino uses the French wheel. On American roulette wheels there is an added feature of the double zero, which is not on the French wheel. The American wheel has thirty-six numbers plus the zero and the double zero. The French wheel only has thirty-six numbers plus the zero. All bets on both wheels are paid at odds as if only the thirty-six numbers existed. The house advantage comes from the zero and the double zero. American roulette places great advantage toward the house winning and gives them a 5.26 percent advantage. With the French wheel, players only face a 2.7 percent edge, and that is lowered to 1.4 percent betting on even numbers. On an American wheel, it is very difficult to win. The roulette game can be played at forty-five spins per hour. At five dollars a bet, the player faces an expected loss in roulette comparable to an unskilled or average blackjack player," Angelo explained.

"I am not a great blackjack player, but my chances are better than roulette," Steve said as both he and Linda listened intently to Angelo's gambling lesson.

"Sun, would you rather play blackjack, too?" Angelo asked.

"Sure. It sounds like I would play roulette as if I knew I would lose. We could use a game where positive thoughts might be more to our advantage."

We four paraded the beige tiled floor to the blackjack table. We occupied a vacant table with a handsome Tico dealer by the name of Armando, in his late forties, who stood in the center of the semicircular table. Two other players, an American couple from New Jersey, named Dixie and Ralph, joined our table. Ralph seemed to be a serious card player, but Dixie was more like me, there for fun. Angelo bought both of us a hundred dollars worth of chips, and Steve and Linda bought twenty-five dollars each. Angelo, Dixie, and Steve all put their chips in the betting box. Angelo's bet was at the front and had control over the position. He also placed his bet into the vacant box without a player. The rest of us played behind.

The very first round the dealer busted, and we all won new chips. The second hand the dealer stood at seventeen, and Angelo won with both of his bets. I busted that round and lost to the dealer twice more. I had lost half of my chips and surrendered the hand, saving what I could. I gave Angelo my remaining chips and moved away from the table, giving my space to someone else. Linda and Steve both cashed out after playing a few more rounds. We all watched Angelo win almost every round, where he would draw down or split, and his chip pile grew. Dixie and Ralph both gave up their seats and watched Angelo, who continued to win. The five of us became Angelo's cheering fans whenever he won. Our enthusiasm generated the attention of other people in the casino, and before long Angelo had over twenty people who watched him and cheered.

This was really fun. I was a better cheerleader than I was a black-jack player. Angelo had an unspoken demeanor of stage presence and maintained a humble glow. He kept his focus but loved the attention he received from his audience. Angelo performed and continued to win while his chips grew taller. The perspiring handsome Tico, Armando, waved to be relieved and was replaced by a middle-aged man named Roberto. I observed the expanding crowd and saw two men who watched Angelo. I thought they were his protection team. The crowd encouraged Angelo and urged him to continue. My ten-dollar-a-piece chips were long gone, and I counted Angelo's winnings without being rude. I counted over $3,000 worth of chips. One of the men I thought was Angelo's man, but wasn't, stepped forward and announced to Angelo and the crowd, "Congratulations, Señor The management of Verde Paloma's invites you and your friends to our restaurant to order anything of your choice including our fine wines and champagne. Tell us, who are your friends?"

Angelo pointed to Steve, Linda, me, Dixie, and Ralph. The man-ager gave us a card to the restaurant. I gave Angelo a hug, and others shook his hand while Ralph and Dixie thanked him for the restaurant invitation. Angelo cashed out, shyly smiled, accepted his honors from the crowd, leaned over, and said softly into my ear, "Sun, this is just a polite way the casino asked me to leave."

Dixie and Ralph didn't join us for dinner, and I was glad the four of us could talk about what had happened. At the restaurant, Linda wanted to take our pictures with the chef, and I noticed Angelo's insistence that he should be the one to take their vacation picture, but Linda was bold and demanded she should take his picture. This was the only picture I had of Angelo. His job restricted his picture from being taken. Later, this picture of Angelo's image was blacked out from the picture Linda e-mailed to me. I had no picture of Angelo.

The menu was fabulous, and the restaurant wasn't a common restaurant, but the dinner was fine dining. Angelo selected the wine, and when it arrived, none of us were drinkers, so Angelo sent it over to the table of another couple that had played blackjack with him.

"How did you learn to play so well?" Steve asked.

"My uncle Enrique started teaching me when I was barely five years old. I count the cards. Some clubs play with only two decks at a time, but tonight they played with five. I have played this club before. By law, clubs can use as many as eight decks, which improves the house edge and makes it difficult for players to count cards."

"I know it isn't illegal to count cards, and I try with one deck, but I can't begin to keep track of more than one," Steve revealed.

"US citizens who play poker professionally online come to Costa Rica to continue legally pursuing their profession. This describes the plight of one thousand poker immigrants, mostly men aged twenty to thirty with a talent for mathematics. I wonder if this is a good thing for our country. I play poker, too, but with a thousand new poker players, maybe it is better I stick with blackjack," Angelo joked.

People congratulated Angelo on his winnings as we left the casino. Our drive back to Casa Ave was peaceful, and we talked about Steve's work with the Austin television station.

"I told President Oscar Arias about your television work, and he is interested to learn anything he can about the subject. Costa Rica is new to establishing its own television networks, and the existing television industry is novice. The president and my father are longtime friends. He was responsible for directing me to the United States for my school training. I can get you a five-minute audience with our president. Would you be interested?" Angelo asked.

"*Oh, good heavens*! Are you kidding? What vacationer who comes to Costa Rica has such an opportunity! An audience would be exceptional. Yes, we would!" shouted Steve.

"Tomorrow will be Linda and Steve's last day in Costa Rica. What an exciting perfect ending to their vacation."

"I will make the arrangements for tomorrow," Angelo assured.

When we got back to our hotel, Linda and Steve thanked us and dashed off to take a midnight moonlight dip in the pool.

"Tonight was an exceptional night for me, Angelo. I got to know you a little better, and I learned one more extraordinary talent you possess," I complimented.

"Sun, you know me better than anyone."

"Can you really get them into the president's office?" I asked.

"Yes, it is possible. I have forms they need to complete. I can fax them back and have their interview tomorrow afternoon. After their meeting with the president, we can take them to the airport."

"I am continually amazed at your breadth of connections. You are a special dynamic man, Angelo," I affectionately expressed.

"Your opinion is the only one that matters to me," he said as he ushered me to my door, turned, and ambled back to his own apartment.

"Thank you for helping me with my tourists. We all had such fun! Good night," I called after him.

By 7:00 a.m., Wyoming knocked on my bedroom door and

presented two white, eight-by-ten-inch questionnaire forms, in English, that Angelo had asked her to deliver.

"Wyoming, please take these directly to the tourists' rooms and wait for them to fill them out. Here, take this pen with you. When they return the forms to you, please take them quickly to Angelo. Thank you Wyoming," I said.

Wyoming served the tourists a hearty breakfast of her famous mango pancakes, topped with a Tico sweet cream cheese, Quetzal Dota coffee from Angelo's family's coffee plantation, and a large platter of fresh fruit from our garden trees. Our jubilant guests were excited about the day's appointment with the president of the country they visited.

"I don't know of any vacationer who has the privilege to meet with the president. I am so excited I can barely sit here and drink Wyoming's delicious coffee. Linda, let's explore the Barrio while we wait for our one o'clock appointment!" Steve suggested.

I was glad for their independence of exploring and told them about a nearby zoo they might enjoy. I had hotel chores to attend to until the scheduled afternoon presidential appointment.

The guests returned to the hotel for lunch, and I saw Angelo walk from his suite toward the lobby and knew by the way he slumped that something was amiss. We ate our lunch with Angelo's entertaining jokes and stories when he softly announced, "I have some disappointing news; the president canceled our appointment."

"Why?" blurted Steve.

"On the form you wrote you both were teachers of Transcendental Meditation, and he was forced to cancel even though he is interested in your television station. The president has a political enemy named, Leonardo Verez, who demands that our country remains under Catholic domination. Several years ago, Oscar Aries invited the world leaders of the Transcendental Meditation group to Costa Rica after he learned the practice, and Verez was outraged because he

believes the TM teachings will erode Catholic influence. Verez circu-
lated rumors the meditators armed our indigenous people with guns
and ammunition, and the entire meditating group was deported. It
happened in the early years of two thousand," Angelo explained.

I gasped with comprehension when I heard Angelo's explanation.
"So that's why I never reached any of the meditating community.
When I first arrived in Costa Rica, I contacted the TM headquarters
in the US to find out where the Costa Rica, TM center was located. I
left many messages with the names and phone numbers I was given,
but no one responded."

Many months after Steve and Linda's visit, I received a call late
at night from a man who said he was the Transcendental Meditation
teacher for Costa Rica. He said, "We knew about you for these past
two years, but we needed to be careful about contacting you. Can
we meet at your house for a group meeting? There are six professors
from the university who are meditators and would like to meet you."

Angelo's explanation gave clarity and confirmed the exact story
I heard from the Costa Rican TM professors.

"It is sad that the Costa Rican government is ignorant to the fact
that meditation is a practice like combing your hair, and has nothing
to do with your choice of religion," Steve said.

"Steve and Linda, I am sorry for your disappointment," Angelo
apologized.

As an American, this was my first experience with political oppression—to be denied the right to openly express beliefs and to
practice what I considered to be inwardly important. I became keenly
aware of my American freedoms formerly taken for granted. To be
forced into secretiveness made me feel unclean, dark, and shameful.
I felt like a sneaky coyote slinking around beloved sheep hoping to
remain unseen. I thought about the many people of different world
religions, such as the Jews, Muslims or Tibetan monks, who are op-
pressed by political rules and required to find ways of being honest

to themselves while skirting the countries' laws they live under. This secret way of life has a strong effect upon an individual's self-image and the way he relates to his fellow countrymen. I have renewed appreciation for the values of my Americanism.

"Linda and Steve, would you like to spend your last hours in Costa Rica touring an herb farm? Herbalists can tell you what plants to use for ailments you might have," I quickly interjected, to help erase the major heaviness of Angelo's news.

"We would like to go," Linda said, as they dejectedly ambled to their room and changed out of their dress clothes into shorts and sandals.

"Sun, while you take them to the herb farm, I will arrange for an escort to the airport in the event they would be detained or held for questioning."

"Oh, yes, thank you, Angelo. You can use your position as Central American authority, which outranks the local authority. Interrogation and detainment would be a tourist's worst nightmare," I agreed.

The herb farm visit was always interesting to me, and Linda and Steve's disappointment was graciously hidden from view. Angelo gave them a book about the history of Costa Rica, and we saw them safely board their plane.

"Thank you, again, Angelo, for the time you gave to my tourists."

"You are welcome, but I did it for you," he said.

"It makes my 'thank you' even stronger. Do you know this entire week, I haven't even thought about our danger? I am grateful none of the violence surfaced while we had guests."

CHAPTER 25

WITNESS PROTECTION

"I need to catch you up to speed. The JIO investigated Valerina Pachona's brutal death and took DNA samples because they believe her beatings started inside her apartment, and she ran out into the street to seek help, where she was beaten to death. The JIO tracked the Colombians who were hired to assassinate you, Sun. They were released, and the police hope they will lead them to their employer and reveal their identity. The Colombians have only been released a few days ago, but JIO let me know they may try again to renew their assassination plan, and since the tunnel has been dynamited, they may become bolder. This year, there were eleven murders of foreigners, and the JIO believes they will be connected to Katerina Meza. Some of the eleven deaths were of people whose names we saw in Katerina's legal books. Even with these statistics, the Tourism Commission continues to depict this country as a safe country for tourism! Are you thinking you should go into the Costa Rican government witness protection program?" Angelo asked.

"I am hesitant about that. What would the government witness protection program be like?"

"Sun, Costa Rica is a country with little money, and they put their witnesses into the regular prison, called protective custody because they can't afford to place them into hotels or remote resorts as they do in the United States. Protective custody for you in Costa Rica would be the women's prison. The women's prison is especially bad because it receives little funding or attention. This year, the US ambassador, Ann Andrew, requested the United States give $800,000 to improve forty-one prisons. It will be a long time before money would be used in the women's prisons when there are urgencies in all the prisons. Let me tell you more. The food is scant and unhealthy, and you won't be able to request a menu for a diabetic. The sanitary conditions are deplorable. Safe drinking water is questionable with eighty-year-old corroded water pipes, and the sewer lines leach into open fields. The inmates are mostly drug addicts, prostitutes, and alcoholics and share a ten-by-ten cell with no less than six other women, which produces inhumane overcrowded conditions. You would not be awarded the luxury of your own cell. You would receive no special requests because there is a scarcity of staff, and we can't risk the inmates finding out you are a witness. There are only a few doctors to make the rounds of the forty-one prisons. How do you think the other inmates will accept a foreigner, with an education, artistic, and appearing successful? Manuel told me you are claustrophobic, and I know you wouldn't do well in that environment. I have done everything to keep us both safe," he promised.

"I admit the witness protection program sounds grim."

"You would need to enter the prison with a new identity, and even if you remained safe, how would your children and friends respond without communication from you? You can't risk anyone knowing your location. This case is large, and it might take eight months, or possibly as long as a year, to close. In a Costa Rican prison, that much time seems an eternity. I want you to understand we have no choice in this matter."

"Angelo, I don't think I need to 'experience the event' to understand it intellectually. I will place a 'no vacancy' tag onto the Casa Ave website until this case is closed. The tag will ruin my business, but it will help save lives and fight crime. My sacrifice seems small by comparison."

"Thank you, Sun; it makes our job easier and reduces your risk of injuries to others. Do you want to hear a really funny burglar story?"

"I don't think so. My experiences with burglaries have strongly thwarted my sense of humor about thieves."

"*No*, no, you will like this story! Do you remember when I took you out to the road construction site, and you stood next to the big side loader. The one with tires two feet taller than you, bright yellow in color, longer than most Tico houses, and that took up the width of an American highway?" he asked.

"Yes, I remember."

"It was stolen!" he said.

"You must be joking!" I laughed uproariously. "You thought I was remiss when my 'little' power tools were stolen. Now this is funny!"

"Last week, when you had tourists, I couldn't tell you about it, but we traced, tracked, and hunted for the loader! It was an inside job, just like your thefts. We took the helicopter and traveled most of Costa Rica looking for it. We found it yesterday a few miles from your hotel hidden in a sugarcane field. You are not the only victim of Costa Rican crime." He chuckled.

"Your story helps me to reduce my complex about being the national crime target," I laughed.

"Sun, our country leads the Western Hemisphere in robbery rates. There are 943 robberies per 100,000 people in Costa Rica. There are even more unreported crimes because victims don't expect results from the police. Authorities believe two former police are involved in 'tumbonazos' (a practice of robbing members of drug gangs). Police are also victims of assault and robbery. Last week a police officer in San Jose, responsible for the American Embassy security, was attacked and robbed by two men who stole his Uzi, .726-millimeter pistols, four bulletproof vests, and the embassy's radio and communication equipment."

"I guess I don't hold a corner of the victim crime market, but it feels like I do," I snickered.

"Sun, I don't want to scare you by telling you details of your case. I need to know if you prefer not to know what is happening?" he asked.

"I want to know as much as you can tell me about everything!"

"That's what I thought you would say. We have started vamping up the security interrogations and investigations on your case. The night we were at the casino, the men stationed in the rented house across the street shot another Colombian in the leg who managed to climb to the top of your gate. They interrogated and tortured him for information," Angelo explained.

"You use torture?" I gasped.

"Sun, this is my job! You said you wanted to know," he snapped.

"Yes, I want to know, but I didn't realize the harshness of violence you would use. I don't want to know about the torture."

"Your property is well protected. The north—the back of the property—has the protection from the campers. The east side has the rifle squad, and the south side also has the team of armed marksmen. Manuel and I cover the west side, since our suite faces that direction, plus the tracking team is housed in the new apartment complex next door on the west side. We have your boundaries secured. When you travel, you have the mobile trackers. We also established a team of decoys. Do you want to go with me now to test them?"

"I don't understand about decoys, but, yes, I want to go with you," I answered.

"We will take your car. I want to buy you some special red flowers called 'Thorns of Christ' to plant along the west side of the fence. My mother has these flowers at her orchid nursery, and I have always liked them."

We left the heavily protected boundaries of Casa Ave and headed down the pink and red oleander-lined street of La Uruka toward the vivero of many plant growers section of the city. It was a beautiful day, and the nurseries were my favorite place to shop in Costa Rica. We pulled into Fauna de San Sebastian, with its tall lovely fountains, lucky bamboo, artistically twisted trees, and mountains of red vinca.

"I am in my natural habitat," I purred.

"Me too, Sun. This is home for me since my parents raised us to appreciate the agriculture of our country."

Angelo smiled as we strolled the many rows of plants. He took my hand and breathed deeply into the many fragrant smells of fresh lemon and wet earth as we passed by the citrus trees.

A young strong Nicaraguan approached us, and Angelo asked to see the plant Thorns of Christ.

"Over here," he said, and we followed like Wyoming sheepdogs following their shepherd.

"Do you like these?" Angelo asked me.

"Yes, Angelo. I do like them. The red flower is shaped like a teardrop, and, wow, are the thorns ever sharp!"

"We will take a hundred of these?" Angelo said.

"A hundred?" I repeated.

"I think we should plant them inside of the fence on the west side, and we will probably need a hundred," he said.

"It would be a lovely border and painful for any intruder," I agreed.

"It would also discourage anything from going under the fence, animal or human. We will also buy a twisted fig tree, one lucky bamboo, three hundred red vinca and four white oleanders. Please deliver all of this to this address." He scribbled it out. Angelo stepped up to the register and paid with his credit card.

"Angelo, this will be beautiful. Thank you."

"I am thanking you for sticking with the case and helping us. When we pull out of this vivero, notice the car that enters." He opened the car door for me, and I slid into the passenger's seat and looked up and saw a white, four-door, model 2000 Suzuki pull into the vivero. The car was the exact duplicate of my car.

"Check out the license plate," he whispered as he saw that I noticed the car.

"This is incredible! That is us! The license plate is mine, the car is mine, and that girl looks like me only cuter," I exclaimed.

Angelo laughed. "Yep, the guy is better looking than me, too, but at a distance they look like us. The team has done a good job with the look-alike decoys, don't you think?" he asked.

"*Amazing!*"

We parked out of sight and watched at a distance.

"Let's watch his reaction."

The clerk waved at them in friendly recognition, approached them, and shook hands. The decoys placed an order from the same clerk that we did to be delivered to Casa Ave Hotel, and they all walked to the cash register to pay.

"He has my duplicate credit card," Angelo said.

"Does she have mine?"

Angelo laughed, "*No,*" he said. "Just mine."

We waited until the decoys were in their car before we pulled away from our hiding place. We left the vivero from the right exit and they left from the left.

"If someone was to follow us, they won't know which one we

are. This is definitely very cool. Angelo, do I need to tell someone when I go out?" I asked.

"No, just go. They will do their jobs. Your car has a tracking device installed," he said.

"There are some fun times in this property scam case. Not just the shopping and the wonderful presents you give to me, but it is the adventure you include," I teased.

"Let's just keep ourselves safe. These events are my daily routine, but your friendship is my extra bonus," he said sincerely.

When we got home, Wyoming was just leaving, and I waved to stop her.

"Wyoming, thank you for the great job you did with the Texas tourists. Would you enjoy going with me to the mall tomorrow to go shopping?" I asked. She jumped and clapped her hands like a child.

"Yes. I will wear my good shopping dress tomorrow," she said.

The bronzed beauty of the morning opened itself like the petals of a blooming American Rose, and midmorning we left for mall shopping in the Suzuki. Wyoming shopped for her granddaughter's second birthday and looked at little girls' frilly pink dresses. She decided on a little lavender plaid dress with matching slippers, and I bought a pair of purple shoes to go with an outfit I already owned. She was pleased; I paid for the child's dress and shoes as appreciation for the many extra things she had done for the hotel.

The mall in Ciudad Colon was nearly always empty. Angelo said it was owned by groups of people laundering money who didn't care if it was successful. I believed native Costa Rican people preferred to shop in the small mom-and-pop shops they knew. They felt intimidated by the large sprawl of the mall. The prices in the mall were not significantly higher than the tiny spaces of the street vendors. The empty caverns of shops allowed Wyoming and me to have the place to ourselves. We shopped until we smelled food odors from the food court and decided to have Kentucky Fried Chicken. Wyoming loved the adventure of eating out and tasted to determine the ingredients.

"Sun, do you like this chicken?" she asked.

"Yes, I like it."

"I will cook this chicken for you in the hotel," she proudly stated.

"Oh, no, Wyoming, your fried chicken is far better than KFC," I protested.

"Why did you buy this KFC, if you liked my chicken best?" she asked.

"Just to have our 'girls' day out' with you, so you didn't need to cook today."

She smiled as big as the Wind River Canyon and thanked me.

I bit into the KFC drumstick and broke out my front tooth. She laughed out loud when she looked at the gaping open space I showed to her. We quickly finished eating and gathered our packages, and she showed me the way to the dentist office. I took her to our hotel and returned to the dentist. I didn't want anyone to see my toothless face.

Dr. Solis took me into his dentist chair without waiting. His office had two dental chair spaces separated by curtains plus the reception area. The medical area was equipped to modern US dental standards. Dr. Solis was a slight, thin man with high-energy movements and didn't look old enough to drive. He spoke great English and suffered through my Spanish without complaining. He was a great comedian and gave a funny performance of how to pucker up your lips to kiss without your front teeth. I laughed myself into a relaxed state. I hardly noticed I had been there for three hours, and he still wasn't finished. Unlike an American office, he prepared an entire front bridge and gave me a temporary that I wore home while I waited for the final completed product.

I arrived at the dentist office a little after one o'clock in the afternoon, and now it was nearly 4:00 p.m. While I lay in the horizontal reclined position with Dr. Solis out of the room, I became aware of my aloneness. My fear rose to panic when I thought about this place as my assassination chair. If I were to be taken out, this would be the perfect time. I struggled for air beneath the bridge dam and forgot to breath. I sweated and gasped for air. I felt my blood boiling in my face, but I was cold even under the hot lights. The KFC was a jumble in my icky stomach. I had to get my fear under control. Get a grip!

My mouth still had the rubber dam clamped around the area of the missing tooth where the dentist fitted the bridge, and I became claustrophobic. I took a deep breath through my nose and tried to relax. I listened for any outside noise indicating the whereabouts of the dental staff. Where were they? I knew about the decoys, but now I was like a sitting target in a Wyoming duck blind ready to be shot. I panicked and grabbed the arms of the chair as I bolted upright.

Breathe, breathe, and deep breathe. Allow air into any open space—take air into your ears, your mouth, your navel, into your trachea and your eyes. I relaxed and lay back into the reclined chair. I tried to meditate. I peeked at the clock, and fifteen minutes had passed. Dr. Solis admitted someone into the nearby chair, and he closed the curtains. I saw two large male feet clad in Italian dress shoes sticking out under the curtain. These were not Tico-clad feet but shoes of a foreigner. My heart pounded at the thought this could be my Colombian assassin. I heard English being spoken, but I couldn't hear what was said. I heard my own curtains open, and Dr. Solis peeked his head in and asked, "How are you doing?"

I gave a thumbs-up, without speaking because of the equipment in my mouth and the fear in my throat.

"I have an impromptu patient to attend, but I don't think it's serious. I will be right back," he said.

In two minutes Dr. Solis returned, removed the dam, did a quick imprint, placed the temporary bridge, and lowered the chair.

"Can you come back for your permanent bridge tomorrow afternoon?" he asked.

I nodded my head, and he ushered me to the receptionist's desk. I saw a middle-aged Tica in the waiting room and assumed she waited for the large dress shoes who was behind the curtains in the next room.

The receptionist spoke. "You can pay tomorrow when you pick up your completed bridge."

"I would be glad to pay the $250 in full tomorrow when I come for the final fitting," I replied.

I sensed the stare on my back from the waiting Tica while I checked out at the reception desk and turned to see the large American GI who came from the curtained room.

"How is your tooth?" she asked him in Spanish, with a tiny smirk and downcast eyes.

He mumbled, as if his mouth was in Novocain, and nodded.

At that moment I smiled, not because I was happy about the reasonable bill still in the hands of the receptionist, but because I knew the Novocain-swollen mouth and large Italian shoes belonged to one of my protectors. I was astounded at what lengths he went through to do his job. He was concerned about me and came to occupy the nearby chair. My fear panic attack turned to sugar-sweet gratitude.

I got home about 6:00 p.m. Angelo opened his apartment door and yelled, "What took you so long? One of my men had to go to the dentist today. How was your day?" he asked with a smile.

"It was a banana split kind of day. Do you and Manuel want one, later tonight?" I asked.

"Manuel left for work and will work late tonight, but I would love one."

"Your special delivery will be in a couple of hours, or would you prefer to come over to the lobby?"

"Thanks, Sun, I need to stay here and monitor the computers in Manuel's absence," he explained.

"Okay. I will be over later."

The banana split was gorgeous. I made it with green tea ice cream, topped with sweet creamed marshmallow, chocolate chip sprinkles, and macadamia nuts, and trimmed with three mint Godiva chocolates with soft centers perched on the side of the plate. I was proud to make the delivery.

"Eureka! Just look at that!"

"Artists work for praise, Angelo, and I have just been rewarded. I will go back and get Manuel's so he has it later."

"Do you trust me so much to leave it in my refrigerator?" Angelo joked.

"Are you asking me if I leave a coyote to guard the hen house? The answer is yes, because I know this coyote is a champion for honor." As I left the apartment, I heard Angelo chuckling, and I thought the cultural gap had its advantages. Who else appreciated my stale humor if not someone who had never heard it before? Maybe he was just desperate for a laugh, but I liked his easy sense of humor.

I returned and delivered Manuel's banana split to their refrigerator. I sat down to watch Angelo finish the remainder of the sweet creation. Through the apartment west window, I saw electric sparks, pops, snaps, and flashes of light radiate from the west side of the property fence. The sound made us both jump. A natural reflex made me hit the wall switch shutting off the lights in the apartment. I heard Angelo's voice in the darkness.

"Thank you, Sun," he said as he was on his way into his bedroom. He returned to the living room with two pairs of night-vision glasses and a pistol.

"Put these on so you can see what happens out there."

I did as instructed and was amazed how clearly the figure at the exterior of the west border was seen. The glasses were like looking in daylight. Angelo and I watched an intruder brace some type of pole into the electricity of the fence, which directed it to the ground.

"That man used professional equipment from ICE Electric Company to short out the current. Sun, get down on the floor and stay there," he ordered as he opened the apartment front door and crawled outside on his belly close to the wall. The fence line of the property stood on the higher crest of the incline, and even though I was on the floor, I could see what happened outside. The intruder continued to wind the pole through the fence wire and fasten it to the side of a nearby tree for support. The electricity was diverted directly to the ground and bypassed the wire intended for continued electrical current. He managed to short out the fence, giving himself safe passage. He cumbersomely climbed the side of the chain link fence without electricity and carefully swung his short legs high over the barbed wire at the top. This man wasn't agile nor was he an athlete, but he managed to tumble to the inside of the property without burns. He stood up. I heard two rapid-fire pistol shots and watched the standing figure crumble to the ground.

From the darkness came Angelo's calm voice. "Sun, are you there?"

"Yes," I said.

"Call the police and turn off the electricity to the fence," he said.

I ran to the lobby entrance in the opposite direction from the west fence, grabbed my cell phone, called 911 (the same as US emergency) and in my best Spanish gave directions to the dispatcher, who repeated it in English.

"Yes, that is correct."

I entered the sentry building near the driveway's main entrance and pulled the lever shutting off the electric fence. I saw red sparks and heard the snapping and popping cease. Still wearing the night-vision glasses, I quickly ran back to the lobby and got the gate controls to open for the police when they arrived. I realized Angelo still lay on the ground next to the wall of the apartment. My heart did the pounding war dance in my chest as I remembered I heard two shots. As I neared the west side of the apartment, I dropped to my knees, slid to my belly as he had done, and crawled to Angelo.

"Angelo," I said softly, lying beside him.

"Yes," he replied.

"Are you hurt?"

He rose up slightly and looked in my direction.

"No, I'm not hurt. I made sure there are no others. I wanted to give you cover, if needed, while you ran to the sentry building," he replied.

"I heard two shots!"

"Insurance. I think the guy is very dead, but I need to see what we have," he answered.

"I'm coming with you," I demanded. He reached for my hand, and with his pistol poised, we walked toward the crumbled heap. Angelo waved to his team of west property protection men, who all wore night-vision glasses.

"You are all clear from this direction, sir. There are no others," called a male voice.

"Thanks," Angelo acknowledged.

I walked closer to the body and saw one small blood droplet in the middle of the dead man's forehead and a larger red stain on his chest. My own system turned rigid as stone, and I needed to breathe. I stopped breathing and gasped for air when my entire body went numb and cold. This was my first sight of human life taken by another.

"Sun, do you know this man?" Angelo asked.

"Yes," I answered without even realizing I looked at the dead face. I didn't know I answered the question. I was no longer in my own skin but watched these events unfold being somewhere else

without a body. I was somewhere floating around. There was de-
tached Me, who watched me.

"Sun, who is he?"

The empty me answered, "Jorge Vargas."

"How do you know this man, Sun?"

The floating Me wanted to come back but remained watching
me look at the body.

"Sun." Angelo gripped my shoulders, but I felt nothing as the
floating Me watched.

"Sun, can you hear me?" he asked.

"Yes," the empty me answered.

"How do you know him?" Angelo repeated.

"He is the man who said he wanted to see our building permits
for the gate the first months after I moved here, and he stole my purse
and passport. I saw him again months later running through our
gardens on the Sunday we had the sugarcane fire with all the soot."
The empty me sat down on the ground. The floating Me circled and
circled but didn't want to come back. The floating Me sobbed, but
the stone me remained seated on the ground. The police car arrived,
and, without awareness, I clutched and pressed the control to open
the gates.

"Good girl, Sun! I didn't know you had the control."

After the two police cars were inside the gates, the empty me
robotically pushed the control and closed the gates. The floating Me
sobbed and floated up and down the fence line in the presence of
Angelo's men. Floating Me franticly searched the fence line like a
panther trapped in a zoo cage.

"Come on, Sun." Angelo pulled me up. I saw him do this, but I
didn't feel him. Floating Me continued to cry as the empty me and
Angelo walked down the hill toward the apartment.

Angelo met the police at the portico.

"I've shot a man up by the west fence line. Here, take these glasses and watch for other intruders," he said, as he removed the glasses from my face and gave them to the police. He removed his own glasses and gave them to the officer from the second police car.

"My men are on the outside of the fence and have not seen any other intruders from that direction," he told the police. "I think Sun is in shock. I will be with you soon."

Angelo and I walked into the house, and I sank down in the warmth of our large overstuffed chair.

"Angelo, I am fine," I said, but I was freezing cold.

The floating Me came with me into the house. I knew Angelo had placed a cup of something warm into my hands, but I felt nothing. I sipped the tea and the two parts of me began to amalgamate. I felt Angelo put a blanket around me.

I heard him ask, "Are you okay?"

"Yes, of course," I answered.

I leaned back into the comfort of the chair and remembered to breathe. I closed my eyes and heard the quiet of the night. I fell asleep and woke when Angelo removed the cup from my hand.

"Angelo, where are the dogs?" I asked.

"Manuel took them with him when he went to work this afternoon."

"Do you want to share Manuel's banana split?"

Angelo laughed. "I hoped you would offer it. We won't tell him, but I think we deserve it."

"I need to turn the electric fence back on. Are the police gone?" I asked as I unwrapped from the tangle of the blanket.

"Yes, I disconnected the attached wedge in the fence and turned it back on. How are you feeling?"

"I am glad I am whole again," I said with relief.

"I am glad we both are without holes."

"Do you need to go back to your computers? What happens when you have an emergency like that?"

"I have an emergency button I tap, and red lights flash on someone else's screen, and they take over. I managed to tap it before you cut off the lights. That was very quick thinking, Sun. What made you think to do that?"

"From practice." I told him about the man throwing rocks, the nights of the bullets hitting the house, and my crawling around on the floor.

"I have had practice."

"Sun, you are a very brave woman! I am glad we are friends," he said affectionately.

"Angelo, thank you for saying those words to me even though I don't feel brave. Tonight, did I cry?"

He looked surprised and said, "No!"

"That's good! Shall I go split the banana split?"

"I will get it. Are you up for talking?" he asked.

"I am Amazon Woman and ready for anything!"

"I thought you would say that. I will be right back." He laughed.

We devoured the banana split. I needed comfort food in spite of the sugar intake. I needed a good jump start. We both were relaxed, and the dim glow from the wrought iron Spanish chandeliers reflected from Wyoming's polished high-glossed floors. We sat in the extra-large, soft, suede tufted chairs with mahogany wood trim matching the ceilings, doors, and baseboard trim. Even with everything that had happened in this house, I still found it to be beautiful.

"Sun, I had a good visit with JIO and Interpol today. This case is much bigger than you suspected. Our group of Ticos are small cogs in the wheel. It appears our Ticos work with a group of Colombians who launder money through banks all over Central America and perhaps even into the USA. Drugs and racketeering as well as money laundering goes on simultaneously with Costa Rican property scams. Your passport and ID were stolen to open bank accounts in Panama, Nicaragua, Colombia, and El Salvador. Mercedes was the person who opened those accounts. We think she opened them for her father, Pablo, and stepmother, Katerina. They were cutting out the Colombians. We believe Valerina Pachona Uribe was killed by Katerina Meza. Our department took DNA samples from Katerina's home and office. It was a match with DNA taken from Valerina's apartment, where Katerina drank wine from a glass," Angelo explained, as he went to the kitchen and returned with two glasses of water.

"Thank you, Angelo," I said, taking the water.

"I'm glad you were able to get two shots off to the front of Jorge Vargas's body." I had read that in Costa Rican law self-defense can be claimed if the perpetrator is shot in the front. Coming forward would show his aggression, but if he is shot in the back, he would be retreating, which meant it is not self-defense, but Angelo waited for the forward position.

"Jorge Vargas didn't see any other cars except mine parked at our hotel because Manuel drove yours to work. He thought I was alone and would not be able to see the west side of the fence. What are your thoughts and feelings about Jorge Vargas?"

"The police told me that Jorge Vargas is Katerina's brother. His death made him the second person from your former board to meet his death because of your property. Tonight you saw a glimpse of the work I do. My feelings aren't involved, and my thoughts are that Jorge Vargas isn't even equal to a nail in the cog. He helped his sister, Katerina, but since he was also on your corporate board, he would get a cut if you were dead. He came to commit a revenge killing requested by his sister. He carried a gun with him tonight. Katerina Meza couldn't get the property legally, and if you were gone, no one would know the truth. Perhaps she would record the unregistered Estate Beneficiary Document you signed for your children as heirs, but she would change the names and register the property to Mercedes Meza, Jorge Vargas, or other board members," Angelo conjectured.

"You are right. The day Mercedes demanded money before she took me home, she asked me if she was in the will. I thought she was joking, and now I understand that her demands that day were made for real."

"You have two people who are dead from your board corporation. The one remaining Tica is Marianela, Katerina's secretary. What usually happens is that internally the criminals begin arguing and disagreeing and kill one another. When the Ticos couldn't gain ownership of your property, it set off a chain reaction of anger. The motivation for Valerina's death? She gave Katerina trouble because she had been promised the biggest share of money since she was board president. We have much work ahead to gather evidence." He sighed.

"I think the sellers of my property, Antonio Lopez and Rodney Lewis, are involved too."

"Why do you think that?"

"Antonio was outraged with the changes I made to the property. At the time I thought his reaction was unjustified, but if he thought he would get the property back, then his reactions were understandable. He also threw a hissy-fit when I wouldn't pay for the security alarm. Maybe it was him who tried to scare me away with rocks and bullets. I wonder if we can dig the bullets out of the back of the house and match them to the gun he carried in the top of his boot?"

"Sun, your words are a beautiful 'probable police report.' You might be right, only Rodney Lewis, Tony's partner, is no longer involved because he died last month of AIDS. I want you to know this case extends all the way to your former hometown of Austin, Texas."

"Really? How can that be?" I asked.

"Remember when we rode in the car a couple of weeks ago, and you told me how you met the Mezas through your friend who took an investment class of Extended Education from the University of Texas?"

"Yes, the instructor was Paul Phillips, and my friend Carol told me that she really enjoyed the class. He recommended Pablo Meza as investment broker," I explained.

"Sun, Paul Phillips was shot to death on the beach in Jaco, Costa Rica, the same week you told me how you had gotten involved. I would have told you sooner, but JIO only gained positive identification today and linked him to our case."

"Maybe the evidence you gleaned from Valerina Pachona Uribe's beating had commonalities with Paul Phillips's death," I conjectured.

"Yes, it does, but the hardest challenge of this case is to arrest all suspects simultaneously so the criminals don't tip off each other and leave loose criminals to mess up our clean catch. This case is big. We must take care to have patience gathering proper evidence first and strike the criminals in Costa Rica and Colombia at the exact time."

"Everyone has cell phones and emails these days, so news can travel quickly," I agreed.

"That is a certainty! Jorge Vargas's death tonight will shake the family tree in Costa Rica and the interrogation of the apprehended Colombians. The surveillance of the three fence-fried Colombians produced interesting results in Colombia. I don't want to be crass or disrespect the value of human life, but it is important to keep a sense of humor, so my question is: What is on the menu? Do we want our criminals fence-fried or sunny side up?" he joked.

"That is a good one, Angelo. How about getting them well toasted and serve arrest warrants?" I smiled as I heard Manuel's car drive in.

"Here comes Manuel. You need to wipe off the telltale signs of banana split on your lips!" I said, as I handed him a corner of my blanket.

The front door to the lobby opened, and Manuel popped in.

"Why are you waiting up for me? Don't you know how late it is? What did you do tonight, have a party without me?" he asked.

"You missed your curfew, young man. Yes, you missed a big party tonight! Come on, let's go home, and I will tell you all about it," Angelo said, as he closed the entrance door to Casa Ave and tucked me in. During the night, both Manuel and Angelo left for Colombia.

CHAPTER 26
SPYWARE

The spying jungle trees around our bowl stretched their crooked, smothering fingers over the hills' rounded tops to confine all living things under their control, but the innocence of the sunny day struggled to squirm free from their grasp and hazed the dark day. The intercom buzzed midmorning, and I looked up the driveway to see who was there as I answered. I saw the Judicial Investigating Organizations (JIO) official vehicle waited at the gate.

"Good morning," I said into the intercom.

"Good morning, Sun. This is Chief Inspector Mario de Luisa. May I visit with you for a few minutes? Con permiso."

"Of course; I will open the gates," I welcomed.

We met in the lobby, and I ushered Mario de Luisa to the large, comfortable, overstuffed settee, where he perched on the edge of the cushioned seat like a jack in the box ready to jump up but was held tightly down by the lid of Costa Rican constraints of its culture, customs, and traditions.

"I made an official visit of my own. Angelo asked me to check on your safety from time to time in his absence, so I combined the two requirements and came today. I hope my presence does not disturb you," he timidly stated.

"I enjoy company," I cheerfully encouraged.

"You look well since we last met. It is my wish that these occurring criminal events have not been too distressing for you."

"I am fine; thank you for your concern."

Costa Rican society had a very difficult custom for me to endure. I knew Mario de Luisa came on business, but the Tico culture required him to delay presenting his intentions. Ticos believed it was abrasive and rude to get to the point too quickly. Ticos resent "pushy" Americans who state their business and depart. Consequently they postponed their business until forty-five minutes passed before disclosing their purpose. This idle chitchat drove me into impatience. This custom brought the difference between our two cultures into a direct clash. I wanted to stand and scream, "We wasted an hour of valuable time. Just tell me what you want." Instead I sat in my jack-in-the-box position and waited, groping to find patience buried deep in my back pockets—somewhere.

At last he said, "Angelo explained he would be in Colombia for an extended period, and he wanted me to find some bullets lodged into your house. Do you know where they are?"

"Yes, I can show you," I said, as I did the jack-in-the-box spring up.

"Thank you. We can do that in a few minutes. I want you to understand your case is a large case. It would take time before arrests are made. We must have indisputable evidence against those involved. Even if the bullets matched Tony's gun, it will be a long while before we have evidence against Pablo; Mercedes; Katerina Meza; her secretary, Marianela; and the Scotia banker, Mr. Gonzales. We don't want to arrest Tony Lopez and risk the others fleeing. I am here to caution you against any associations with these people," he said.

"I had a phone call this very morning from Marianela, who

told me Mercedes had her baby in Spain and would be home in two weeks. She said Mercedes wants me to see her baby, and Katerina would like to see my hotel. Marianela thought it would be a festive occasion for us to get together to celebrate, since she also has a new baby. She said she would call me when Mercedes arrived, and we could make plans."

Chief Inspector Mario de Luisa looked startled, took out a notepad from his briefcase, made some notes, scribbled a phone number on a piece of paper, and handed it to me.

"Sun, when she contacts you again, please call me at this number. *Under no circumstances* should you meet with them. We have strong evidence Katerina was in Valerina Pachona Uribe's apartment the night she was beaten to death. We believe she is directly responsible. We don't want to arrest her at this time because other evidence is being gathered against her in another murder in Guanacaste. She was involved with an older man and his son, who were found dead in their swimming pool with unregistered property. Katerina was the transferring property lawyer. There is a strong possibility she is linked to a total of nine murders of foreigners all involved with unrecorded property," he explained.

I gasped. "I will not meet with any of them."

"Good. We have good support from the Argentina-based Interpol, and they found four new bank accounts opened in four different countries in your name by someone who had your passport. The passport number was from your old passport, stolen by Jorge Vargas and given to Mercedes. Interpol confirmed her airline travel dates with the dates of the account openings in Panama, El Salvador, Spain, and Colombia. We suspect Katerina helped with legal details to money launder for the Colombians but decided to create her own operation. She had Mercedes set up new accounts, used your identity, deposited Colombian laundered money into those (your) accounts. We made progress, and perhaps Angelo will make the needed connections to determine what Colombians are involved. He started with the two names on your corporation board, Mauricio Machado Santos and Leonardo Garzon Serpa."

"Do you know a man by the name of Paul Phillips?" he asked.

"Yes, I know the name, but I don't know the man."

"He was shot execution style on the beach in Jaco last week. How do you know his name?"

I explained that Paul Phillips was the University of Texas extended studies instructor who introduced my friend Carol and me to Pablo Meza. Chief Inspector Mario de Luisa's information supported what Angelo had already told me.

"We gathered evidence that Paul Phillips was killed by the same Colombian hired to assassinate you. When he was in the Costa Rican hospital with third-degree burns from your fence, we questioned him and released him in hopes he would lead us to his employer, which may still happen. We believe he is associated with a larger money-laundering group in Colombia. Interpol has tracked them.

"We think this larger Colombian group disposed of people who became obstacles to their progress or demanded their commissions. We think Paul Phillips and Valerina Uribe got in their way. Your corporation's former president, Valerina Uribe, was also a Colombian, and when her husband came to Costa Rica to claim her body, he also was killed in a drive-by shooting. Whoever shot him knew he probably would talk to us about his wife's death and would give us helpful information. We are determining the connection between the Costa Ricans you knew and the arrested Colombians. That's about all we have for now. Are you ready to show me the bullet holes in your hotel walls?" he asked as he stood and brushed the wrinkles from his pants. I led the way to the back of the house.

Mario De Luisa, JIO chief investigator, carefully removed three bullets logged into the walls of the hotel facing the river.

"These are from a .26 Glock pistol," he said, as he placed them into his case, and we ambled to his official car that waited in the driveway.

"Sun, thank you for your help, and please believe that we are working your case as high priority. It is important that you avoid placing yourself in harm's way by accepting Marianela's offered invitations," he cautioned.

"Señor De Luisa, I value my life," I said, as he drove away.

I had anxiety from the report Chief Mario De Luisa had given. The removal of the bullets from my hotel walls, and the information Amon had given about Tony's concealed .26 Glock in his boot top, confirmed for me that he was the man who committed the nightly rampages. He hoped to frighten me to return to the States, and he would get his property back.

My fear would be deterrent enough to keep me away from Mercedes and her family. I was drained by Mario De Luisa's report and plopped down to watch the new TV Angelo gave to me before he left for his work-related trip to Colombia. I never experienced relaxation or comfort from TV, but Angelo assumed I might enjoy it. After ten minutes, I switched it off, scuttled to the art studio and sculpted a new piece. Sculpting was an activity where I gained strength and clarity. It worked every time to rid my heebie-jeebies. After a few hours passed, I stepped away from the sculpture, where a "happy, fat Tica" emerged from the supple clay. I smiled as I saw the compassion she reflected back to me.

I walked the red pathway from the art studio to the back patio of my bedroom and saw a large delivery truck parked at the entrance gate, and a man used the intercom. I ran the last few steps of the pathway to the lobby and quickly answered the call.

"This is Sun Richards, may I help you?" I panted.

"This is the Fauna de San Sebastian Vivero with a plant delivery from Señor Angelo Lopez." The delivery is for Doña Sun Richards. Con permiso."

"Yes, mucho gusto!" I replied as I pressed the automatic gate button for entry. The truck entered and unloaded the plants Angelo bought from the nursery when he showed me our look-alike decoys.

The plants were even more beautiful than I had remembered. I looked at the overwhelming amount of delivered vegetation and realized I had an enormous amount of work ahead of me. Angelo and Manuel were both gone to Colombia and no telling when they might return. Wyoming had a full day's work ahead of her created by the departed Texas tourists, and she wanted to complete her work first. Again, another occasion to miss Amon. I placed the hundreds of plants into the area of the garden that showed their splendor and created a delightful design. I moved the large twisted fig tree three times before its decided location was found. I struggled with its placement when I noticed an SUV parked at the gate, and Orlando, one of Angelo's men, smiled and waved to me.

"Let us in, Sun; you cannot do the planting by yourself. We are the landscape crew from Angelo's highway project. These guys, five of us, have been sent to help you," he shouted.

I recognized Orlando as one of Angelo's friends and opened the gate with relief as the "cavalry" arrived to help with the landscape. The five men worked to transform the gardens into a magnificent manicured mini-resort. While the men sweated and labored, I went into the kitchen and made large pitchers of lemonade. While I prepared their drinks and sandwiches, I thought about the culture differences between my US home country and my new home in Costa Rica. Their culture got in the way of production, and people didn't understand the efficiency of "time," at least not by American sensibilities, but unlike Americans, Ticos understood how to serve, and they gave it from their hearts like the men who helped today.

Besides the uneasiness of adjusting to Costa Rican cultural traditions, I was aware of yet another discomfort. I noticed my computer, email, house phone, and Skype phone systems were used by

someone else, or under someone's control other than mine. I could
tell my communications were compromised. Being spied upon created yet another worry. Emails didn't show up for two or three days,
and then several days later they all appeared. Friends told me they
sent emails I never received, yet the sender received no messages as
undelivered. My family thought I hadn't responded when the truth
was, I hadn't gotten them. I checked with my service provider, which
reported everything operated in good form. I had three accounts
each with the same problem, and each provider reported its system
worked perfectly.

On the Skype phone there was a menu that showed the countries
I called in order with the most frequently called listed first. Usually
the USA remained in the top most-called position. Yesterday I used
the Skype, and the country of Nagorno Karabakh showed up as most
frequently called. I didn't know anyone in that country and I didn't
even know where the country was located. Nicaragua, Mexico, and
Argentina were also listed as frequently dialed countries.

The most clandestine event occurred when I used the World
Wide Web. A strange message appeared in code. It was a series of
dashes and stars with numbers and letters mixed in. I worked for
Western Union as a schoolgirl, and the message I received looked like
the ticker tape of dots and dashes, but was different from my understanding of Morse code. It included random symbols and letters, and
I couldn't understand it. I interpreted these unreadable messages as
some type of government codes that needed cryptology.

On another occasion while I wrote a document, my screen was
under someone else's control, who wrote something that made no
sense to me. I needed larger print to see the screen with ease, and
this print came in so very small, as if the person who typed was
farsighted.

After Angelo moved into Casa Ave and transformed the apartment into his communications base, my private communications

were no longer private. I received an email from a male musician friend that included pictures from his gigs. The next thing I knew, Angelo told me he had his own band, and he played keyboard. I lived with family musicians all my life, and they made music every moment of their waking hours. They strummed, composed, rehearsed, performed, or jammed, and Angelo exhibited none of those characteristics. He indicated no interest in our hotel orchestra pit.

Another male friend showed his "biker" life on email photos, and suddenly Angelo told stories about his biker days. Did he believe these activities "tripped my trigger"? Did he think he had to invent these activities to gain my attention? I was not attracted to an image of a rock star or a "hog rider" or any image. A man's good character was what held my attention. Angelo remained a mystery to me even though he told me he was an agent; he didn't disclose in which branch of government he was employed. I suspected he was with the National Security Agency, which explained his assumed privilege to snoop into my communications.

It was no mere coincident my emails and his personal stories were similar. He read my mail! He spied on me. I was cleared of any suspected involvement that pertained to the two murdered people from my corporation board. Was he spying on me in official capacity for the National Security Agency? Who gave him latitude to disregard privacy rights? He spied on me out of his own curiosity! I considered this invasion as a high-tech form of stalking. I was flattered by his interest in my personal life, but I was American enough to cherish my privacy rights.

Angelo once told me that whenever his name was typed onto any computer anywhere in the world, lights and signals appeared on the headquarters computer analyst's screen. The agency wanted to know who checked on their operatives. I told my sister, Ann, in California about this and explained never to use his name. I told her to use ******** (little stars) in place of his name. She laughed and said, "I think he should be called Shooting Star."

I read in a prominent US newspaper, which obtained a National Security Agency internal audit and other top-secret documents, that the agency had broken privacy rules and overstepped its legal authority thousands of times each year since Congress granted the agency broad new powers in 2008. Angelo's boundaries of professionalism and personal stalking became blurred, and I resented my loss of privacy. Was this the price I paid for my appreciated protection?

In 2009, Angelo told me private details that involved my son: how much money was in his bank accounts, that his wife was online and researched sanitariums, and private details about their family ski trips that revealed infidelity. He told me about questionable business practices that involved bonds and insurance. Angelo knew the names of detectives and the amount of money my son spent hiring them to visit Costa Rica to shield me from harm. My family's involvement heightened my concern for the seriousness of the experienced communications invasion.

I was frustrated when the website went into a scramble of colors and later corrected itself. Before Angelo left for Colombia, I asked him about the unusual computer events, and he shrugged and replied, "We know the Colombian suspects have very sophisticated equipment much more advanced than ours. Maybe they infiltrated your systems."

I confirmed my suspicions about being a victim of communications infiltration and surveillance. I learned that my communications systems were infiltrated with the help of special equipment called XKEYSCORE. The National Security Agency built a building located in Bluffdale, Utah, that sprawled one and a half million square feet and was filled with super-powered computers designed to store massive amounts of information gathered secretly from phone calls and emails. The collection included basic call logs of phone numbers, time, and duration of calls, and could be used, or misused, by any snooping agent.

The XKEYSCORE program determined which computers visited certain websites, apparent from the gathered information from my daughter-in-law's computer. The program tracked a person's private interests and followed the history of his or her website searches. The US government spent $14.7 billion for spy satellites, high-tech equipment, analysts, linguists, cryptologists, and cyber specialists. The amounts of information the XKEYSCORE searched and stored was massive, easily over forty-one billion total records.

The Kaspersky Lab listed Costa Rica as one of the countries hit with spyware.

I was afraid of the power my US government had, and I was a victim who experienced its misuse. I feared with anxiety that I could be framed for murders in Costa Rica, or alleged money laundering because the XKEYSCORE had information. An agent could manipulate information against me even when I was innocent.

I experience misgivings, and was poked by intuition that concerned the toiling men who arrived, dug, and planted. My disquiet came from inherent eruptions and not from the intellect, which advised acceptance and gratitude. Intuition and intellect played their old game of tug-of-war and pushed and shoved me around until logic reasoned that my negative thoughts were nothing more than my own "new country" insecurities. Rational thought and subconscious directives were out of sync with each other, and I accepted the intellect side of the debate rather than listen to my faithful intuition.

I looked out the window and completed my task of preparing lemonade. I applauded the arduous sight of five sweating, exerting men who diligently worked to beautify the hotel grounds. I questioned Angelo's character, and allowed my negative thoughts to color his thoughtful gift. His bestowed gift nullified any possible wrongdoing or character flaw he possessed.

I picked up the freshly made lemonade and took it outside to our bench in the shade below the mango tree. I gave Orlando a wave, and the five men came to rest while I poured them each a tall glass.

Orlando spoke a smidgen of English, and I spoke a smidgen of Spanish, and together we managed to communicate in Spanglish.

"You beautiful; why you live in Costa Rica with no mens? Do you not like mens?" Orlando asked.

"Of course I like men, but I need to find a special man."

"What you want? Many presents?" he probed.

"Yes, presents are great, but it is the man's character that interests me," I explained as I offered snacks to everyone.

"I am character, would I do for you?" Orlando asked earnestly.

I smiled about the translation error. "Angelo told me you are married."

"Yes, I have seven wives. One for each day of the week, but I make you number eight," he offered.

"Thank you, but there are only seven days in the week," I laughed.

"I do my best to fit you in."

"I love the garden you and these men made, and your efforts are appreciated. Thank you for your help today. If you want more lemonade or sandwiches, please bring the empty trays to the door for a refill." I felt uneasy with the line of Orlando's conversation, and from the incongruent, unexplainable thoughts tugging me between distrust and gratitude. Intuition spoke loudly and told me the men were planting a clandestine technical communications system into the ground as they planted the beautiful garden. I retreated into the hotel. It was after dark when the tired men finished their work. They trudged up to their van parked at the gate and disappeared into the secretive black leafy space of rural jungle.

The next morning, the beautiful glow of day radiated through me and brought waves of happiness as I looked outside at the splendid new

"Orlando-created gardens." For some unexplainable reason, I experienced Angelo's incisive good thoughts. I strolled from my bedroom suite into the lobby and noticed a small three-inch square box that rested on the dining table. There was a pink card behind the gift, labeled: "To Sun, Fondly, Angelo." I dashed to his apartment and found it empty but knew he arrived during the night. I rushed back to the dining room and reached for the labeled card and opened it, to read:

> My dearest Sun,
> I arrived late in the night and left this gift for you, which reminded me of your eyes. I am called to Washington for a meeting after resting at your resort for only three hours. I will return in a few days and would like you to go to lunch with me. Fondly, I remain, yours, Angelo.

I carefully unwrapped the little pink box and sighed at the sight of the elegant, deep-green emerald earrings. I realized such guilt from the dark thoughts I had about his integrity. *Angelo, please feel my love and my thanks and receive extra energy to do your Washington work.*

I ran to my office to answer the ringing phone. I tried to meet people and joined a variety of women's clubs. One of the groups I liked the most was a spiritual group, led by a saint named Didi, but the phone call was not from her. It was from one of my new friends from Bloomers, a garden club. "Where we are planted, we will Bloom" was on the phone.

"Hi, Sun, this is Beverly from Bloomers. I need to get my passport stamped for my ninety-day Visa requirement, and I wondered if you want to go with me to Nicaragua for the weekend," she asked.

"I surely would. It sounds like fun. Let's plan on going!" I accepted quickly to silence my jabbering intuition. My indecisiveness between gratitude and suspicion dueled again.

CHAPTER 27

ESCAPE

The special mysterious Angelo went great lengths to arrange a trip into Nicaragua with my new friend Beverly. He arranged with his department for me to experience fun, travel, and protection without the usual confinement of the Costa Rican witness protection program. The expense of enlisting a team of experienced protection professionals to keep me under their watchfulness was enormous, and before I left Costa Rica, Angelo cautioned me not to talk about my case or to reveal I knew I had an army of men tracking my whereabouts or knew where I was every minute of the day and night.

I dismissed the thought that a listening device could be placed into the alarm control attached to the car keys we used to drive to Nicaragua. I erased the idea that sophisticated technology could be used to monitor our travels and location. I was an American who took the rights of privacy for granted.

I listened carefully to his instructions, but in my mind all of the cautionary lecture about not talking about my case, level of danger, or about revealing the many people risking their lives protecting mine seemed oppressive and controlling. I was feeling smothered under the weight of protection. I had never harbored secrets or lived a life behind a veil of obscurity. Expression was the need of my soul, and I wanted to feel freedom I hadn't enjoyed in months. I was so excited to be replacing this dark weight with lightheartedness and girlish laughter. I shook off his lecture and replaced it with antici-pated wild dancing.

Beverly and I left Casa Ave mid-afternoon. It was our goal to reach the border crossing of Nicaragua before dark. The day was sunny bright, as were most days in Costa Rica. We drove north through the winding, pothole-marred, narrow roads, lined with lush thick trees and tropical plants and trimmed with borders of natural volunteer pink, orange, and white impatiens. Those flowers grew in colorful profusion outlining the roads and separated the various gradations of greens until they blended into solid walls of emerald green as they fortressed into the distance, not unlike the perspective of old master painters.

As we drove, Beverly commented on how the fences (trees strewn with barbed wire) were all so straight that farmers used them as fences. This was one of the miracles of Costa Rica. The trees didn't comply with the farmers' wishes for a straight fence, but the ground was so fertile that farmers simply cut branches from trees, stuck them into the ground, and strung barbed wire, and later those planted branches grew into trees all in straight rows. The trees made a natural fence and became a practicality for the landowner. The soil was so rich that most plants grew because they were stuck into the ground. The grounds at our Casa Ave Hotel were entirely landscaped from existing plants and trees that were cut and stuck into the desired design. Within two weeks, the gardens looked as if they had been there forever.

Stories about Wyoming and Amon and Costa Rican observations made for good travel conversations with Beverly as we drove the miles north to the border. The Costa Rican government required foreigners to leave the country for seventy-two hours every three months. This rule required Beverly to travel into Nicaragua for the weekend to receive a passport stamp and made a pleasant weekend travel adventure for me. I went along to keep her company, and I wanted to experience the country of Nicaragua after living in Costa Rica for two years. My travel companion required frequent bathroom breaks, and I welcomed the chance to experience the peace and beauty of the Costa Rican hills and valleys. We found beautiful places to consume our snacks, but the light of day was nearly gone, and the border crossing was another hour in the distance. I believed the border crossing would be the most dangerous if violence pertaining to my case were to occur.

It was totally dark by the time we were met by rushing young men with various forms and outstretched hands for payments. They spoke in rapid Spanish, of which I understood six out of ten words. Beverly waited in the car to protect our luggage and car from theft while I tried to understand the requirements for border crossing.

I stood alone in total darkness and waited for various officers to receive the paperwork, which heightened my sense of vulnerability. My small stature was accentuated by the large, coarse, dark-eyed truck drivers, who scanned my body as they waited beside me. After an hour, it was my turn at the officer's desk. He asked for a hundred dollars for the required papers. I refused. He requested seventy-five dollars; again I shook my head, *no*. I feared he could arrest me for vagrancy. I accepted his request for twenty-five dollars and ran back to the car. Beverly was crying because she thought something had happened to me and didn't know what to do.

While I drove across the border of Nicaragua, my emotions soared! I felt waves of terror mount and wash over me and drown my breath. I felt mountains of gratitude toward Angelo, who arranged this trip. I was enamored with his intellect, his position of command,

and his elegance. I saw traces of his etiquette and the privileged childhood he had, but my terror incapacitated me, and that, mixed with infatuated excitement, equaled a hormonal teenager, producing a strange state of surrealism. I could be assassinated at any minute while my grown son and daughter, who lived in elegant secured US homes, would know nothing about what happened to me. I wanted Beverly to tell my children about the peril and my death in the event it occurred. I selfishly purged my tremulous stream of boiling emotions to Beverly and disregarded the consequences those words had upon Angelo and his team of agents who protected me.

The blonde, plump, fiftyish face of Beverly's froze in opened-mouth disbelief. I wanted her sympathy and her promise she would contact my children in the event I was killed. I wanted her to know about the fear I tried to conquer at the border crossing. Beverly understood nothing nor accepted my fear-laden concerns.

I had done most of the driving up to this point. We traded places because I had poor night vision from a childhood injury to my left eye and asked Beverly to complete the drive into the city of Rivas, Nicaragua, where we looked for a hotel. The town of Rivas looked unappealing to both of us, so we traveled on to Managua. Bev wasn't the best of drivers, and our speed ranged between thirty and forty miles per hour on the open straight road. We found a hotel late in Managua, and Beverly wanted to share the cost of one room. I knew I wanted my own room because few people understood the level of silence needed for meditation. She insisted her finances required us to share the cost of a room, and I relented. We shopped several hotels before she selected a large lovely hotel. We ate a simple soup supper and went to the room after midnight. Angelo called and inquired why it took so long to cross the border. He explained his men were ready to intervene to expedite the process but refrained. He wished us a pleasant trip and assured that I was safe.

That night my mind wouldn't be still. Beverly wanted to listen to music and watch TV, and she rejected my preferences. My body and mind were restless because I didn't erase the mind chatter with my evening meditation practice. Unable to sleep, I realized I inadvertently transferred my fear—no, terror—to Beverly. She absorbed my level of consciousness like I absorbed the collective consciousness from the third world country I determined would be my home and occupation. The collective consciousness of these two countries of Costa Rica and Nicaragua were steeped in the vibrations of fear. Fear from insecurity, hunger, the safety of their children and families, from unemployment, the lack of clothes, home, or money. There was fear of petty theft from people who had less and were driven to desperation, committing violent crimes. They were afraid of being humiliated or feared unconventional thoughts of nonconformists. They feared breaking a morality standard, for low living standards, or fear of being found stupid, unworldly, and uneducated. They experienced fear from lack of materialistic objects, and feared breaking the churches rules, and they experienced self-loathing because they couldn't accumulate wealth. Money, money, money—the strife to gain it and the anxiety produced to protect it—seemed to be the motivational factor of the culture.

I listened to Bev's heavy sleep and realized I was a victim of the country's crimes but also a victim of the avalanche of human collective consciousness. I was challenged to conquer fear before adopting Costa Rica as my home. I must learn to unplug from the collective consciousness. I was determined to live my life from the level of peace, and repelled the collective consciousness of fear I possessed. I wanted to unlock the *divine* within every individual including myself.

I felt inner conflict from gratitude toward Angelo and discomfort from his control. My childhood in Wyoming raised me to be free and independent. I suffered from lack of privacy. Angelo produced a conflict in me between respect and submission, and I felt a growing sense of oppression.

The next morning I had a better attitude. Beverly and I became regular tourists. Our morning started separately because she left the hotel early to get breakfast while I did my meditation program. I arrived later at the hotel café, where Bev had finished, and engaged in conversation with a religious, English-speaking group of men traveling doing missionary work. One of the male missionaries looked directly into my eyes for several seconds, pressed a handmade tiny cross, made from palm leaves, firmly into the center of my hand and said, "May God bless you," and disappeared into the street crowd. My intuition told me who he was.

Bev and I strolled among many small shop-lined streets of Managua and walked several miles to a pleasant park. I welcomed this opportunity to walk. I missed my regular sessions where I trained in Austin, Texas, with "Team in Training." The training provided endurance to complete a twenty-six-point three-mile marathon to raise money for leukemia. My Austin friend Molly and I became close friends through the many hours of six shared marathons. I missed her friendship and our training time. Beverly had different energies from the "eager to be of service" angel, Molly. I had moments during this trip when I knew I preferred to remain at home with Angelo. I missed both of my angel friends, Molly and Angelo.

The best thing to connect with inner calmness and disconnect from the surrounding human consciousness was to walk. I discovered walking barefoot proved the most satisfying benefit. Soaking up earth energy into the soles of my feet fed my body with renewed energy. This satisfaction occurred because earth was one element that was part of the natural environment. Connection with this element allowed removal of obstacles that blocked my path and helped to use full potential. Practicing this theory produced personal pleasures of peace. Anyway, it probably wouldn't hurt to try.

I walked along, thought these most lofty thoughts, applied my training techniques of tucked butt, kept my eyes lifted to the horizon, and fell straight down into a three-foot-deep pothole with my arms and legs flailing. I hit my nose on the edge of the asphalt, dripped blood everywhere, and scattered my purse, bags of new purchases, and sunglasses through the air in a high arc that sent them flying across the street, and my delicious mango smoothie landed in my hair. I completed the perfect pratfall of an old vaudeville act. I jumped up and looked to see if anyone saw the spectacle, only to discover a Nicaraguan man had hurried over and retrieved my scattered articles. I took them from him in haste, and thanked him with great gusto and many expressions of "gracias, gracias."

He said, "That will be five dollars, please!"

His statement wounded me worse than the deep bloody gash on my nose because of its clear message. I was an aging woman, no longer radiating signals of a beauty in distress. *Up his!* Well, so much for attempted disconnect from the level of human collective consciousness!

Bev came out of a shop and joined up with me, stared at the blood on my shirt, the sticky stuff in my hair, and asked, "What in the world happened to you?"

"I don't really want to talk about it," I muttered.

As we walked along, I had a fleeting thought that all of this would be chuckled over during Angelo's daily office reports. I wondered if the missionaries we met at the breakfast cafe were connected. I knew that each time he called he asked pointed questions such as, "How do you like the white dress you bought from Wappa's? Someone told me you had the most beautiful penetrating emerald green eyes he had ever seen."

Thank goodness he didn't mention my bloody nose! I knew I received devoted attention, but it didn't reduce my fear. Fear or not,

I was determined to see as much of Nicaragua as possible while I was here.

Bev and I decided to go to Granada. I had heard about its beauty, and we drove there the next day.

Granada was truly the most beautiful city of all Nicaragua. We ate delicious food, wandered through art shops, tried on colorful clothing, walked through festive flower parks, and arrived at the location to board a small motorboat bound for Isla de Ometepe. This island was residential and strewn with magnificent brick and stone mansions. Our boat careened through small canals and waterways that surrounded the peaceful natural gardens. Marco operated our boat and told us many stories of gained or lost fortunes, about love and unrequited love, adventure, sorrow, and the mysteries about the people who owned these beautiful properties. This was a romantic setting. I thought about my benefactor who made this trip possible and wished he was here.

We returned to central Granada and managed to find our way to the little suburb of Messiah to experience the markets, which were a maze of many small stalls side by side similar to office cubicles, but instead of florescent lights they had natural light from the main entrance. Unlike a cubical office building, which would be covered by a stationary roof and air conditioning, these cubicles were covered with a tent that served as rain shelter but intensified the heat and lacked ventilation.

We walked farther into the maze of shops. It became darker and denser with heavy, claustrophobic, stale closeness of shop vendors, merchandise, dogs, and children, and the entrance was no longer visible or remembered. The shops were abundant with creative handmade crafts, but the artistry of these products was overpowered by my urgency to locate the exit. The heat stifled and intensified the smells from food vendors' cubicles, who cooked products to sell or to feed to their families. The size of this area was hard to determine, but I guessed the entire marketplace was over ten blocks without exaggeration. Only one exit indicated there was no local fire marshal. My American sensibilities raised their serpent heads to overshadow the unique artistry on display before us.

I looked at Bev's sweat-soaked blouse and felt the trickle of saltwater stream down my own face, which indicated that locating the exit was way overdue. After my panicked escape, we refreshed ourselves with a lemonade at an open-air table. The anticipated and restful twenty-minute lemonade pause gave time to notice a crisp-looking, well-groomed young man between the ages of twenty and thirty sipping a drink at the table near my left shoulder. Intuitively, I knew this African American impeccably dressed man, out of context with the surroundings, with excellent composure, Italian shoes, a starched pale yellow shirt and dark brown pants, was not your local businessman or tourist. I waited for the servers to pass from Bev's line of vision to tell her to notice him. By the time I finished my sentence, and when she was able to glance in that direction, he was gone. She looked at me bewildered. I knew he was an agent, and she knew I was deranged.

That night after I finished meditating, and Bev finished her dinner, we had time to walk to a theater, where I was eager to observe and evaluate the Nicaraguan performing arts. I had recently resigned from an equity theater in Austin, Texas, where I served as the director of the performing arts school. Theater had been a long thirty-year career, and I enjoyed the benefits of a successful resignation. I wanted to see productions from other countries and disengage from the role of theater critic. On our way to the theater, we heard the most beautiful choir of voices coming from a large marble-titled foyer. Bev's and my eyes met. We were drawn to enter a hall and hear a choir rehearsing. They were wonderful. While my knowledge of choir music was quite unlike my knowledge of theater, we were dazzled by their vocal abilities. We stood as an innocent audience and applauded wildly at their conclusion. The choir director was amused at our impromptu reaction and beamed his approval to us and to his choir.

I had great expectations for the theater production, where we paid ten dollars to attend. This low fee compared to the price of American theater was a bargain. The production was advertised as a well-known national acting group that produced original works. The theme was "domestic violence." Bev walked back to the hotel within the first twenty minutes of the production. I was "theater-trained" to never walk out during a performance and forced myself to wait until the intermission that never came. I concluded, based upon one production, that Nicaraguan theater was in its infancy. .No, that was understated—the production was far below any American high school or junior high level of acting and production skills. OOOOps—so much for enjoying the production as art and not from my professional background. There wasn't any art either!

I arrived at the hotel around eleven and was amused by a feuding backpacker couple who obviously were tired and cranky. They checked into the hotel. They both seemed to be in their mid-thirties and spoke English. He was a GI type, with military crew cut, drab camouflage-colored clothes, stern facial features, and without a sense of humor. She appeared to be of Latin American heritage. He chastised her for being wimpy without camping skills, and she remained quiet and remorseful. She was attractive but obviously looked forward to a warm-water shower, which made me smile, knowing this hotel had cold water. I was tired myself and didn't wish to get into the middle of their quarrel. I squeezed past them and continued on my way to my room.

In the morning we started on our return trip via San Juan del Sur. Bev and I discussed visiting this quaint village on our return to Costa Rica, and we both wanted to experience the seaside. This clean pleasant touristy village was noted for its seaside restaurants and Catholic influence. The gigantic cross on the hilltop gave its peaceful blessings to the villagers below. I felt the peace of this hamlet and was excited to walk the beaches with craggy rock jetties beside the beautiful seaside.

I felt the exuberance of freedom and walked rapidly to a distant rocky inlet that formed a point by the sea. I felt like a freed wild bird absorbing the energy from the sea and mother earth. I was filled with unexplainable energy even after running barefooted in the sand for over three miles. I slowed to put on my shoes to comfortably scale the sharp craggy rocks of this inlet surrounded by the aqua blue water that formed the point of the land. It was absolutely blissful to rest feeling the breeze on my skin and hair while I waited for Bev to catch up. The breeze was full of fresh smells from the sweetness of some nearby jasmine mixed with the salty smell of the sea. The sun was sharp bright since it was past two in the afternoon, and the water looked like widths of silver lame fabric moving in choreographed rhythms. It was beautiful.

CHAPTER 28

CAPTIVE

Out in the distant water, I saw what I thought looked like gray dolphins, but they swam like humans. As they got closer to shore, they stood up, and I saw clearly they were men who wore gray hooded wet suits and carried underwater spearguns. They began shouting something, but with the ocean sound of the waves crashing on the rocks, I couldn't tell what they said. I didn't respond, and they came nearer. One of the men spoke American English and said, "You should not be out here!"

The other one said, "Do you know many tourists are kidnapped from this very spot? Go back!"

I resented the interruption of my exuberance for nature and freedom. I disliked the controlled domination that injected fear for assassination into the energizing warmth of this beautiful piece of natural creation that blanketed my well-being and cuddled my spirit. I resented these two men that sought to shatter the magic like destructive vandals, who felt nothing for this natural masterpiece. Their words flung a net over me like a captured wild bird that could no longer experience the rapture of freedom. I was caught and re-strained. What were the consequences if I didn't comply?

Bev approached, and I told her what they said. She saw the two men but was reluctant to leave the enchanted spot or to believe they had spoken to me. I retraced my steps, but Bev reacted as if she was not to be bossed around by me or by anyone else. I felt the same. She was indignant and perturbed but followed me back. She resented and disbelieved me. Now she was certain that I was bonkers.

Before dinner, Angelo called me on the cell phone and asked, "Just what were you doing out on the rocks?"

Childlike, my response was, "Nothing!"

After dinner, again I tried to explain my case and the protective witness program to Bev and the unprecedented latitude Angelo gave for me to take this trip and experience this country. I wanted Beverly to know my situation, partly because my personal pride and credibility were at risk and partly because crossing the border again made me insecure. The more I told her, the less she believed, and I felt desperate to be validated.

Crossing the border in exodus was effortless and uneventful. I didn't talk to Beverly again about my situation. I knew if something happened to me she would never tell authorities or my children. She believed none of this happened, and she was not a person who took action to seek justice.

At last, our little white four-door Suzuki arrived at Casa Ave Hotel's entrance with the large black wrought iron security gates. We waited a few seconds while I fumbled around the inside of my handbag to find the gate control. After the third push, the gates swung open, and we descended the sloping driveway to stop at the main entrance. Bev was in a hurry to drive to her own home. It was dark, and only the hotel's security lights permitted enough light to transfer her shopping bags, luggage, and magazines into her vehicle. We exchanged hurried good-byes, and she drove away.

I was tired. I transferred my bags into the lobby and noticed the staff had long gone to their own homes after their workday. I was aware Angelo and Manuel's apartment was dark and indicated no one was there. During the last phone conversation with Angelo, over two days ago, he told me he was helping a neighbor of ours repair a well.

I unloaded the rest of my stuff and sank into the large oversized beige, soft, fabric chair. I pressed Angelo's number to thank him for our trip and to tell him I was safely home. No answer. I remained sitting there for a few minutes when the gates flew open, his car sped down the driveway, both car doors flew open, and he and Manuel leapt out leaving the car doors wide open. I jumped up in alarm and darted outside to the entrance to see what was wrong.

Angelo was in a wild rage of anger, shouting, "How could you do this to me! I was trying to make nice for you—and you betrayed me. Everything that you tell—had been recorded, and the department and all our men were at risk. Three agents were sitting across the room in the restaurant where you ate. They put a chemical into the water glasses that allowed them to hear your entire conversation through tiny transmitters they carried and augmented by the chemicals in the water. They gave the recordings to JoSam. You jeopardized everyone's positions and their lives. These men had given months for you. Do you care nothing! I fear JoSam. I am now at great risk."

Usually, Angelo's English was very correct, but in anger his English slipped into broken English and revealed the height of his rage. At that moment our two worlds collided. His was the need for secrecy and mine had been the need for expression.

"Angelo, I am so, so sorry!" I took steps to approach him, and he shrank from me like an injured wild animal and shouted, "Don't you touch me."

Manuel was in pursuit behind him trying to calm his rage.

Angelo shrugged him off, backed away from me and disappeared into his apartment, slamming the door.

I didn't comply with Angelo's instructions. My cowardliness caused me to betray my friend. Looking into Angelo's angry eyes was like the wild eyes of my mother when I was a child and knew her anger meant I would suffer broken bones, and swelled lips and ears. Angelo's eyes and shouting face showed the same rage mother expressed when she hit me across the face with a chair and knocked me down a flight of stairs! She threw the chair at me, and the chair leg broke across my face, piercing my eyelids and nose as a piece of wood and paint lodged into my left eye, causing a lifetime injury.

"Mama, I can't see," I said calmly and quietly.

"Faker, faker, you little faker!" mother shouted.

I lay at the bottom of the stairs and wished I was dead. Not from the pain of the injuries but from the humility for what I had done to cause my mother's rage.

Now, I caused someone else to feel anger toward me, and I felt the same humiliation. My guilt for betraying Angelo because of my weak character was insurmountable. My demand for attention and understanding was larger than my loyalty and love for Angelo. All my self-righteous theories had desolated to ashes because of my small egocentric character. I was only thinking of my fear, my safety, my future, my validation, my need for approval, my, my, my, my—

"Oh, Manuel, I am so riddled with guilt for what I have done. Please be my priest and forgive me of my wrongdoing. I was egocentric, weak, selfish, and full of fear. I regret I have injured those who tried to help and protect me. Please, please forgive me. I am so very sorry!" I was reduced to tears and sobbing.

"Sun, I am not a priest," he mumbled.

"Yes, I know, but I need you to forgive me," I sobbed.

"Sun, what you have done is a mistake, but it is not a sin."

"Please hear my prayer." Manuel made the sign of the cross over me.

I said, "Father, forgive me, for I have sinned. I betrayed the most respected of men. Please hear my confession and relieve me of the guilt I carry in my soul."

It was unexplainable how in times of great stress I resorted to childhood teachings to regain balance. Now, I just wanted rest, seclusion, and to meditate. Later, I managed to unpack my bags in silence. I tried to implement consciousness energy transfer through self-referral to provide comfort and forgiveness for myself, and found it difficult to self-love. Instead all I felt was great remorse for the transgressions I had done. I also felt a great disappointment in myself for not being more in touch with natural law that previously promoted spontaneous right action. I allowed my ego to be fed by selfish needs for validation. I fed the hungry ego again when I sought compassion and sympathy. I allowed my ego to soak up my love and gratitude for others, and it grew to enormous proportions. Ego made me forget to protect those who protected me. I failed to be strong in all that I believed.

Done was done, and I couldn't take back what had happened. I refused to wallow in self-pity but accepted my character flaw and took what would come.

The following day was beautiful and brought new hope that Angelo forgave me. We remained isolated in our separate domains until four o'clock after Wyoming had gone home for the day. Angelo came running to the lobby shouting my name. I had never known him to make such an entrance, and I had never seen him in such a state of fear.

'Sun, Sun, Sun, where are you?"

"I am here," I said coming from the kitchen. "Sun, he is coming for us both. I no longer can protect you. I don't know what to do. We have to get out of here, but I don't know how. We only have three hours, and he will be here," Angelo said, as he paced up and down the lobby floor like a wild animal. I had never seen him display such lack of composure and to be so full of fear and urgency.

"Angelo, please tell me what is happening," I begged.

"JoSam is on his way to put you into the Costa Rican Women's Prison, and, as far as I know, he may shoot me execution style. I saw him do this to his own men before, and I know he may kill you too. JoSam said he would let you rot in prison," Angelo said in nervous, rushed English.

"We need to decide where to go."

"We will be running and hiding from my own men, who know how to find people. JoSam gave new orders and reassignments to those men who protected us. Now they will be hunting us, and we have no more protection from the criminals. We have two groups to hide from, the Costa Rican criminals and the US government. JoSam can manipulate the evidence he has to prove it was you who opened all the bank accounts in other countries for money laundering. I know a priest in a monastery who may hide us. My men don't know of that place. I need to make us new passports. You need to go to a hotel and not be here when he comes," he said, as he ran back to his suite.

I knew how to pack for living in the wilderness. I removed all nonperishable food supplies from our cupboards plus a can opener, put them into a box and placed it into the back of the Suzuki. I knew we couldn't eat in restaurants or go to grocery stores. I grabbed blankets and sleeping bags, two towels and two washcloths, matches, flashlights, wading boots, and rope. Sleeping in hotels would also not be an option. I knew we would be traced by our ATM withdraws and could not use credit cards.

I dashed to every place I had stashed money to pay Wyoming's salary, hidden reserves to feed unexpected hotel guests, unexpected maintenance costs, and counted out a total of $425. Angelo's money came from his company credit cards, which would be unusable. I could use my jewelry to pawn or bribe. I put the jewelry into my sports socks and hid them inside my tennis shoes. I packed clothes for wilderness survival. I packed my overnight bag with my medications, vitamins, three bottles of bug repellant, disinfectants, and Band-Aids. I knew we would need a different vehicle, but for now the white Suzuki was all we had, and it was loaded ready to flee. A stroke of luck was given this afternoon when Manuel filled the car with gas, and we could drive for five hours before it needed to be refueled. Forty-five minutes had passed, and I was ready to hide. I stopped by the apartment, where Angelo worked on the computer.

"I am going to the Casa Tranquil and hope they will take me without reservations."

"That's good, Sun. That hotel is enclosed, and your car will be hidden from view. I am online and asked my friend, Montgomery Summers, for his help. Don't use your cell phone and stay hidden in the motel until I come to get you. If I don't come, wait for three days, and then leave the country the best way you can. I think Manuel will agree to bring you a new passport. We are making them now. They will watch all borders."

"Angelo, I am so sorry for what I have done. This is not what I wanted for you. I wanted for you to know peace, and I have made things in a mess for you."

"We will do whatever we can."

"Please be safe," I said, as I walked to the packed car, opened the gates with the remote control, and drove the winding roads to the remote hotel.

The Casa Tranquil had a sentry posted by the gates, and I asked if they had vacancy. The guard said they did and opened the gates for me. I smoothed my hair, straightened my skirt, and walked to the front desk, where a friendly small woman asked if she could help me.

"Yes, please. I want a single room for three nights."

"Yes, we have a room. What is your name?" she asked.

Oh, Oh. My mind raced forward. "DeLila," I said.

"Last name?" she asked.

"DeLila Sampson." I knew Angelo wouldn't know how I registered, and this was our first mistake, but registering in my name was not an option.

"How would you like to pay?" she asked.

"I will pay with cash. Is it possible for me to pay for each night separately?"

"Yes, that will be no trouble," she assured.

I signed the registry as DeLila Sampson with my left hand. Even, if Angelo may never find me, the name on the registry would be known to my children. When they were young I took them to swim meets and they yelled, *"Mom,"* and two hundred moms would all turn to answer. I told them, if they yelled, 'Mom,' I wouldn't know my child in a sea of children's voices. My son laughed and said, "Okay, we will call you DeLila."

DeLila was the name my sisters called me when we were little girls playing dress up. If something happened to me, I left a clue.

"Did you wish a wake-up call?" she asked.

"No, thank you. This will be my three-day vacation," I said, as I picked up the key for number six on the first floor, a few doors down from my parked car.

I took out only enough clothes for one night, quickly walked to room number six, checked the lock to see if it locked properly and dumped my stuff onto the bathroom counter. The room was small with only a twin bed, but it was clean with crisp sheets and towels. I felt the terrible stress of tension, hurry, and anxiety lessen a bit as I adjusted the clock beside the bed and began to meditate. Meditating was a welcomed pleasure. I felt the high level of blood pressure drop and the rapid heart rate slow down, and the exhausting short breaths began to elongate and deepen. My fast, wild thoughts minimized and settled into empty spaces between thoughts, which produced peace, bliss, and comfort. I peeked at the clock, and forty minutes had passed. I lay down for a peaceful rest with rejuvenated awareness. After I completed my rest, I gathered my money stash and followed the brick pavers to the hotel restaurant for registered guests. I slurped and gobbled a delicious lobster bisque soup and a house salad, previously unaware of my hunger. I paid for the meal with cash and returned down the walkway. Outside my room, I quickly stepped back into the shadows of the palms to watch the young couple moving into room number seven. My heart rate jumped higher, and my breath stopped completely.

The young couple was the same feuding backpacker couple that checked into the hotel in Granada, Nicaragua, after we had attended the bad theater production. They both seemed to be in their thirties and spoke English. *Yes*, they were the same ones! He still wore the drab camouflage-colored clothes. She was Latin American and was tired and unhappy because he now chastised her for being unable to open the door with the given key. There was absolutely no doubt in my mind this was the same couple. They must have been agents. What were the chances of random travelers being in the same hotels twice in a span of two days in two different countries? Not much! They were assigned as protectors, and now they had new orders to stalk. Maybe their job was to locate me before JoSam arrived and convey my location. They tracked me from the tracking device Angelo placed in my car, and we neglected to remove it. I was caught!

I waited until they were in their room and pulled their curtain closed to the outside courtyard before I stepped up to number six and entered as fast as my shaking hands allowed. Inside, I paced the floor as Angelo had done in my lobby hotel. I knew exactly what he had felt not knowing what to do or where to go. I looked at the clock. It was 8:30 p.m. Angelo had said JoSam would be here in three hours, and that was at four o'clock. I assumed JoSam would be in Costa Rica by now but maybe not to Casa Ave Hotel if they had flown in and waited for airport pickup. I paced, planned, and worried over what I should do. I listened with an empty glass against the wall. I heard voices, but they talked in low volume, and I couldn't hear what was said. If they selected their room to be next to mine, I would make noise to indicate my presence. I opened and closed doors, sang songs, hummed, coughed, banged drawers, showered, flushed the toilet, and ran sink water. Finally, at 9:30 p.m., I opened the hotel door to the outside and looked to my left and saw their room lights were turned off. I closed the door without sound.

I gathered my things and had everything in a heap by the door for fast departure. I assumed my capture would be in the morning when the backpackers reported my location. They might have checked with the hotel receptionist and learned I had reserved for three days. I lay down on the bed fully dressed and waited to make sure the backpackers had time to fall asleep.

I had a plan that gave my mind focus. I couldn't just do nothing and be taken to the women's prison. I had to attempt to save myself even if my plan was faulty. Angelo could no longer protect me when his focus was to save himself. The strongest and most knowledgeable protectors who once gave me security had become my most feared enemy. JoSam seemed not to be held accountable for anything and made decisions based on his anger. I felt greater danger from my own American government than I felt from the vengeance of the Costa Rican criminals who plotted my death.

JoSam held evidence that could easily be twisted against me. Two people who were my corporation board members were murdered, one before and one after I created a new board where I was president, and that could easily be viewed as my motive. My passport and identity opened four bank accounts in four different countries where $700,000 was the balance in each of those accounts, which clearly pointed to money laundering. I also bought a house where payment didn't go through an escrow bank. The large sum of money deposited into four foreign banks made me one of the wealthiest single women in Costa Rica, and that action confirmed tax evasion.

I was no match against the power and technology of the US government, and flight seemed to be my best option. The feuding backpacker agents in room number seven knew I still drove a white Suzuki, which had a tracking device installed. The device was how they found me so quickly. If my departure from this hotel could go undetected (which would be an error on their part) it would be a gift for my survival. If they woke from the car alarm that notified my movement, they might be confused when I returned to Casa Ave. When I reached home, I would leave the white Suzuki packed with supplies for Angelo. I hoped he remembered to remove the tracking device! The car would also signal Angelo that I was not at Casa Tranquil. I would leave my house on foot and go to another hotel. Presently, this plan was the best I could create.

At 10:30 p.m. I gathered my stuff placed beside the door, twisted the lock noiselessly, turned the door knob so slowly without making any sound, left the room key on the table, and left without closing the door in the event my departure plan must be quickly aborted. I walked past the backpackers' room, opened my car, and backed out to the sentry station. The Tico at the gate approached and said, "Is something wrong with your stay at our hotel?"

"Oh, no, everything is wonderful. I am bored and need a little action." I said this like a girl of the night. In Costa Rica, prostitution was a thriving business.

"I will be back!"

He winked at me and replied, "I understand. Have fun."

Tonight was especially dark without moonlight or stars. The streets were quiet with loitering men and street gangs who cut deals on the corners at intersections. The potholed streets were passages no wider than the alleys of American cities. It was much harder to drive at night. The landmarks I knew in the daylight were unseen, and my night vision was terrible. My car careened through the maze as if it was in charge of itself and knew the way home.

I turned off the car headlights as I arrived at the top of the driveway where the familiar black wrought iron gates prevented entry to intruders at Casa Ave, and tonight I was the intruder. I looked down the driveway while my fingers searched the bottom of my purse for the successfully found control. My heart leapt, and I gasped when I saw the black Lincoln Continental four-door sedan we drove to the restaurant where Angelo's brother was killed and remembered he told me JoSam always drove this car when he was in Costa Rica. Now it was parked like a stalking black panther under the beautiful entrance portico of my hard-won hotel.

Tears wetted my face as my thoughts filled the dark corners of my mind without knowing if Angelo was alive. Maybe his death transpired hours ago. I knew I had to save myself. I listened for voices and heard at least three or four voices speaking in both English and Spanish, but none was Angelo's. The men's voices were not shouting but discussing. I turned off the car engine, coasted down the driveway, and poked the remote button to close the gates. Maybe they hadn't heard the gates opened or closed.

I parked on the east side of the hotel away from Angelo's suite. I grabbed my purse that held the stashed money, ran through the lobby into my bedroom, and changed my white skirt and blouse for flexible black pants and T-shirt and black shoes suitable for hiding. I rummaged through my office desk drawer to find the large master set of hotel keys. I put them into my pants pocket and noiselessly opened the back lobby door leading to the pool.

I ran through the darkest part of our gardens masked by shadows from the tall banana and enormous hardwood trees to the back of the property, which had a walk-through padlocked gate in the electric fence leading to the tropical jungle. I found the correct key and unlocked the Yale lock on the third try. I knew both of these "never to be used" gates had electric wires planted at the bottom of the fence line to prevent intruders from attempting to cut off the padlocks and enter through the normal-looking open entrance. I pushed open the gate, backed up and took a running leap to jump the wired area. God, give me the strength and agility of a Wyoming antelope.

I felt my body fly through the open gate and land safely. The dogs, Tico and Rex, came bounding to the fence line. Tico started barking loudly, and Rex went into stalking position. I whispered as loudly as I dared risk the volume of my voice.

"Rex, go home. Tico, be quiet."

The dogs knew me, and Tico reduced his bark. I crouched in the thicket of tropical plants and watched Manuel as he came from their apartment suite and looked around for the dogs, who were confused. They didn't know if I was an intruding bandit or their friend. They behaved as if they didn't know what to do. I saw Manuel and another man come from their suite carrying large handheld searchlights. I remained still. I knew if JoSam was inside, these two men had to do their jobs. The dogs quieted and obeyed Manuel's call.

"Benga, Tico; benga, benga, Tico. Benga, Rex," Manuel and the other man called in their tenor duet voices as the dogs ran from my hiding place.

I remained hidden in the shadows while their searchlights made white pathways across the gardens in wide sweeps like lights from an airport signaling aircraft. It was heart-wrenching to remain hidden from Manuel, but I couldn't compromise his position with JoSam as I had done with Angelo. I have had months to know this terror, but I couldn't let it consume me now. I couldn't trust anyone. I stayed motionless as I thought about the large snakes that frequented the trees where I crouched away from the searching lights. I took the risk of snakes over JoSam's threat of prison. The searchlights continued to probe and poke the darkness until they turned off, and both men went back inside. Neither Manuel nor the other man seemed diligent in their search. I pushed my way through the tropical thicket westward, not knowing exactly where the road to the barrio began.

I felt tall plants brush my face and arms as I forced myself through the vines, roots, and barbs of bougainvillea. I guessed I swathed at least a city block in the thicket away from my hotel toward the anticipated road.

I knew I found the road when I was blocked by the five strands of a barbed-wire fence. I was small and had practice as a child climbing through these fences. I successfully climbed between the second and third strands of wire as one leg reached the ground on the opposite side of the fence. I kept my head and butt low. I protruded my upper body through the wire first while balancing on the grounded leg. I carefully pulled my other leg through the wire. I snagged my pants and punctured my arms with barbs, but this was small payment for freedom. I was out of the thicket, and all that remained was a seven-mile walk in the barrio to Casa Silencea Hotel.

I was in a part of the city known for the worst violent crimes, but I had no other choice. I remembered that Carmen and Mark cautioned me to stay out of this area known as the Inferno. The only safe hotel was on the other side of this crime-riddled area. The night was dark, moonless, and after midnight. I walked in the center of the empty streets. I reasoned that if someone approached me from either side, walking in the middle of the road gave me an edge to outrun the perpetrator. There was occasionally a single street light lighting the intersections of the acne pockmarked, winding ribbons of streets I navigated. I was a fast walker, but now this neighborhood prompted me to run. I wasn't a runner, but I ran.

A slow-moving car without lights approached from the back. I moved to the far right side of the street, jumped a deep ditch that prevented the car's pursuit, and hoped it would pass without incident.

The car didn't pass but slowed, and the lone driver rolled down the window.

"Sun, it's me, Angelo, quick get in. It isn't safe where you are."

"I know it isn't safe. I'm not safe anywhere! Have you come for me?" I asked, as I stayed with the ditch and the car width between us.

"Yes, but I have come for you because I care for you. I will not turn you over to JoSam. Please get into the car; neither of us is safe in this neighborhood. If you walk one more block, you will be in the Soto drug cartel's territory, and your kidnapping would compromise our operation even more than you have done. Sun, I love you, and I allowed my feelings for you to get in the way of my job. I am partly to blame for the reason we are in this mess. Please get in," he begged.

My fear melted like chocolate in sunshine. My heart liquified to sweet syrup by his sugar-coated words and persuaded me to get into the car. He drove through the barrio to safer streets and parked.

"I am relieved to see you, Angelo. I was afraid for your life. How can you be here now? What happened?"

"Sun, JoSam is enraged into a temper tantrum. I called two of my friends, Montgomery Summers and Colonel Hollander, to fly here with him. They calmed him, or he would have shot me on sight. Concerning my two friends, Montgomery Summers is equal to my position, and the other has been JoSam's longtime friend, who owed me his life. They both calmed him and discussed what to do. I am under house arrest. The agent assigned to guard me gave me his car to find you. I have men who know and trust my honor. They know JoSam is too old and senile to be in his position, and they look to me for direction.

"Sun, I was humiliated because I broke my own rule of never allowing wives or girlfriends to know about our work. I broke the rules I taught the men to uphold. I disgraced myself."

"I disgraced myself too by what I did to you, Angelo."

"Why did you leave the Hotel Tranquil, and where are you going?"

"I saw the same backpackers in Nicaragua, and they checked into the room beside me at the Tranquil Hotel. I believed the couple were your agents. I couldn't stay there to be delivered to JoSam tomorrow morning."

"Oh, Sun, you are very observant to notice them. Yes, they are our agents, and we are lucky you left the hotel, but where are you going?"

"I am walking to Casa Silencea Hotel."

"It is at least five more miles from here. It is nearly 1:30 a.m. Do you think the hotel will open for you since you have no car and no luggage?"

"I had over two miles to think about that, Angelo. I was going to tell them I needed to leave a drunk, angry husband and would pay them cash."

"That is a good one, Sun. I will take you there," he said, as he started the engine.

"Sun, I am afraid of JoSam. The first day I met him he handed me a book of poems, which I learned was his way to enforce mind control, and tonight reminds me of one of those poems."

> "This Night"
> By Nicola
> Tonight the streets run thick with blood.
> Tonight the blood runs here.
> It becomes a roaring, silent flood,
> And paralyzes with helpless fear.
> Tonight another is committed to fire.
> Tonight another dies.
> When is it your turn to be laid out on the pyre?
> When your soul to the demons flies.

"Angelo, please! This isn't helping my fear!

"I expressed my fear to you too, Sun."

"Angelo, I am so sorry for what I have done."

We drove in silence for several blocks, and then I said, "I registered as, DeLila—"

"Samson," he interrupted and smiled. "We know how you registered. That was quite the name. Manuel, told JoSam one of your friends delivered your white Suzuki to the house. They all believe you are asleep as DeLila Samson at Casa Tranquil. Manuel caught your escape on the video camera and clipped out the film. I am lucky to find you before the Soto Cartel did. No one passes their territory unnoticed. If you had walked one more block—it is no telling—what they might have done. You, a foreigner, are the perfect material for kidnapping."

"I am more afraid of JoSam, and I decided to take my chances with the Inferno and the Soto Cartel."

"That's a tough choice you had, Sun."

We drove to the entrance of Casa Silencea, and Angelo flicked his headlights into the office windows. Several minutes passed before a security guard arrived. Angelo got out of the car and walked toward the office.

"My friend DeLila needs to leave her husband for a few days until he sobers up; she will pay cash. Can you help her?" Angelo asked.

"Yes," the guard said. "I must have the money in advance, and I will get the key."

Angelo took the key from him and walked me to a quaint little *cassita*.

"Thank you, Angelo, for helping me—again."

I hugged him and said, "I love you, Angelo."

He hugged me in return, held my hand, looked into my eyes, and said, "Stay here until I come for you, Sun. Don't go with anyone else. I will remove the tracker chip from the Suzuki. If I don't come in three days, leave the country! I had Manuel put your new identity and passport into the glove box. I can't begin to predict what JoSam will do. I have looked after your safety for many months, and I can't leave you alone now."

"Thank you, Angelo. I love you for who you are," I said through tears.

"Angelo, wait. One more thing," I said, as he turned to go. "The Suzuki is all packed with provisions for wilderness survival. Please use it for yourself if you need to."

"Thank you for thinking of me, Sun. If I can't sort this out, I too might need to hide. I wish safety for both of us. I have to leave now, so not to worry my men."

I went into the cassita of Hotel Silencea and collapsed onto the bed without looking around or even turning on the lights. I slept in my clothes, too tired to take them off. I slept to midday and needed to find food. I brought no change of clothing and was in a state of restless anxiety. I meditated. I walked to a nearby grocery store and bought two apples and some cheese. The walk calmed me, but I was still too upset to eat. I force fed myself one of the apples and some of the cheese. I saved the rest for tomorrow in case I should still be here. I meditated. I spent the remainder of the day and night restlessly waiting for Angelo and thought through a plan in the event he would not return. I didn't think it was a good idea to walk about the town in case some of JoSam's agents looked for me. The waiting—not knowing whether to run or to hide—was the worst. The lack of transportation pointed to the resolution of continued hiding—and waiting.

Midmorning of the second day, there was a soft knock at my door, and I heard Angelo's baritone voice.

"Sun? It's Angelo."

I opened the door. He looked as rough as I felt. We both stood there in silence. Many thoughts collided with each other, and I didn't know where to begin.

"Let's go home," he said.

I took five seconds to grab my purse, and I was out the door. I saw a gray van waiting with license plate beginning with nine in the parking space in front of the small cassita that served as my refuge. Neither of us spoke while we walked to the car. He opened my door, and I stepped up into the van.

"Were you crucified, Angelo?" I asked, after the van moved down the road.

"Not hung on the cross but definitely at the foot of it."

"Can you tell me about it?" I asked.

"*Yes*, parts of it, but let's wait until we get home because I am required to present you with papers for your signature.

"Are you okay, Angelo?" I asked.

"I haven't slept for two days, and it is hard for me to focus. After I have a little sleep, I will meet you in the lobby, and we can talk. I just can't do anymore right now; I'm sorry," he said.

We didn't talk the rest of the way back to Casa Ave Hotel. He parked under the portico, opened my car door, and went into his suite as he said, "See you soon."

I was anxious about what happened in these past two days, but I was glad to be back into my own hotel and relieved JoSam committed no atrocity.

Wyoming believed that Angelo and I were on some overnight holiday, since we both were gone at the same time, and these past two days hadn't been our normal routine. I spent the day helping her with the gardens and house chores, and did my own office work, which wasn't much since I stopped taking reservations until my case closed. The day dragged on while I waited for Angelo to wake. At four o'clock, I walked Wyoming to the top of the driveway gate, and she hugged me after her day's work.

"Hey, beautiful woman, are you ready for a meeting?" Angelo shouted from his front door.

"More than ready. Were you able to sleep?"

"*Yes*. It feels so good! Sleep is a luxury not a necessity for me, and this place is the perfect sleep inducer I relish. May I come to the lobby?"

From the top of the hill, I shouted, "I'll race you to the front door," as I took off on a sprint.

"That's unfair—I have to get my briefcase out of the car!" he said, as he scrambled.

I was in the lobby and sitting in the settee chair when he entered.

"Yep, I am just a slow old soapyloaty," he laughed.

"It's good to hear you laugh and see you standing upright. Please tell me everything."

"If there is one man on earth to fear for me, it is JoSam. He knows no restraints, and he truly is the most powerful man on earth because he isn't accountable to anyone, any law, or any country. He does what he wants and has done it his way for over fifty years. His senility makes him a dangerous man where once he was bright, courageous, and reasonable, but now he cares nothing for 'the little man' who gets in his way. For many years he took me under his tutelage, but yesterday I was 'the little man' that got in his way," Angelo elaborated with humility.

"What happened to you since you got in his way?"

"I received a demotion, admonishment, and was charged with 'abuse of power' because you were to go directly into Costa Rican custody protection, which is the women's prison. It is a terrible place with filthy conditions, full of drug addicts and prostitutes, and I couldn't do that to you. I wanted you to have your freedom and enjoy yourself. I used my department to accomplish that end. I felt you took a great personal risk with your life by staying and serving as our 'case bait,' and I gave you protection while you remained your free spirit. What you did for us was brave and noble. I knew you faced frightening events. No one I know would have done as much. I am sent here today to present you with these papers to sign. I am doing my job. They are for your admittance into protective custody."

I took the papers Angelo handed to me and stared at them.

"Angelo, I feel your demotion will only be temporary. My intuition tells me you are valued in your position, and JoSam will restore it. I saw your leadership with your men, and your system seems to work smoothly with you at the helm. Besides, I believe in the old adage, cream rises!"

"Thank you, Sun, for your encouragement. Can I make a recommendation about these papers, as your friend?"

"Of course!"

"Don't sign them!" he said. "This is your home, and I require a regular level of protection. Since we share this space, you receive the same level of protection I have. The outside teams of trackers, river campers, the sharpshooters across the street, and decoys have all been pulled off. We are on our own! We have Manuel for our house and car security, but there are times when we both need to be gone, and you will be alone. You could leave if things got to be too much for you. Can you temporarily stay with family or Molly in the United States? After the danger passes, or when Manuel and I return to Costa Rica, would you come back?"

"Yes, I will stay, but I want to tell my children about these papers. I will conceal the case number at the top of the form to protect your agents, but I want my children to know what is happening to me. Is that acceptable?"

"Probably not, but you have your responsibilities too. If you don't sign the papers to enter protective custody, there are no rules for you to follow. Sun, I know you are a person with idealistic views about your country and want to help others who had the same bad experience you had. You gave the families of the murdered victims comfort to learn the criminals will receive justice. Jorge Vargas's death shows how intent Katerina Meza is to remove you. Are you aware you risked your life to do this?"

"I have never known the reason I came to Costa Rica, and maybe this is the cause that gives me purpose and direction."

"You will never receive acknowledgment for your sacrifice. You know that don't you? There will be no reward except your own personal satisfaction that you did a good thing. I guarantee your family won't understand this commitment," he warned.

"I feel some honor in staying. I don't want to be in the protective custody program while the main suspect in my case is the Ministry of Justice and indirectly supervised Costa Rica Directorate General of Social Rehabilitation, the entity that oversees the prison systems. How long do you think it would take for her to learn I am under her nose? I would be her bird in the net."

"*Bingo!* Sun, I didn't want to remind you of that scary thought. I am glad you will stay. You are really a special, brave person. My own family understands nothing about my job or why I can never be with them. Your decision will build a wall between you and your family that takes years to be repaired—maybe never."

"I trust their love for me."

CHAPTER 29

VALOR

The beauty and brightness of Costa Rican mornings affirmed "life everlasting" and restored my spirits after the devastating experience of Skyping my son the witness protection papers I was given to sign that placed me into Costa Rican protective custody. I wanted him to know the peril I was in. My fear of prison and its restraints terrorized me more than Colombian assassins, JoSam, or Costa Rican criminals. My son refused to believe any of the terror I had known last night and told me I printed out the papers from some government website. My turbulent story was unbelievable, but his reaction shocked me. It was the same reaction shown when I confided in my traveling friend Beverly. Both people, my son and Beverly, emphatically rejected my story that was my truth. They said my story was one of total disbelief and emphasized they wouldn't listen to any more of my "dramatic lies." I felt discredited, unvalued, and alone.

If ever there was an empty hole in my life, it happened to me then. None of the fear or terror I experienced these last two years matched the sorrow I felt from my son's unbearable rejection. If ever there was a time I needed support, it was now. I needed my son's love and encouragement but received neither. I had been a devoted and supportive mother, always there for him with love, comfort, nurturing, security, and stability. As a mother, I believed the childhood years of raising, guiding, and caring for him, his injuries, and his heartbreaks would never be forgotten. Unlike the umbilical cord, the subtle ties between mother and son could never be severed, but I was wrong. My only consolation was knowing that if something happened to me, I tried to tell my son my story.

After a sleepless, soul-searching, and sobbing night, I needed to summon my own internal strength. The warm morning sunshine poured through my windows, affirming that I could do what was necessary, and natural law supported me. I shook off last night's crippling emotional events and found my resolve and determination.

This morning, I was "case bait" for the arrest of Katerina Meza, Mercedes Meza, and Marianela. I packed my suitcase, placed the plane ticket Angelo gave me carefully into my passport, and called my loyal longtime friend, Molly, and asked her to pick me up at the Austin airport. All was set for my departure after the arrests. I dressed for travel in comfortable black pencil pants, a flowing blouse, and comfortable black walking shoes. I was ready to do my part.

Joseppe, one of Angelo's agents, left his car someplace in the barrio, walked into the property, and arrived first. I had never seen him before, but I greeted him at the lobby entrance and was surprised by his youthfulness. He was a handsome man, refined, polite, and self-assured. The other men that came later were Roberto Zamora from the Fuerza Publica and Mario de Luisa from the Judicial Investigating Organization, who I knew well from previous meetings at my home. They were accompanied by one other officer from each of their departments, which made a total of five men who arrived by foot. They showed me where to usher in my three female "guests," then hid in the lobby behind the wide brick pillars that screened them from the entrance where the three women arrived. Joseppe didn't hide but went to my old stereo and put in a tango disk.

"This is a gift from Angelo. Would you enjoy practicing your tango while we waited?" Joseppe invited, as he held out his hand. The music was Argentinian and was what I needed to relax. The music blared as we danced beautifully around the lobby's polished burnt-orange tiled floor. This was the prescription that soothed my heebie-jeebies. Good grief, Joseppe could dance! He was a performer, and the knot of fear in my stomach disappeared like the officers hiding behind the pillars.

"You are as good a dancer as Mrs. Serpa," Joseppe complimented.

"Who is Mrs. Serpa?" I asked as I practiced my flicks.

"She is the wife of the man we are arresting in Colombia this morning." Hearing his words resurrected my fear, and I missed a step.

"I'm sorry," he said, as I looked up to see my three nemeses' car at the top of the driveway. We danced over to the intercom and I poked the button for the gates to open.

"Keep dancing with me," he instructed, as Mercedes's blue "Alegre" van descended the driveway and parked under the portico. Joseppe twirled, swooped, and kicked to the tango music. His body shielded me from the guests' entrance.

"Let them wait a minute," he directed. He hesitated before the open entrance door and called to them, "We are just finishing our tango lesson," as he gave a dancer's lead for me to greet them at the doorway, while he "side stepped" beside me.

Mercedes was as attractive as when I last saw her over a year ago. Her son's birth didn't change her figure or her elegant style. She wore designer jeans and a purple blouse with cute sandals. She was slimmer than she was before the birth of her son. She looked great!

"Mercedes, Katerina, and Marianela, I am glad to see you all again; please come in," I greeted in a gracious and relaxed tone.

"Where are your babies?" Coming to my house, without their babies confirmed the real purpose of their visit. My heart pounded as I wondered if they planned my death the same as my former board president, Valerina Pachona Uribe. The thought drove icy terror through me.

"Oh, they are both asleep, and we didn't have the heart to wake them. Besides, Marianela and I needed a mother's reprieve and decided today would be a girls' day out," Mercedes covered.

"I really wanted to meet your new children," I said, as I ushered the three women into the chairs that Inspector Louisa had positioned.

"Wyoming made cakes and coffee for us. Would you all like some?" I invited.

"Yes, please, and later we want a tour of your hotel," Katerina asserted in Spanish.

I walked the sixty-foot distance across the brilliantly polished floor into the kitchen where there was *no* cakes or coffee while Joseppe removed the tango music from my old stereo.

"I'll see you next week!" he shouted, as I heard the front door close, and the electric gates open. The four policemen jumped from behind the pillars with their pistols pulled as Roberto Zamora from the Fuerza Publica shouted, "You are under arrest!" The two officers pulled the women to their feet and handcuffed them from behind.

I waited in the kitchen. I didn't want to see the startled, shocked expression on Mercedes's face as she realized my betrayal. I knew she might not see her baby for a long time.

"You are all pigs!" Marianela spat as she realized there was no escape. Katerina, even though she was handcuffed, made a dash for the door, but the officer grabbed the elastic cinch-belt on her wide body, intended to shape her waistline, but instead made her look like link sausage. The wide belt stretched from his grasp like a blimp attached to a bungee cord.

"Hold it right there, Ms. Meza, or I will shoot you for attempted escape," Roberto Zamora shouted in a deep Spanish voice of authority.

Even though my Spanish wasn't the best, it was impossible not to understand Katerina's foul language, heated by hate, vengeance, and anger. I didn't believe a minister of justice capable of talking such trash toward her fellow justice workers. The La Uruka local police car quietly descended the hotel driveway, and an officer got out and opened all four doors of the patrol car that waited for the apprehended criminals. From the kitchen window, I watched the police secure the women into the backseat with bars and an iron mesh screen, leaving me inside my hotel with a symphony of silence. The only sounds were the natural whispers from the bamboo to the bougainvillea, gossiping about "arrest day's" morning event. I stood motionless and stared out the kitchen windows, transfixed on the opened gates at the top of the driveway, and realized my role was finished!

I saw JoSam's familiar long black Lincoln Continental coming through the opened gate and down the driveway. My heart painfully pounded, and my empty stomach retched and tried to escape as my fear erupted as quickly as it had dissipated moments ago. The black car evoked stressful memories of the terrifying night when I ran for my life from JoSam. Riveted to the kitchen window paralyzed with fear, I remembered that Angelo told me JoSam had died. I recoiled into past fear, which shut out my presence of mind. I was surprised by the effect many fearful months had taken on my nervous system. I recognized Joseppe's handsome young face behind the wheel of JoSam's car and was relieved to see him. I crumpled over the kitchen counter as my lungs inflated again when I remembered to breath. I gathered up my limp body, ran to my bedroom, closed and locked all the hotel doors and windows. I slid my suitcase across the slick floor to the entrance where Joseppe stood.

"Thanks for the dance," he chirped, as he picked up my bags and placed them into the phantom black Lincoln.

"Thanks for your great help, Joseppe," I replied, as I slid into the car that once was my predator and that now served as my coach to freedom.

I was grateful for being alive but drained of thoughts or emotions, and was incapable of superficial chitchat with Joseppe. I wanted to escape onto the airplane and sleep. On board the flight, I felt the presence of an escort agent a few rows behind me, but I didn't care. I was tired of being watched, followed, advised, cautioned, and protected. I suffered over two years of this oppression, and I just wanted my life back. I yearned for independence, freedom, and seclusion. I was tired of dealing with fear, and I was unsure I would ever be myself again.

Energy rejuvenated and lifted my spirits when I saw my friend Molly waiting at the Austin airport, but I felt my frisky effervescence dissolve into the shadowy muck of low consciousness where I had lived for the past years. Molly realized my personality change, as I was dark and silent, but I couldn't explain about the week's terrible events. I needed to heal my wounds and recover my energies by being with this exceptional friend. I needed to sleep in her safe home where I knew no one watched for an opportune moment to pounce.

My week in Austin was joyously spent sharing time with Molly and friends while I waited for the Costa Rican property scammers to be incarcerated. I walked Town Lake and ate at scrumptious restaurants and saw movies. I took a road trip to Dallas to repair the tattered relationship with my son, Matthew, but my intentions didn't work out. It only widened the canyon of our relationship.

My son told me about a Dallas detective agency he hired to check on me in Costa Rica and explained the report's conclusion:

Angelo was a ten-cent thug, without any property, no means of support, and his single possession was a 1978 Ford (one of the first cars that Angelo owned and wrecked sat without wheels on fallow ground near his father's plantations) with a license plate of 264YL and was seen parked at my hotel. (Costa Rican vehicle plates never combined letters with numbers until 2013.)

The date the Dallas detective agency reported seeing the 1978 Ford car parked at my house was the same date that Fuerza Publica Roberto Zamora and Judicial Investigating Organization Chief Inspector Mario de Luisa were parked at my hotel, collecting evidence and interviewing me. (This information revealed the detective agency's faulty report because there were six cars parked at my house on that date.) The Dallas detective agency reported contacting the American Embassy on specific dates and reported that Angelo Lopez was unknown. (The embassy would never compromise the identity of operatives. The dates the Dallas detective agency gave for the embassy visit were dates it was officially closed for the many Christmas holidays.) My son reasoned that Angelo Lopez was a loser and took advantage of his mom. I painfully realized that my son had hired a company that never came to Costa Rica and charged him $7,000 for an investigation that didn't take place. Again, I felt violated by my own son and his private-licensed detectives who spied on me. I knew his concern was genuine, but he didn't trust what I told him about the witness protection program.

Our opposing points of view were a heated exchange that tore us further apart. One of the truths the Dallas detective agency found was that a $350,000 lien was placed on my property by Angelo's Road Construction Company and recorded with the Costa Rican Public Registry. This was the protective lien that Angelo placed on the property over two years ago, which I knew about, but supposedly where no money was exchanged and that only served as paper to protect the property from future attempted scams.

Angelo recovered the books of title from Katerina, filed the proper papers, and halted foreclosure, and I gave him power of attorney to pay property and municipality taxes, which he did. Would he put a *real* lien on my property? Why would he do something unfavorable toward me now? Intuitively, I knew something was wrong. Was it Angelo who may not have told me everything? I loved and trusted Amon and Mercedes, but both of them proved false. I was filled with self-doubt about my abilities to see truth. This new doubt put me off balance and created a big concern for me, and the lien was definitely a red flag for my son.

I left my son's beautiful Dallas mansion and returned to Austin with great sadness, but with strong conviction that I would never give up the challenge to make amends and show him maternal love. One of the known truths was that both my children expressed disrespectful behavior toward me on the same energy level they absorbed it from me. I was in a fearful, guarded, tired, insecure, unacceptable, low-level-of-consciousness place, and it was this darkness they absorbed. It was not their natural characteristics but my reflection. I learned it must be the parent who sets the thermostat for child behavior. If I could emanate love and good will, love and good will would be returned by my children. At the moment, my connection to source of creation, where I tapped the creative supply of love and nourishment, was clogged by knots of negativity caused by fits of terror.

Parents must be the originator of this "gleaned from source," transferred love. I needed to be the receiver, which was out of alignment with natural law. I vowed to strengthen my own conduit and unplug from the negative energies I endured for two years. I believed Molly trusted our bond of friendship and accepted the reality that I needed some repair.

When I returned to Molly's house in the little green 2000 Toyota truck lent for my Dallas trip, Angelo called. "Hi, Sun. I hope you enjoy your US visit. We had a very successful arrest operation in Colombia;

Mercedes underwent maximum interrogation and needed a doctor, while Pablo and Katerina were forced to watch. The investigation officials extracted more information from her about the hiring of the Colombians to assassinate you. The three Colombians were apprehended and charged with attempted murder. While Mercedes was held for interrogation, her husband, Apollo Hernandez, drove to a store to buy diapers for their baby and was shot to death in a drive-by shooting. We believe it was a warning to the Mezas not to talk."

I was appalled when Angelo told me of torturing Mercedes and the violence and cruelty taking place because of my case. The thought of my former friend being tortured completely revolted me. The antiquated barbaric forms of forcing a confession were stupid and inhumane.

"Angelo, you must stop Mercedes's interrogation *now*! Please, Angelo, I don't want anyone suffering to resolve my case. I would rather all criminals be turned free than to think of Mercedes, with a new baby, enduring such atrocities. "Promise, promise to stop!"

"Yes, okay, Sun, I promise all extreme interrogations will stop. Mercedes faced charges of bank fraud, money laundering, and theft of your cargo from customs. Mr. Gonzales, the bank escrow manager, lost his job with the bank under the charges of deceptive bank practices. I'm sorry if the details of my job upset you."

"Yes. It's very upsetting, Angelo! How is everything at Casa Ave going without me?" I quizzed to change the subject.

"Sun, we miss you, me most of all, and I will be glad when it is safe for your return. Wyoming had visitors from CAJA (Social Security Office) who delivered routine papers concerning your employees, and she told them you were gone to the USA, but they didn't believe her because they checked immigration records and found you were reported as being in Costa Rica."

"I don't understand," I admitted.

"The papers they delivered weren't important—just routine

census taking, but they were required to talk to the employers. When they couldn't reach you, they checked with immigration, which reported you being in Costa Rica because I erased your exit records to prevent you from being followed. Not only is it my professional responsibility to keep you safe, but I have a personal interest as well."

"Angelo, it is shocking how much power the US government assumed over *this* American citizen's life. How is that possible?" I demanded

"The United States has worked on the world's largest computer system since the early sixties, Sun. A friend and teacher of mine, David Allen, who has since passed on, was the primary designer of the XKEYSCORE database system. In 2008, the US Congress secretly gave the intelligence community and operatives authority to use this XKEYSCORE, and now we have access to the world's largest infiltration computer system. It is easy for me to erase your records using this equipment."

As Angelo spoke, my mind questioned the boundaries and the integrity of agents who had the power to stalk anyone, conduct warrantless searches, wiretap, read emails, manipulate computers holding true evidence, or erase materials proving or disproving innocence or guilt. That kind of power could easily become self-serving for users of the XKEYSCORE system. It would leave common people powerless.

"Sun, are you still there? Hello, hello," Angelo shouted into the phone.

"Yes, Angelo, I am here."

"Would you like to know about the other arrests in Costa Rica?" Angelo asked.

"Yes, of course, Angelo, but all of this information is overwhelming."

"Yes, I understand our modern times are fast and perplexing. I want to tell you about Pablo Meza. He elected to wait for his trial in the hospital under guard because his diabetes was advanced. Placing him in a Costa Rican prison would mean certain death for him because the prison system is inhumanely overcrowded, and cannot administer health care for him or any inmate. Pablo spent six months in the hospital waiting for his trial. The Costa Rican prison system is in such a deplorable state that they released prisoners back to the streets with armbands because the prison system is overcrowded." Angelo paused but continued.

"Tony Lopez was arrested for fraud and armed violence for shooting at your house but elected to enter a halfway house for AIDS because he is in advanced stages and possibly dying. During the Lopez investigation led by Roberto Zamora with the Fuerza Publica, a curious event placed Tony Lopez at the center of suspicion. It seems Tony hired a sixteen-year-old boy to help with the gardens, and he became a missing person. I conducted an interview with the boy's mother, who explained he left for work at seven in the morning and never returned. Her son was her oldest boy of six children, and she grieved for her firstborn. She didn't report him missing because he often stayed overnight at work if he had major tree trimming or other large projects. When her son failed to return after the second day, she began to worry. She called Tony, asking where he was and why he hadn't come home. Tony told her he left work at seven fifteen two nights earlier and didn't return the next day. It was four days of unsuccessfully searching with relatives and friends before she called the police and filed a missing person report." The phone connection clicked and hummed.

"Hello, hello, Sun? Are you still there? Oh, now I hear you. I thought I lost you! Anyway—I investigated the boy's social life at his school and found out he told his friends about wild sexual parties. Tony invited the boy to attend. I think the party got too rough, and the boy came to an unpleasant end. I searched your property with the help of the Fuerza Publica and our special equipment. We looked for a body but didn't find one," Angelo continued.

"Katrina Mesa was extradited to four different countries where she committed bank fraud, serving four years in each country before she returned to Costa Rica, where she faced eleven charges of murder involving foreigners who were victims of her property scams. Sun, I am calling you from a plane on the way back to Costa Rica, and the connection isn't great. When will you come home? I am ready for you to return soon."

"I'll be home in a couple of days, and I look forward to resuming my hotel business," I stated with enthusiasm. The purpose of Angelo's arrest litany was to assure me that I was safe, but all it did was confirm how I desperately needed to return to the life that once was mine. Molly and I enjoyed Jack's last home-prepared gourmet dinner before we said good-bye and I returned to Costa Rica.

CHAPTER 30
HOMELESS

Costa Rica, in my vision, remained the most beautiful in the months following the heavy rains, and this sunny day was proof when Manuel picked me up at the airport. The landscape was accented with many varieties of pastel orchids that grew as wildflowers upon the ground, tree trunks, creases of tree branches, and sometimes even upon fence posts. The sprinkling of these soft-colored orchids was accompanied by the dense, blanketed fields of red, pinks, lavender, orange, and white vinca. All this colorful profusion was laced with tall, expansive, florescent, vibrant colors of red, fuchsia, and white bougainvillea. The entire country looked to be one giant bouquet tied up with gaudy madigras pieces of chiffon scarves ready to gift the eyes of humans.

The incongruent beauty of Costa Rica rivaled the harsh, dark underbelly of the country's crime. Angelo and his teams were trained to understand the criminal mind, but how long could crime fighters wallow in the dark muck of their jobs before they absorbed the same criminal tendencies?

Manuel told what happened in Costa Rica while I was away and explained Angelo's absence as he drove me home.

"Angelo is very sorry he could not pick you up from the airport himself, but he was called out to Nicaragua again to face a problem. I am glad to do this task because I have the fun of seeing your reaction to the surprise Angelo left for you." Manuel's delighted eyes lit, and his nose crinkled in anticipation.

I had viewed the beauty of Casa Ave from the entrance vantage point many times as I entered the high driveway, but this view today, as Manuel pulled next to the electronic black wrought iron gates and paused while the gates opened was the most spectacular I had seen. The many gardens were newly manicured with birds of paradise, large red roses and tropical greenery designed into graceful curved lines. The entire property was touched with an artist's brush of red, white, and green.

"This is magnificent," I whispered in a hushed tone of adoration.

"Angelo hoped you would like it," Manuel stated as he remained parked to allow me the joy of a prolonged view.

In the center of the property was a thirty-foot-high fountain that spewed cascading water down its center pillar into smaller bowls of ponded water with three bowls. Each bowl became larger until the water reached the largest bowl, which easily measured ten feet in diameter. The cascading water sounded like water rushing from a river, which calmed everything within hearing range. The birds enjoyed bathing in the smaller bowls and chirped their pleasure. The fountain itself was created of white stone that matched the white stucco of the house, and its base was bordered with burgundy red vinca the color of the rooftops of the property's buildings and walkways. The sun dropped behind the hills, and the fountain was lit in elegant blue and white floodlights. Manuel watched me admire the property's transformation when he put the car into gear and descended the driveway to park under the portico. Manuel, said softly,

"Angelo asked me to deliver a message from him. The fountain is a token of his friendship."

"Manuel, Angelo's message and gift means a great deal to me. Please tell him how touched I am for his thoughtfulness," I emotionally said. I wondered what the truth was about Angelo, the $350,000 lien on my property, and the reason behind the beautiful gardens and fountain. What was buried beneath this beautiful vegetation? Intuition told me it was communication equipment for espionage.

"Sun, I will tell him tonight because I am driving up to meet him in Nicaragua," Manuel explained as he helped me into the house with my luggage.

My own home gave me a sigh of snugness and ease, impossible to obtain while visiting or traveling. Familiar surroundings of my hotel gave me comfort, but the foreignness of the country still felt— foreign. I didn't feel Costa Rica gave the same warm security as my country even though I lived here three years. The United States provided my sense of country, but it didn't provide the contentment this house gave. I had one foot in each country, and the position stretched my being to the point of discomfort.

I attempted to put down roots in Costa Rica by attending meetings of organizations that gave a sense of belonging and acceptance. Every Sunday I traveled to San Jose to take part in a spiritual group, organized by my friend. Didi was a beautiful, willowy Irish woman over six feet tall with a thin, graceful body; large hands, feet, and face; and medium brown hair and eyes. She served as a mother figure to nuns, homeless women, and children alike. Didi's group wasn't my regular Transcendental Meditation group, but it offered friendship, music, and dancing with other spiritually friendly Tico people. Didi fed, clothed, and schooled over 250 women and children, and I invited her group to use my hotel for their workshops, teachers' retreats, children's field trips, arts and craft classes, or whenever she needed a larger space. Didi traveled worldwide, gave workshops and retreats to other nuns, and told me she planned a retreat in Austin, Texas. I made a mental note.

I had only been back in CR for a few weeks when my younger sister, Ann, called from California.

"Hi, Sun. As you know, our mom is doing fine in the nursing home a block away from our house, and I check on her twice a day. Ben and I wondered if you would come here to house sit and do Mom care while we took a two-week vacation to Peru?"

"Of course, Ann. I'd love to spend time with Mother. Thanks!"

"Sun, why not invite your friend Angelo to come with you to keep you company! He would be welcome," Ann nudged, unable to conceal her curiosity about my male "of interest."

"What a fun idea! I will invite him. Thanks!" I gladly accepted.

When Angelo returned, I extended Ann's invitation, and he enthusiastically agreed. He had vacation time coming from his job, and we made plans for our California trip. I arranged for Casa Ave staff to be paid and planned their work schedule. Manuel agreed to look after the property in my absence. The days whirled around, and we both packed our bags. Excited in anticipation of our first trip together, I bought lacy underwear, and Angelo bought the plane tickets.

We trudged the hill to the top of the entrance, toting our bags to where Manuel waited to take us to the airport. Angelo's cell phone rang.

"Sun, I am sorry, but you need to go without me. I will come in a few days," he said, handing me my ticket. "I have an emergency with the Honduras team and need to be there. I will call you when I can." He ran back down the driveway and disappeared into his apartment. My disappointment was paramount as I stood with my bag in my hand, but I went to California alone.

Ann's California home was located in a balmy paradise with serene flower gardens and plenty of fresh tomatoes. Ann was disappointed that Angelo couldn't make it because she looked forward to meeting him, but she and Ben nevertheless departed for Peru. I spent the time enjoying my mom, who had dementia, and I visited her all day, every day for two weeks. Angelo called several times to see how I got along and repeated he would come in a day or so. I told my mother about Angelo, and she liked listening to the stories. I was saddened he wasn't there, but I knew firsthand the intensity and the demands of his job.

When Ann and Ben returned from their trip and met Angelo—over the phone—he asked if it was possible he could come next week. She welcomed him, and I stayed a total of three weeks. Angelo explained," Sun, I sent you $1,000 by Western Union; please use it to go shopping or whatever you want. I will be there soon," he promised again.

Ann and I visited Mom together the next morning. Mom asked Ann, "Did I have a husband?"

Ann answered, "Yes, you did, Mom."

"What was his name?"

"Mom, what do you think his name was?" Ann asked, testing her memory.

"I think it was Angelo," Mom answered.

"No, Mom, it wasn't Angelo," we laughed.

"Who is Angelo?" Mom asked.

"Angelo is Sun's boyfriend," Ann chuckled.

"Oh my goodness, that will never do," laughed Mom. While Ann and I walked back to her house from visiting Mom during the late afternoon, several big military planes kept buzzing low over her neighborhood. She told me her house was not near an airport, and she had never experienced anything like this during the many years she lived there. The impromptu air show continued for over an hour. I wondered if this was Angelo's promise to pay us a visit.

Angelo's gift of $1,000 arrived at Western Union on the last night of my three-week stay, so I invited my sister, my brother-in-law, both my nieces, and their three children to a fabulous Mexican restaurant with a lavish tip and spent almost the entire sum. The loneliness and waiting for him these three weeks was a repeat of the many times I waited for him at immigration appointments, at offices in Costa Rica, and on tourist outings, and he never came. I had a great time visiting my family, but I regretted I was always alone and waited for him.

I returned to Costa Rica the next morning and resumed my responsibilities of property management but was prohibited from operating the hotel business until the criminals' trials were over. Angelo called, and from the now familiar static—static—pop—bang—static—click, click—pop I knew it was Angelo calling from an airplane phone.

"Hi, Sun, I miss you so much. I have business in New York in a few days—static—static, and I wondered if it would be possible for you to spend time in New York with your daughter? I will come and get you, and we can spend time together in New York City. Would you like that?"

"Thank you Angelo, I would love to visit my daughter. It's been a long time since I'd seen Sage."

"Good, then it is settled. Manuel will bring your airline tickets, and I'll call you to make arrangement for our meeting—static—static—click. Sorry to be brief, but I am on assignment. Ciao."

Sage is a reflection of her name, philosophical, and a natural healer. She was happy about the news of my impending visit. I made preparations for the trip to upstate New York while Manual delivered the tickets, and I left within the week.

The flight from balmy to freezing was a severe adjustment, but Sage outfitted me with warmer clothing while I took care of my three-year-old grandson. Sage was the senior veterinarian at a nearby animal clinic, and her hectic work schedule provided pleasant play time for me and my grandson, Alexander. Angelo called and left messages: "Hi, Sun. I wished I heard your sweet voice. I am unable to come and get you, but I made reservations in your name at the Kingsley Hotel in Manhattan. I look forward to seeing you there. I left my credit card on file with them; use room service, the spa, hair salon, or whatever you want. I will be there in two days. Ciao."

Sage and I were disappointed he wasn't coming to her house. I sang his praises, and she looked forward to meeting him. I thought he would arrive as a surprise. He didn't! I accidentally erased the voice mail messages, causing Sage to doubt his existence, and she thought he was a byproduct of my imagination.

In the city, anticipating Angelo's arrival, I bought a new winter dress to go with the lacy underwear from the California trip. I looked cute in my daughter's fashionable coat and knee-high boots. Angelo called, and we met in the Kingsley Hotel Cafe for lunch, where he handed me $1,000 to buy tickets to Broadway shows.

"Sun the reason I asked you to meet me here today was to tell you in person what has happened with my job. This week during our Washington Pentagon meeting, JoSam died, and the members promoted me to his position. I have been groomed for his job for over thirty years. The council members demoted me one month and promoted me the next. I am back at the top of my game again. The salary, the perks, and the material gifts are luxury. I have my own plane and limitless amenities."

"It is as it should be Angelo. I told you they would soon promote you because 'cream rises.'"

"Sun, I am sorry that I can't stay. I need to leave within the hour, but I promise to return in two days. I stayed in New York for two weeks waiting for Angelo to come. He sent more money, for theater, and to shop or visit former theater students. Angelo called every other day and assured me he would be there soon. At the end of the second week, he called and begged me to stay for a third week to wait for him.

"Angelo, I live the lonely life of luxury, ran up a two-week hotel bill of $3,000, which you graciously paid, but I can't live life as an entertainment sponge, and I can't assume the role of a professional vacationer. New York City needs to be shared with a special friend, and I am alone waiting for you. I need to feel productive and contribute to my own existence, and I want to finish a sculpture I started in Costa Rica. I want to go home! My stay in New York has shown me that the idle life of the rich isn't for me. I feel shallow and need to be of service for someone, or make some creative contribution for others." He heard the determination in my voice. Angelo arranged for my Costa Rica travel plans.

The next two months in Costa Rica were happily spent sculpting, gardening, and fidgeting while I waited to resume my hotel business. I had trouble with my eyesight, and a local doctor told me I needed eye surgery. I called a well-known eye surgeon in Austin, who informed me he had a six-month wait list. For some unexplainable reason I didn't understand myself, I felt an urgency to leave Costa Rica. I didn't feel any medical emergency. It was something else! Intuition drove my behavior. I became an aggressive wild woman. I maneuvered receptionists, nurses, doctors' assistants, or whoever would talk with me to get a prompt appointment. I got one for the following week, and back to the USA I went.

I stayed with Texas friends, who drove me to appointments while I had expensive eye surgery on my left eye, the one most damaged from childhood. I would correct only one eye and wait until I had money to pay for the second surgery, but Angelo called.

"Sun, you should get the other eye corrected too while you're there. I wished I could be with you, but I will come later. I will send you the money to cover your medical expenses." Angelo promptly sent the money. I remained in Austin, Texas, for one month and recovered from the surgeries. It was then that I discovered the reason for my urgent need to flee Costa Rica. The Tico criminals were released! I followed the Costa Rican news and learned the criminals involved in my case were released with tracking bracelets because of the overcrowded and unsanitary conditions of the prisons.

This month in Texas I felt safe, but now fear jumped on my chest like a starving animal, ripped into all my internal organs, and clawed them to pieces. Fear consumed me, stole my breath and mind, and left me shaken and limp like an empty sack. My eyes healed, and my sight was perfect, but I had no desire to return to Costa Rica to be stalked and slaughtered by revengeful Ticos.

I called my sister Ann and discussed our mom's condition. We decided I should go to Wyoming and remodel Mom's house for handicap access so we could move her back into her home, where she wanted to be during her final days. I flew to Wyoming where friends lent me a car and parked a camper trailer on her property so I would be comfortable while the remodeling of the bathroom took place. I lived there for four months. It was surprising that Angelo kept in contact with me through my travels, and he continued to call. "Hi, Sun, how are you coming with the remodel?" he asked.

"Angelo, how did you know I worked on my mom's house?" I asked.

"I always know where you are and what you do! I know because I care for your safety. I can describe your mother's big white house with the black lions sitting beside the steps. I sent a man to help you with your mom's paintings for the art show," he revealed.

"I knew he was one of your men when I saw his disguised over-the-top hippie bus, with the love wreath on the front. A one-ton dually pickup truck with gun racks would be a better fit for Wyoming, Angelo. He asked me to remove my sunglasses so he could check out my eyes and told me I had very green eyes! I knew for sure you sent him. Angelo, I want to talk to you about something else. The solitude of Wyoming gave me pause to consider my future, and I decided it is time for me to sell the Costa Rican property. I listed it with a well-known worldwide franchise that has an agency in Costa Rica."

"Yes, I know. You listed it with Coldwell Banker," he boasted.

"Angelo, how do you always know everything I do?" I demanded.

"Sun, the Realtor is a crook and took advantage of you. He already charged you to advertise. Don't sell it yet; we had so many good memories there," he coaxed.

"Neither of us lives there. You work in the States, and I wire money to pay staff while the property sits empty and makes no income. This is not good business practice. I signed the 'for sale' contract by fax. Angelo, you know I can't come back because the criminals were released!"

"I hoped you didn't know about that. They think you are still in Costa Rica because I erased your exit visa, so they wouldn't follow you. Sun, I need to go into a meeting now, but I will call again another day. Ciao." He clicked off.

Despite my feelings of gratitude for Angelo, my intuition pinched my behind and told me something was wrong. I emailed the Costa Rica lawyer, Robert Galverez, and asked him to retract the power of attorney I unwittingly had given to Angelo. The lawyer promptly replied that the expeditiously rescinded POA would cost $1,500, and he further explained he had a client from Norway that was building a new port dock in southern Atlantic Costa Rica. If his Norwegian client should buy my property, would he receive a sales commission? I wired the money and contact information to the receptive Realtor, who agreed to share the commission, and Roberto Galverez promoted Casa Ave to his client.

The freedom of Wyoming's spirit soaked into my system, prompting tranquility, lightheartedness with childhood friends, and giving me calmness. I was reconnected with quiet mountain trails beside clear streams, and I never experienced a flicker of fear. I was steeped in nature's healing medicine and found myself again.

I deliberated for days about my friendship with Angelo. I made up my mind to disconnect from him and his country. My decision was strong and pushed me to write an email that established my independence. The day I sent the email that ended our friendship he called me thirty-three times, and I cried with each call, but I remained strong. There wasn't a day passed that I didn't think about him.

My sisters and I agreed to give 'Mom Care' in Wyoming for three months each. I spent four months remodeling my mom's house, and my sister Ann brought mother to Wyoming from California. Ann remained to do her three-month term first. Mother was upset by chaos or activity, and we knew she was uncomfortable with more than one caregiver. I needed to relocate, and now I was among the homeless.

I was fortunate to be accepted into a program at Fairfield, Iowa, that gave a grant to cover living expenses in return for meditating with a group of five hundred women, seven hours a day, seven days a week. I flew to Iowa without telling Angelo where I was, but he knew! Another three months passed where I lived the life of a sequestered nun while I monitored Casa Ave.

The sale of the hotel was a disaster! Whenever we had a showing, I wanted the Realtor and the lawyer together to maintain transparency. It was important for me to know the date and time of each showing, so I protected and prepared Wyoming to ready the hotel into "show" condition. Someone sent fraudulent emails to the Realtor, after I confirmed the showing dates, with cancelations or time changes. Realtor and lawyer angrily blamed each other. I resolved the problem by calling them for each appointment. I told them not to travel to the prospective appointment unless I confirmed by phone. Prospective buyers were routinely mugged at the gate and discouraged from buying the "unsafe" property.

One night the surrounding area of the hotel was set ablaze. Manuel hosed down the property and fought the high flames with the fire department. Another time, gallons of liquid silicone from my art studio were poured down all the outside drains and clogged the system. I remained determined to sell the property.

Roberto Galverez had a prospective couple from Norway, Evelina and Tutu, who were qualified buyers and looked at the property three times. They agreed to meet Mr. Galverez for dinner at a restaurant to sign earnest papers. He did not show up!

Evelina sent me an angry email about his absence. Four hours later, I received an email newspaper picture and article from Mr. Galverez's son that showed him as a victim of a hit-and-run accident that resulted in his hospitalization and unstable condition. I asked Manuel to go to the hospital and report his condition.

Manuel reported that he was not admitted into Mr. Galverez's room. It was guarded by the local police, who determined the hit and run was deliberate. I kept in constant email communication with Roberto Galverez's son concerning his hospitalization and condition. It was reported that both Roberto Galverez's legs were severely crushed, and surgery, steel plates, and pins, were necessary for recovery, but he was expected to walk again.

Evelina and I kept in email contact for months concerning Galverez's recovery. During this time, I gave her permission to visit the property again. The police and the buyers reasoned that the hit and run was caused by one of Galverez's angry law clients seeking revenge and had nothing to do with buying the property. Their thoughts were to my advantage. The buyers loved the property and offered full price.

In Costa Rica, property transactions were conducted by lawyers not real estate agents. Evelina and Tutu, the buyers, liked Roberto Galverez and wouldn't consider a different lawyer because he was also the lawyer for their new Costa Rican port business.

I remained in Fairfield, Iowa, meditating the days away while I waited for Roberto Galverez's recovery and the pending sale of the Costa Rican property. In the middle of the night, my cell phone rang:

"Hello, is this Ms. Sun Wren Richards?"

"Yes," I replied. I thought it might be the male voice of a doctor concerning my mother's health.

"My name is Leonardo DeLancy. I hold the lien on your property Angelo Orlando Andres Lopez placed in the amount of $350,000, and I called to ask you to please pay it off before we foreclose in two months," he stated flatly.

"Sir, please explain to me what you are talking about," I gasped as my heart pounded.

"Angelo Lopez presented documents that showed he had power of attorney and your permission to place a lien for $350,000 on your property. He paid interest on the lien for over a year, but he hasn't paid the interest for several months, which has a very high interest rate. We can't locate Angelo. Do you know where he is?" he asked.

"No," I answered. "It has been over four months since I ended our communications. What was the last date he made the interest payment?" I asked and heard Mr. DeLancy shuffling through papers.

"His last payment was over four months ago," he reported. My mind quickly correlated the timeline. It matched the email that I sent disconnecting from Angelo.

"Mr. DeLancy, I am sorry for your troubles. If I had the money I would pay you, but I don't have anywhere near that amount. I invested everything into the Costa Rican hotel. I essentially live in a convent here in the United States because I'm not safe in Costa Rica. I tried to sell the property, and I have an interested qualified buyer. How did you get my phone number?" I asked.

"I saw an ad where the property was for sale and your Realtor gave me your number. The Realtor explained he had difficulties showing it to prospective buyers."

"Yes, we had troubles, but I hope to sell it soon, and I ask you to give me time," I begged.

"I don't want to foreclose, and I don't want the property. I need the money because it is family money."

"I will rush the sale if you can please wait," I pleaded.

"I will stay in touch with you to see how the sale progressed," he graciously said.

"Thank you for your kindness and understanding," I appreciatively stated.

It was a good thing I was in this secluded safe place with loving, warmhearted people around me meditating, or I would be crushed under the mountain of stress heaped upon me. I was fortunate I learned the Transcendental Meditation technique, which helped to clear the useless mental chatter and rejuvenated my energy. I knew everything would be okay, and I trusted my strength to persevere.

The long-deliberated decision to disconnect from Angelo promoted "spontaneous right action," a gift from natural law. Strength did come, and it was a needed commodity. The following night I received a call from my sister Ann, who told me our mother wouldn't be with us much longer, and I needed to come back to Wyoming the first thing in the morning. I left Iowa on Valentine's Day. I arrived in time to spend two days with my mother before she passed. I stayed in Wyoming for another two months and prepared mother's house for sale.

I received an email from Lawyer Roberto Galverez explaining that his recovery was completed, but he waited for the pins in his legs to be removed, and then he would be released from the hospital. His email shot up my spine like a red flag for a bull at a Wyoming rodeo! I called my son, Matthew, the orthopedic surgeon, in Dallas.

"Hi, Son. I have a medical question. If a person has pins placed into his or her legs, is it necessary to remove them?" I asked.

"No, usually pins are placed and remain forever. Why do you ask?" he questioned.

My son's valuable help went a long way to mend our torn

relationship. I related the lawyer Roberto Galverez's hit-and-run ordeal. Matthew researched the story and found a picture from a recent traffic accident that involved a twenty-five-year-old that was "Photoshopped" and rewritten using Roberto Galverez's name. I reviewed emails from Roberto Galverez's (alleged) son and spotted traces of Angelo's words and personality. I checked out Evelina's and lawyer Galverez's many emails and determined those too were written by Angelo. I once commented to Manuel that Evelina seemed very masculine.

All the emails came from different email addresses and returned with quick replies whenever I wrote to them. All of this time I wrote to three different people, four if you counted Manuel, who were all Angelo's posturing. I didn't know if Manuel lied to me about visiting the hospital to check on Mr. Galverez or if his email was also from Angelo. I assumed this was Angelo's way of postponing the property sale so I wouldn't find out about the lien, or that he used the property for espionage. I needed to find an honest lawyer and a buyer before Mr. Delancy foreclosed.

I received another email from Evelina asking me to meet her in Cheyenne, Wyoming, where she and her husband wanted to vacation for a few days, and they were ready to give me the earnest money for the property. If my conclusions were wrong about the emails being from Angelo and my refusal to travel to Cheyenne would cause the loss of an honest buyer, my refusal wasn't worth the risk. Always the optimist, I accepted, but I knew the predicted outcome.

I borrowed a friend's car and asked permission to drive 350 miles to Cheyenne, which they graciously granted. I waited to hear from Evelina and Tutu. This was Angelo's continued method of operation. I was never told where to meet the buyers, and I waited at my mother's home for instructions that didn't arrive.

Meanwhile I was busy with the sale and the "make-ready" on

Mother's house. The house looked artistic when the listing Realtor showed it. After a few days passed, I received an email from Evelina:

> Dear Sun, I am so sorry for your inconvenience. My husband could not make the trip to Cheyenne, and we wondered if you could meet us in Denver where we would both have access to our banking needs. Respectfully, Evelina

> Dear Evelina, Thank you for your invitation and your continued interest in the property, but my bank is Bank of America, and there isn't a Bank of America in Denver, Colorado. Please advise. Sun Wren Richards

> Dear Sun, Our bank is Bank of America also, and this would make an easy money transfer from our bank account to yours. You were right about there not being a Bank of America in Colorado; the nearest is a small town in New Mexico. My husband and I have our own private plane, and we can pick you up in Denver with Roberto Galverez, our legal representative, who has all the paperwork on your property ready for us to transfer. He has fully recovered from his accident. Would you be agreeable to this plan of flying to New Mexico? Waiting for your reply, Evelina

All my mental alarms went to red alert as I remembered Angelo's story about how his agency pushed people out of airplanes, and I had no desire to experience the New Mexico landscape face-first.

Dear Evelina, My mother's house has a buyer, and I
need to return to Austin, Texas. Bank of America is
very accessible in Austin. Austin is a fun city—being
the music capital of the world. I would love to be
your hostess and tour guide. We can walk Town
Lake every day and go to theater productions, where
I have access to free tickets. I know the city well, and
we can spend the time getting acquainted, if your
husband or Mr. Galverez got delayed again. Would
this work for you? Respectfully, Sun.

Evelina, who I knew was Angelo, accepted my terms. We agreed
on dates and times and chose to meet at the Holiday Inn on Town
Lake in Austin, Texas. I drove the many miles in the 2000 green
Toyota truck, sleeping in it some nights and eating fast food.

When I arrived in Austin, I couldn't afford to stay at the Holiday
Inn while I waited for *Evelina*, so I chose a nearby Motel 6. Predictably,
Evelina, Tutu, and Roberto Galverez didn't arrive, nor did they send
any emails, phone calls, or text messages. I sent notes of inquiry, but
they all vanished never to be heard from again. My mother once told
me that I was like a cat. She could throw me out the window, and I
would always land on my feet. I hoped she was right! I formed a plan
to save my property from foreclosure.

My Costa Rican friend Didi was to attend a retreat and workshop
in Austin, Texas, and I thought of a plan that concerned the property
foreclosure. I drove the smooth ribbon of undulant roads through
the green, sweet, fresh-cedar aromatic west Texas hill country to
meet Didi. I belonged here in my own country with its security and
freedom. I felt safe and knew my problem was solvable. I felt exuberant that what I had in mind produced spontaneous right action.

"Today, Didi, I realized how much I missed our delightful and
spiritual Sunday events. I have so much to tell you." I told her the

unbelievable long story while she listened intently and never once doubted me.

"Didi, I want to give you my property in Costa Rica. I want the beauty of the hotel to go for a good cause for Costa Rica. I don't want it to belong to undeserving people who have selfish motives. You do wonderful things to make people's lives better, especially the poor. You are established, speak the language, and administer love to all you contact. You would use the property for the good of your nuns and for your school. Please accept it as my gift," I begged.

"Sun, you can't walk away from your beautiful hotel after you worked so hard on it. Your story makes me angry, and I urge you to fight for what is yours. I have a trusted lawyer I have known for sixteen years who will help you, if you allow me to tell him about your situation. Please allow me to call him," Didi offered.

"Didi, you are an Amazon woman, but we fight a manipulating man who has power over many countries. I am no match against him, and I am out of time with the threat of foreclosure."

"Sun, Angelo intimidated you, and he made you afraid of him." I didn't tell her Angelo was a US agent. "No one has power over the courts of Costa Rica, and my lawyer is ferocious. I will serve as your translator because he doesn't speak English. Please let him help you. You must save your place," Didi strongly urged.

"We have to work very fast!" Her energy rekindled mine and made me hopeful.

"I am calling my lawyer now when you are with me, in case he has questions for you." Didi moved into action and made the call. Speaking Spanish into her cell phone, she explained my situation to her lawyer, Jorge Rivera.

"What is the name of the lien holder? What is the full name of the person who deceptively placed the lien?" she translated.

"Leonardo DeLancy is the lien holder, and the perpetrator is Angelo Orlando Andres Lopez," I answered.

"Sun, Jorge wants me to come to his office when I return to Costa Rica. What will you do now? Where will you go, now that you are homeless?" Mother Didi inquired her concern for me.

"I am fine. Didi, please don't worry about me. You helped me already even if Mr. Rivera doesn't take my case. Knowing you want to help me is help enough. I love you Didi, just like all of your nuns. Thanks for helping me. I am fortunate, Molly, my dear friend in Austin, gave me back my Toyota pickup, and I have safely spent a couple of nights sleeping in the truck, and Motel 6 is always a familiar bed. Tomorrow I need to return to Wyoming," I related.

My little green truck took me 1,266 miles back to Wyoming to pick up a few of my mother's paintings and keepsakes my children and I wanted before the new buyers took possession of my mom's house. After I drove to Wyoming and gave the keys for my mother's house to the new owners, I drove the 1,566 miles to Galveston, Texas, to stay with my longtime friend Clair, who was my boss twenty-three years ago when we worked together in an equity theater in Austin. During this homeless period of my life, I found Clair's exceptionally gracious hospitality comforting. Clair told me I could stay with her until I found a safe place of my own.

The drive to Wyoming and back to Texas was filled with the usual sleepovers at Motel 6, truck stops, gulping fast food, missed exits, and maps locating my travel position, and I enjoyed the ordinariness of the entire affair. I had enough intense adventure for one lifetime.

I was welcomed to Galveston by "The Kleenex Lady." Clair was a very unique person. Kleenex ads read, "with the strength you need but the softness you like." She naturally exudes that kind of comfort. Clair softly took charge with inner strength and skills acquired from years of theater directing. Our years together in theater afforded our friendship unspoken attachments.

We set out on a mission to find a beach cottage affordable from the money of my mother's estate. Clair spotted several small east- and north-facing bungalows. She knew my Wyoming heritage requirements, and we house hunted with a delightful fluffy-haired Realtor named Sue.

After I relocated into my own cottage, in Galveston Texas, Didi and I began in earnest the arduous task of preparing my Costa Rican court case. Jorge Rivera explained that to stop the foreclosure, I must file a criminal case against Angelo. I protested because I knew agents had immunity, and I didn't want to hurt anyone. The lawyer declared he wouldn't be able to stop the foreclosure unless we showed criminal cause. I gathered a pile of two hundred incriminating emails, money wires, canceled checks, proof of ownership, and payments to Roberto Galverez for legal work never completed, and many emails of untruths from Angelo.

Didi's efficient lawyer, Jorge Rivera, outlined his presentation to the Costa Rican courts. He presented proof I was an elderly single woman and was a victim who had trustingly and unwittingly signed misrepresented documents without proper translation under false pretenses. He told me the courts were swayed toward older women being victims of the many Costa Rican property scams. He assured Didi and me that we had a strong case, and it was filed in the courts on time. It hurt my pride to be called an elderly woman, but I sucked it up.

The foreclosure date arrived, and I was represented well, but the judge ruled in favor of the lien holder, Leonardo DeLancy, with the stipulation he could not take possession for seven years, when the overbooked courts would review the criminal case against Angelo. This meant Mr. Delancy and I would be sitting in limbo for seven years.

I was privy to Angelo's abilities to receive special favors from judges when he helped me with the original sellers' scam, and I suspected bribes were given, or the judge protected a double agent's identity. I received no definitive answers. No matter the reason, we needed to solve the problem between us, and the resolution was in Didi's blessed hands.

Didi prepared a proposal for her foundation and asked permission to buy my property, Casa Ave, appraised at $850,000 for the cost of the $350,000 lien. The foundation granted her request. New facilities were needed to accommodate her many expanded projects.

I returned to Costa Rica and stayed with Didi while we settled the case out of court. I willingly dropped the criminal case against Angelo. I knew Costa Rica had a law protecting agents' identities. Angelo had demonstrated power to sway the judges during the Meza case. I would never receive justice. I signed papers that agreed to never sue any of the involved participants, and they signed papers to never sue me.

I suspected Mr. Delancy was one of Angelo's agents. He was a handsome man from Argentina who looked like other agent types I saw at our hotel. He was a big man, thirty-three with blond hair and brown eyes. During a break in our legal meeting, I quietly asked Leonardo DeLancy a direct question.

"Why did you ask me if I knew a man by the name of ****************?" This was the name Angelo told me would be his new US name. Leonardo Delancy looked surprised, stammered, stuttered, and answered, "I thought it was Angelo." Only another agent would have known his new identity.

The property settlement was peaceful, and it was a quadruple win. Didi received a large estate for her charitable projects, Leonardo DeLancy recovered his money, and I received security and freedom, but Angelo was the biggest winner of all because he escaped from any punishment for his wrongful actions and he had $350,000 in cash without consequences.

CHAPTER 31
TRANSCENDENCE

December 2013 marked two years since I found peace and safety without the oppressive, black, paralyzing bouts of fear experienced in Costa Rica. I found my creativity again and mended the connection to the source of creation where the waves of happiness and contentment were regained by grounding from beaches and the perpetual motion of the sea. Bliss in life and individuality were realized and appreciated on new levels of understanding with each glorious orange and pink sunset. Contentment of the soul and quietness in the nervous system were more valued than any property needing to be guarded against the tide of desperate people.

Today, sitting on the deck of my tiny beach bungalow, I received a RESTRICTED text message on my cell phone that interrupted the flock of sea gulls that gleaned food at the water's edge. In past years, Angelo only communicated with restricted cell phone messages, and it had been two years since he made contact. The message read: "Located: Angelo Orlando Andres Lopez," and gave an address.

I was bewildered as I closed the cell phone and pondered the message. A restricted call provided no opportunity for any follow-up. I stretched out on the sun-filled deck, lathered in lotion, closed my eyes, and felt contented basking in sunshine, but my mind continued to dwell on the message. In past years, after accepting Angelo's many invitations, I spent days that grew into weeks waiting for him to show up. He even sent me money to pay my expenses, but he never arrived, not once.

I felt peaceful alone, without the worry for my safety. I created sculptures, made new friends, formed new social circles, and lived with my feet stuck into nature's pockets with no thought of my security because it was always within me. There was no need to even think about Angelo Orlando Andres Lopez again—but I often wondered if he was alive or if the perils of his job claimed their prize.

My cute, tiny bungalow was no more than three hours from Austin, and it could be a pleasant, easy drive in the 2000 little green Toyota truck that Molly and Jack returned to me when I became homeless. What the heck! I might as well respond to one more wild goose chase. Good grief, I had a great deal of practice with Angelo's invitations to empty rendezvous.

Two days passed, and I was on the road to track down an address to an unknown, from an unknown. For me? That too was unknown. It was hard to believe I was doing this, but my days were my own, and my curiosity was stronger than my common sense.

After living in Austin for twenty years, I had no problems finding the address. I expected to find a home or condos and was amazed at the grandeur of the building at the given location. It was a stately old Texas southern mansion constructed from the beige Texas limestone. The building was four stories tall with the center of the building designed into four stories of open-air balconies. It was a beautiful old building used for some type of government offices.

I found parking in a visitor parking lot and looked out over the walkways of expansive green sprawling St. Augustine grass dotted with scores of large three-foot-diameter, tall, thick, live oak trees typical of Texas native landscape. An impressive fountain similar to the grand fountain that Angelo had given me in Costa Rica splashed in front of the building, but this fountain wasn't as tall, had no graceful bowls, and was surrounded by a railing to keep people out. No, this fountain was certainly not as beautiful as the one from my past. I followed the walkway to the entrance and read the large limestone sign: AUSTIN STATE HOSPITAL.

I doubted the correctness of the email-texted message and wondered if there was a mistake. I ambled into the lobby, where an older woman with swept-back brown graying hair and a pleasant heart-shaped face looked up at me and removed her glasses.

"May I help you?" asked the chatty receptionist.

"Thank you; I hope so. What kind of hospital is this?" I inquired.

"It is a mental hospital for people with acute psychiatric illness, and we serve three hundred patients. What hospital are you looking for? Do you have the correct hospital? Are you in the right place?" she asked.

"I'm not sure. I was given this address." I showed my cell phone to her.

"Yes, you have the right location," she assured.

"Do you know someone by the name of Angelo Orlando Andres Lopez?" I asked.

The easy-going, talkative woman behind the desk looked through some papers in a vanilla-colored folder and on to her computer. She looked at me perplexed.

"We have a new patient admitted two days ago by that name. Are you a relative?" she asked.

"No, we were friends when we both lived in Costa Rica," I answered.

"What is your name?" she inquired as she filled in a visitation form requiring extensive personal information and my signature.

"Costa Rica? This hospital is for Texas state patients. Let me take a minute and review his file," she said, returning to her computer. "Our files are empty in his regard. Can you contribute any information that may be helpful for a treatment plan?" she asked hopefully.

"I knew him when he worked on highway construction projects in Costa Rica," I answered openly.

"Is he married with children or other living family?" she continued to inquire, taking notes.

"No, he only expressed interest in his work. Why are you asking these questions? Are they requirements for visitations?" I asked, unsure of my circumstances standing at the reception area of a state mental institution.

"Your friend was committed by a government court, and we don't have any history for him except he was admitted without designated local mental health authorities. He had an emergency medical screening in compliance with EMTALA and in consultation with the LMHA, and the admitting doctor authorized his admission. His history reported everything as unknown: unknown family, unknown employment, unknown level of education, and unknown prior health and mental history. His services are paid by a Washington agency," she read.

"Do you know which agency?" I asked.

"No. I'm sorry; our information is limited. If he is from Costa Rica, he must speak Spanish, right?" she assumed.

"Yes, Spanish is his native tongue, but he speaks fluent English." I tried to augment her file information.

"Oh yes, he talks constantly in English, like a malfunctioning computer. I assumed you wanted a visitation?" I nodded assent. "Your visitation will be monitored by doctors observing behind glass, where they can see and hear what is said in the hope of learning something about him," she disclosed.

"Did your hospital send me the text message concerning his location?"

"No, the only thing we know about him is his name, and the information you gave today. We didn't know he had any friends. The only reason for allowing your visit is the hope it may help him. The doctors may want to visit with you following your visit. Have a seat, while I arrange for your visit. It may take ten to thirty minutes," the receptionist cordially added.

I was in no mood to read any of the mental health magazines, for parents, loved ones, or friends, strewn on the low tables in the area where I waited and felt trepidation and sorrow for Angelo's plight. It was too difficult for me to imagine his extraordinary mind becoming bent, broken, or shattered.

The hospital's interior designer made a heroic attempt at cheerfulness with the use of a soothing pale blue color scheme with mauve-colored throw pillows tossed in the chairs and on the sofa. Everything seemed to be coated with an unseen, gray, dust-like energy, similar to smog residue that absorbed into my skin. The unnatural intense energy seeped from the walls of this hospital and competed with the human attempted "mood made happiness." It produced a weird state of unrest that gave a jolt of uneasiness.

The smell of the waiting room was the smell of old men with soiled underwear, whose clothing exuded the odors of fried food and unwashed hair. The benevolent hospital staff made a valiant effort by providing aromatic fragrances of furniture polish, dusting oils, and Clorox cleaning sprays. A bowl of dried flower petals sat on the small table to mask the accumulation of centuries old, collected human stress and misery dating back to the 1860s when the building was known as the Texas State Lunatic Asylum. The feelings of centuries old human turmoil and suffering were unnerving, despite the staff's determined efforts. Sadly the superficial and pretentious endeavors only made the environment worse.

The only satisfaction this visit could bring was to add a frame around the two-year-old puzzle with its missing pieces pasted in my mind. I couldn't imagine what purpose this visit had for Angelo or me except for my continued compassion for his past exhausting lifestyle, and the belief there was a reason he committed the infractions against me. Only Manuel or the Costa Rican lawyer could have known Angelo's location, but only Manuel would have had the thoughtfulness to share this information with me.

My thoughts were interrupted by a tall, slender, blonde woman who wore casual street clothes and sensible shoes and carried a folder.

"Ms. Sun Richards? I'm Doctor Sally Hill. I'm glad you've come to visit our patient Angelo Lopez. We want to observe any recognition he has of you or what his reactions might be. Follow me, please? Please leave your purse or any items in your pockets in this locker and leave the key at the front desk. Your visit must be limited to thirty minutes." She cordially directed me into the visiting room and then walked farther down the hall into the observation room that the receptionist told me about.

I forced myself to open the door and step into the naked, bald room that gripped two lonely rocking chairs. When I closed the door, I saw Angelo as he paced and talked out loud to no one. He was dressed in clean, casual street clothes of khaki pants and a yellow short-sleeved shirt and was well groomed as I remembered him. He turned to face me, and I never would have recognized him! He gained over 350 pounds. He showed muscle loss and was going bald. His deep chocolate eyes were sunken into the roundness of his fleshy face, and the eyelids fluttered and hid their color. I remembered his full beautiful lips, which now seemed to be stretched or misshapen. I sucked in air at the sight of his size as he turned still talking to himself and paced toward me. I walked up to him and tried to take his hand in friendship while he continued to talk, but he didn't feel my touch. I released his limp hand and let it drop to his side as he continued to roam and rant.

"Angelo, I am glad to see you again. Do you remember me? I am Sun Wren Richards; we were friends in Costa Rica." I thought reintroducing myself and saying my name might make an impact. It didn't. I sank down into the mauve, cushioned, overstuffed rocking chair while he walked and talked. I was absorbed by the intensity of the moment, and I wasn't distracted to know we were monitored. A hundred questions raced through my mind about what I wanted to know.

He cocked his head like a bird, waddled, and monologued. I continued to talk over his voice, and we both were in a miserable overlapping verbal duet. It must have been impossible for the doctors to understand anything either of us said, and this was good because what I had to say to Angelo was intimate and private.

"Our agency team was assigned the secret return to Honduras for President Manuel Zelaya, September 21 of 2009. The country's near revolution was ignited by Manuel Zelaya's attempt to rewrite the constitution of Honduras to allow him to run for another term. The country was outraged and may have assassinated him without our intervention. Honduras had no clear constitutional process for removing a sitting president and planed to do it with violence. We rescued him and later had to take him back. Our team returned him clandestinely to the Brazilian embassy in Tegucigalpa. Nikola's poem said: 'I tolerate no betrayal: No tarnished loyalty. If my trust in you does fail, you die like dethroned royalty.' In 2010 President Zelaya was exiled to the Dominican Republic. Now he represents Honduras as a deputy of Central America Parliament, and his wife ran for the presidency. Our work meant nothing and would circle around again." Angelo monologued continuously, and his higher-pitched words were slurred and rambled together.

"Did you know you were only the second man in my life that

I loved? I think you knew it, but I wanted to repeat it again now. I loved you, Angelo, and I trusted in your honor to do the right thing toward me, but I ended up homeless with a financial mess and left with nothing because I gave it all to you. I haven't told you this out of anger or applied guilt, but I was here today because I hoped you would tell me what happened to you and why our friendship didn't grow into permanency."

"We all knew the USA had oil interests in Nicaragua. The border dispute with Costa Rica intensified daily, and the USA took sides with Nicaragua. I chose to be loyal to my job while I was labeled a traitor to Costa Rica. The issue was under consideration by the judge of the International Court of Justice in The Hague. The Ministry of Foreign Affairs in the lawsuit maintained the decision granted greater maritime sovereignty to Nicaragua but ruled the power of the keys included the disputed island of San Andres, and it remained with Colombia. In the coming days we made a comprehensive review of the judgment to determine the scope it had among the Republics of Nicaragua and Colombia and how that related to the interests and rights that Costa Rica had in the Caribbean Sea. I'm going to fight you. Nikola's poem said: 'You know I don't like you: I will slam you and strike you: I will kick you and bite you.'" Angelo recited, paced, and mumbled over my voice, and our dual orations flooded the abused trodden beige carpeted floor.

"You knew my thoughts had always been respectful toward you even during the year I was a vagrant, Angelo. I had never harbored ill will or bad thoughts toward you, and I thought you were one of the most interesting people I had ever known. You were a very gifted man with a superhuman mind, and you were everything I waited to find in a companion. You were aware of your abilities, and I believed you were a rare individual whose goal was to use his full potential. I continue to purge my pent-up emotions to you, Angelo, but I don't think you hear me. This is a strange situation we both experience today because I don't understand anything you tell me, and you can't hear or understand me. Aren't we symbols for all of humanity who can't understand, can't hear each other, can't see each other, or feel each other?" I desperately challenged. I poured out my discourse uninterrupted, and so did Angelo.

"'You will be banished to Lucifer's fiery domain. Your soul for love famished: Abandoned, dying in the rain.' That was what the poet Nikola told us. Costa Rica had a deplorable overcrowded prison system where 326 prisoners were presently stuck in holding cells of the Judicial Investigation Organization (OIJ) because the national prison system refused to accept new inmates. The OIJ cells were completely full, and lacked beds, adequate ventilation, and access to sunlight. The country's prisons were an echo of the holding cells. The courts gave bracelets to prisoners and released them to the streets. The US ambassador, Mrs. Andrews, had given money to the correctional segment of the judicial system, but the money was never realized to relieve conditions. Convicts spread terror for tourists in the southern Caribbean, and police suspected a gang of heavily armed convicts were responsible for causing panic in the Caribbean zone of Costa Rica, where in the last two months there were twelve assaults on foreign tourists. Leaders in the tourism industry related that gangs became more organized and were better armed than the police." Angelo paced and ranted relentlessly and became intense and emphatic.

"Wouldn't it have been delightful for us to have experienced the beauty of Costa Rica with its lush greenery, its beautiful waterfalls, and its oceans and powerful volcanoes? I wanted for us to enjoy those things together, Angelo. Our time together was such a waste of a rare moment, where the universe gave us a chance meeting, but the window of opportunity closed without us seizing its gift," I emphasized as I stood and walked with him up and down the small carpeted room while our overlapped word cannons continued their volleys.

"Drug lords laundered money and transported drugs in vacuum-sealed packages covered with blue tape inside human body cavities, or surgically placed inside the lining of human bellies. Our human race became piggy banks for the drug cartels. The Costa Rican president supported extradition of its nationals wanted in other countries for organized crime and drug trafficking, but drug production and transporting became big business to the country's economy. We could clean up this mess, but the country's economy would plummet, and the poor would starve because of our efficient work. The line of right and wrong disappeared." Angelo rambled on unaware that I kept pace with him.

"Why did you put the lien on my property? I want to know why things turned out as they did. Did you lose the money gambling? Do you still like to play blackjack? I chose to believe you used the money to buy Manuel a home so he could get out of the job because you knew it wasn't good for him. Angelo, I don't think your job was good for you either, and I wanted you to resign. Did you resign? I wanted to help you find quiet inner peace and feel relaxed. I wanted you to know the beauty of our world, but most of all I wanted you to experience restful sleep. You never got enough sleep when I knew you. You were always on the edge of turmoil and anxiety. I am glad to have this chance to tell you what my heart felt. I wanted good things for you! I loved you, Angelo. Do you not know we both tried to make our world a better place, but we had opposite strategies of approaching the problem? I tried to change human behavior at the cellular level through meditation, and you tried corporal force, which seemed to have destroyed your sense of purpose and your great gift. I begged you to consider other methodologies. I wanted you to resign," I orated over his voice.

For a moment I stood and watched him walk and noticed that his heavy body distorted his normal turned-out-toes gait. I tried to stop his walking by standing in front of him and grasping both his forearms, but his stride continued uninterrupted, and if I hadn't stepped out of the way, he would have pushed me over totally oblivious of my presence.

"Could you please stop walking and talking and look at me? Do you see me, Angelo? Do you hear me, Angelo? Do you know me, Angelo? Angelo, do you feel me taking your hand?" I released his hand without receiving any reaction or change in the stream of his words.

My grief brimmed over from the void of his presence of mind. I grieved for his unawareness of my presence. I felt compassion for the inner turmoil he went through and knew his stress existed years ago during our first meeting in the Casa Ave hotel kitchen.

"Angelo, I am sorry for your troubles. I am saying good-bye, and I wish you well."

I felt the smallness of the room; the pulsating accumulation of centuries of human distress oozed into the atmosphere and pushed me toward the door. I had to leave. I walked to the lockers with the key the receptionist held out for me without speaking. I retrieved my purse and cell phone. I left the building. My eyes flooded over, and my sobbing body made sounds so that the whole outdoors knew my bereavement.

I cried for the pain, suffering, and ignorance of humanity. I cried for their strife for unimportant material happiness. I cried for the crimes, sickness, and unkindness delivered by human hands. I cried for the senseless wars and the devastation heaped upon citizens by self-serving leaders. I cried for individual egos that were fed to enormous proportions while their universal love, their heart centers, had shrunken to minuscule pinpoint size. I cried for tiny children whose parents nurtured their self-importance and smothered their innate compassion. I cried. I cried. I cried.

I cried while I stumbled down the cement walkway and sat on a bench under the condolence of a large live oak tree. The tragedy of what our culture had done to God's perfectly created specimens of humanity, such as Angelo, had been rolled onto life's theater screen, and I was forced to be its audience. The grief spilled from my heart like wine from a broken glass, leaving only the pain from its shattered, sharp shards.

I suffered the multifaceted responses from the loss of Angelo's astonishing mind. I wept for the bond I felt toward him for the many times he protected me and for the circumstances that tied us together. The heartache I felt was from witnessing another of God's creations crumble into disrepair because of his personal life choices, self-neglect, and the appropriate suffered consequences. I held fast to the idea the body must be in perfect health to function and receive intuition, spontaneous right action, and happiness. Every person remained responsible for his own welfare and maintained his own channels to the source of his creation, and my sorrow was not for myself but for Angelo's agony. I vowed to remain resilient against this devastating grief.

I felt the comforting warmth of afternoon sunshine filtering through the spaces of the live oak tree's immense sympathizing branches, and I breathed its mint green, menthol, medicinal vitality. The deep pool of my compassion drowned my sorrow and nurtured the natural law of poetic justice. I remained absorbing the healing elements from nature for over an hour when my thoughts about poetic justice expanded to include Angelo.

Angelo took pride in his photographic mind that had given him advantages throughout his life, and now he was cared for by Austin State Hospital. How many people he scammed in the name of his US government agency throughout his career was unknown. I gave him everything I had under false pretenses, and no court of law restored the loss or brought justice. Under man's law he knew no consequences and was shielded by government's protection, but poetic justice balanced the scales. Angelo was deprived of his most prized asset—his mind.

The young lien holder, age thirty-three, who gave Angelo the cash for the property and foreclosed, was also an agent. He knew the property rightfully belonged to me. He had the courts' law in his favor with the papers I signed, but he also was served by natural law. Four weeks after the Costa Rican government awarded the case to him, his young wife died of cancer.

Amon the gardener, who stole and betrayed me to the original property sellers, was deported by the Costa Rican justice courts, but his stronger consequences came when nature delivered a drought to the plantations where he worked and left him destitute and begging on the streets of Nicaragua.

Mercedes served time in a Costa Rican prison for her wrongful actions, but her true pain came from natural law with the death of her innocent husband. She also suffered from the loss of precious "mom time" taken from her baby son.

I held no satisfaction or pleasure from any of their misfortunes, and I remained in awe witnessing the swift power of nature correcting imbalances by the delivery of its own justice. I felt no pangs of loss from my own Costa Rican misfortunate or misadventure that evoked fear and terror. I was grateful to poetic justice and the laws of nature that blissfully took my mother while she gifted me the means to buy my tiny, simple beach house, where I could strengthen my soul and recover using the natural elements of the sea, sand, and sun. It's time for me to go home.

The giant consoling live oak whispered the poet Rumi's words to me as I walked away: "You have escaped the cage. Your wings are stretched out. Now fly."